# The Highland Henchman

## Highland Force Book 2

# Amy Jarecki

Rapture Books

Copyright © 2014, Amy Jarecki

Jarecki, Amy

The Highland Henchman

Print ISBN: 9781495947247

First Release: April, 2014

All rights reserved. The unauthorized reproduction or distribution of this copyrighted work, in whole or part, by any electronic, mechanical, or other means, is illegal and forbidden.

This is a work of fiction. Characters, settings, names, and occurrences are a product of the author's imagination and bear no resemblance to any actual person, living or dead, places or settings, and/or occurrences. Any incidences of resemblance are purely coincidental.

To Bob. I'm Glad we're together!

# Chapter One

*The Firth of Clyde, Scotland ~ 1st April, 1568*

The activity on deck stilled when the ship turned east and sailed into the Firth of Clyde. All eyes cast to the inlet. Entering Lowland waters always bore a risk.

A golden eagle perched on his shoulder, Bran scanned the waterway with the bronze spyglass. "Ruairi's galley sails ahead." He strained to identify pennants on the ships beyond. "MacNeil of Barra and MacLeod of Harris as well."

Laird Calum MacLeod grasped the ship's rail beside him. "Do ye see the MacDonald pennant?"

To allay all doubt, Bran surveyed the Firth waters one more time. "Nay."

"Cannons stand down," Calum bellowed, and circled his hand above his head. "Continue on, Master John."

Bran turned and leaned his backside against the galleon's hull. "I never considered I'd become a knight."

Calum smoothed his hand over the eagle's brown feathers. "A Highland henchman needs a title to garner respect in the Lowlands."

Knighted by the Highland chieftain only a few hours prior, some might view the honor as contrived, but Bran's chest swelled. He owed his life to Calum. With his father dead, the clan had considered Bran an outcast, until he turned twelve and the laird took him under his wing. Now one and twenty, Bran's dedication to the clan had been rewarded.

Griffon's claws clamped into Bran's shoulder harness as the eagle stretched his back. Bran chuckled. "I aim to win the tournament and show all the might of Raasay."

Calum's weatherworn hands grasped the rail beside him. "'Tis what I like to hear. I didna train ye to be me henchman for naught."

"How many contestants do ye think there'll be?"

"We'll find out soon enough. Lord Ross invited all the Hebridean clans. I'm sure there'll be quite a gathering."

"Why do ye think he's holding the tournament?" Bran slipped a piece of bully beef into Griffon's beak. "Lowlanders hate Highlanders."

The salty wind picked up and Calum tugged his feathered bonnet lower on his brow. "Me guess is he's up to something."

"Then why'd we come?"

"And miss a chance to gain respect for me clan?" Calum shook his head. "Never. Besides, Lord Ross would have anarchy on his hands if he lifted a blade against us. He wants something, mark me."

"Are ye inclined to give it—ye ken, what he wants?"

"Have I taught ye nothing since yer father passed? Ye never give something for naught, lad."

"I'd consider no less. Ye have me sword, on that there will nay be a question."

The ruddy chieftain leaned in, his warm breath skimming Bran's cheek. "Stay close. Keep yer eyes open. The tournament will be over soon enough and we'll be back in Raasay with Anne and the boys."

"Drop anchor," shouted John Urquhart, Calum's quartermaster and right-hand man. With John on Calum's right, Bran now occupied the left—a fearsome trio they made.

Bran counted the galleys moored at the estuary of the River Clyde, which flowed into the firth from the town of Glasgow—six boats, all laden with cannon, but none as impressive as Calum's *The Golden Sun*. With eighteen guns, the galleon and crew would lie in wait should any skullduggery arise.

Once the skiff had been lowered, Bran stood behind his laird with Griffon perched on his shoulder. He wrapped his fingers around the basket-weave pattern of his hilt, scanning the sea and shore for suspicious activity. Instructions were to gather with Sir

George Maxwell at Newark. Horses would be provided for the short ride to Halkhead House in Renfrewshire.

Bran didn't like it. Though every Hebride chief was accompanied by his henchman, they were leaving their greatest weapons behind. *The Golden Sun's* cannons would be of no use ten miles inland.

Enya squinted at the target. Pulling the string of the longbow even with her ear, she held her breath. The string rolled to the tips of her gloved fingers. She released.

A quick flutter of her heart accompanied her grin. "Spot on the middle."

With his breeches a tad too small and his new boots oversized for his body, Rodney ran up to the target and yanked out the arrow. "Hells bells, you should've been born a lad."

Enya walked up and stuck her finger in the hole. "Wouldn't that have been something? Instead of picking fabric for fancy dresses, I'd be on a ship sailing for the South Seas right now."

The young squire's eyes popped. "And miss the tournament?"

"Well, perhaps after the tournament. I would never be able to resist an opportunity to show up a gathering of brawny knights."

Rodney flexed his muscles. "Do you think I'll be a knight one day?"

"Of course you will. 'Tis why Robert named you squire." She squeezed the lad's scrawny arm. "You have strong bones, and at two and ten, you're nearly as tall as me, I'll say."

"But not as dead-on with a bow as you."

"Yet."

Together they walked back fifty paces, and Enya held out the bow. "Your turn. Let me see your best."

Rodney concentrated on the target. White lines strained around his lips as he let his arrow fly. It hit the target inches below the bull's-eye.

"Not bad." She pulled another arrow from her quiver and handed it to him. "Try again, and this time, keep your fist even with the top of your ear."

He grinned and followed her instruction. *How long will the young laddie listen to the likes of me—a mere woman?* Soon he'd be off patrolling the borders with her brother, Robert, and she'd be left behind at Halkhead while her father arranged her marriage. *Oh, what a wretched parcel of miserable affairs I have to look forward to.*

Enya wanted to patrol the borders—see the world, or Scotland at least. She loved to listen to tales of Robert's travels. She dreamt of riding a white steed and saving the poor from starvation. But she was stuck at Halkhead House, the youngest of Lord Ross's six daughters.

Her mother always berated Enya for daydreaming. "You must take more interest in your embroidery, dear," Mother scolded endlessly while tearing out Enya's horrific mistakes. *Embroidery. Bah.*

"Did you see that?" Rodney asked.

Enya snapped her head toward the target. Rodney's arrow stuck in the bull's-eye—not in the middle like hers had, but close. "Excellent. See? All it takes is a little adjustment and you'll hit your mark every time."

The muffled rumble of horse hooves echoed in the distance. Rodney gaped at her as if it were Christmas morn. "They're coming."

Enya grabbed his hand and headed through the copse of trees. "Let's watch from atop the hill. They'll not see us up there."

Nearly out of breath, they reached the crest just as the long line of horses carrying robust Highlanders ambled into view. Large men rode toward them with plaids draped across their shoulders, helms on their heads, targes in one hand and pikes with deadly spearheads in the other. Some had their claymores strapped to their backs and others carried the large swords in scabbards on their belts.

"They all look so...inexplicably tough," Enya said.

Rodney peeked out from behind an enormous oak. "They look like a mob of heathens if you ask me."

With their long hair and massive exposed legs, Enya could see his point. Lowland men would never be caught baring their knees or wearing kilts. But a basal stirring swirled deep inside. These sturdy men were proud, strong and focused.

Enya watched an imposing warrior ride directly beneath her hiding place. Unable to look away, her breath caught. He was even bigger than the others, and his chestnut hair curled out from under his helm. On his broad shoulder perched a great golden eagle. She'd seen falconers before, but never one with a bird as impressive as an eagle.

He grasped the reins easily, as if he were holding a thread of wool. His plaid covered his thigh just above the knee, leading to a powerful calve that rested against the horse's barrel. Gaping at the warrior's exquisitely muscular frame, Enya covered her open mouth with her palm.

He rode beside a man with an ornate breastplate, and Enya guessed the warrior was *An Gille-coise*—a henchman paid to protect his laird and his clan. His gaze flicked across the scene like a hunter, or the hunted. Simply looking at him made her stomach tense.

His eyes darted up the hill. Enya froze. Crouching behind the clump of gorse in full yellow bloom, no one should have seen her, but the warrior's gaze fixed on her as if she were waving a torch. In the flicker of a heartbeat, time slowed. Her mouth went dry as their eyes met. His jaw tensed and his line of sight trailed to the bow in her hand.

"That's got to be the biggest man in the entire world." Rodney's amazed voice broke through her trance.

Enya's hand flew to her chest to quash her pounding heart. "You think so?" Taking a deep breath, she wouldn't let on the warrior had affected her in any way. But her fingers trembled as she watched the parade proceed through the heavy iron gates of Halkhead House—until he turned and regarded her over his shoulder. *Does he think I'm going to pull out an arrow and shoot him in the back? Perhaps he does.*

Rodney yanked her hand. "Come. Let's go watch."

Enya hesitated and stared down at her olive-green kirtle. A plain day dress, her hem was caked with mud. She ran her hands over the simple white coif she'd slapped on top of her head that morning.

She looked frightful and knew it. "You go. I'll spirit round the back. If Mother sees me like this, she'll have one of her spells."

Rodney shrugged. "Och, you look fine."

Enya feigned a smile. "You ken Mother. She ordered all that fabric for me."

The lad blew a raspberry and raced down the hill without her. A long breath whistled through Enya's lips. At eight and ten, she'd been to court on a number of occasions. Mother had always made her put on a show of finery, but she didn't care for it. She preferred simple kirtles allowing her more freedom of movement for things like archery and horseback riding.

However, that brawny warrior's eyes raking across her face and fixating on her longbow made her cheeks burn. She didn't want him or anyone else gawking at her dirty gown. Besides, Enya's mother would be furious if she raced into the courtyard with a bow and quiver of arrows slung over her shoulder. A folly to use the secret entrance in daylight, she'd skirt through the woods, head around back, go in through the kitchen and tiptoe up to her chamber.

Edging around the woods proved the easy part, but once she hit the rear side of the manse, her brother, Robert, popped in front of her. "There you are."

*Caught.* Enya snapped her hands to her hips and challenged him. "Why are you not in the courtyard greeting our guests with Father?"

"Why aren't you?"

"I am not the heir."

"Touché." Robert raked his hand through his hair. Enya was well aware he didn't approve of her father's reasons for holding the tournament. "Actually, I heard the horses and was heading there now. Must welcome the barbarians, you know."

"Don't let Father hear you say that."

"And why not? He feels the same."

"Not when we're asking them for help."

"Very well." He licked his finger and rubbed Enya's cheek. "How do you manage to turn into a guttersnipe every time you venture outside?"

Her hands flew to her cheeks. "Really?"

"You'd best not let Mother see you."

"I was just heading in to clean up."

"Hurry. Father wants us all in the great hall for supper. The Hamiltons will be here. You dare not be late."

Enya cast her gaze skyward and headed for the door. She wanted to forget about Lord Claud Hamilton and his supposed interest in her. The few times she'd seen him, he'd reminded her of a rooster strutting amongst a gaggle of hens.

Heather shook her finger under Enya's nose. "I've no idea how we'll turn you into a beauty by supper. Your mother will take it out of my hide for certain."

Enya wrapped her hands around the accusing finger and kissed it. "You worry far too much."

Though she adored Heather almost as if she were a second mother, Enya hated to be doted upon. She looked at the torturous fine-toothed comb in her serving maid's hand and took her seat at the vanity. Heather started at the ends and yanked the comb through Enya's red tresses. "You should have put your hair in a snood before you went out this morning. There wouldn't be half the knots. How you manage to mess my handiwork as soon as you leave the chamber is a mystery to me." She let out a noisy sigh. "You should have been born a boy."

"That's what Rodney said when my arrow hit the bull's-eye." Enya flashed a challenging grin in the looking glass. "Wouldn't that have been a boon? I'd be free to travel, see the world." She swung her arm through the air with an imaginary sword. "Fight duels, and win this fanciful tournament."

Heather groaned and jerked the comb harder.

"Ow."

"You'd do very well to stop your dreaming and face the fact you are a lass, and a grown one at that."

Enya folded her arms and glared at her reflection. It wasn't that she didn't like being female, but it was so *limiting*. One by one, she'd watched her five sisters marry. Her father was close to negotiating her betrothal to the pompous Claud Hamilton—heir to an earldom. She should be overjoyed. At least that was what her mother said.

Enya hardly knew Claud. Friends with William, he hadn't been to Halkhead since her closest brother left for his fostering a few years ago. Father had invited Claud to the tournament, just as he had every other able-bodied knight who sympathized with Queen Mary. Enya blinked at her reflection. She'd best give the young lord a chance. Besides, she was curious to see him after so much time had passed. She fidgeted with her skirt. Of course she wanted to see how he'd changed. Perhaps with time to mature, he wouldn't be so full of self-importance. After all, she might have no choice but to spend eternity with him.

*Saints preserve me.*

Heather pulled a small clump of hair from Enya's temple and started braiding. Nice. She loved it when Heather wove her hair through her bronze tiara. Though unpretentious, it was her favorite piece of jewelry. Enya glanced over to the bed. Heather had set out her gown. It was beautiful. Mother had picked the emerald damask to match Enya's eyes. She bit the inside of her cheek. If she was to see her future husband this night, she should look her best.

## Chapter Two

Bran rested his fingers on the pommel of his sword, his gaze darting across the great hall. Thus far, the whole affair seemed like the mustering of a flock of sheep—or several unrelated flocks of varying breeds. When he spied the line of "black sheep" Lowlanders in their finery across the room, his fingers tightened. "Look at the peacocks in their ruffled collars and fancy breeches."

Calum leaned close and mumbled in his ear. "What did ye expect? Ross is a bloody Lowlander himself."

"At least he had the sense not to invite the MacDonalds. A blood feud would erupt before the tournament began."

"Aye, ye have that right." Calum elbowed him in the ribs. "If I'd seen the MacDonald pennant, I'd have turned the ship around and headed back to Raasay."

They moved toward the dais, where Ross sat beside his wife and a retinue of his highest-ranking men. A line of tables had been prepared for the visiting Highland chiefs, and facing it was a similar table for Lowland lairds.

Calum sauntered up to his brother, Ruairi, Chief of Lewis. "What do ye think of all this?"

Ruairi wrapped his arm around his brother's shoulders and kept his voice low. Bran strained to listen. "Regent Moray still has Mary, Queen of Scots locked away in Lochleven. My bet is Ross is suckering us into siding with the Marian Party."

"'Twas as I thought as well. He wouldna just extend an invitation to this tournament without attaching a few strings."

Bran stepped back while Calum and Ruairi took their places on the bench. He nodded a subtle greeting at Ruairi's henchman, Rewan. They both folded their arms across their chests. At a meal like this, Bran stood guard behind his chief, just like every other henchman in the room. The threat of something going awry was too great, and there were very few men present he could trust, especially not those milk-livered Hamiltons seated across the hall.

Lord Ross stood and pounded the hilt of his dirk on the table. "Welcome, my Highland friends and my Lowland neighbors. I trust your accommodations are acceptable and I invite you to enjoy my hospitality during these days of challenges for brawn. I've invited you here to improve relations, to foster the concept of one Scotland..."

Someone across the hall cleared his throat. Bran homed in on the source of the sound—a fair-haired man, solidly built with narrow eyes. Though he was sitting, by the breadth of his shoulders Bran could tell he'd come for the tournament. The man scanned the room and his gaze collided with Bran's. He tipped his blond head back in silent challenge.

Vehement was the misplaced contempt Lowlanders had for Highlanders, and it didn't surprise Bran to see it here. The tension hung in the air with apprehension akin to the night before a battle. This might be a tournament of skill, but everyone knew it was more. Ross was rolling the dice in a high-stakes game that would match Highlanders against Lowlanders. Lord Ross would be lucky to see out the games without a full-on altercation erupting.

As if he could hear Bran's thoughts, Ross continued. "I ask you all to cast aside your prejudices and join with me in this week of games to determine the best warrior in our beloved Scotland." He held up his tankard and looked straight at the fair-haired Hamilton. "The victor will receive a sword forged by the master smith of Glasgow."

A servant placed a claymore in a bronze scabbard in his hands. The weapon hissed across the metal as Lord Ross drew it. He held the sword high and assessed the shiny new blade with appreciation. "On one side it reads, 'Unite and Protect.'" He turned it over and ran his finger along the flat side. "The reverse side is the same motto in Gaelic, '*Aonaich Agus Dìon.*' I commissioned this claymore to honor both our Lowland knights and our Highland warriors."

Calum and Ruairi exchanged smirks, but Bran kept his eyes on the Lowlander. Unperturbed, Blondie took a long draw of ale from his tankard. Bran didn't care for the idea he and his clansmen may have been invited for their entertainment. But one look at the piece of fine weaponry and Bran wanted it. He glanced at Rewan beside him. "I'd like to take that back to Raasay."

Rewan wore his scraggly hair straight. His thick beard made him look like a Highland barbarian. "Why waste it on your puny isle? It should be in Lewis."

Calum leaned back and eyed them both. "Let it be won by a MacLeod. That is for certain."

Ruairi raised his tankard. "These Lowland nobles are no match for a rugged Highland warrior. They'll be sleeping in their warm beds while we camp on damp straw in windblown tents. 'Twill go to Rewan, mark me."

Calum raised a brow and glanced back at Bran. Words were unnecessary. Bran understood the challenge. Calum purposely kept his guard hidden on Raasay so no one would have an inkling of their might. He worked his men hard. Unbeknownst to all outside Raasay, the laird and his men had embarked on several privateering missions, from plundering English ships to seizing a Spanish galleon filled with treasure in Tortuga. Bran had been there for it all and Calum had driven him like no other—as if he expected more from Bran. The hard work had paid dividends. No one on Raasay could best him, including his revered chief.

Lord Ross sheathed the sword and returned it to his squire. "Eat, drink, my friends. Let no one say they were not offered hospitality from my hand." He clapped, and servants laden with trenchers of food swarmed across the hall. Bran salivated at the smell of roast meat and freshly baked breads. His stomach turned and he swallowed hard. The Highland henchmen would have their supper in the kitchen after their chieftains dined. He would have it no other way, for he would defend his laird and see to his safety or die in the process. This was the price of belonging. Bran held his appointment of knight—of henchman—with pride.

No sooner had the meal begun than a rustle of skirts came from the wide stone stairwell. Every head in the hall turned. A spry lassie wearing a bronze tiara, with exquisitely long auburn tresses, hastened toward the dais. Her cheeks flushed with a healthy glow, her green gown clung to shapely curves. The lass was tall for a woman—she might even come to Bran's chin if she stood beside him.

Bran's folded arms tensed against his body while his hungry stomach flipped upside down. He had only seen one woman in his entire life who could compete with this maiden's beauty, and that was Calum's wife, Anne. But this lass, this *woman*, was far younger and had a spring in her step reminding him of a butterfly flitting between daisies.

With practiced grace, the lovely—but late—young lady danced up the steps to the dais and pecked Lord Ross on the cheek then kissed his wife. By the stern look on Lady Ross's face, Bran realized this must be the Honorable Enya Ross, their youngest and only unwed daughter. Enya patted her mother's shoulder and slipped into the seat beside her. She scanned the wall of Lowlanders first, her gaze stopping for a moment at the Hamilton man, and then continued around the room.

Bran forgot to avert his eyes when her gaze met his. Once connected, he could not look away. His stare held as if a lightning bolt arced between them. Though he couldn't hear her over the crowd, her red lips parted and she gasped. Something deep inside stirred, as if his heart had actually fluttered. Was she the same lass he'd seen on the hill? The one he thought just might load an arrow into her longbow? She smiled. The right corner of Bran's mouth ticked up. She snapped her gaze away and looked at her mother. Bran's eyes traveled to the frowning matron—who was glaring directly at him.

He shifted his attention across the room—anywhere but the dais. He wasn't there to wench. With clenched teeth, Bran scanned the great hall for possible threats. He had no business ogling a baronet's daughter. His duty was to watch Calum's back, win the tournament for the clan and return to Raasay with the prized sword. That was all.

The blond Lowlander scoffed and raised his tankard.

Rewan leaned in. "Ye have some sort of barney with Claud Hamilton?"

Bran swallowed. That was Claud Hamilton, heir to the Hamilton earldom, sitting across the room eyeing him like a caged dog? "Nay, never seen him before in me life." Did the bastard have some sort of claim on the lass? That would be right. Lord Ross would be looking for a highborn match for his beauty.

"Mayhap he's sending a challenge across the hall," Rewan said.

Bran clenched his fists. "I'd wager every man in this room is ready for a challenge. 'Tis why we're here, no?"

"Aye." Rewan nudged him. "And I'll show ye something about the might of Lewis." He chuckled. "Br-ä-n." Rewan drew out his name. "Yer mother should ha' named ye Snowflake."

"Stuff it in yer arse. We'll see who's stronger soon enough."

Frowning, Rewan assessed Bran's folded arms. "Why don't ye spare yerself the embarrassment and concede defeat now. I'll be happy to take that claymore back to Lewis."

"Not on yer life." Bran glanced to the dais. Enya pulled a piece of meat from her eating knife with her teeth. Her gaze floated his way and she smiled and slowly chewed. A rush of heat prickled across Bran's skin. How could she make eating look so—*delicious*?

Every time Enya looked up, that Highlander was staring at her—or was it her gaze kept straying toward him? It mattered not. The man standing behind the redheaded laird was the same warrior she'd watched when he rode past the hill. And he made her so self-aware. Aside from her unbearable etiquette lessons, she'd never thought twice about cutting up a piece of roast lamb and placing it in her mouth. But now she studied her meat, cut it precisely and took every care to lift it to her lips. With each bite, her eyes drifted to the north wall, where he stood with his muscles practically splitting the seams of his linen shirt. It was impossible not to stare.

Enya's mother touched her shoulder, cutting through her thoughts. "I was looking for you this afternoon."

"Oh? I managed to squeeze in a bit of target practice with Rodney." Enya swallowed her grin, fully aware it would irk her mother to know she'd been doing something unladylike.

"Honestly. Must we put a leash and collar on you during these games?"

Enya sighed. The same old talk on "refinement" again. "Of course not. I shall play the part of the delicate maid and do you proud."

"You had better." Mother leaned in. "I've noticed Claud Hamilton looking your way. He won't want a woman who trudges through the mud with a bow and quiver of arrows over her shoulder."

Enya arched a brow. "Have you asked him?"

Mother's jaw dropped. "My heavens, you are insufferable."

Enya patted her mother's hand before the matron had one of her spells. "I was teasing." But she couldn't resist one more ribbing. "I promise not to let on to Lord Hamilton I could skewer his heart from one hundred feet."

Mother grasped Enya's hand and squeezed her fingers. Hard. "I'll hear no more of this. Do you understand? Your father is in negotiations with the Hamiltons and it could mean a great alliance for you as well as the family. You do know Lord Claud is third in line to the throne?"

"Aye, Mother. I'm aware." Enya cast her gaze to the south side of the wall. Claud chatted with his brother. From a distance, he appeared reasonably attractive, though aloof in an aristocratic way, not unlike her father. Her wayward eyes panned across the hall. Larger than the others, the Highlander was anything but aloof. But he looked like he could best anyone in the room and she doubted he needed to prove it, though she wouldn't mind if he proved it to her.

*And where did that entirely inappropriate thought come from?*

Enya cleared her throat and focused on her trencher. She didn't want to admire any man—not until she found adventure.

Making his way to the dais, Enya watched Claud climb the stairs then bow before her father. "The meal was splendid. You did quite well to accommodate such a diverse crowd, my lord."

"These times require one to be, shall we say, open-minded." Lord Ross raised his tankard. "Are you ready for the tournament?"

Claud's gaze shifted to Enya. "I am looking forward to it."

Lord Ross inclined his head. "I'm sure you remember my daughter."

She smiled and held out her hand. Claud clasped it with warm fingers. With grey eyes, his gaze roamed from her face to the flesh of Enya's breasts exposed by the square neckline of her stomacher. Bowing, he pecked the back of her hand. "So good to see you again, Miss Ross."

Enya pulled her hand away and rubbed it. "'Tis a pleasure, Lord Hamilton."

His eyes remained on her cleavage. "I noticed the tulips in the garden. Would you like to take a stroll?"

Heat spreading across her cheeks, Enya tried not to cringe. "That would be *lovely*." She shot a panicked glance to her brother. "Robert, would you care to join us?"

She could tell he tried not to laugh, the heartless barnacle. "Perhaps not this evening. I'll leave you to entertain our guest." He regarded Claud. "But I shall be within earshot if you should need my assistance."

Enya swallowed. She would much prefer Robert to join them. *I'll wager that was Mother's doing.* Enya glanced to the north wall. The Highlander and his laird were gone—just as well. She didn't need a rugged warrior distracting her. She stood and placed her hand in the crook of Claud's arm. "Very well. A stroll through the gardens should be quite pleasant."

The cauldrons blazed along the stone garden path, though a chill iced up her arms now the sun had set. An involuntary shiver trickled down her spine and Enya rubbed the outside of her shoulders.

"Are you cold?" Claud asked.

"A bit. I should have brought my cloak."

"Please, allow me." He removed his grey woolen mantle and draped it across her shoulders.

Enya pulled the sides closed and clasped it under her chin to cover the flesh above her bodice. "You're very kind. Thank you." The heavy cloth smelled a tad musty, but the body heat that remained warmed her. She had walked this path countless times, even in the dark. Never had it given her unease. Tonight, however, she imagined the garden to be a dark forest filled with vile creatures hidden in the shadows.

Enya desperately tried to think of something clever to say, but only came up with an insipid question. "What is it like being the heir to the Hamilton earldom?"

He chuckled. "'Tis most likely boring to a lady like you."

"Like me? Whatever do you mean?" Enya tensed. There she went, challenging him. Mother told her to be demure. Right. Her sister, Alison, was demure. *How would she act? She'd probably turn red, bat her eyelashes and giggle.* Enya didn't giggle, nor did she bat her eyelashes.

Claud puffed out his chest and frowned, making his slender nose appear a bit too long for his face.

*Oh dear, I've put him off straight away. Definitely not the way to begin a courtship, Enya.*

But then his mouth curved up. "Apologies. I suppose I should not make assumptions. How about if you start? What is it you like to do on a sunny afternoon?"

She couldn't hold in her wicked smile. Oh, how she wanted to shock him with her real idea of fun, but she cleared her throat. "There are so many wonderful things to do when the sun's out." She drummed her fingers against her lips. "Hmm. I suppose if I had my choice, I'd go riding."

"A worthy pastime. Do you prefer to ride sidesaddle or in a hackney?

*In a saddle, my legs either side, galloping with my hair flying in the wind.* "I like the feel of a horse under me."

"Ah, do you prefer a spirited mount?"

"Aye, I do. Very much." They passed a statue of cupid with his bow and arrows, and she eyed him. "Now 'tis your turn."

He plucked a yellow tulip from a raised flowerbed and twirled it between his fingers. "I do not have a great deal of idle time. My father's given me a fair bit of responsibility, keeping the crofters in place and collecting their rents."

"That does sound dreary." They walked a bit farther until they reached the pinks and reds of azalea blossoms looking like a splay of confetti in the dancing firelight. "Do you ever have a yen to travel?" Enya asked, hopeful.

He brushed the tulip across her cheek and then held it out to her, his gaze dipping to her breasts. "Whatever do you mean?"

Enya reached for the flower, realizing the cloak had opened. She squeezed it closed. "I've heard tale of the South Seas and the riches of the New World."

Claud laughed and continued along the path. "Your brother warned me about your fancy for adventure. No, I daresay there is quite enough to keep me busy right here. Besides, when I marry, I wouldn't expect my wife to accompany me on any necessary trips abroad. They're fraught with danger and abominable sicknesses like scurvy."

Enya pursed her lips. Robert probably made her out to be daft dreamer. That was what everyone thought of her. Why couldn't she be *normal* like her sisters? She stole another peek at his face. And why couldn't Lord Claud make her insides flutter like they had when she looked at the Highlander? Here she stood beside a perfectly eligible courtier, and all she wanted to do was turn tail and run for the solace of her chamber.

He stopped and faced her. "You've gone quiet. Have I said something to offend you?"

"No, my lord."

"Good." He stepped closer, fixating on her mouth. "Are you looking forward to the tournament?"

Enya crushed the tulip stem between her fingers and stepped back. "Very much. I shall watch with great interest."

"May I..." He hesitated, and then looked her in the eye. "May I carry your kerchief?"

Enya didn't know why she wanted to refuse, but her shoulders tensed. She cast her eyes to the sleeve where she kept it and pulled. What harm was there in giving it to him?

Claud snatched the white linen trimmed with lace and held it to his nose, taking a deep breath. "It shall bring me luck, my lady."

Enya turned toward the manse, but Claud caught her hand and pulled her uncomfortably close. "Why the hurry?"

At eye level, he stood no taller than she. "I thought—"

He pressed his lips to her ear. "You are very pretty."

Enya dropped the tulip and stepped back. "Th-that is kind of you to say."

He held her hand to his lips and kissed, holding it there far longer than necessary. "I will look forward to seeing you often throughout the games."

She gulped. "I'd best return before Robert comes searching for me."

## Chapter Three

Before dawn the next morning, Bran hummed his lullaby for Griffon, his prized golden eagle. Bran chained his jesses to a perch when traveling—the bird's mews was far too big to transport. Though the leather hood covered his eyes, the eagle responded to Bran's voice and pecked against the chain that held him captive.

"Are ye hungry, laddie?"

He held out his gloved hand with a nibble of dried meat. The bird swiftly snatched it. With a practiced flick of his wrist, Bran fastened a lead to the leather jesses. "What do ye say we hunt a pigeon before I break me fast?"

The sky glowed orange against the wisps of spring clouds as Bran headed for the woods with Griffon perched upon his shoulder harness. Aside from a lad scurrying with an armload of firewood, the estate remained quiet, having slept through the night, awaiting the excitement of the day to come.

Marching through a copse of willows, Bran found an open paddock and pulled the hood from Griffon's head. "Arm," Bran commanded.

The eagle hopped from his shoulder perch to Bran's gloved forearm. In one motion, Bran whipped his hand forward. Bran's heart always raced when Griffon spread his wings, spanning a massive six feet. With a flap of Griffon's wings, Bran's hair blew back as he watched the majestic launch—slow at first, but then quickly shooting straight up.

In seconds, Griffon soared at the end of his hundred-foot lead. As if holding on to a kite, Bran watched him fly in great circles. He sang his song. It wasn't necessary to belt it out. The eagle's keen sense of hearing would bring him to the tune from a mile. Griffon inclined his head toward the music and dove. Bran chuckled. The bird looked as if he would dive into Bran's skull like a cannonball, but Griffon always pulled up and clamped on to his forearm in expectation of a reward.

Bran didn't give him a morsel every time. It was important to earn the bird's respect. Eagles would try to dominate and fight if they lacked respect for their handlers. Well aware raptors had no capacity for affection, and harbored no love for their falconers, Bran never fooled himself into thinking Griffon loved him. He had trained the eagle by becoming his most reliable source of food and rewarding good behavior. Bran had created a lifetime bond through discipline, and the two would only be separated by death.

The bird's feathers bristled and Griffon's yellow eyes met Bran's. A warning pricked the back of his neck. The heather rustled. They weren't alone. Bran inclined his head and used his ears to mark the position of the spy—directly behind him. After transferring Griffon to his shoulder, he slid his claymore from its scabbard.

In one swift move, he whipped around and slashed his blade through the brush. Muscles steeled for a fight, Bran glared into the shadowy trees. The stunned form, clad in a hooded cloak, crouched and scooted backward. He had a bow slung over his shoulder, no weapon in his hand. Bran hesitated.

"Please don't kill me."

The soothing pitch of a woman's voice made Bran's heart race. "Ye shouldna sneak up on a man like that, lassie. Ye're likely to have yer throat cut. Now come out here where I can see ye."

A pair of emerald-green eyes peeked from under her hood. "Sheathe your sword."

Bran glanced at the blade in his hand then back at the trembling lass crouched in the dim light. A slender thing, she was about half his weight and posed no threat. He complied and placed his fists on his hips. "All right, now tell me what a wee lass is doing—"

Bran's mouth fell open. Holy Mother Mary and all the saints, he'd nearly skewered Miss Enya. Bran dropped to one knee and bowed his head. "Dear Lord Jesus, if I'd known it was ye, I'd have..." He would have dove behind a tree and let her pass unawares, but she'd think him an utter simpleton if he said anything the like.

"Please forgive my impertinence, Miss Enya. I'm no' accustomed to seeing highborn lassies roaming about the trees."

She smiled and pulled the hood from her auburn tresses. Her hair gleamed like a new copper farthing, but Bran's gaze was immediately pulled to her emerald eyes. They glistened with her wily smile, as if telling him she relished adventure. A faint splay of freckles stretched across her petite nose, which ended in a teasing point.

The hood of her cloak slipped low on her shoulders when she turned her attention to Griffon, giving Bran an eyeful of silken ivory skin that flushed down Enya's slender neck with the chill of morning air.

Her gaze flashed back to his, almost as if she were flirting with him. "I'm afraid we haven't been properly introduced." She curtseyed deeply and bowed her head as she would to a chieftain. "I am Miss Enya, daughter of Lord Ross."

"I ken who ye are."

Rising, she ignored his remark and gestured her hand toward him with an expectant look.

"Sir Bran of Clan MacLeod." Not entirely comfortable with his new title, he gave her a stiff bow. "At yer service, m'lady."

Her gaze slid down his body and back up again. "A Highland knight?"

Though bold, she most likely was assessing his fitness for the tournament. Bran pulled his shoulders back. "Knighted by me chieftain, Calum MacLeod, Laird of Raasay." He wasn't about to say Calum knighted him hours before the ship sailed into the Firth of Clyde. Bran was Calum's champion and that was all that mattered, at least in Renfrewshire.

Enya pointed to the eagle. "And who might this be?"

"Forgive me." He held out his forearm. "This is Griffon."

She admired the bird as if he were the crown jewels. "He's enormous. Usually only kings have the pleasure of hawking with golden eagles. Is this your laird's bird?"

"Nay. I nearly broke me neck pulling him from a nest when he was but a wee chick. Trained him meself."

Enya held up her hand. "May I touch him?"

Bran slipped the hood over the eagle's eyes. "Now ye can. His beak's a bit vicious."

She stroked her fingers along the eagle's brown feathers. Bran arched his back as if her hand had touched his skin. He imagined her fingers running along his back and a soft moan escaped his lips. Bran cringed.

If Enya had heard him, she didn't let on. "He's beautiful."

"Aye, and a great hunter."

Enya's green eyes met his again, making Bran's insides roil. "What's it like in the Highlands?"

Heaven help him, he could stand there and talk to the lassie all morning. "Ye've no' been there?"

"You must be jesting. My father scarcely allows me a carriage ride to Glasgow."

"Me clan's from the tiny Isle of Raasay, sandwiched between the Isle of Skye and the northern mainland. 'Tis a rugged piece of rock, but we make do."

Enya assessed him like a woman would a piece of fine cloth. "Rugged land for a rugged man." Her voice sounded like warm cream. The silken ivory on her cheeks flushed and Bran wished he could run his fingers across the searing warmth of it.

Heat radiated below Bran's belt and he clenched his gut to gain control. If he'd been at an inn, he could have easily mistaken the half cast of her eyes and parted lips as an invitation, but this lass probably didn't even know how much her bonny expression tempted him. He cleared his throat. "And what brings ye walking so early this morn?"

"I always rise with the sun."

"As do I, but 'tis probably no' wise to be wandering the woods when there are so many warriors mulling about."

"Oh? But they're here on my father's invitation."

"Aye, but they're no' all as good-natured as I."

She pointed to the bow on her shoulder. "I can take care of myself."

Though tall for a woman, her delicate limbs were too fine to wield a weapon of any weight. But the haughtiness of her arched brows reflected misplaced self-assurance. Bran frowned to suppress the laugh tickling his insides. "Can ye now?"

Enya rested her hands on her hips. "I can hit the eye of a target at one hundred and fifty paces."

Bran scratched his chin appreciatively. "Had a bit of practice with the bow?"

"Aye."

"Ye sure ye could take on a warrior like me?"

She blinked once and looked him directly in the eye. "I can with my bow."

Aside from being foolish, the lass's overconfidence could be dangerous for her. Mayhap she needed a quick lesson to set her to rights. Bran moved Griffon to his shoulder. "But what if someone crept up and snatched ye like this?" With the speed of a viper, he grasped her shoulder and wrapped her in a firm hold before she could open her mouth to protest.

Bran closed his eyes. He inhaled the sweet perfume of rose oil as the warmth of her back pressed against his chest. Everything about her was soft, supple. *Woman*. Rather than a lesson to teach her caution, he wanted to take Enya's hand and lead her into the tall grass—forget about the tournament and show her exactly how good-natured he could be.

Enya struggled against his arm, but he held her firm.

"Unhand me."

Bran flinched at the scolding tone of her voice, released his arm and resumed a proper distance. His heart pounded in his chest and he studied his boots. Had he ruined his chances to befriend her? He hoped not. She seemed quite...*normal*, almost like a Highland lass. "Apologies, Miss Enya. I shouldna been so brash."

"No, you shouldn't have." Enya brushed her arms, but did not storm away as he expected.

"But 'tis me point. It is dangerous to be in the brush alone."

She clasped her hands together. "Mayhap around someone as enormous as you."

"Ye have nothing to fear from me."

"But you look frightening."

Boar's ballocks, he'd really startled her. Why did he always have to be so overbearing when it came to the lassies? "Good."

Enya dropped her hands to her sides and stepped toward him. "Why do you say that?"

Bran caught the hint of rose oil again and his heart thundered in his ears. "Because I dunna want someone charging out of the brush and skewering me with an arrow."

She pushed her bow up over her shoulder. "You'd kill them if they tried, would you not?"

"Nay—well, mayhap. At least afore they killed me." His fingers twitched. He ached to reach out and run them through her silken tresses.

Her gaze slid down his body as if she were deciding if she wanted to continue the conversation. Bran liked having her eyes on him, though she thought him frightening. She probably thought him unsightly too, with his hard features compared to her delicate ones.

"Did you sail a galley from your island?"

At least she was still willing to converse. "Most came down in galleys, but Laird Calum brought his galleon."

"A tall ship?" Her eyes popped. "Oh my, I'd like to see it."

*Och, she is an inquisitive lass.* "'Tis quite impressive, with three masts and eighteen guns."

Her eyes grew even wider. "Are they all manned?"

"Mostly. The laird wouldna risked sailing down to the Clyde without a bit o' black powder in the hull." Wanted by the English, the Spaniards and quite possibly the Dutch, Bran had no intention of revealing the MacLeods notorious reputation. There was no need for the lass to know about his privateering adventures. She'd shun him for certain.

"But why?" she asked. "We're not dangerous."

"Mayhap no' *you*, but one can never be too careful or have too many guns in these times."

The sun sparkled in Enya's eyes when she looked up again. "So, where else have you sailed in your laird's galleon?"

Bran shouldn't let out too much about Calum's skill at plundering on the high seas, but she looked so interested. He removed Griffon's hood and lead, and sent the eagle soaring as he gathered his thoughts. "We recently returned from Tortuga in the Caribbean." He wouldn't mention they were plundering Spanish silver before Francis Drake and John Hawkins could lay their thieving hands on it. After all, Drake and Hawkins had beaten them to the booty many a time.

Enya clasped her hands to her lips. "An adventure on the high seas? That must have been unbelievably exciting."

"Aye, and a fair bit warmer than it ever is in Scotland."

"What is your favorite memory?"

Bran gave her a twisted smile. He couldn't say "the women," though he'd had his first taste of love with a harlot who fancied him—taught him everything he knew about...

He looked at Enya's angelic face and altered his line of thought. "The water is warm as a bath and the color of the sky on a cloudless day."

Enya turned a circle and her skirts swirled outward. Leading her to that tall grass looked all the more inviting. "It sounds heavenly. How lucky you are to go on exotic adventures. You must tell me more."

Bran smiled and glanced back toward the manse. He knew he shouldn't be standing there talking to Lord Ross's daughter, especially without a chaperone—and especially with the twists his mind was taking. "Mayhap I will someday."

Griffon screeched above. Together they looked up to watch him dive and nab a pigeon.

"Good laddie, bring it here." Bran sang, his voice warbling a bit with Enya watching.

"He's amazing."

Bran wished she were referring to him. "No better hunter exists."

"Why did you choose an eagle and not a falcon or a hawk?"

"Golden eagles nest on Raasay." Bran grinned. "Eagles are at the top of the raptor food chain, but they're very hard to catch."

Griffon soared down with the pigeon and dropped it at Bran's feet. The neck was broken. Bran used his dirk to remove the pigeon's heart and held it to Griffon's beak in reward.

"Why did you do that?"

"'Tis the falconer's reward. The eagle always receives the heart. 'Tis like a sweet to him." Bran eyed her bow and arrows. "Did ye come out here to hunt?"

Enya pulled the bow from her shoulder. "I usually shoot at targets, unless I'm hunting with my brothers."

Bran reached for her weapon. He ran his finger along the wood appreciatively. He chuckled at the painted purple thistles carved on its spine. "'Tis nicely crafted, though the flowers are a bit dainty."

"My father made it for me."

"A man of many talents, aye?" Further delaying his return to the tent, Bran pointed at a tree fifty yards away. "Can ye hit the knot in that oak, yonder?"

The corners of Enya's mouth pulled down. "You're not disgusted that I like to shoot?"

Holy Jesus, she was adorable. "Why should I be disgusted? If ye have a skill, ye should no' be ashamed of it."

Her eyes raked over his body again. This time she had a proud tilt to her chin. She pulled an arrow from her quiver. Her expression turned serious and intent when she aimed at the target. Bran's stomach flipped. She looked incredible, focused like a female eagle diving toward her kill. He liked that. Though clearly protected by her family, Enya was no delicate rose tucked away inside a richly decorated mansion. Bran could tell she had heart and a passion for life. If only he could find a woman like her—someone who wasn't afraid to shoot a bow or sail to exotic isles.

Enya released her arrow. Bran's gaze followed its flight straight to the center of the knot. "Spot in the center." He pointed to her quiver full of arrows. "Do ye think ye can do it a second time?"

She snatched another arrow. "Of course."

Bran watched her intently. Clearly, Enya enjoyed hunting—a great deal. She released her arrow and it skewered the knot directly beside the first. Bran trotted up to the tree and examined the shots. "I couldna done better meself."

Enya walked up and pulled the arrows from the target. "The question is, can you do as well?"

The lass was confident. He liked that too. With Bran's uncanny eyesight, he had no doubt he'd be able to hit the same two marks, and proving it would give him more time to flirt with Enya, though he knew better. But how often did he have a chance to spend a morning with a lass? "I'll have to give it a go."

She held out her bow and Bran's fingers brushed hers. The softness of her skin stopped him. He wanted to reach out and touch her again. They locked eyes, and then Bran remembered to inhale. Enya's cheeks flushed as she lowered her lashes.

With a glance at the tall grass, Bran counted fifty long paces, which took him past where Enya had shot her arrows. He gave the string a test pull and held his hand out for an arrow. She drew one from her quiver and placed it in his hand, keeping her fingers far away from his.

He pulled back the string and aimed. For a moment, he considered missing on purpose, but then a woman like Miss Enya would probably respect a man more if he were her equal. He swallowed—equal in archery, perhaps. Bran's father had been a mere fisherman, drowned when Bran was just a wee lad. His mother worked in the kitchen of Brochel Castle, and by the grace of God, Calum MacLeod had seen fit to foster him. Enya was born into nobility, untouchable to a Highland henchman, even if he could best any man on his island.

Enya held her breath when Bran pulled the bowstring back. She had nearly thrown her arms around his neck and squeezed him when he'd admired her shooting. His dark features made him look so *dangerous*, but Enya could tell his looks were deceptive by the way he handled Griffon. She watched the vein in his neck pulse as he lined up with the target.

When he released the arrow, her heart leapt. She gasped. The shot could not have been more perfect. "You've had some practice." She smiled at her use of his words.

Bran flashed a devilish grin. "Calum used me in the crow's nest during battles when I was a cabin boy. He'd be dead if I missed me target."

Enya gaped at him. "You fought battles as a boy?"

"Aye. Fought the tyrant Thomas Wharton in the bay right in front of Brochel Castle."

"Wharton? Why, even I've heard of *him*. He burned out the Douglas keep at Solway Moss."

Bran nodded as if he had a million things to say but thought better of it. "I doubt an angel wept the day he died."

Right in front of her stood a Highland warrior who sailed the high seas and fought monstrous tyrants. She could spend the entire morning asking him questions. With his dark hair hanging in waves to his shoulders and the shadow of a beard along his jaw line, he could pass for a cutthroat pirate. Why couldn't Claud Hamilton have a teaspoon of Bran's *manliness*?

"Enya?" Robert barked from behind. "What are you doing out here...with *him*?"

Bran wrapped his fingers around the hilt of his sword and Robert yanked his from its scabbard. "No." Enya jumped in front of him. She didn't want her oldest brother killed by the Highlander, and she knew he could do it. "I was out for a stroll and surprised Sir Bran with his eagle, 'tis all."

Robert held his gaze even with Bran's. A thin line formed across his lips. "You shouldn't be wandering about with so many barbar—er, guests here. I'm surprised Heather let you out of her sight."

Enya wrapped a lock of hair around her finger. "Well, she didn't exactly see me."

Robert tugged on Enya's arm and pulled her behind him. He pointed his sword at the Highlander's heart. "You stay away from her."

Bran stood his ground, his face dark, as if he might issue a deathly blow at any moment. He didn't say a word. Robert took another step back and Bran's eyes shot to her. His features relaxed as if the sun had burst through a gathering of clouds. He blinked an unspoken thanks.

Enya pulled her arm away from Robert's grasp. "It has been a pleasure meeting you, Sir Bran. I hope you will dance with me after the tournament."

As Robert marched her to Halkhead House, Bran's gaze seared into her back. She wanted to slap her brother. For heaven's sakes, all she had done was talk, and Bran had been a perfect gentleman—aside from when he snatched her in his arms and turned her knees to mush. *Barbarian? There's nothing barbaric about Sir Bran. He's skilled in so very many things. Look how gentle he is with Griffon.*

*For pity's sake, Highlanders live only a day's ride from Renfrewshire, yet everyone on this side of the Great Divide considers himself superior.*

She eyed her brother, who looked like he could blow steam out his ears. "He did nothing to incite your ire."

"He looked at you. For that I could have killed him."

"Except you would be dead, not him."

"Pardon me? What are you saying?"

"Did you have a look at him? He's enormous. He's a henchman."

Robert stopped and balled his fists, his face turning as red as an overripe tomato. "That's exactly why you should not keep company with a bloody barbarian. We asked them here for one purpose, and that's the only thing they're good for."

"War? Fighting?"

"Aye."

"You're wrong." Enya marched ahead.

"I'd better not catch you speaking to him again," Robert yelled as she disappeared inside.

Enya stomped up the stairs to her chamber. How dare her brother interfere? Could she not talk to someone without her entire family having kittens? She pushed through her door and tossed her bow and quiver onto the bed. She would speak to whomever she pleased. Meddling Robert would have no say in it.

She would dance with Sir Bran and show Robert how civilized Highlanders could be. Catching her reflection in the mirror, Enya steepled her hands to her lips. Claud Hamilton would be there. She let out a sigh. It would be expected she would mostly partner with him. *Heaven help me.*

## Chapter Four

The clans gathered on the estate grounds in anticipation of the day's events. Bran stood beside Calum and assessed his competition. Lord Ross had assembled an impressive collection of warriors. Rewan glanced his way and raised his chin. Bran's gut clenched. He'd like to best the arrogant bastard, even if he was kin—besides, he was a most distant relation, if the generations even counted at this point.

Riding a white steed, Lord Ross cantered up to the fancy podium, festooned with pennants and draped with blue and white striped cloth. His full coat of armor glistened so brightly in the sunlight, Bran had to squint to look at him.

Ross strode up the steps and held out his hands to the crowd, requesting silence. "Warriors of Scotland, it is with a heavy heart I commence these games."

Calum leaned in and whispered. "Here it comes."

"As you are aware, Queen Mary has been wrongly incarcerated at Lochleven Castle under orders of the usurper, self-appointed Regent Moray. This is a travesty against Scotland and against all of us. As you take part in this tournament to find the greatest warriors in Scotland, look into your hearts. Will you sit back while the true queen suffers in her prison?"

"But the queen conspired with Bothwell in the plot to kill Darnley," a voice hollered from the side.

Ross drew his dirk and pointed it at the outspoken warrior. "There was no evidence upon which to convict her." The man opened his mouth to rebuke, but Ross sliced his knife through the air. "We are not here to debate our sovereign's innocence. When these games are over and we have determined the victor, I ask you to weigh your conscience and decide if you will stand beside me and take up arms, or if you will turn your heads and succumb to the edicts of the bastard usurper, Moray."

Lord Ross looked beyond the crowd as if searching for something, and then smiled. He beckoned with his hand and Enya trotted up to the podium on a high stepping white Galloway mare with yellow ribbons woven through her mane. Enya wore a sunflower yellow gown with ample skirts that fluttered across the beast's rump. "My daughter has come of age and will soon wed..."

Bran's heart lurched in his chest. Would the winner of the tournament have a chance at her hand?

"...and her mother and I will be left with no children at home. I have asked Enya to cut the ribbon to commence the games."

Lord Ross nodded to a man at the front of the crowd. Craning his neck, Bran caught a glimpse of Claud Hamilton's smirk. As he'd guessed last eve, Lord Ross would be seeking a highborn heir for his daughter. *What chance does a henchman have at winning the hand of a lassie like Miss Enya?*

*None.*

Enya accepted the shears from her father and held them up. As if she knew where he was standing, her gaze snapped straight to Bran. She smiled, making his insides churn with pent-up nervousness. In a heartbeat, her eyes dropped and she cut the ribbon to the roars of raucous cheers.

Calum slapped his hand against Bran's back. "Do me proud, laddie."

"Och. 'Tis no' today I'm worried about."

"The joust?" Calum hung his thumbs on his belt. "How hard could it be to knock a man off his horse with a pole?"

"I dunna ken why they canna stick to Highland games."

"Because Lowlanders have their noses up English arses."

Bran scowled. "The sooner these games are over, the sooner we'll be back in Raasay."

Rodney took a seat on the bench beside Enya. She eyed him with surprise. "Why are you not helping Robert?"

"He said he doesn't need me during the archery."

"Humph." Enya tugged on her tatted lace gloves. "I should be down there."

"Aye. That would be a sight in all your finery." Rodney gave her an elbow in the ribcage. "I think you're a better shot than your brother."

"If Father wouldn't lock me in my chamber for life, I'd hit the bull's-eye while galloping my horse."

"Why do you not?"

Enya folded her hands in her lap. "I promised to behave myself."

Rodney flicked the silk wimple that covered everything but Enya's face. "I'm glad I'm not you."

Enya watched the archery tournament unfold, and as she expected, Bran made it to the final elimination. It quite surprised her that his opponent was Lord Hamilton. She sat forward with her spine straight.

"I see Lord Claud has made a fine effort," her father said from his red upholstered chair across the aisle—Enya always thought it looked more like a throne.

"I'm not sure he's a match for the Highlander." Enya enjoyed watching the crease that formed between her father's thick eyebrows. "He hasn't missed the bull's-eye yet."

"And whom, may I ask, are you for, my dear?"

"For?" Enya pushed an errant strand of hair under the silk. "Why, the best archer, my lord. Is this not a contest of skill?"

"You always seek to raise my ire. You know very well what I mean."

Lord Claud fired his arrow and hit clean, on the outside edge of center. Enya leaned into Rodney and whispered, "The Highlander will best that shot."

The lad tapped her with his elbow. "You want to place a wager?"

"Ladies do not place wagers."

"Aye, and ladies don't beat their brothers at archery either."

Bran stepped up to the mark.

Enya couldn't resist. "A farthing."

"Two."

"Agreed."

Enya held her breath. Her bow fingers tensely pulled back in concert with the Highlander's. She jolted in her seat as Bran's arrow snapped from his bow and skewered the bull's-eye exactly in the middle. Enya clapped, but when she caught her father's frown, her fingers immediately resumed their folded position in her lap. Rodney reached in his pocket, and Enya gave him a nudge. "Not here. Father will murder me if he discovers we made a wager—especially one against the venerated Lord Claud Hamilton."

"The way you say it, I'd think you didn't like him."

Enya thumped the top of Rodney's woolen bonnet. "'Tis not a question of like or dislike. I simply do not care to be used as a pawn to increase the holdings of men."

Rodney's eyes glazed and he stood. "I'd best see to Sir Robert. He may need a drying cloth for the swimming competition."

By the end of the day, Bran had won the lot, with Rewan MacLeod of Lewis taking second in everything except the archery. Enya was indeed impressed—and to think, early this morning, she'd shared a brief contest of her own with the rugged victor.

Lord Ross grasped his daughter's elbow. "The Highlanders may have come out ahead today, but tomorrow will be an entirely different matter."

Enya curtseyed. "Yes, Father, but I should like to dance with the victor. After all, we ought to show our support for his efforts."

"One dance, aye. That would be diplomatic. But I fully expect you to flourish your attentions on Lord Hamilton. He will sup at our table this eve."

---

Reclining in Ross's solar, Claud Hamilton sat across the writing table from his future father-in-law. "What else do the Highlanders have to do but flex their muscles? 'Tis why we brought them here."

"Yes, but I expected more of a showing from our men." Lord Ross eyed him beneath thick beetle brows. "And I expected more from you."

"Tomorrow will be our day." Claud waved his hand through the air. "Highlanders don't joust, and since you invited men from the Hebrides, their horse skills will be lacking. They're seafarers."

"You had better be right. I want that sword kept in the family. Do you know how much it cost me?"

Claud admired the sword in its brass scabbard, resting on the sideboard. Hewn with a hammered, blackened iron hilt with a glistening golden pommel, the sword would be impressive on any man's belt. But he hadn't come to Ross's solar to discuss the tournament. Two things occupied his mind—both grave, though the first he believed could be settled quickly. "I sense Miss Enya's interest in our union to be tepid."

"Aye? And what would you expect from a young lass?" Ross stood and poured two tots of whisky, then handed one to Claud. "I've married off five daughters, and all were fickle at first. 'Tis your job to charm her. Enya is as shrewd as she is adventuresome. I wouldn't expect her to swoon over your handsome face."

Unconvinced, Claud accepted the cup. "You believe her not to be indifferent?"

"I believe she is terrified."

Claud tossed back the drink and savored the bite. "I saw her watching one of the Highlanders."

"Is that surprising to you? Those men are quite beastly looking. I would expect her to assess them with curiosity."

Though Ross's argument had merit, Claud's gut burned. "I would prefer it if she would not."

Ross grasped the back of his chair. "Hamilton, are you a man or a blubbering nitwit?"

"I beg your pardon, sir, but I do not wish for my intended to shamelessly gawk at commoners."

"My daughter did not gawk."

His gut twisted tighter. "Apologies." This conversation had turned down a path Claud preferred not to pursue. He would win Enya's heart and he would do it without the assistance of her father or his insults. "We must discuss a more pressing matter."

Ross resumed his seat. "You've news of the queen?"

"Yes. As we thought, she's won George Douglas's affection."

"Is he on board to spirit her away from Lochleven?"

"Preparations are underway. Lord Seaton is seeing to it." Claud examined his impeccably groomed fingernails. "When this tournament charade is over, I must return to Rutherglen. In addition to my five hundred foot soldiers, I have fifty elite cavalry men primed and ready to march against Regent Moray, and I expect you to prepare to follow with the same."

"The Ross army will be there, fortified by our Highland neighbors."

Claud stifled his shudder. He'd just as soon the Highlanders march back from whence they came, but then they had their purpose. "I'd expect no less. I shall send word as soon as we know the time and place."

"The queen will want a treaty."

"I doubt she'll receive one. This is a battle that must be won by force." Claud stood and bowed. "God save the queen and restore her to her rightful throne."

Once outside Lord Ross's solar, Claud adjusted his sword belt. Above all things, Claud was a Hamilton, an aged and revered Scottish family, a family that needed to push aside the Stuart line and claim their royal lineage. Claud and his army would first see Mary, Queen of Scots regained her throne, and then they would ensure their line of succession claimed superiority over all others.

Naked, Bran poured water into a wooden bowl provided by Ross's hospitality. He held his bar of cinnamon-scented soap to his nose and inhaled. Cinnamon. Once rare on Raasay, but no more—not since they'd hauled back a cache of it from Tortuga.

Calum pushed through the flap of the tent door. "Cleaning up for the gathering, are ye?"

Bran pulled a pieced of green slime from his hair and held it up. "Aye. I think the loch had more lake weed than water."

"The swimming competition wasn't only cold, aye?"

Bran poured the chilly water over his head and let it dribble into the bowl. "Did ye think more on Ross's call to arms?"

"The chieftains met. We agreed to lend Ross our henchmen, but we're no' bound to him to provide armies of men. We all have keeps to defend. Dunvegan's in the midst of a blood feud with the MacDonalds, and ye ken as well as I, Raasay's a target with the riches we've built."

Bran stood while water streamed down his torso. "Ye mean to leave me here?"

"Ye say it like ye're a lad pining for his ma." Calum swatted him on the back. "Train with Ross's men. It will be good for ye to taste a bit of battle with the Lowlanders."

Bran didn't like it. He bent over and rinsed out the soap. "I've no business in these parts. Me life is with ye and the clan. How am I to protect ye if I'm here and ye're home at Brochel Castle?"

"Ye think I canna watch me own back for a time?" Calum gave him a stern, fatherly look that told Bran not to argue. "I seem to recall many a year where I watched out for *yer* bony arse."

Bran ran his cloth over the offending body part. "Aye, but 'tis anything but bony now."

"No argument there." Calum chuckled. "It has been decided. Ye'll return to Raasay once the queen is back on her throne."

Bran balled the cloth in his fist and scrubbed under his arms with a bit more vigor than needed. Train with Ross's scrawny men? Ride into battle to support a queen who existed more as a fairytale than as his sovereign?

He ran the drying cloth across his groin. He stopped. If he were to stay in Renfrewshire, he'd most likely see Enya. Frequently. *Boar's ballocks, I need to stay away from the likes of her.*

Enya tried to listen while Claud carried on about his endless responsibilities. Honestly, he put more importance on collecting the rents from a parcel of poor crofters than reasonable. She'd rather talk about the events from the day. After all, this was the first such event held at Halkhead House, and it had been quite an extraordinary display.

Seated beside her, Claud grasped the handle of his tankard. "The next crofter who pays me with rabbits will see them thrown back in his face."

"Aye, but at least they're paying something," Lord Ross said.

Enya raised her eating knife. "Today's tournament was quite an impressive exhibition of skill, would you not agree?"

Lord Hamilton sniffed. "A display of brutish talents, I suppose."

"Are you brutish, Lord Claud? I couldn't help but notice you scored quite highly in most of the day's contests." Aside from the caber toss, which took unimaginable strength, and at which the Highlanders bested every single man in her father's guard as well as Lord Hamilton himself.

Claud ran his finger around the inside of his oversized ruff and stretched his neck. "Tomorrow will be more favorable for the Renfrewshire men."

Enya lifted her goblet. "You're more skilled at knocking a man off his horse, then?"

"Jousting." Claud met her gaze then dipped his eyes to the flesh swelling just over her square neckline. "'Tis a gentleman's sport of unprecedented skill."

Enya chuckled into her wine. Oh, how she would dearly love to take that remark and mention the civility of riding at breakneck speed and ramming a ten-foot lance into your opponent's chest. All while trying to stay mounted on your terrified horse, laden with ten stone of armor—the animal hardly able to huff its way to the far end of the arena. "I'm sure tomorrow's activities will be quite invigorating."

"I will do my best to ensure you are entertained." Claud's knee brushed against hers beneath the table.

Enya crossed her ankles away from him. "Gratitude, my lord." She bowed her head to appease him, however. "Perhaps tomorrow will be as amusing as this day's activities."

Enya's gaze strayed to the dour frown stretching her father's jowls. She knew her conversation bordered on impoliteness. Lord Ross was giving her a warning. She'd seen that look hundreds of times. *Curses, why did I have to be the daughter born with a sharp tongue? Why not Grisel or Jean? What would Alison do?* Enya drummed her fingers. Alison would keep her mouth shut and fixate upon Claud's every word as if he were sermonizing during Sunday mass. *How utterly dull.*

"I'm looking forward to seeing you in your full armor. You will make an imposing sight, of that I am certain." *There. Curses to Alison.*

Claud beamed and rubbed a lock of her hair between his fingers. "I shall carry your kerchief."

"You honor me."

Lord Ross smiled, as did Lady Ross. But Enya did not share their pleasure. This feigned adoration soured her stomach.

Across the hall, the henchmen were seated with their chieftains this eve. Evidently the threat of attack had been reduced. Bran pulled a bite from his eating knife and looked her way. He gave her a quick nod then turned his head toward his redheaded chief. She watched the two men talk and wished she could be at the table with them. They most likely had far more interesting topics to discuss than collecting rents from starving crofters.

"Do you find today's victor striking?" Claud asked with an edge to his voice.

"Interesting, mayhap. Different."

Claud leaned in and whispered in her ear. "And what of me? Am I all those things?"

Enya would have thought the son of an earl would be more self-assured, but the man beside her wore his confidence upon his shoulder. She met his grey-eyed stare. "My lord, I find you more familiar, much more in line with a gentleman from Renfrewshire." She was certain her words weren't precisely what he wanted to hear, but it was as much as she was willing to give.

Claud bowed his head politely. "'Tis good to hear."

When the tables cleared and the pipers took their place for the evening's dancing, Lord Ross called for attention. "The first dance will be a strathspey. My daughter has agreed to partner with the winner of today's games."

Bran's horrified gaze shot to Enya. His chieftain gave him a shove. Tripping over the bench, Bran shook himself and walked toward the dais. He adjusted his sword belt and managed to make it the rest of the way without incident. Enya held her hand over her mouth to stifle her urge to laugh.

But Bran looked anything but amused. His powerful legs stretched against his kilt with each step and his eyes did not waver from Enya. Though he'd just eaten, she was sure the look on his face resembled hunger, almost like a Pointer fixated on a mallard he'd just retrieved for his hunter.

Bran stepped onto the dais and bowed. "Miss Enya."

Claud's eyes narrowed as if he were going to leap across the table and challenge the Highlander on the spot. "Do not tell me you're going to lead her to the dance floor with that mammoth claymore swinging from your hip."

Bran frowned as he regarded Claud, but he reached for his buckle and unfastened it with one tug. "I shall leave it here on the dais for safekeeping." He turned to Enya and offered his hand. "Shall we, Miss Enya?"

He wore his damp hair combed back away from his face. Enya placed her palm in his much larger, very warm hand. Cinnamon—the rare fragrance of delicious, delectable cinnamon pleased her as she stepped beside him. "Do you like to dance?"

Bran glanced down the length of his straight, bold nose, a masculine nose that rested above full lips that turned up at the corners. "I danced quite a lot as a lad, no' so much now."

"Why not now?"

His eyebrows arched with his sideways glance. "Guarding me chief has its responsibilities. There's no' so much time for niceties."

She liked that she had to look up to face him. "But you enjoy dancing?"

"Aye."

They stood across from each other in the line of dancers. Bran bowed and Enya curtseyed. The piper's music filled the hall and Bran executed the first sashays of the strathspey with practiced precision.

Enya grasped his hands for the circle. "Someone has been taught well."

"Laird Calum's wife, Lady Anne, saw to it I learned refinement."

"She sounds quite accomplished."

"She is. Her da was an English earl."

"English?"

Bran turned away, not missing a step. Enya watched him across the aisle as couples sashayed through. Sir Bran had quite a number of talents one would not expect in a barbarian. And his laird, married to an English lady? How that union came about would be a story she'd love to hear.

Her shoulder brushed his, sending her insides aflutter as they took their turn stepping together down the aisle of dancers. Enya stole a glance at him and her palms moistened. "I quite enjoyed the tournament today."

His fingers clutched hers a bit tighter. "'Twas a good match."

"Are you looking forward to tomorrow's games?"

"No' so much."

She stretched out to match his long strides. "And why, may I ask?"

He released her hand and took his place at the end of the line. "I dunna see much sport in jousting."

Enya faced him. "Interesting. I have reservations about jousting as well." She raised her voice a bit to be heard across the aisle. "I'd much prefer a hunt."

His gaze focused solely upon her. "Aye, a hunt with raptors."

"Or dogs."

"That'd be something I'd enjoy."

Enya's stomach lurched when she had to take a turn with the man to Bran's left. She glanced over her shoulder at him. Bran's hungry stare made her skin prickle, as if every inch of her flesh had heightened in sensitivity.

All too soon, the music ended. Bran took her hand, then bowed and touched his lips ever so softly to the back of it. The heady scent of cinnamon wafted over her as if in a dream. Slowly he straightened, his lips slightly parted, and then his tongue slipped out and moistened his bottom lip. A fire ignited deep inside and rose quickly to her cheeks.

Enya's pulse beat rapidly where his lips had been and she held her hand tight across her waist. She could scarcely breathe as he led her back to her father's table. If only the dance hadn't ended.

Bran blessed her with a devilishly handsome grin and picked up his sword. "Thank ye for the dance, Miss Enya."

"'Twas my pleasure."

Enya's stomach sank when Claud rose and pulled out her chair. "Thank heavens you shan't have to dance with him again."

Enya wanted to give his smirk a firm slap. She'd dance every tune with Sir Bran if it were permissible. "Oh?"

"I shall rescue you from graceless brutes for the duration of the games."

Enya slid into the chair. She'd had just about enough of Lord Claud's self-importance for one night. "If it would not offend, I rose early and am quite tired. I believe I'd prefer to watch the dancing for the rest of the eve."

---

After he'd escorted the beautiful maid to the dais, Bran buckled his sword belt and headed back to Calum's table. He couldn't bring himself to turn and look at Enya, though the prickles at the nape of his neck told him she was watching. So was Claud Hamilton. Bran had no intention of pursuing his attraction for the lass. Lord Ross had made it clear the couple was betrothed, or close enough to it.

Calum filled Bran's tankard with ale. "I think the lassie enjoyed yer dancing by the blush that crawled up her face."

"Nay, 'twas just the exertion."

"A strathspey?" Calum smirked. "A reel I would believe, but Lord Ross's daughter clearly flushed when she looked at ye, though dunna ask me why."

Rewan leaned across the table. "She doesna ken what to think of a rugged Highlander who's so light on his feet."

"Aye." Ruairi held up his tankard. "Ye most likely frightened her walking up there with yer claymore."

Bran guzzled his ale and poured another. He glanced to the dais. Holy falcon feathers, why did she have to be looking his way? Every time her skirts had brushed against his calves, his knees turned to jelly. How could he carry out his duty and protect Calum with a sweet-smelling woman sapping his wits? He inhaled deeply. The warm air in the hall choked him. "If ye dunna need me, I think I'll head for me pallet."

Calum reached for the ewer and started to pour. "So early? Are ye worried about tomorrow?"

Bran held up his hand. "I havena even a coat of armor." The joust was the last thing from his mind, but it was easier to admit to nerves than admit the lassie had riled him. The softness of her touch, the emerald eyes gazing into his when they held hands and circled, attacked his defenses and flung them aside as if he were a helpless lad. If she'd come at him with a dagger, he might have let her stab him in the heart.

Bran pushed outside and headed toward the tents. He needed to find a way to convince Calum to allow him to return to Raasay with the others. If he remained behind and trained with Ross's men, he'd surely see Enya. And as a member of Ross's guard, he'd have no access to her. He'd watch Enya from a distance and the sickly feeling would eat away at his gut. Christ, he'd probably have to watch while Lord Claud came calling.

"Highlander."

Bran stopped.

Claud Hamilton tugged on his silk doublet and sauntered up to him. "I hoped you enjoyed that dance, because it will be the last time you touch a lady as fine as Miss Enya Ross."

Oh, how gratifying it would be to slam his fist into that smug face. Crossing his arms, Bran stepped into the future earl and looked down. "I generally dance with whomever I please." Bran sniffed the air. "But the stench of this Lowland air is disagreeable."

"You'd best head back to the Highlands where you belong."

"'Tis my thought exactly." Bran studied the ruff encircling the pompous man's neck. "But our host has other ideas."

"He'll be fine without you."

"Aye? By the look of his men, they could learn a few Highland tactics."

"Mayhap with Highland games, but tomorrow you'll lose and you can return to rutting the sheep on your godforsaken island."

Bran clenched his fists and leaned in. "Perhaps we should have a tournament of our own."

Claud's eyes widened. Bran detected a flash of fear that Claud quickly covered by tilting his chin up and taking a step back. "I'd dearly love to oblige you. However, I've more delicate matters to attend to this eve." Claud looked back to the double oak doors of the hall. "Miss Enya will be wondering to where I've disappeared."

Bran rubbed his palm over the pommel of his dirk and watched Lord Claud amble back into the hall. If he hadn't promised Calum he'd stay out of trouble, he would have challenged the fool-born bastard and shown him exactly how Highlanders fought.

He pulled the dirk from its scabbard and held it up to the moonlight. Bran's memories of his father were few, and keepsakes fewer, but this was one possession he treasured, one that had served him well in many a fight. Claud Hamilton would eat his arrogance one day, but whether Bran would be the one to feed it to him was yet to be determined.

## Chapter Five

Calum buckled the breastplate in place and stepped back. "'Tis only a wee bit too small."

Bran stood with his arms straight out to the sides. "It feels like death linen."

"Pardon me? This armor is forged of the finest iron."

"Aye, so said the bastard ye took it from."

"Won it, mind you."

Bran could barely move once Calum finished buckling all the metal pieces to his limbs. "I look like an overstuffed sausage."

"Ye look fine. Besides, the armor's covering all the important parts."

Bran glanced down at the cutaway over his unmentionables. "Not quite everything."

"The saddle pommel will protect ye there." Calum stood back and eyed his work. "The most important thing to remember is holding the lance level and aim for yer opponent's heart. Hit him square and he'll fall off his horse every time."

"Aye, and how do I keep from being knocked off me own steed?"

"'Tis easier than fighting two at once. Keep one eye on yer target and the other on his weapon. Dunna let it hit ye or ye'll be mighty sore for days."

"Or dead."

"Aye, well, then there's that."

Bran hated the way the armor constricted his movement. Though a good idea in theory, he realized why he never saw a full coat of armor in the midst of a battle. A warrior's strength would be sapped before he raised his sword. Besides, Bran would never be able to afford such a luxury. Bran was content to fight his battles protected by his chainmail and helm—it gave him far more freedom of movement.

Forced to use a mounting block, he climbed aboard the warhorse provided by the host. Bran ran his hand along the stallion's mane and leaned toward his ear. "Yer armor fits better than mine, but if ye ride without fear, I'll see to it ye have an extra ration of oats."

Calum led the horse to the field. "Yer up against Robert Ross first. They're running Highlanders against Lowlanders in the elimination."

"Och aye, the heir himself?"

Eyeing his opponent, Bran preferred to feel the reins against the pads of his fingers, but the iron finger gauntlets prohibited it. The horse lined up at the south end of the arena and Calum handed Bran a lance. He inserted the thick end in the iron lance rest attached to his breastplate. He glanced down to the top of Calum's red-haired head. "Any last advice, m'laird?"

"Remember what I said. Focus on yer opponent and dunna get hit."

"Sounds easy enough."

Bran flipped down the visor of his helm. Through the slits, the world around him focused on the mounted knight straight ahead. Hot breath filled the metal, turning cold and moist against his chin. Lighter than he'd imagined, the jousting lance weighed about as much as his claymore, though awkward and much more difficult to balance.

Bran watched his target at the far end of the run. Sir Robert had been none too friendly since finding Bran talking to Enya. These Lowlanders thought they'd push out the Highland contestants with their fancy games? How hard could it be to knock a man off his horse with a stick?

Standing in the middle of the jousting run, the squire raised a flag. Bran's heart lurched. The flag dropped. Bran clenched his legs around his steed and leaned forward in the saddle. The warhorse bounded into a full-out gallop. The slits in the helm bobbed up and down, impeding Bran's line of vision. His opponent deathly and impersonal in his shining coat of armor, his lance trained on Bran's heart. Two steps to collision. Bran leaned back and thrust his lance forward.

It struck solid and splintered. Bran teetered as the jarring impact reverberated through his shoulder. He pulled the horse up and spun. Robert Ross lay in the sand, struggling to right himself. He tugged the helm from his head and glared at Bran—a look of complete contempt. At least the Ross heir wasn't badly wounded.

Calum raced in. "Not a bad try for yer first time."

Bran's armor cut into his flesh as he dismounted. "'Twas like swinging into battle from a ship's rigging. No time to think, just hold on and pray."

When his feet touched ground, he glanced to the stands. Enya sat beside her mother with her hands covering her mouth. A lead ball dropped to the pit of Bran's stomach. Enya would probably never speak to him again. Bran looked to Robert, who was up and being tended by his young squire. It was just as well. Bran had no business talking to the lass, and besides, he'd see trouble for certain if she kept flirting with his sensibilities.

Bran and Calum viewed the remaining first round from the sidelines. Rewan was smashed to the ground by Claud Hamilton and Ruairi helped him limp back to the tents. Enya continued to watch from her perch on the dais, her eyes not once straying Bran's way. By the end of the joust, Bran had made it to the final run, and would face none other than Lord Claud Hamilton.

---

Enya nearly lost her wits when Robert and Bran sped head on in the first joust. Her heart betrayed her family, wishing for Bran to win, yet wanting her brother unscathed. After Bran had won his round with Robert, she couldn't bring herself to look at him. Too many emotions roiled inside. She hated jousting and its barbaric pummeling. It was no better than Roman gladiatorial sport.

Worse, both Bran and Claud now readied their horses for the championship. Claud had his visor pushed up and smiled at her, waving the handkerchief she'd given him as if it were his claim to her. Enya wanted to march over and yank it out of his hand, but then Claud tied it to the end of his lance. Wonderful. Her "almost" betrothed was going to smash his lance into Bran's chest, with her kerchief giving *her* blessing.

She studied Bran, who looked gargantuan under a coat of armor that must be two sizes too small. With no squire, Laird MacLeod patted Bran's shoulder, imparting final advice. Bran closed the visor of his helm and steadied the big horse beneath him.

As Rodney raised the flag, Enya clasped her hand over her heart and held her breath. Bran kicked his heels. The warhorse bolted forward, only to skid and whinny like he'd been skewered. The miserable stallion threw its head and reared dangerously. Bran's lance flipped out of his hand while he tightened the reins to regain control of his mount. Claud sped forward. Bran raised his head just as Hamilton's lance struck him. The blow lifted Bran from his horse and he careened through the air. He crashed to the ground with a clanking thud.

Enya stood, fists clenched under her chin. Calum ran to Bran, who lay motionless. She raced down the steps. Claud rode his warhorse into her path. "Come to congratulate my victory, Miss Enya?"

She snapped her gaze up to him. "Congratulations on bludgeoning a man whose horse spooked."

"Ah, my lady, one must be able to control his mount in tournament or a fight." He leaned down. "If you falter, you lose."

Enya pushed past him and dashed to Bran's side. His eyes were closed. She held her hand to his nose. Warm breath caressed it.

Calum signaled to Rodney. "Bring the board. We'll need to carry him to the tent."

Enya wrung her hands. "Will he be all right?"

Calum's brow furrowed. "Only time will tell. Do ye have a healer?"

"My serving maid Heather can help."

"Meet us at the tent."

Enya didn't look back to regard Lord and Lady Ross's expressions. They most likely disapproved of her display of concern, and they most certainly would disapprove of her taking Heather to the tents.

"The baroness will have my hide if she knew I allowed you to come with me." Heather clutched her medicine basket, waddling as fast as she could, cheeks flushed.

"You haven't *allowed* me. I demanded to accompany you, and will attest to it." Enya hurried ahead. "Come along."

Rushing into the corridor of tents, Enya had no idea which one housed Bran. She stopped and turned full circle and spied the henchman from Lewis. She hurried up to him. "I've brought the healer for Sir Bran. Can you tell me which tent is his?"

The man gave her a lecherous smirk. "Dancing with him and then tending his wounds as well?"

"I shall find him with or without your help, but the healer is waiting." She looked through the gap of the nearest tent and saw nothing. "Which one is it?"

He pointed. "Second from the end."

"Thank you," Enya clipped, caring not for the man's impertinence.

With no place to knock, Enya reached for the flap, but pulled her hand back. He could be indecent. "Hello?"

"A moment." Laird Calum popped his head out and looked her over from head to toe. "Have ye brought the healer?"

Heather huffed up from behind. "Where's the patient?"

After stepping inside, Enya made the introductions. "This is Mistress Heather, Laird Calum MacLeod of Raasay." She moved to the pallet where Bran lay unconscious, still clad in his armor. "And this poor, unfortunate soul is Sir Bran."

Heather bustled in and set her basket beside him. "The first thing we must do is remove that constricting armor." She pointed to the leather strap cutting through his side. "He's not taking in enough air."

Calum knelt behind Bran and lifted him by the shoulders. "I'll hold him up if ye can make quick work of unfastening the buckles."

Without a second thought, Enya tugged at the leather straps and released the bindings of his breastplate while Heather knelt beside him. Calum laid Bran back down and Enya went to work on removing his leg armor.

Pulling away the leather straps belted atop his quilted doublet had not caused Enya's body to react, but when her fingers brushed his exposed calves, her breath caught. His flesh warm to her touch, she slowly pulled away the leg iron and studied the powerful muscles beneath. His calf alone was at least as big as her thigh. It narrowed to a sturdy ankle that sloped into a well-worn leather boot.

"Is something amiss?" Calum asked.

Enya snapped her head up. "He has no foot armor?"

"'Tis a borrowed suit that barely fit."

"Was too small, I'll say." Heather put a foot on Bran's shoulder and tugged off his helm. "I never thought I'd lever it off."

Enya made quick work of removing the other pieces of armor until she reached his thighs. Though Bran wore a pair of knee-length leather trews, the muscular form beneath was a sight of pure mastery. Enya unfastened the thigh piece and admired the snug fit to the leather that outlined Bran's physical power. She reached out, placed her hand on his thigh and gasped. The muscle beneath the trews was as hard as the armor she'd just removed, though far warmer.

The muscle twitched beneath her hand. Her gaze shot to Bran's face. His eyes were still closed but his muscle had tightened. Enya left her hand there while Heather opened one of his lids and peered into his eye. The old woman then gave him three smacks to the face. "Wake up, young man."

Bran's leg twitched again. Calum bent down and shook Bran's shoulders. "Come on, lad. 'Tis time ye woke."

Heather lifted his eyelid with her thumb and leaned forward. "We need to raise him up. His eyes are dark. 'Tis not a good sign."

Calum grasped Bran's shoulders, but Enya couldn't imagine trying to force Bran to sit up in his condition. "Let me try."

Heather wiped her hands on her apron. "What good do you think you can do, child?"

Enya pushed her way to Bran's shoulder and knelt. "Just let me speak to him before you shake him up more."

Enya had no idea what she was doing, but the thought of Calum setting him upright and shaking him while Heather smacked him across the face didn't bode well. His muscle had twitched beneath her hand. Twice. Something told her he was trying to come around.

Enya leaned forward and whispered in his ear. "Sir Bran, 'tis time to wake. You will miss the gathering if you do not..." Enya glanced over her shoulder at the two people eyeing her with incredulity. She could do nothing with them staring. "Leave us."

Heather wrung her hands. "But my lady...'tis not proper."

Enya spread her palms to her sides. "Does he look like he's going to brandish his sword and take advantage? Please, just give me a moment."

Heather hesitated, though Calum tugged on her elbow. "Come, mistress. We'll be right outside. How could a few moments hurt?"

When the tent flap closed, Enya returned her attention to the patient. Pausing, she studied his face. Hardened by the sea and battle, Bran's rigid features were tempered in slumber. With his hawk-like eyes shuttered, he was as beautiful as a sleeping babe. She placed her hand on his forehead then traced her finger down the length of his nose. Caressing her thumb across his lips, Enya did not expect the velvety smoothness—nor did she expect the heavy swell in her breasts.

As if compelled by a force outside her body, she leaned forward and touched her lips to his. The air from his breathing tickled her cheek. Closing her eyes, she kissed him again. A soft groan, almost a whisper, came from his throat. Enya pulled up, but a hand caressed her neck and coaxed her back to those full lips. This time she wasn't kissing a piece of silk cloth. The lips parted and Bran's tongue brushed her mouth ever so softly. Enya's lips tingled. *Holy sweet Mary*. Her entire body tingled. She joined her lips with his.

With a hint of cinnamon lingering, Bran tasted fresh, like water from a clear stream. She hesitated when his tongue met hers but when he swirled it in a delicious loop, Enya melted into him and followed his lead. Her body on fire, she couldn't breathe, couldn't think. Every inch of her flesh tingled.

His hand skimmed to her shoulder and his eyes opened. "Am I in heaven?"

Enya surveyed the tent as if she were spinning while ropes unwound on a tree swing. *I'm most likely as dazed as he.* "Nay, Sir Bran, you had a fall. Do you remember?"

"Ah, Lord Hamilton and his vicious lance."

"I'm afraid so."

He tried to sit up, but Enya held her hand to his chest. "You must rest."

His forehead creased between his dark brows. "But why are ye in me tent? 'Twill be a scandal."

"Not to worry, my serving maid and Laird Calum are right outside."

As if she'd beckoned them, the tent flap opened and Bran threw his arm across his eyes. "'Tis too bright."

"He's awake?" Calum asked.

Heather stepped beside Enya. "How did you do that?"

Enya glanced at Bran. He winked with a rakish smile stretching across his lips, and Enya twirled a lock of hair around her finger. She could never lie to Heather—the woman always knew she was fibbing before the words got out. "I kissed him."

"What—"

Calum swatted Heather on the back with a hearty laugh. "A kiss from a bonny lassie will fix up me henchman every time. Now why didna I think of that?"

Heather shot Enya one of those "wait until I see you alone" looks and reached for a vial from her basket. "I'll rub some marjoram oil on your head and will send you a flagon of rosemary tea."

"I'll bring it," Enya volunteered.

Heather rubbed in the oil like she was trying to remove a stubborn stain from a silver dish. "I believe you've done quite enough."

Bran closed his eyes and grimaced. "I think I prefer Miss Enya's healing methods."

"You shan't find yourself in such close proximity to the lady again." Stoppering the vial, Heather regarded the patient with a dour frown. "I think you'll live."

Bran pushed up onto his elbow. "I'm sure of it. Thanks to ye ladies, I'll be right in no time. It takes much more than a fall from a horse to keep me abed."

## Chapter Six

When he sat up, Bran swallowed back a heave.

Calum plopped on the edge of his pallet. "So ye got a kiss from the baron's daughter?"

"Och, 'tis the last thing I need." Bran unfastened the top button of his doublet and stretched his neck. "Ye're leaving me here with a mob of unfriendly Lowlanders and *her*? Calum, I kissed her back. That could see me thrown in the pit, or worse, strung up on the nearest tree."

"'Twill be a good lesson for ye, learning to control those hot-blooded MacLeod urges."

Bran wished his head wasn't throbbing so much, and he wished he could say something to the chieftain to make him understand Bran could not stay at Halkhead. "She flirts with me."

"Aye? When has a lassie batting her lashes and stealing a kiss caused ye consternation?"

"This is different."

"Bran, I cannot go back on me word. Ye'll do the MacLeod proud, ye understand? I need ye to gird yer loins, train with Ross's men, and hightail yer arse back to Raasay." Calum cuffed the back of Bran's head. "Can ye do that for me?"

Bran's brain rattled with the thump and his teeth ached like they would fall out. "Och, ye ken I'll do anything ye ask of me."

"Then there's nay question. Ye must dress. We've a gathering to attend."

Bran swayed a bit when he stood. Gathering? He'd rather take Griffon and spend the evening riding.

Before the feast, Baronet Ross called the chiefs together to hear their decision on his request to support the queen's cause. Claud Hamilton stood beside him as the dozen lairds filed into his solar and took a seat at the long cherry wood table. He'd expressly asked for the chiefs to leave their henchmen behind. The size of the room was his excuse. The real reason he wanted the chiefs separated from their musclemen was to meet with them without the added virility acquired when one had a young buck ready to wield his sword in one's defense.

Of course Ross had Malcolm, the captain of his guard, his son and Claud Hamilton beside him. Ross addressed the future Earl of Arran. "'Twas a good win for us today."

Claud tugged on the hem of his doublet and stood a little taller. "Thank you, sir."

Malcolm, a sturdy man with dun eyes, ran his fingers down to the point of his black beard. "It didn't hurt that we put Bran on Spooky."

"Nor did it make any difference I had deerhound piss sprinkled on the Highlander's side of the field," Robert added.

Ross wondered if there had been some interference on the part of his men. He'd made it clear a Lowlander was to win the joust. "'Tis good we showed that young buck a Highlander's place." Ross shook out his ruffled sleeves and turned to Claud. "When will you return to Rutherglen?"

"On the morrow."

"Very good." Ross leaned so his lips were a half-inch from Claud's ear. "And once we've got the queen back on the throne, we shall resume our negotiations regarding Enya's hand."

"I will look forward to that with great anticipation."

Lord Ross watched the Highland chiefs file into the room in a wave of color, all shrouded in plaid. Ruairi from Lewis wore yellow, Calum from Raasay red, MacNeil from Barra blue and dark green.

It looked like a mob of court jesters had come to call. "My lairds, please be seated."

Ross waited until the noise of seats scraping across the floorboards subsided. "It has been a fine tournament with great skill on display. I have been impressed with the substance of the Highland warriors."

Heads nodded. Ruairi MacLeod piped up. "Did ye think we were a bunch of laggards? Have ye forgotten the wars with the Lords of the Isles? Those men were our ancestors."

"Of course not. Your reputation as fighting men is why I brought you here." Lord Ross rested his palms on the table. "Now tell me, how will you help restore Queen Mary to the throne?"

The room erupted in a cacophony of braying voices. Everyone spoke at once. Ross was not a patient man, and he didn't like the excuses he was hearing. "Silence. Ruairi, since you seem to have a lot to say, you shall be the first to speak."

"We've considered yer request with great concern." Ruairi gestured to the Chief of Dunvegan. "Hector is in the midst of battle with the MacDonalds, and we all have our keeps to protect."

Calum MacLeod cleared his throat. "'Tis no' that we dunna support the queen, 'tis just the law of Edinburgh and the Lowlands doesna impact us overmuch."

Claud shook his fist. "But in the name of King James V, Mary's father, we are bound to be one Scotland."

Ruairi sliced his hand through the air. "Aye, and that's why we've decided to leave ye our best men to fight by yer side. My Rewan is as good as ten pikemen. Let our henchmen train with yer army and ye'll have a force to be feared in anyone's eyes."

Ross needed a draught of whisky. This wasn't at all what he'd expected. They'd taken advantage of his hospitality. He'd shown them the finery of the Lowlands and welcomed the barbarians onto his lands as if they were equals. Well...almost equals—he'd had them sleep in tents, but they hardly would have noticed any resulting discomfort. "We need an army of thousands."

Claud stood. "We'll have it. My family alone will bring six hundred men. In addition to Ross, we've Argyle, Eglinton, and Cassillis to name a few—all with numbers as great as Hamilton."

"Ye see?" Ruairi and all the chiefs stood. "Ye've nothing to worry about. Our offer still stands. Our men will remain behind to train with yers."

Ross glared at Claud. He'd not appraised well, standing and bragging about how well fortified the Marian Party was. Moray had a number of strong families behind him as well. With the Hebrides clans behind the queen, the country would be further divided. Hell, Ross was ready for a full-out civil war if that was what it took to dethrone the usurper. Ross looked to Ruairi and Calum. Their faces were grim. He harbored little hope he'd change their minds after Claud's remark. "Very well. Training will commence in the courtyard at dawn."

---

Enya didn't know why it irritated her when her father announced the first dance would be with Lord Claud, but her stomach twisted in a knot all the same. Claud grinned and took her hand. His fingers were soft like hers, not rough as Bran's had been. Together they strolled past the table where Bran sat. Engaged in conversation with his laird, he appeared completely recovered from his calamity earlier in the day. If Heather had known he was sitting in the hall, she'd shoo him back to bed straight away.

On the dance floor, Claud stood across from her, but fortunately the piper launched into a reel, which meant vigorous steps with little hand holding. Enya plastered on a smile and picked up her feet, but every time she turned toward Bran, she checked to see if he was watching. Something must have been wrong. Queen's knees, he'd even turned his back. Finding it nearly impossible to smile, Enya pretended to concentrate on her feet.

Her mind rifled through their encounter in the tent...for the hundredth time. Of course she'd been undeniably bold by kissing Bran, but he was *unconscious*. He wasn't supposed to wake and attempt to *eat* her. And what made him put his tongue in her mouth anyway...and why did it feel so inexplicably good?

Enya twirled in another circle. Bran had turned around and his hawk-like gaze now focused on her as if she were the only dancer on the floor. Heat rose to her cheeks.

"Well, do you?" Claud's voice cut through her thoughts as they danced across from one another.

"Do I what?"

"I believe you've not paid attention to a word I've said this entire dance. Do you need some air?"

Claud had been talking? No matter, Enya had no intention of leaving the hall on Lord Hamilton's arm. "Not at all." The music ended and she curtseyed. "I'd like to inquire as to Sir Bran's health."

"He looks well to me."

"Nonsense. The poor man was knocked silly...and by *your* lance. 'Tis only proper to ask how he fares."

Claud rolled his eyes. "Very well, if *we* must." He clasped Enya's arm a bit too firmly.

Enya smiled as they approached. "Sir Bran."

The bench scraped against the floorboards when Bran stood and bowed. "Miss Enya. Ye were as light on yer feet as a fairy princess."

She actually giggled. "'Tis very kind of you to say so. Might I inquire—"

Claud gave Enya's arm a firm squeeze. "The lady would like to know if your head has recovered from our jousting round. I trust I didn't cause any permanent damage."

Bran's eyes narrowed with the thin line of his lips. "As ye can see, I'm fighting fit."

Claud dropped Enya's arm and stepped toward him. "Aye? We'll have to have another match."

Bran closed the gap, his nose an inch from Claud's. "It would be me pleasure."

Loud tapping came from the dais and Enya's father stood. "The time has come to present the victor's sword." Malcolm stood beside him holding the trophy.

Both Claud and Bran folded their arms and turned their attention to the dais.

"With all the points combined from yesterday's tournament, and his undefeated win in the joust, I present this award to Lord Claud Hamilton."

Enya's jaw dropped.

Aside from applause from the Hamilton contingent on the south side of the hall, the room fell silent. Claud grinned at Enya and marched toward the dais.

Calum shoved back his bench and stood. "What of Sir Bran? He took the entire games, and only fell in one jousting round. I say he's the winner."

The hall erupted in a resounding "Aye."

Enya's father ran a hand across his ermine cap worn only by chartered baronets—the cap that gave Lord Ross final word regarding every issue upon his lands. He would have thought this through, no doubt.

"The Highlander performed very well indeed. I can assure you this was a difficult decision."

Calum dropped back to the bench with a grumble. "The whole thing seems bloody rigged to me." He bowed his head toward Enya. "No incivility to ye, m'lady."

"None taken. If my father would have consulted with me, I would have asked the same question, my laird." Enya watched as Claud held up the sword to a tepid applause. "'Tis clear a great many guests feel the same."

As the music resumed, Bran leaned down, his lips brushing her hair. "Ye rewarded me with the greatest prize this afternoon. I will never forget yer kiss."

Enya gasped and met his gaze. If only she could wrap her arms around him and kiss him again, right there in the hall with everyone watching. Her eyes drifted to his full lips and her insides danced in concert with the piper's tune. Not trusting her voice to speak, she forced a curtsey and returned to the dais.

# Chapter Seven

After the tents were struck, Bran found a place to set up his pallet in the stable loft. He preferred not to bed down in the tower with Ross's guard like Rewan and the others. The solitude of the stable enabled him to keep Griffon away from prying strangers who knew nothing about raptors. Besides, he was used to the privacy of his cottage on Raasay. That was the one condition he'd insisted on when Calum appointed him henchman. He only stayed in Brochel Castle's tower when necessary for the clan's protection.

He'd been training with Ross's guard for three days, and hadn't even seen Enya in the great hall for meals. It was for the best. Seeing her only twisted his insides. However, he'd never forget awaking to her delicate, bow-shaped lips teasing him. Dropping in and out of consciousness, at first he'd thought he was dreaming. He had some idea a healer tended him, but when Enya's lips touched his, he woke as if someone held smelling salts to his nose—though a bouquet as pleasant as heaven.

A stall door opened below. "Good morn, Maisey." A woman's voice…a young woman.

Careful not to make a sound, Bran crawled to the trapdoor and peeked down. Dressed in a simple kirtle, a linen coif upon her head with a long braid trailing down to her beautifully curved hips, Enya fastened a bridle on a sorrel mare. His heart skipped a beat.

"Good morn, Miss Enya." The words came out before he had a chance to think.

Enya snapped around but didn't look up. "Who's toying with me?"

"Sorry to startle ye." Bran's feet hit two rungs of the ladder as he hopped down. "I've made me pallet in the loft."

Enya glanced up at the opening. "Why not the tower? Would that not be more comfortable?"

"I prefer the quiet, and the animals dunna talk back."

Enya slipped the snaffle bit into the mare's mouth. "If it were up to me I think I'd stay in the stable as well."

"And where are ye off to this morn?"

"I was planning to slip out for an early ride." Her eyes shifted to the stable door. "Father never allows me to ride alone. I can only do it when I spirit away before dawn."

Beyond the open door, the sky had taken on a pre-sunrise violet hue. "Yer da's right. Ye never know what's lurking in the shadows."

She swung a saddle blanket across Maisey's back. "But Father's guard patrols."

Bran still didn't care for Enya's overconfidence, no matter how bonny her smile. "Do ye think they catch everything?"

Enya picked up her sidesaddle. Bran stepped in and grasped it, but she pulled back and hung on tight. "You cannot stop me."

"I aimed to heft it for ye."

"Oh." She released her delicate fingers. "Thank you."

Bran fastened the girth, knowing he should climb back up to the loft and mind his own business. "I'll ride with ye as yer guard. Besides, Griffon needs to spread his wings." Bugger his business—he also had a responsibility to see to the lady's safety.

"Splendid. Perhaps you could show me more about falconry."

In no time, Bran had Griffon on his shoulder and they rode out toward the forest. "I havena seen ye since the last night of the tournament."

"Between my mother and my maid, I haven't many opportunities to escape—especially if I value my sleep."

"I canna imagine being kept inside. I love a biting sea breeze on me face and the feel of a ship rising and falling with the waves."

"What's it like, being a sailor?"

"'Tis a lot of hard work, that's for certain. But Calum's a good captain—treats his men fair, and I'd sail into hell with him if he asked."

"Where do you sleep when you're at sea?"

"With the men below decks." Bran waved his hand through the air. "Swinging to and fro in a hammock."

"How adventurous." She tapped her heel against her mare, requesting a trot. "In all your travels, what is your favorite place?"

"Me favorite is me own cottage on Raasay, but sailing into southern seas is a wonder. The sea is blue as the sky on a clear summer's day, and the air so warm ye dunna need a cloak." He chuckled. "Ye dunna need clothes, really."

"No clothes? How preposterous."

"Aye, well, no' stark naked, but woolens are certainly uncomfortable there."

She gazed beyond him with a faraway gleam in her eye. "Sounds like a dream."

Enya leaned forward and cued her horse to a canter. Bran followed, staying close behind. She laughed when the linen coif flew off her head. Bran pulled up, but Enya galloped ahead. As one of Ross's guards, he couldn't allow her out of his sight. Griffon's claws dug into the leather harness on his shoulder as he raced his old gelding after her, wishing Sir Malcolm had appointed him a spry young Galloway to ride, like Enya's mount.

Enya reined her horse to a sliding stop and threw her head back with a hearty laugh. "There's nothing better than a gallop at sunrise."

Bran pulled up beside her. God, she was ravishing with her wild red locks tossed about by the wind. "Ye sit yer horse well."

She beamed. "Do you think so?"

"I wouldna said it otherwise." Bran dismounted. They'd arrived at an open lea speckled with daisies and tall grass. "This looks like a fine place to let Griffon do a bit of hunting."

Enya slipped her leg over the lower pommel.

In two steps, Bran had his hands on her waist—her very small, very warm waist. "Allow me."

When she rested her hands on his shoulders, Bran detected a slight tremor.

"I can dismount on my own."

"I have no doubt, but I'd be no kind of gentleman allowing ye to do so."

Hit with a heavenly bouquet of rose soap sweetened by the intoxicating smell of woman, Bran tightened his thighs to keep his knees from buckling. Enya slid down the length of his body, again attacking his senses and his sensibilities. He lengthened with every progressing inch as she skimmed along his flesh.

If only her lithe body could brush against his all morning, but her feet touched down and she stood, unblinking. Those emerald-green eyes looked at him with wonder—and desire. Bran's heart thudded against his chest with such force, he was sure Enya could feel it, though her body was not quite touching his now.

Eyelids fanned by long lashes shuttered her eyes. She leaned in, chin up. No words were necessary to tell him what she wanted. Bran tilted his head down and caressed his lips over the petal-soft skin that parted for him. Every inch of him came alive. So intense was his reaction, he could no sooner control his urges as he could control the tides.

His hands still grasping her waist, a voice at the back of his mind told him to stop, but she felt so incredible. The voice again reminded him this was forbidden fruit. A guardsman was bound by an oath of loyalty not to touch, hold, kiss, love the baron's daughter. Their lips merged with passion that made Bran's blood run hot and his heart thunder. Enya's hands found his waist and slipped around to his back, pulling his body into hers, his cock hard as the wood of an oak. Bran could think of nothing but the sweetness of her mouth and the wickedly soft breasts plying his chest.

He rubbed against her. Oh, how easy it would be lead her into the copse of trees and raise her skirts. Her fingers clamped into his back and she moved with him, returning his kisses like a woman who needed to be bedded. Holy Mary, she would unman him if she kept rocking her hips.

*Caw.*

Griffon squawked in Bran's ear. Enya squeezed him tighter. Bran ran his hands along her slender spine and cupped her lovely bottom. Enya moaned. He moved his lips to her neck and tickled her with kisses.

*Caw.*

If only he'd left Griffon in the barn. But the bird was his voice of reason. He must bear down and regain control. Clenching his teeth, Bran grasped Enya's shoulders and inhaled, though it was a moment before he found his voice. "Please forgive me. I-I must have lost me head."

Enya reached out and slipped her fingers along the plaid Bran wore across his shoulder. "Did you not wish to kiss me?"

"Och, of course I wanted to kiss ye. Who wouldn't want to kiss a bonny lass with hair of fire and eyes that light up the forest?"

"But the look on your face—'tis as if you did not like it."

Bran glanced down to the protrusion under his kilt and then reached out and cupped her face. "I liked it too much, m'lady. But I'm yer father's guardsman now. 'Tis no' right for me to take advantage."

Enya turned her back, her braid swinging out, brushing Bran's arm. "You are accomplished, a knighted henchman." She whipped back around. "You are no commoner."

Bran's gut twisted. "Tell that to yer father—and to Lord Hamilton."

Enya's eyes flashed with a challenging spark, but she quickly diverted her attention to Griffon. "Will you show me how to handle him?"

"Aye." Bran removed the eagle's hood. "I attach the lead to his jesses and let him soar, then I call him back and give him a morsel. Once I've reinforced the fact he's rewarded when he returns to me, I give him his freedom."

"May I try?"

Bran pulled his falconer's glove from his belt and handed it to her. "Ye best wear this." With a stern command, he transferred Griffon to her forearm. "Take up a firm hold of the lead."

Enya wrapped the end of the leather strap around her hand. "My, he's heavier than he looks."

"He weighs near three stone, but less than a female eagle." Bran braced his hand under Enya's elbow. "Swing yer arm forward to command him to fly."

With Bran's help, Enya sent Griffon sailing to the skies, the breeze from his wings blowing her hair back. "He's magnificent."

Though alluding to the bird, Bran could hear her words again and again. He wished she had referred to him. After the bird took a good number of turns on the lead, Bran sang his lullaby. He used the Gaelic words rather than humming. Enya's gaze slipped from the eagle and rested upon Bran's face.

Griffon landed on her outstretched arm as Bran resumed his support. "I didn't even see him approach."

Bran popped a piece of bully beef into the raptor's beak. "The song calls to him."

"I know, you told me before." She stroked her hand along Griffon's feathers. "May I remove the lead?"

"Sing to him first."

"But I do not know the words."

"Can ye hum the tune?"

Enya regarded the bird for a moment. When she opened her mouth, a sweet soprano sang the notes perfectly to a "fa-la."

The sound of the supple, feminine voice trickled along Bran's skin, sending it proud with gooseflesh. He leaned down to her ear and whispered, "Now release him."

Spreading his huge wings, Griffon's initial takeoff was slow and majestic, but soon he soared in a circle above them. Bran knew the bird spotted prey when he climbed so high, he appeared no bigger than a hummingbird. Griffon headed south, and Bran scanned the sky. "There." He pointed. "A flock of ducks flying in formation. Do ye see them?"

"Aye. Do you think he'll nab one?"

"Griffon rarely misses. He flies above them and dives. The prey have no idea they're under attack until 'tis too late."

"I can barely see him now."

"He's almost over them."

"There he goes!" A gasp squealed from Enya's throat. "He's diving as if he's falling from the sky."

"Watch this."

Griffon hit the duck with a powerful blow, latching on to the unsuspecting mallard with his great claws. The formation scattered with honking squawks, ducks flapping everywhere. Bran sang his song.

Enya joined in with her fa-la's, laughing in between breaths. "I have never seen such a thing. He must be the most feared hunter in all of the skies."

The eagle dropped the duck on the ground, its neck broken. Bran called Griffon to the harness on his shoulder. "Do you think cook could make use of duck?"

"I'm sure he can. Duck soup shall be on the menu tonight."

---

Enya watched Bran reward Griffon and tie the duck to his saddle. When they had sung together, his deep voice rumbled through her, filled her breast with delight. The singing was nearly as exciting as watching Griffon dive through the air and snatch his prey.

Bran treated the eagle with a firm hand, yet there was a mutual bond between handler and raptor. It was if the two understood each other's thoughts. Bran was so unlike anyone she'd ever met. He hadn't scolded her when she galloped her horse like Robert would. He simply urged his horse faster and kept pace.

Bran patted the rump of the aging gelding that Malcolm had assigned to him. "We'd best go back, lest they send a search party for ye."

"Back?" Enya clenched her hand, the one still inside the falconer's glove. "I want to stay."

"And have yer brother catch us again? He's likely to have me thrown in the pit."

"That's absurd. I enjoy your company." *And I want you to kiss me again—and again.* "I should be free to enjoy a hawking expedition with whomever I choose."

Bran grasped Maisey's reins and led the horse to Enya. "Highborn women have few choices as to whom they can befriend. You said yerself ye're rarely alone, rarely able to spirit away time."

"That is exactly what frustrates me continually." Bran held out the reins, but she didn't take them. "How am I supposed to become 'worldly' if I am not allowed to experience the world?"

"I dunna ken. But if yer father's words are true, ye are betrothed."

She stepped into him. "I am not betrothed."

"But what of Claud Hamilton preening his feathers at the tournament?"

"My father is negotiating with the Hamiltons for my hand. Nothing has been finalized." *And if I have any say in the matter, nothing will be.* "Nonetheless, I am free to be upon my father's lands hawking with you."

"Robert—"

"Robert is not my father." After one more step, Enya craned her neck. If she moved any closer, her breasts would brush against him. "You are a knight, be it Highland or Lowland it matters not to me." *And kiss me, please kiss me now.*

With a line of concern deeply creased between his brows, Bran looked in the direction of the manse, though the view was blocked by the forest. When he spoke, it was but a whisper. "I wish I could stay too, Miss Enya. But even if ye are no' sorely missed, I shall be, for I'm here on loan from my chieftain and I've sworn fealty to yer father. 'Tis a vow upon which I canna turn me back."

"Then why are you here with me now?"

"I am protecting ye, m'lady."

She leaned in so only the tips of her breasts touched just below his chest. She could scarcely breathe. "Is that what you were doing when you kissed me?"

Bran lowered his gaze to her lips. "Apologies." His voiced turned ragged. "That was a mistake."

Enya reached up and traced the dark stubbled line of his jaw with her finger. "I think not, Sir Bran. Kiss me again, and then we shall return to break our fast."

As his gaze snapped up and met hers, Enya read a maelstrom of emotion—anger and desire melded into luscious golden hazel. She knew she was brash, knew she shouldn't be there at all, but if she did not seize this moment, she would forever regret not having done so.

Bran's powerful hands clamped on to her shoulders and the unmentionable intimate flesh at the apex of her legs coiled into a fiery ball. His full lips parted. Never in her life had she felt this alive. Her breath quickened, her heart thundered and she slid her hands around his waist and pressed her body against his. They melded together as if they were two matched pieces of a cypher. She rose up on her toes and closed the gap to his lips.

Savory male entered her mouth, his body steely against her soft. A gentle groan escaped Bran's throat, telling Enya how much he wanted to kiss her, compelling her to seek more. Her flesh melted into him. Was this what her sisters meant when they spoke of passion? Could anyone feel it more strongly than she at this very moment?

Her breasts straining against her stays, Enya could have continued kissing him for an eternity, but all too fast, Bran eased the pressure with gentle kisses caressing her lips. He rested his forehead against hers. "This is no' right, Miss Enya."

"But it feels right. How could it be wrong?"

"For all the reasons I've mentioned and more."

# Chapter Eight

Lord Claud Hamilton sat at the table in his library with the Earl of Argyll, Lord Seaton, and his father, James Hamilton, second Earl of Arran. At the opposite end sat Claud's uncle, the Archbishop of St. Andrews.

"Has the queen recovered fully from her miscarriage and the ailments that cursed her after she signed the letters renouncing the throne?" Lord Seaton asked.

The archbishop, seen by the enemy as a harmless third party, had arranged for Marian Party spies to infiltrate the queen's island prison at Lochleven Castle. "Thockmorton reports she's fully recovered, and of late has attempted to charm her captors."

James Hamilton stroked his fingers down to the point of his beard. "I still cannot believe she abdicated the throne in favor of her infant son."

The archbishop leaned forward. "What was she to do? She was weak from loss of blood when Moray's vulture forced her to sign. She has no allies in Lochleven aside from the two *femmes-de-chambre* they allowed to accompany her from Holyrood."

Lord Argyll removed his feathered cap and tossed it on the table. "And now Moray's men cling to the charges she conspired to kill her husband."

The Earl of Arran shook his finger across the table. "We all know that's false. The letters were copies. Besides, who could blame her? Though he may have had impeccable lineage, the duke turned out to be an unmitigated arse. I have yet to meet a nobleman who believes otherwise."

"Gentlemen." The archbishop rapped his fist on the table. "We cannot allow her royal highness to remain single. I suggest we select a worthy suitor before George Douglas bends his knee."

Claud licked his lips. Could a kingship be within his grasp? He could push his negotiations for Miss Enya's hand aside if it were necessary for civil duty. Though he had been so much looking forward to claiming the beauty's maidenhead—perhaps he could have both?

Lord Argyll raised his flute of port wine. "My brother would suit. He's a Stuart, after all."

Claud's father sat erect in the leather chair and puffed his chest. "We are all aware my Claud is the most apt and well-bred candidate to become king."

The archbishop's gaze met Claud's. "What say you, young man?"

Claud salivated and sipped the sweet liquor while scanning the expectant faces. "I would never be one to shirk my bounden duty to Scotland, your grace."

Given a choice between a life of royalty and a life as a future earl, Claud could push his desire to bed the auburn-haired maid aside and alter his plans. Besides, there was no need to make known his candidacy as Mary's possible suitor until the queen had shown interest in his suit. "Why not bring her to Rutherglen once we spirit her away from Lochleven? It will give us a chance to become better acquainted."

"Archbishop, do not place favor for your blood relations ahead of matters of state." Argyle slammed his fist on the table. "I assure you, my brother is equally willing to sacrifice for Scotland."

The archbishop opened his mouth, but Lord Seaton intervened. "I also offer up Lord Methven. The queen has an eye for pretty men."

"Damn this charade." Claud's father pushed his chair back, rose and paced. "Every one of you is aware my son should sit on the throne. Look at him."

Claud arched one brow and made a show of sipping from his goblet as if he hadn't a care in the world. He wanted power more than anything—though the decision would not be resolved here in this room.

He made eye contact with his father then lowered his lids in an unspoken vow. They would both stop at nothing to make this alliance. The Earl of Arran reached for the ewer and poured. "We cannot allow that woman to choose her king. She's nearly ruined herself twice by doing so."

"Upon that we are agreed." The archbishop stood and shook out his robes. "Bring your suggestions to me and I shall make a decision for Queen Mary posthaste. Once she escapes, we shall hide her in Rutherglen, as Claud suggested."

Claud smiled inwardly. With his uncle overseeing the selection, his suit was already won. Besides, he still had pretty little Enya Ross's dowry dangling should something go awry.

---

A burden eased from Enya's shoulders when the gates of Halkhead came into view from the carriage window. She and her mother had been visiting her sister, Alison, who had just birthed her first child. A boy, the babe seemed to cry endlessly, and his lungs grew more powerful by the day. With everyone from Alison and her servants to Heather and Lady Ross tending the bairn, Enya had been completely useless, listening to her inconsolable nephew, biding her time.

When they approached the courtyard, Enya craned her neck. The guard was sparring, as they did every morning, but this sight was like nothing she'd ever seen. Wearing no shirt at all, Sir Bran wielded his claymore encircled by five men. He moved like lightning. Over the sound of horse hooves and creaking carriage wheels, she could hear his deep bass rumble, bellowing orders while he deflected each attacking strike.

The carriage stopped a mere twenty paces from Bran's sparring lesson. Enya leaned further out the window. The muscles in Bran's bare back flexed with his movement, his arms sculpted like a Greek statue. He spun, displaying his glistening, powerful chest, leading to his rippling abdomen. She focused upon the thin line of dark hair below his navel that trailed beneath his kilt. She couldn't move, nor could she breathe.

"Enya." Mother's voice came from behind. "Ladies do not gawk."

Enya snapped her gaping mouth closed. "'Twas merely admiring a skilled warrior practicing his trade." She accepted the hand of the footman and alighted from the carriage. "Sir Bran has become a worthy trainer for Father's men."

"That he has," Lord Ross said, swallowing Enya in his embrace. "And how is my youngest? And my grandson?"

"I'm happy to be home." Enya grimaced. "That bairn had us all fussing over him into the wee hours."

Father led them into the manse. "I would expect no less from a healthy Ross lad."

"He's a beautiful babe. The colic never lasts." Mother kissed Father on the cheek. "And Alison will make a wonderful mother."

Her parents headed into the library and Enya dashed up the stairs to the second floor alcove above the courtyard. Bran now sparred with Sir Malcolm, Halkhead's best. The clang of swords clashing resonated through the window. Enya twitched and her gut clenched with each resounding blow, her fists moving in concert with the contest.

"He's quite skilled, the Highlander."

Enya jumped and faced her father. "W-we're fortunate to have him join us."

"Yes." Lord Ross brushed her chin with his forefinger. "But more than once I've noticed your eyes stray his way. Must I remind you he is a commoner?"

"Of course not, my lord."

"Once we see the queen back on her throne, I will resume negotiations with Lord Hamilton for your hand."

"The talks have stalled?"

"They're merely on hold."

Enya cast her gaze out the window, but Lord Ross pinched her chin and turned her head to face him.

"Lord Claud expressed his concern about your wayward eyes, and now I see his worries are founded."

A tense flare burned the back of her neck—yet another saw fit to complain about her. "No, my lord."

"They best not be. Must I restrict you to quarters?"

"For watching the guard sparring?" She clenched her teeth—that shouldn't have slipped out.

His grip tightened. "I'll not stand for your impertinence. You know exactly what I mean."

Enya winced. She knew better than to answer back to her father, but her temper had the most maddening way of getting the better of her. "Yes, Father. I'll see if Heather can use some assistance making her rounds."

"That's better. Besides, I like it when my daughter is seen visiting the sick. It much improves the crofters' opinion of our household."

Enya watched her father until he disappeared into the solar. The baron treated their tenants like dirt, and then expected her to rebuild relationships by visiting with Heather. Though Enya enjoyed calling on the crofters and learning about healing, she did not care for her father to use her as an offering of goodwill. All too often she had listened to the woes of the poor souls who farmed her father's lands, woes that had nothing to do with their health.

After casting one last glance at the captivating Highlander in the courtyard, Enya headed for the kitchen. As she expected, Heather mulled over the contents in her basket. "Are you departing soon?"

"Aye, lass. Will you be going with me today?"

"Mm hmm."

"Well then, would you please fetch the guardsman while I replenish my supplies?"

Enya's stomach flipped. "Of course." She skipped to the back door before Heather could change her mind.

The sparring session had disbanded when Enya arrived in the courtyard, but she spied Bran heading toward the stables with his shirt in his hand. She broke into a full-out run. "Sir Bran."

"Miss Enya?" A smile stretched across his face. "I've no' seen ye in some time. Are ye well, lass?"

Over the past few days, she could think of little else than the memory of his kisses, and now he stood before her, keeping a safe distance. Enya's eyes trailed to his heaving chest and the bands of muscle beneath. Unable to pull her gaze away, she clasped her hands behind her back to resist her temptation to touch him. "I've been visiting my sister. She recently birthed a son." Enya scarcely recognized her own voice or the palpitations thundering beneath her stays.

"Ah, that explains it." He shook out his shirt and wiped it across his exposed skin. "Apologies. I need to fetch a clean one."

Enya stared at definition of the thick muscles over his chest. "After, will you accompany Heather and me on our rounds?"

"Do ye often go out with Heather?"

Her gaze trailed over the bands rippling across his tight abdomen, which led to a dark line of tight curls. Was the hair as downy soft as it looked?

Bran cleared his throat.

With a jolt, Enya snapped her eyes up. "Aye, Father says the crofters like it when I call with the healer."

"And who is yer usual guardsman?"

Sir Malcolm stepped out of the stable. "'Tis usually me."

Blast. Why did Malcolm have to be within earshot? "I thought Sir Bran might enjoy accompanying us today."

Malcolm shrugged and shot an apologetic look to Bran. "'Twould give me time to visit the blacksmith, if ye don't mind spending the afternoon traipsing over the countryside."

"Very well." Bran held up his shirt. "Give me a moment to dress."

Enya's heart fluttered. "I shall wait here."

When Bran left, Malcolm stepped in. "I'll allow the Highlander to accompany you this once, but keep in mind, I am the man responsible for your safety, Miss Enya. You should have been looking for me."

---

"Where is Sir Malcolm?" Heather asked as Bran approached.

Enya blessed him with a warm smile. "Sir Bran will be our guard today."

He knew Enya had been up to something when Heather frowned. After their last encounter, he'd thought of little else than Enya. He constantly mulled over all the reasons why he should stay away from the lass, but his heart tirelessly warred against his logic.

That same heart practically leapt out of his chest when she called his name. Provide protection for the lass and the healer? What harm was there?

When they'd walked about a half-mile, the first cottage came into sight. "Why dunna ye take a horse and cart on yer rounds?" Bran asked.

Heather gestured to the cloudless sky. "When it's not raining, I prefer breathing the fresh air."

Enya skipped alongside him. "Me as well, though I like riding my mare."

Bran loved the way the world brightened whenever Enya was near. "Yer white Galloway?"

"Aye, Maisey."

"She's a spirited filly."

"That she is."

Bran studied the bow and quiver of arrows slung across Enya's back. "Do ye always take yer bow when ye visit the crofters?"

Enya ran her thumb under her bowstring. "Do you always carry your dirk and sword?"

Bran chuckled. "I do." She would draw connection between his need to carry weapons and hers. The lassie certainly had mettle. He liked that a lot.

A portly woman hobbled up the path, panting heavily. "Mistress Heather, Miss Enya, come quickly!"

"Mrs. Armstrong." Enya rushed forward. "What is it?"

"Graham has taken a tumble off the crag. I think his leg's broke, but I cannot reach him." She motioned them ahead with a wave of her hand. "Hurry."

Now Bran really wished he'd brought a horse and cart—the crag was a good half-mile ahead. "The lad's stuck ye say?"

"Aye, he fell trying to fetch a lamb." Mrs. Armstrong pointed. "He's just below the highest rock."

Enya grasped his arm. "You must do something."

"I'll fetch him. Dunna worry." Bran raced ahead, leaving the women in his wake. As he ran, he studied the outcropping of stone jutting over a ravine below. He'd seen the formation on his patrols with the guard. The lad couldn't have gotten himself into a more precarious spot in all of Renfrewshire.

Bran quickly planned his ascent and attacked the crag. As he climbed, the boy's small boot came into view. "Graham. Are ye all right, lad?"

"'Tis me leg," the boy responded in a ragged, youthful voice.

Bran steadied himself on a ledge and caught full sight of him. No older than nine, Graham crouched under an alcove, clutching the lamb.

"Hold on, lad—I'm nearly there."

"M-mind your step. 'Tis a long drop."

Bran slid a foot onto a ledge and transferred his weight. It was hardly wide enough for him to take another step. "Ye scurried up here without a rope?"

"Aye."

Bran forced himself not to look down. "I'd wager ye wouldna do that again."

"N-no, sir."

Bran skirted across the narrow rim, pressing his body against the cold stone. One missed step and he would tumble down the steep drop—at least two hundred feet. Though accustomed to heights from climbing ships' rigging, the prospect of plunging into the stony ravine below made him queasy. Nearly to the lad, Bran steeled his nerves. With a hop, he landed on the boy's ledge.

"How are ye holding up?"

Graham grimaced, shaking his brown curls. "My leg's throbbing a bit." Blood soaked through the lad's chausses and his foot hung at an odd angle.

Bran surveyed his options to descend. Without a rope, he wouldn't be able to traverse the narrow ledge carrying a child. "Do ye think the going might be easier if we climb over the back of this rock?"

"Aye." The boy pointed. "I came that way."

Bran gauged the alternate route and saw no narrow ledges—if only he'd known that to begin with.

"Ye hold on to the lamb and I'll keep hold of ye, all right?"

"Aye."

He slid his arm around Graham's waist, the lad crying out as his leg jostled. "Here we go."

Movement in the distance caught Bran's eye. He clutched the boy against his body and watched a row of men clad in blue tunics carrying the Saltire, the flag of Scotland. *Regent Moray's men, no question.*

Bran carefully climbed over the stone with the lad in his arms, the lamb kicking its legs and bleating a ruckus.

Enya and the women stood at the base of the outcropping, watching with stricken faces. Bran slid over a boulder, rested Graham atop it, and clutched the bleating lamb under his arm.

Mrs. Armstrong reached out for her son and cradled him against her bosom. "Thank the good Lord you're safe."

Bran turned to Enya. "I saw Moray's men. It looks like they're heading for Halkhead."

Enya pulled the squirming lamb from Graham's hands. "Oh, my heavens. We must warn Father."

He turned to Mrs. Armstrong and slipped Graham into his arms. "I'll take the lad to the cottage and then run ahead to sound the warning. But ye must stay with Mrs. Armstrong until I can return with a cart."

Mrs. Armstrong led them along the path to the house. Enya reached over the stone fence and set the lamb down. Bleating like he'd just had his tail docked, he ran to his mother, who boldly charged the fence.

Once inside the two-room cottage, Bran rested Graham on the bed. "Yer going to be all right, lad."

"Thank you, sir."

Heather pushed him aside and bent over little Graham. "Let me have a look at your leg."

Bran and Enya exchanged worried glances when Heather tugged his chausses from beneath his tunic. Blood seeped from a deep gash, the shinbone clearly visible.

Heather placed her hand on Graham's forehead, checking for a fever. "Enya, find two sturdy sticks of equal size. Mrs. Armstrong, boil a kettle of water, and then I'll need you both to help me set this leg."

Bran followed Enya into the main room. "I dunna like leaving ye here."

"Heather and I will be fine—besides, it will take her some time to tend to Graham's leg."

"Very well." Bran held up his finger. "Do no' leave the cottage until I return. Do ye understand?"

"Aye." Enya nodded. "Come back quickly."

---

Bran cursed himself for not insisting they take a horse and cart to make Heather's rounds. An easy afternoon, following Enya around with her serving maid? He should have known something might go awry. He ran through Halkhead's gate and found a sentry. "Where is Sir Malcolm?"

"How should I know?"

"Moray's men approach."

The guard glanced back to the manse. "He's most likely meeting with Lord Ross."

Bran rushed into the great hall. Upon finding it empty, he headed toward the library.

Lord Ross and Malcolm pored over a map. Ross snapped his head up. "What the blazes are you doing here?"

Ignoring Ross's affront, Bran stepped forward. "Moray's men approach. I saw them near Armstrong's place."

"How many?" Malcolm asked.

"A dozen."

Ross adjusted his sword belt. "That doesn't sound like a war party."

Bran spread his palms to his sides. "Nay, but it looked like they're heading straight for Halkhead."

"Where is Miss Enya?" Malcolm asked.

"She and Heather are safe with the Armstrongs until I can return with a cart."

Ross's hands flew to his hips. "You mean to say you left my daughter unguarded with enemy soldiers about?"

Bran held up a calming hand. "With strict instructions no' to leave the cottage until my return."

"I see you do not know my daughter, do you?" Ross pressed his finger in Malcolm's sternum. "And why in God's name did you allow a Highland rogue to escort Miss Enya?"

Malcolm shot Bran a panicked look. "She asked Sir Bran to take her."

Lord Ross's thick brows drew together. "She asked? Since when does she make such decisions?"

Malcolm jerked his hand through his hair and cringed.

"It cannot be helped now." Lord Ross paced. "Malcolm, I need you for our meeting with Moray's men."

Malcolm bowed. "My lord."

Ross turned to Bran. "Highlander, take a cart and fetch my daughter."

"Yes, m'lord."

Ross grabbed Bran's arm and squeezed. "If one thing goes awry, I'll have your head."

"I'll protect her with me life, m'lord."

"You had better."

With a quick bow of his head, Bran raced to the stable, biting back his ire. Ross was probably right. He shouldn't have left Enya, but the lord's lack of trust ate at his pride.

---

Lord Ross watched the Highlander drive the two-wheeled cart out the gate just as the soldiers approached. "Don't ever let him guard my daughter again."

Malcolm bowed his head. "Apologies, my lord. I'll see to it."

"I do not trust that man. He doesn't know his place, walking into my house without leave."

"He's a damned good warrior."

"And that's all he's good for." Ross turned his attention to the enemy sergeant at arms, leading a procession of the usurper's soldiers. He folded his arms and glared down from the portico.

The sergeant reined his horse to a stop. "Lord Ross, how fortunate to see you out this afternoon."

"I received notice of your arrival long before you crossed through my gates." Ross smoothed his palm across his sword's pommel. "And what brings the regent's guard to my doorstep this fine spring day?"

"We've word the deposed queen is organizing troops to mount a rebellion."

Ross arched one brow. "Is that so? Did she not abdicate?"

"Yes, she did, though we have reason to suspect rebel activities to reinstate her are underway right here in Renfrewshire."

Ross exchanged a glance with Malcolm. "'Twould be preposterous to suspect Halkhead and the Ross family of such lawlessness."

"As I expected, my lord." The sergeant scanned the courtyard, which was now surrounded by Ross's guard. "I see you have a healthy contingent of men."

"Yes. 'Tis necessary in these unsettling times."

"Quite." He ran his reins through his gloved fingers. "Have you heard no word of rebels in these parts, Lord Ross?"

"Not a single rebel has crossed through these gates. I assure you." *Aside from those who are presently mounted before me.*

"Very well." The sergeant tipped his feathered cap. "Do send word to our regent should such activities become known to you."

Ross offered a quick bow of his head. "That I will." He watched the sentry ride out the gates and turned to Malcolm. "Double the guard. They suspect something, and it would not surprise me if they posted spies."

"Yes, m'lord."

Ross started toward the door and stopped. "If you catch a spy, hang him. I'm fully within my rights to post any trespasser's head on my gatepost."

Enya watched out the window and drummed her fingers on the sill. Bran should have returned by now. "I think we should start back."

"Without a guard?" Heather asked.

"Have you ever been in danger in all the years you've been tending the crofters?"

"No, but these are perilous times." Heather pointed toward the outcropping. "Moray's soldiers are about."

"Attacked by the regent's soldiers? I think not. That would cause an insurmountable uprising." Enya slid her bow and arrows over her shoulder and paid her respects to Mrs. Armstrong.

She tugged on Heather's sleeve. "Come. We should have just enough light to reach Halkhead before the sun sets."

Heather shook her head and trudged toward the door. "This is against my better judgment. We should wait until Sir Bran returns."

"What if he was delayed?" Enya picked up Heather's basket. "Poor Mrs. Armstrong cannot accommodate us overnight. 'Tis best to leave now."

Heather followed, grumbling under her breath. Enya was well aware her serving maid often visited these farms with no escort at all. Lord Ross only demanded an escort if his daughter ventured out. She hated double standards, always being under scrutiny. Yes, her father insisted the guard was for her protection, but honestly, what did she need protection from?

Arriving at a copse of trees, not far from the place where Bran had pulled Graham off the cliff, Heather stopped. "As long as we're here, I'd like to collect some willow bark."

Enya set the basket down and fished for a leather pouch. "Splendid idea."

Heather pulled down the end of a branch and examined the buds. "By the looks of these, the flowers will be out in a week, mayhap two."

Enya rubbed a finger over the tight blossom. "For your willow flower remedy?"

"Aye, it helps rigid people relax."

"I should slip some of that into mother's ale."

Heather released the branch and chuckled. "You are incorrigible, child."

"How can you say that? Mother surely could use it. Father as well."

Heather took a small knife from her pocket and Enya held the pouch up to the tree's trunk. "Your parents want the best for you."

"Did I say otherwise?" Flecks of bark cascaded into the pouch. "It's just they fret over me as if I'm a crystal vase."

"So they should. Besides, you're their last daughter and you're soon to be married. 'Tis very hard for a mother to say goodbye."

"I think Mother would be happy to have me gone."

Heather stood straight and pocketed her knife. "Why would you say that?"

Enya tied the thong to secure the bark within. "It seems she's always in a dither over something I've done—or haven't done."

"Aye. That's her job."

A twig snapped. Enya froze. Her gaze darted to Heather. "Bran?"

He'd said he would return with a cart, but that sound wasn't rackety enough. Crouching, Enya slipped her bow from her shoulder and loaded an arrow. She crept toward the sound.

Heather grasped the back of her skirt and tugged. "No."

Enya glanced over her shoulder and shook her head. She wasn't about to cower behind a willow tree. Besides, the sound most likely came from a rabbit or a deer.

Enya crept to a clump of heather, pulled back her bow and stood. A dark-headed man bellowed and launched himself at her, arms spread wide. Before she could blink, she released the arrow and skewered him straight through his chest. With a chilling cry, the man dropped facedown only feet from where she stood.

Enya recoiled at the sight of him, the iron stench of death pervaded her nostrils. Blood seeped into the ground all around the man's writhing form. Her hands shook but she couldn't tear her eyes away. She'd just killed a man.

Heather screamed behind her. Enya snapped around. A one-eyed Gypsy slapped his hand over Heather's mouth and dragged her away. Enya reached for an arrow. Three more vulgar brutes burst through the trees, lunging straight for her. Enya's hand quaked as she raced to load her bow.

Unable to move fast enough, powerful arms thick with black hair, wrapped around her torso. Air whooshed from her lungs. The bow dropped. Shrieking, Enya thrashed and kicked, fighting against her captor. A hand slapped over her mouth. She bit down and tore away a piece of vile, salty skin. The attacker howled and swung a fisted punch into her ribs.

Thrown facedown to the ground, Enya fought as they yanked her arms behind her. She opened her mouth and screamed until her throat burned.

# Chapter Nine

Bran slapped the reins against the horse's rump and hoped to God the bloodcurdling screams hadn't come from Enya. Up the path, four horses stood, hitched to a rickety Gypsy caravan. Dread snaked up his spine. *Gypsy slave traders*. Bran reined the horse to a stop and jumped from the cart, drawing his sword.

Another shriek came from beyond the trees. If he hesitated the woman could be killed—or worse. With no time to think, Bran ran into the brush, bellowing his war cry. Rage steeled his grit. Enya lay on the ground fighting like a cat, two men on top of her. Beyond, a man lay face down, the tip of an arrow skewered through his back. Another had Heather in an arm lock.

Bran planted his foot and spun, swinging his claymore. Whipping his head around, he targeted the exposed neck of Enya's nearest attacker. The man turned, his eyes bulging just as Bran's razor-sharp sword sliced through his neck. Enya shrieked and covered her face.

The other Gypsy sprang up with his dagger drawn. The two men circled. Enya scooted away. Bran lunged, but the Gypsy dodged the blade and darted in with his knife. With a flick of his wrist, Bran deflected the blow and slammed his fist into his opponent's jaw. The Gypsy toppled backward. Claymore over his head, Bran lunged for the kill, thrusting his blade into the bastard's heart.

Bran whipped around, crouching. Enya dove for her bow. Heather's attacker tightened his grip on the cowering older woman and chuckled. He pressed his knife into her neck. "I'll kill her."

"Ye do, and ye'll no' live to tell about it."

Bran crouched lower, slipping his hand down to his hose.

Sweat streamed from the Gypsy's brow. "Stay back."

Bran brushed his knife with his fingers and gripped. In one move, he threw the blade, hitting the Gypsy in the throat.

"Behind you," Heather yelled.

Bran spun and faced a madman, bellowing, bearing down, sword over his head. Raising his claymore, Bran braced himself to deflect the blow. The man stopped short, his eyes stunned. Blood oozed from his mouth and he fell face first into the dirt, an arrow lodged in his back.

Bran glanced up. Enya stood, clutching her bow against her chest, shaking like a leaf in the wind.

Bran dropped his sword and rushed to her. "Miss Enya."

With a sob, she threw her arms around him.

He held her against his thundering heart. "Are ye all right, lass?"

"I-I don't know." She took in a stuttered breath. "I heard a twig snap. All of a sudden they were attacking us."

"Why didna ye stay at the cottage like I told ye?"

"'Twas growing dark. I was afraid you were detained."

Heather scurried beside them. "Enya, are you hurt?"

Enya buried her face in Bran's chest. "Mayhap a bit bruised."

"Ye were very brave, lass." Though he wanted to lift her into his arms, it wasn't proper. "And how are ye, Mistress Heather?"

Heather thumped her chest. "Me? I'm unscathed thanks to your fortunate timing." She reached for Enya's arm. "Come here, child. Let me have a look at you."

Enya took a step and fell against Bran. "My knee."

Heather raced to her basket and started tossing in the scattered vials and leather pouches. "Take her to the log over there." She pointed. "I need to tend it."

Enya smiled up at him, causing his heart to race again—though a much more pleasant sensation this time. "Mayhap I should carry you." He scooped her into his arms and cradled her against his chest. "I daresay ye dunna weigh much more than Griffon."

Enya inclined her head into his chest. Her fingers disappeared under the laces of his shirt. "I feel safe with you."

Bran's skin tingled beneath her touch. He glanced toward Heather. She'd nearly finished collecting her remedies. He kissed Enya's forehead. "'Tis my duty to protect ye, m'lady." He gently set her on the log. Enya reached out and grasped his hands, holding them tightly under her chin.

Heather bustled over with her basket. "Sir Bran, you'd best turn your back."

Enya frowned, but gave him a squeeze and released her grip.

Bran retrieved his knife and complied. "Yes, mistress."

Skirts rustled. Aware that Heather's back was to him, Bran couldn't resist peeking over his shoulder. His knees turned molten. Both Enya's long, slender legs were exposed clear up to her thighs. Heather slid the hose from beneath the garter, blessing him with an eyeful of creamy white skin that could have never seen the sun. Transfixed, Bran's heart thundered. He rubbed his fingers together, longing to touch her.

Heather examined the offending knee. "It looks like bruising is coming up." She straightened Enya's leg. "Does this hurt?"

"A little. Not too badly."

"Good. 'Tis not broken, then."

Bran snapped his head back and faced the trees.

"That is a relief. I could not abide being abed with a break," Enya said.

"Did I say you wouldn't have to take to your bed?"

"Oh no, please, Heather."

"We shall see. You need rest, that's for certain."

The sun hung low in the sky. Bran worried there could be more Gypsies roaming about. "If Miss Enya is set to travel, we'd best be going."

"Very well," Heather said. "I'll just rub in a salve and we can be off."

Skirts rustled. "You can turn around, Sir Bran," Enya said. She held out her arms. "Would you assist me to the cart?"

His eyes darted to Heather, who nodded.

"Of course, m'lady."

Bran's chest swelled as he stooped to lift her. Enya wrapped her arms around his neck and touched her lips to his ear. "I want to remain here in your arms forever."

He glanced over his shoulder to ensure Heather wouldn't hear. "Nothing would make me happier. But ye've had a terrible fright."

She shuddered. "I killed two men."

"Two thieving Gypsy slave traders."

Heather bustled in behind them. "I cannot believe Gypsies are here in Renfrewshire. Do you know what would have happened if you hadn't come along?"

"Ye'd be shipped abroad and sold to the highest bidder."

Enya curled against him. "Filthy pirates."

Bran cringed. He'd been called a pirate. Often. He climbed into the cart and placed Enya on the bench. "Ye're looking a bit pale."

"My head's spinning. It must be the aftershock."

Heather handed her basket up. "Straight to bed with you as soon as we return to Halkhead House."

"Let me assist ye, mistress." Bran hopped down to help Heather aboard.

She bowed her head and clasped his hand to her heart. "You are a good man."

"Thank ye, mistress." Bran held her hand while she lifted her skirts above her ankles to climb the cart steps. "We need to hurry and inform the guard. There could be more Gypsies about—and here I was more concerned about the rebels."

---

Sandwiched between Heather and Bran, Enya snuggled into Bran's warmth. Her fingers still trembled. The Gypsies attacked so fast, there was no time to take them all with arrows. Enya had never been this close to death. Every time she blinked she saw the stunned face of the Gypsy as her arrow skewered him—hit him straight through the heart with a perfectly aimed shot. How easy it was to release the arrow, yet that flash in time she would not likely forget. Robert had never talked about the ugliness of death.

Bran drove the cart straight up to the manse. When he jumped down and ran around to lend a hand to Heather, a clammy shiver coursed across Enya's skin.

Heather took her time alighting. "Thank you, Sir Bran. I can see someone's taught you manners."

"I wouldna be able to live with meself if I did no' see ye fine ladies properly taken care of."

Enya liked that Heather had developed a fondness for Bran. At least someone in her household recognized his virtue.

He lifted Enya from the cart. "I shall carry ye inside."

Henry, the head valet, opened the big oak door. "Miss Enya?"

Heather pushed past. "She's twisted her knee. Alert the lord and lady." She turned to Bran. "This way."

Closing her eyes, Enya inhaled Bran's masculine scent laced with cinnamon. His sweet fragrance calmed her. This was a man who could protect her from anything—a man who would hold her in his arms and give her comfort in the most trying times. Touching him afforded her mind peace.

All too soon, Heather opened the door to Enya's chamber. "Rest her on the bed."

Bran hesitated in the doorway.

Heather rolled her hand forward. "Go on."

His gaze darted across the room, filled with her pretty things. At the far end of the wall, her mahogany bed sported pink silk drapes. "A chamber for a princess," Bran mumbled.

After four long strides, he placed her on the bed. Enya clutched her arms around her ribs. She needed his strong arms encircling her. "'Tis cold without your heat."

Bran reached for the plaid draped across the bottom of her bed. "This will warm ye until Heather has a chance to tend yer knee."

Heather pushed beside him, basket in hand. "How are you feeling now, Miss Enya?"

She reclined into the feather-down pillows. "Just a bit light-headed and sleepy."

"What are you doing in my sister's chamber?" Robert marched across the floorboards and glared at Bran. "Leave this instant."

"As ye wish, sir." Bran bowed. "We need to send out the guard. We were attacked by Gypsy slave traders."

Lord and Lady Ross bustled in. Enya's father assumed the same hateful glare she'd just seen in her brother's eyes. "Why the blazes are you in my daughter's chamber, Highlander?"

Heather pushed between them. "He rescued us from thieving Gypsies."

Enya flung her legs over the side of the bed. "Please, Father."

Lord Ross sliced his hand through the air, his eyes trained on Bran. "You're dismissed to quarters. Remain there until I decide what is to be done with you."

A flush spread up Bran's face. "Someone needs to patrol—"

"I've had quite enough of your insolence." Ross pointed to the door. "Get out."

"Bran!" Enya tried to hobble after him, but Robert clipped her shoulder and forced her back on the bed. "He rescued us. If it weren't for him, Heather and I would be tied up and shipped away as slaves."

Father marched to her bedside. "If it weren't for him, you wouldn't have been left alone at the Armstrongs' cottage."

Enya crossed her arms. "'Tis my fault. I told him we would wait."

"And when he came storming into the library, I told him you would not." Father paced. "Damn it, Enya, are you to be the death of me? Come, Robert, we must alert the guard."

Lady Ross wrung her hands and stepped to the foot of the bed. "Enya has had quite a scare. Heather, give her a tincture to calm her nerves."

"Yes, m'lady." Heather curtseyed and headed for the kitchen.

"You're the one who needs the tincture, Mama." Enya lay back and stared at the canopy above. "I'm fine, truly. I just twisted my knee." She wasn't about to mention the two men she'd shot. Lady Ross would swoon on the spot.

"You could have been killed. What were you thinking, leaving the Armstrongs' cottage?"

Enya tugged the plaid over her lap. "No one has ever been hurt on the grounds before."

"You think not?" Mother paced to the head of Enya's bed. "You are very young, and not privy to everything that happens on the estate. Why do we insist you travel with a guard?"

"I always thought you were overly protective."

"'Tis only for your safety, and you go about as if you can conquer the world with that silly bow of yours."

"But—"

Lady Ross held up her hand. "I'll hear no excuses. You've had your taste of danger and are lucky you came out of it with a mere twisted knee. In the future you shall use your head and act like a proper lady."

*I stopped two with the bow. I am not as incompetent as you believe.* "Yes, Mama." Enya reached for her hand. "Please don't let Father punish the Highlander. He fought with the heart of a lion. Without him, things could have ended very badly."

"I may mention leniency to your father. But he's right. The Highlander should never have been guarding you. That is the responsibility for the captain of the guard." Mother walked toward the door and stopped. "If it were up to me, I would punish them both."

Enya sat bolt upright. She wanted to scream, but the door slammed closed. "Blast you all. Can no one in this household see reason?"

---

Griffon clamped his talons around his perch and watched Bran as if he knew something was amiss.

"Ye can stop looking at me with that glint in yer eye right now. The lassie is poison to me. 'Tis as if I canna even think when she's near." Bran rolled to his back and laced his fingers behind his head. "It grows worse when she touches me—and when I saw those bastards on top of her, I could have killed a hundred of them."

He sat up and looked at the eagle. "'Twas as if they attacked me own kin—but worse." He pulled the dagger from his hose and threw it into the floorboards. "God's teeth, I'm smitten by a highborn woman. At least Calum was a laird when Lady Anne caught his eye. Me? I've only a sword and an eagle to me name."

Griffon squawked.

"I'm no' saying it's bad. I like being free of burdensome responsibilities." He yanked his dagger up and sheathed it. "Bloody hog's breath, could ye see me sitting in the laird's chair listening to the clansmen moaning all day? Och. I was born for a quieter life."

"Bran?" Malcolm called from below.

"In the loft."

Malcolm poked his head through the trapdoor. "I thought I'd find you here."

"Where else? Ross banished me to quarters." Bran waved him up. "Did ye send out a patrol?"

"Aye."

"I dunna think there are any more of the bastards, but we need to be certain."

Malcolm took a seat beside him. "I've come to dish out your punishment."

Bran crossed his arms. "Help me understand exactly why I'm being punished. Miss Enya and Mistress Heather would be on a ship headed to purgatory by now if I hadn't arrived when I did."

"Lord Ross doesn't see it that way. You never should have left the women behind."

Bran's shoulders slumped. "So what did Regent Moray's soldiers want?"

"They're looking for rebels."

"Did anyone tell them they're the mutineers?"

"I'm sure Lord Ross would have liked to." Malcolm thumped him on the arm. "You got me off task, Highlander."

Bran laughed. He'd grown a fondness for Ross's captain. A worthy warrior, his mastery of a two-handed sword rivaled his own. "Wouldna ye try to postpone the torture?"

"It could have been much worse." Malcolm stood, planting fists on his hips. "First, you will never again guard Miss Enya and you are not allowed to set foot in the manse."

Bran nodded. A tic twitched below his eye.

"To ensure you comply with Lord Ross's edict, you will be assigned to permanent patrol."

"I can bear me arms?"

"Ross said nothing of disarming you, especially since he needs your muscle. But once this business with her royal highness is over, you will be banned from returning to Renfrewshire."

"All of Renfrewshire? That's a bit harsh, wouldna ye say?"

Malcolm held up his hands. "Take this as a warning. Lord Ross will see you hanged if you show your face on his lands. He'll do it. I ken him well enough."

Bran ran his hand across his throat. An imposed separation was probably a good thing. God knew he couldn't resist Enya Ross when left to his own devices. "I start the patrol in the morning, then?"

"I need your muscle for our ride to Renfrewshire in the morning. But when we return, you'll be sleeping on the rocky ground with your plaid over your shoulders." Malcolm cast his gaze to Griffon's perch. "I'd say you're lucky to get off so easily. Ross could have escorted you to the Firth of Clyde and made you swim home."

"I'd be good with that. If I hadna pledged me fealty, I'd be heading for Raasay anon."

Malcolm clapped his shoulder. "Well, I'm glad you haven't. There's a battle coming, and I'd be proud to have five of you standing next to me."

"It better happen soon, else I'll be bent over a walking stick afore I see me cottage again."

Malcolm stepped down to the first rung of the ladder. "Get some rest. You'll need it."

"One last thing." Bran scooted toward the trapdoor. "How is Miss Enya?"

Malcolm frowned. "You must block the lassie from your mind. To you she does not exist."

# Chapter Ten

Bran loved to dream, and tonight his dream became so surreal, the sweet rose bouquet of Enya's scent flooded through his senses with every breath. Without tiring, he walked for miles with her soft body cradled in his arms. She tucked her head against his chest, and her delicate fingers toyed with the laces on his shirt, slipping beneath and caressing his bare flesh.

The fluttering of her fingers against his chest made his skin erupt in gooseflesh. And something else rose. He moaned, delving deeper into the dream.

Bran glanced down, admiring her delicate features and that teasing splash of faint freckles across the bridge of her nose. Enya watched him with those emerald-green eyes, studied him, as if she wanted to remember every facet of his face. He liked it when she looked at him that way. It made him feel like a man—mayhap a king. He bent his head and brushed his lips across hers. Oh, how marvelous this dream. The warmth of her lips melted into him.

His cock thrust to a full erection when he tasted her. Sweet as molasses spiced with cloves. He swirled his tongue in harmony with hers.

His dream took him back to his pallet. Bran lay on his back kissing her, his hips rocking. Her kisses grew frantic, her hands caressing his face, running down to his chest. Bran arched his back. He must feel her body over him, pressing against his. He reached up and grasped her shoulders, drawing her atop him like a blanket.

Her body enveloped him in warmth and she mewled with pleasure. Moving like a cat, her mons slid across him with enticing friction. Bran's cock throbbed.

"Please kiss me again," she pleaded.

Bran searched with his mouth and brushed his hips against hers. A dream had never been this vivid. His seed would soon spill.

"Bran?"

His eyes opened. And though the light was dim, there was no mistaking the outline of her beauty. Enya actually lay atop him while his cock pressed into her skirts. "Am I dreaming?"

Enya covered his mouth and kissed him with fierce passion. She slowly slid her hips down and then up, caressing his aching manhood. She pulled back, the white teeth of her smile stretching all the way out to her dimples. "Now do you think you are dreaming?"

Holy Mother Mary and all the saints, he scarcely could believe she was over him. Bran ran his hands along her back. Her weight upon him, natural as if she were meant to always be there. But she wasn't—she shouldn't. "Merciful Jesus, Enya. Why did ye come here?"

Enya arched up, looking suddenly hurt.

Unable to bear to see her unhappy, he clutched her against his chest. "Not that I'm upset 'bout it. Ye just shouldna come. 'Tis too dangerous."

"I wanted to see you."

He ran his hand across her silken hair. God, it smelled like a garden of roses. "How did ye get here with yer sore knee?"

"'Tis not all that bad—just a tad swollen, but I can walk on it."

"If ye're found missing, yer father will string me up for certain. The only reason I'm still alive is because of the war." He inhaled her scent again, hoping the memory would last a lifetime. "I've been forbidden to see ye ever again."

"But I am not prevented from coming to you." She swirled her lithe fingers down his shoulder and squeezed his arm. "I cannot stop thinking about the attack and how you fought—you risked your life for me."

He kissed her forehead. "Aye, lass. I would do anything to see ye safe."

Enya rested her head on his chest. It made him feel powerful, protective. She rocked her hips. He wanted to explode.

Bran arched his back and moaned. "Do ye ken what that does to me?"

She didn't stop. "Nay, but it rains fire across my sacred woman's place." A low chuckle escaped her throat. "It turns me wild with yearning."

Bran was past becoming consumed by lust.

All he had to do was hike up her skirts and slide inside her. In a blink of an eye, he could relieve the throbbing that had tortured him for weeks. And Enya wanted it as badly as Bran did. He covered her mouth and moved his hand over her breast. Another jolt shot through the tip of his cock. His palm filled with succulent unbound flesh. "Ye have no undergarments?"

"I slipped away in my shift and dressing gown." She ran her hand over his chest and kneaded him as he did her. Holy falcon feathers, she was wanton.

Bran pulled the bow at the nape of her shift. God forgive him, her pert breast was too ripe to be ignored. He had to taste it. Swirling his tongue across her skin, he drew the cloth aside and trailed kisses downward until her nipple teased his lips. Moaning with need, he took her breast in his mouth and suckled her.

Tantalizing her nipple with light flicks of his tongue, Enya mewled and rocked her hips harder. "I want to lie with you."

Seed leaked from the tip of his manhood. But he could not take her innocence. Not like this. He squeezed his bum cheeks to quell his yearning. "It would ruin ye."

He cupped her face directly above his. Her eyes glistened, almost black in the darkness.

She turned her head and kissed his palm. "But I choose you."

Bran could scarcely see the outline of her face in the dim light. "Ah, Enya, if this were another time, it might be so, but this can never be. Yer father would see me hanged."

"But I have come to you. Surely he will punish me."

He brushed his fingers across the petal-soft skin of her cheek. "Ye ken he will punish us both."

Sighing, Enya rested her head upon his chest. "Let us steal away—go someplace far from here."

Bran cradled her, as if the Holy Father created her to lie atop him. "'Tis a fanciful thought. But ye would have to give away all yer precious things, yer gowns, this stable full of fine horses."

"I care not for finery."

"And what of...what of yer father's wishes? He will no' allow ye to choose. Will he?"

Enya groaned. "He only cares to use me to increase his wealth."

Bran caressed his hands along her spine. "That's the lot highborn lassies must endure."

"I would rather be ruined than wed Claud Hamilton."

He could scarcely swallow. "Do ye ken what ye're saying?"

"Aye." She ran her lips along his jaw line. "Kiss me, Bran."

His ballocks were on fire. He loved how his name sounded when she uttered it, her voice deepened with desire. Bran wrapped her in a tight embrace and took her deep into his mouth. Her body perfectly molded against his. Only Enya's shift and dressing gown separated them from joining. His cock thick with lust and aching to take her, he was on the brink of losing control.

Bran ran his fingers through her silken hair and squeezed his eyes shut, willing his strength to return. "Ye are so fine to me. But ye must go before the stable boy wakes."

"I will come again tonight."

"I'll no' be here. I'm off to Rutherglen with the guard." It was best to keep quiet about the patrol—at least for now. She'd have him betraying his oath of fealty, which would bring unmitigated shame to his clan. That, he could never abide.

"I want to stay—"

Bran tapped his finger to her lips. "Enya, I must take ye back."

***

Bran helped Enya down the ladder and she showed him how to creep around the gardens to the hidden passage. "This is how I steal away for my morning jaunts. Heather almost never misses me."

"Where does the passage lead?"

"The solar—'tis on the same floor as my chamber."

Bran turned full circle. Though the entrance was shrouded with ivy, using the passage was still a risk. "Anyone could see ye once ye're in the open."

"You mustn't worry. I always wait until 'tis clear and then I skirt through the shadows." She twirled in a circle. "I've done it countless times."

"And why doesna that warm me heart?"

"Kiss me and bid me goodnight."

Bran's concerns melted away when he took Enya in his arms and gave into her sweet lips. "Will I see ye in the window when I next spar with the guard?"

"I wouldn't miss a chance to watch you."

"Ye are as precious as a hundred golden eagles." Closing his eyes, he touched his lips to her forehead. "Go now, afore I lose me resolve."

Enya kissed him one last time and disappeared into the wall of vines.

After Bran returned to the stable loft, he fell on his pallet and groaned. He was still as erect as a Pict standing stone. Sampling her forbidden fruit ignited a fire within he'd never experienced before. Enya Ross had been every bit as enticing in the dark as she was in full daylight. Simply touching her skin sent him mad with longing.

He closed his eyes. Her scent still lingered on him. If only their love had a chance. But he knew his unquenchable desire for Miss Enya Ross could never be satiated.

How could a highborn lassie like her look twice at the likes of him? He had no lands, no riches. She had risked much coming to him in the wee hours of the night. Had she learned nothing from her altercation with the Gypsies? A drunken guardsman could have crossed her path, or worse. Enya's disregard for her personal safety worried him. Many a man would not think twice about taking her to satisfy his own pleasure.

Bran shoved his fingers through his hair. He'd been warned. Lord Ross already distrusted him. And what had compelled Enya to come to him? She said she'd chosen him, yet she was so innocent. Did she know what that meant, or had she simply wanted more delectable kisses? She must be aware their love could never be. So young and inexperienced, Enya had no inkling of what life would be like with a henchman. He had little to give her but his protection.

He must not encourage her advances—no matter how much pushing her away would tear shreds from his heart.

Adept at slipping in and out of the manse undetected, Enya crept through the same secret passageway she used for her early morning jaunts. Not even Heather knew how often she slipped away and stole time for herself. But this was the first time she'd ever actually done something sinful.

As if floating on air, she had no idea how what had just happened could be a sin. Bran was nothing like any man she'd ever met. He accepted her as plain old Enya without scolding her and launching into a chain of prattle detailing all the reasons why she needed to change.

Whenever he placed his hands on her, Enya's body quivered, her breath quickened and heat pooled in her sacred place, coiling so tight, she wanted to burst. She could not breathe in enough of him. Every waking moment her mind was consumed with thoughts of Bran. Enya imagined him kissing her in her chamber, even on her bed. Yet the more she kissed him, the thirstier her body became.

And oh how delectable he had been this night. Enya should never have spirited away to the stable loft, but she had to ensure he was all right. No one had told her what his punishment had been for leaving her with the Armstrongs. She balled her fists. It was her fault they had set out. If she had only stayed at the cottage, the whole debacle with the Gypsies never would have happened.

And when she'd found him sleeping, his shadowy features softened in the dim light, the memory of kissing him in the tent came flooding back. Unable to resist temptation, she knelt beside him, his chest rising slightly with each soft breath.

She stretched out her fingers and rested her hands on his hard belly. A welcome warmth spread through her insides. She'd teased Bran with her kisses, and rather than shoo her away, he'd wrapped his arms around her and pulled her over his hard body.

Entering the solar through the secret door hidden behind the cupboard, Enya tiptoed past Heather's small room. She stopped for a moment and held her breath. Silence.

Enya placed her hand on her chamber latch. The door creaked. She opened it only wide enough to slip inside. Crossing the room, she slipped under her bedclothes and nestled into her pillows. Her father had told Bran to keep his distance? Well, she'd see about that. Enya could no sooner stay away from the Highland warrior than she could food or drink. Bran had become her sustenance.

She ran her hand over the smooth linen sheets. Once the queen was reinstated, she would ask Bran to take her far away from Renfrewshire. Sail to a place where it did not matter if her father was a powerful, landowning baronet.

Enya had barely drifted off to sleep when her chamber door burst open. Heather pulled aside the heavy drapes, revealing the morning sun. "Enya, are you ill?"

"No." Enya stretched. "Just tired."

Heather placed her hand on Enya's forehead. "Rarely have I seen you abed this late. Of all of us, you're always the first to rise."

Wishing Heather would leave her to sleep until luncheon, Enya sat up. "I had trouble sleeping after yesterday's ordeal."

Heather pulled a corner of the bedclothes down and frowned. "Why are you wearing your dressing gown?"

Enya prayed she wasn't blushing. She covered her face with her hands and thought of a reasonable response, praying Heather would leave her be. "I paced the floor for hours."

"Your knee won't heal with you pacing about." Heather pushed up Enya's skirts and examined the offending body part. "The swelling has gone down, but the bruising is worse." She picked up her jar of salve from the bedside table. "Sit back while I rub this in."

"'Tis much better today."

"I shall be the judge of that."

Enya reclined against the pillows. Though intuitive, Heather had believed her lie. This time. Enya would need to be more careful in the future.

After convincing Heather she was well enough to walk down to the hall to break her fast, Enya found only her mother at the table. "Where are Father and Robert?"

"Rode out this morning."

Ah yes, the reason for Bran's ride to Rutherglen. "Are they meeting about my betrothal?" God, she hoped not.

Mother spread cream on her scone with quick flicks of her wrist. "Unfortunately, not this time."

A sickly knot dropped to the pit of Enya's stomach. The edge to her mother's voice told her it had something to do with the queen and the awful split between the Marian Party and Regent Moray's usurping King's Party.

Enya knew the answer, but needed to ask the question. "War is imminent?"

"It appears so. Your father has been summoned by the Hamiltons." Mother grasped her wrist. "Speak of this to no one."

---

Enya climbed into the window well overlooking the courtyard. Though she knew Bran wouldn't be there, her stomach sank, as if she'd hoped there had been a change of plans and Bran had stayed behind.

*Curses.*

Heather ambled past with her arms full of linens. "You'd best stay inside for a few days and work on your embroidery. That knee will heal much faster if you stay off it."

Enya groaned. "I'll go mad cooped up inside."

Heather leaned in. "You might consider making a keepsake for Sir Bran." She lowered her voice. "Lord Ross treated him badly, if you ask me. He fought for us like a true knight. I've no idea what we would have done without him."

Enya beamed. "'Tis so true Heather, and no one sees it but us."

"Be mindful of these walls—they have ears."

Enya glanced sideways. "What would suit? A kerchief?"

"A kerchief is always nice, but I recall him mentioning his cottage. Why not a panel for the wall? Do you not have one of Halkhead House already started? With it, he would always remember his time here."

"Yes. I've been working on that panel for some time." Enya bit her thumbnail. The one Mother was always tearing out the stitches on. "But 'tis quite an undertaking."

"I could help."

"Really?" Enya clapped her hands. "Do you think we could have it ready before he returns to Raasay?"

"If what the servants say is true, then yes."

Enya didn't like the foreboding tone in Heather's voice. "What are the servants saying?"

"Lord Ross is meeting with the nobles for Queen Mary. Once the queen makes her escape from Lochleven, the troops will assemble."

"Where?"

"I have no idea."

"Do you know when?"

"Henry said mayhap a week or two."

"A week?" Enya's spirits dove. "I cannot finish the panel in a week."

"You can if you put your mind to it. Your problem is you cannot sit still."

"True—and I hate embroidery." Enya wanted to know more about this secret coup the barons were planning. "And how did Henry come by his information?"

"Your father is quite careless about leaving missives on his desk. 'Tis nearly impossible not to notice them."

"For servants who can read."

"Of course there's that. Fortunately, Henry can, otherwise we'd all be in the dark."

Enya squeezed her arms across her midriff. "I only hope we can avoid bloodshed."

"Unfortunately there are always losses when men take up arms."

"I pray Sir Bran will fight well."

"Sir Bran? And what of the other Ross men?" Heather narrowed her eyes. "You have feelings beyond friendship for our Highlander."

By the fire burning in her cheeks, Enya knew a blush had given her away. She hung her head. "Yes."

Heather raised her chin. "Your father will never stand for it."

"I ken."

Heather transferred her linens to one arm and patted Enya's shoulder. "There's nothing wrong with admiring a handsome knight from afar—but you ken a man like him is not meant for a noble lass such as you."

Enya studied her folded hands. "I am painfully aware."

"And what are your feelings for Lord Hamilton?"

"Honestly?" Enya met Heather's gaze. "I wish he could make my insides flutter as they do when I look at Sir Bran. 'Twould make this whole marriage business far more palatable."

"Mayhap your heart will find love once this conflict between the queen and Regent Moray has ended."

Enya forced a smile. She doubted she'd ever feel anything more than a tepid fondness for Claud Hamilton.

Alas, her rugged Highland knight might soon exist only in her memory.

# Chapter Eleven

Rutherglen ~ 30<sup>th</sup> April, 1568

Claud Hamilton sat beside his father at the head of the long table. Armed with pikes and battleaxes, his most trusted guards stood at the barred doors. Only nobles, bishops and lairds who had sworn an oath of fealty to the queen were allowed within the walls of Rutherglen Hall. The information Bishop Hamilton, who sat at the far end of the table, was about to disclose was far too sensitive to risk falling on capricious ears.

Archibald Campbell, the fifth Earl of Argyll, stood. Full of self-importance, Claud despised the man. "We must first decide who will captain the queen's army."

Claud ground his knuckles into the palm of his hand. The bishop had not called the session to order and Argyll was already posturing for power. The hall flared in an uproar.

The Earl of Eglinton stood, raising his hands in the air. "I have the greatest army of men. I should be the one to lead."

How the blazes did Eglinton know who had the greatest contingent? That had not yet been discussed. Besides, the earl was the supreme, most damnable fool in the room.

Claud brushed his fingers across his ruff. "I bring an elite cavalry of fifty horse in addition to five hundred foot soldiers. And I am nearest the throne in rank."

At the far end of the table, the archbishop frowned at him. Claud eyed his uncle with contempt. The holy man had best take charge of this meeting, else the hall would soon erupt in a full-on brawl and there would be no noble peer to lead the queen's army.

Archbishop Hamilton pounded his staff on the floorboards. "Silence!" Glaring across the stern faces of the queen's men, he waited until all resumed their seats. "No doubt the queen will choose her own lieutenant of the kingdom. I've brought you here today to advise her escape is imminent."

"When?" asked Lord Ross.

"The date will not be disclosed, but be forewarned it is very close. Very. I need each of you to declare your numbers to the scribe. The queen will want to know the strength of her army straight away."

Lord Sommerville placed his palms on the table, leaning in. "Where and when shall we assemble?"

"Unless you receive word otherwise, all soldiers shall gather here at Rutherglen nine days hence."

Argyll bounded to his feet again. "Nine days? That gives us very little time—"

Every man in the hall stood and shouted protestations, except Claud. He leaned back, folded his arms and grinned. The inner circle of lords had chosen Rutherglen as the site to plan the uprising. Mary, Queen of Scots would soon be within his grasp.

Claud watched Lord Ross across the table. Fortunately, Enya had inherited her mother's good looks from the Semple side of the family. Of late, Claud had more difficulty pushing Enya from his thoughts than he cared to admit. Thank heavens he'd not spent more time at Halkhead House during the tournament, else this business with the queen would be far less palatable.

---

Bran kept his eyes on Claud Hamilton. The snake glared at him from the portico, standing beside Lord Ross. Bran would have thought the nobles had enough sense to keep their voices lowered, but he could hear every word.

Claud tilted his chin upward. "I see you still have the Highlander in your guard."

Ross regarded Bran over his shoulder. "The beast is the best sword. He and the others will be gone soon enough."

"I'm glad to hear it."

Ross rapped Claud's shoulder. "You're still harboring a bit of jealousy, are you?"

Hamilton shot him an edgy glance. "Not at all."

Ross started down the steps. "Good. It doesn't become a well-bred man."

Bran turned his attention to his reins and walked his horse beside Malcolm. "I've watched the peacocks long enough."

"Aye, if we dunna leave now, Hamilton will be asking for another joust to prove how big his cock is." Rewan reined his horse alongside Bran, and the three of them led the party back to Halkhead House.

Having left Griffon in the stable boy's care, Bran wasn't upset they were returning this soon, but it did confuse him. "It makes no sense to me—we rode all the way to Rutherglen just to turn around a day later. What's going on?"

Malcolm slid his fingers under his helm and rubbed his forehead. "All I know is we've little time to prepare. They will be calling for us soon."

"To fight for Queen Mary?"

"Aye."

Rewan steered his horse around a boulder. "But she's still imprisoned in Lochleven. Will we storm the castle?"

Malcolm shrugged. "I know not. We shall gather the troops and meet at Rutherglen on the eighth of May."

Bran grumbled under his breath. "It all seems a bit muddled, like the sails of a ship bearing head on into the wind."

Malcolm slapped his reins against his mount's shoulder. "War always does."

"I'll just be happy to go back to Lewis," Rewan said. "I've got a bonny lassie waiting for me."

Surprisingly, Bran did not share in Rewan's enthusiasm. The end of his tenure with Ross meant the end of his affair with Enya. He doubted he'd see her again once he left for Rutherglen, and with his patrol duty, mayhap not at all. His heart twisted. It was for the best. He needed to spirit away from the temptress before their relationship went further. He'd almost given into his basal desires when she'd visited him in the loft. He didn't know how long he could resist her, and the bonny lass obviously had no intention of resisting him.

Enya was as free as a Peregrine falcon, flying through life, wanting to experience all of it with a wild abandon he'd never before encountered in a woman. If only he could throw caution aside and follow his desires as she did hers. But his loyalties bound him to a code of behavior upon which he could never turn his back.

"On the morrow, you'll ride out with patrol after the guard spars," Malcolm said.

"Very well." A breeze picked up and Bran sniffed. "I'm looking forward to a bit o' rain on the trail. It reminds a man of the comforts of home."

Malcolm chuckled. "You're not going soft, are you, Highlander?"

---

True to her word, Heather helped Enya embroider the panel. Her serving maid had been right. It went faster when Enya focused and worked on it for more than ten minutes at a time. The past few days she had set the piece down only for meals and sleep.

Embroidery of the manse was finished and she only had the gardens to complete. Enya took her shears to her dressing table. She lifted up the back of her hair and pulled a small clump from underneath. Holding her breath, she snipped. The long red lock fell to the floor. Enya smoothed down her tresses and surveyed her work in the mirror. Her hair was so thick, the small clip she'd made wasn't noticeable.

She picked up the lock and threaded several strands through her bone needle. *This will be perfect for the azaleas and Bran will always have a part of me.*

After making the painstakingly small stitches, she completed two of the flowers and held her work to the light streaming in through the window. She smiled and ran her finger over the tiny azaleas she'd just created. Yes, she could have used silk thread died fuchsia or red, but her own hair blended well with the greenery, and to Enya, it made the keepsake far more personal.

She held her breath when the faint rumble of horse hooves clomped just beyond the gate. Butterflies of excitement tickled her insides. Had the men returned? They weren't expected for at least another day.

She put aside her work and dashed to the window in the corridor. The sun had set, casting long shadows across the courtyard, but Enya could see clearly enough. She liked what she saw. Leading the guard beside Malcolm, Bran rode tall in his saddle. His broad shoulders were square and he was armed to protect and defend her father and brother, who rode behind. She doubted there was a soul in all of Scotland who would want to face her Highlander in battle.

Approaching the house, Bran looked up to her window. With a flutter of her heart, Enya waved. Bran's teeth flashed with his grin. Then her father's scowl caught her eye, as did Robert's.

After stopping only long enough for Lord Ross and Robert to dismount, Bran rode straight to the stables. Enya craned her neck to watch him. The stairs below creaked and Enya moved to the landing to greet her brother. "What news of Lochleven?"

Robert's eyes registered a hint of shock. "Mother told you?"

"Aye." Enya had learned far more from Heather, though she would never admit to that fact. "Well?"

"You should not be privy to such news. The more who know, the more precarious the queen's position."

Enya grasped the banister. "Will there be civil war?"

"Aye."

"Soon?"

"The nobles will assemble with their armies within a week."

Enya gulped. Only a week? Such a small amount of time before he would be gone—never to return to Renfrewshire.

Robert patted her shoulder. "No need to fret about me. Father and I have troops to fight before us. We will be well away from the battle."

Enya blinked. She had little doubt Robert and Father would be safe, using Bran to assure it.

Robert bent forward and eyed her. "That is what's got you so worried, has it not?"

"Of course—I care for all our men." A tear stung the corner of her eye, and she sucked in a breath, willing it away. "I shall pray this hostility is soon ended."

"So kind of you, sis." He chuckled. "And while you're at it, pray that big Highlander of yours meets a swift end. One wouldn't want to see him linger with his gut run through."

"I never considered you to be black-hearted, Robert. It doesn't become you." Enya turned and headed for her chamber before Robert could sense exactly how much his words had affected her.

---

Heather had long ago come and gone after helping Enya change into her linen nightdress. Planning to steal away, Enya worked on the panel until the moon rose to high point. Certain all were asleep, she crept to the solar and opened the false cupboard door. She had to talk to Bran, had to warn him about the fighting, and most of all, she needed his arms to wrap around her if only one more time.

Carrying a candle, she tiptoed through the passage, sure she had been the only person to use it since—well, since her father built the manse before she was born. Enya often wondered if Father even remembered the secret passage's existence. Surely he did, though its use would only be necessary in times of war—possibly times that were coming.

It was camouflaged so well, anyone looking for a secret entry would not discover it in the garden. Enya left her candle in an alcove just behind the door, as she always did. As a safeguard, she kept a flint there too.

Wispy clouds sailed overhead, and Enya didn't have to wait long for her eyes to adjust. She listened for sounds of the night guard and heard nothing but the mating calls of frogs. By skirting around the garden, she could avoid being noticed by using the back door of the stables.

Golden light streamed down from the loft opening. Bran must still be awake. Unfortunate. Enya had so enjoyed waking him with kisses.

Enya climbed the ladder. "Sir Bran," she whispered, popping her head through the trapdoor. The scent from a tallow candle hung in the air.

Bran snapped his head up and stuffed something under his pallet, sheathing his dagger in his stocking. "Miss Enya? Och, I thought ye wouldna come—what of the dangers we spoke of?"

He offered his hand and helped her climb up. Enya's heart thundered as she fell into his embrace. "How could I stay away?"

She rose up on her toes and kissed him. When she closed her eyes, a river of emotion coursed through her blood. Enya slid her arms around Bran's powerful back and held him against her body. She wanted to melt into him. So warm and huggable, she kneaded her fingers into his back, kissing him as passionately as she knew how, hoping he could tell how much she missed him.

"Och, Enya. Ye're on fire."

"I couldn't sleep at all when you were away." The bovine scent of a tallow candle hung in the air. "Word is war is near—very near, and you will be at the head of the Ross army."

"Aye. Did ye expect yer father to put *his* men on the front line?" Bran gestured to his pallet. "Would ye care to sit? I'm afraid I've no chair to offer ye."

Enya cast her gaze down. A bit of wood stuck out from under the pallet. "Are you working on a carving?"

"What makes ye think that?"

"You stuffed something under your pallet and sheathed your knife when I ascended the ladder."

Bran tapped the object with his toe. "Ye're too observant." With a devilish grin that attacked her insides, he sat and pulled her onto his lap. "'Tis far too dangerous for ye to be stealing to the stables."

"I couldn't stay away."

He ran his fingers through her hair, his eyes dark. "I missed ye—thought of ye every moment I was away."

Enya cupped his face between her hands. "I thought the days would never pass."

Bran closed his eyes, his brow furrowing as if in pain. "On the morrow, I'm to patrol until we leave for battle."

A lump formed in her throat and she grasped his hands. "You shall be gone again?"

"Aye."

She squeezed his palms, not wanting to release him. "But I cannot bear it."

He brushed his lips across her cheek. "We must enjoy the moments we can take." His eyes drifted to her mouth. "I shall cherish them always."

Enya could wait no longer. Her heart raced as she lifted her chin. Bran's mouth covered hers. Enya's breasts screamed to have his hands on them again. Kissing him, she ran her fingers along the length of his arm and grasped his hand. Slowly, she led it under her dressing gown and to her unbound breast. Bran's strong fingers kneaded her, his lips moving along her jaw line. "I canna resist ye."

"I do not want you to."

He pulled back and gazed into her eyes, the hazel glistening with the flickers of candlelight. His eyebrows ticked up as he pulled the string that closed her nightdress. Enya watched him, her lips parted.

Bran gently pulled the thin fabric aside and exposed her. Praying Bran would not be disappointed, Enya watched the brown rims of his eyes grow dark. His tongue tapped his top lip as he cupped her breast in his hand. "'Tis *bòidhche*—beautiful."

Enya's breath sped as the ache between her legs coiled tighter. Bran dipped his head and licked her nipple. Enya threw her head back and moaned. He took the tip into his mouth and suckled. Enya slipped her shoulders out of her dressing gown and pulled her nightdress down, completely exposing herself. Her breasts swelled with desire, as if they would explode at any moment.

Bran spread his hands over her, framing her breasts between his large palms. "My God, Enya, ye are perfect."

Beneath her buttocks, Bran grew rigid, and heat coiled in Enya's sacred spot—a longing so intense, she feared it would never ease. As Bran's kisses swirled across her breasts, Enya had never been so alive. She gently pushed on his shoulders and tugged his shirt free of his waistband. "I want to see you too."

Bran pulled the shirt over his head and Enya stared. A chiseled Roman statue sat before her. She had never been this close to his bare chest. Peppered with white scars that contrasted with his lightly tanned skin, he was more magnificent than her wildest imaginings. A gush of longing moistened the sacred flesh between her legs. Enya pushed him back onto the pallet and straddled his waist. Her breasts ached to brush across his flesh, but she wanted to suckle him first. When her mouth met his dark nipple, he groaned and thrust his hips up, torturing the coiled need between her legs. Unable to control her response, Enya moved her hips against him, the friction sending waves of unquenchable longing through her core.

After lowering his head to the pallet, she leaned forward and joined her mouth with his. Slowly, deliberately, she caressed his taut flesh with her breasts. Ripples of excitement sent shivers across her body. But it only increased the burning pull of desire.

Bran's hands slid to her buttocks and he held her against his hard manhood. "Ye are as sweet as God's nectar."

Enya gazed into his eyes. No words could express the connection there. Something deep inside stirred. The power of the bond between them could move heaven and hell. "We are meant to be joined. Why else would you be in Renfrewshire?"

"If it only could be so."

Enya kissed his forehead. "We will find a way."

"But yer father—"

She didn't want to hear it, and smothered his mouth, clamped on to it, showing him the power of the love that beat with rapid pulses under her skin. He relaxed beneath her, gently rocking. She slid over the length of him and it touched her—right in the sacred spot where hot longing coiled so tight, she thought her body would burst. Enya tried to steady her ragged breathing.

Bran moaned and Enya again slid her sex up and down his manhood. She'd seen horses mate in the paddock, and Bran's manhood felt as erect as a stallion's. He wanted her as much as she wanted him. Unable to stop, she rocked her hips against him and moaned. But she needed something more. "I want you," she uttered in a husky voice she hardly recognized as her own. "Show me."

# Chapter Twelve

Enya practically unmanned him when she spoke the words. *I want you. Show me.* Nothing else existed but the exquisite, bare-breasted woman who relentlessly rocked her mons across his cock. He had to touch her. Reason no longer needled at his mind. Bran slid his hand down and grasped the skirts of her nightdress. Their mouths joined. Ever so slowly he hiked up the linen until his hand found her silken, bare buttock. He had never been so hard, never allowed a woman to control him, but Enya owned his very soul. She moved against him as his fingers found the heavenly wet core of her womanhood.

Her body shook with every breath. Enya arched her back. "Yes."

He pulled back and gazed into the face of the Madonna herself. God had given him a gift when she ascended the ladder to the loft, and he would not misuse it. "I willna see ye ruined." Uttering these words took more restraint than he'd ever exercised in his life, but he would not throw her down and plunge into her no matter how much he wanted to. Enya needed to be guided into the world of sensual pleasures—and her maidenhead must be kept intact, lest they both meet their ruin.

"Please." She panted and rocked in concert with his teasing fingers.

He rolled with her so she lay on her back with him beside her, pressing into her hip. He smoothed his palm between her thighs. "But I can show ye pleasure. Spread yer legs for me."

Enya clutched his shoulders. "I want to lay with you as a woman would her husband."

"Trust me."

He kissed her and slid his finger between her legs. With a gasp, she opened for him, slick with ravenous longing. Bran could slide into her with ease. Oh, to watch the ecstasy light up her face. He wanted to witness her first taste of pleasure. He pressed his cock against her hip as he worked his finger around the place of a woman's delight. Enya grasped his shoulder, rocking her hips, her tongue all over him. He slid his finger inside her tight, ribbed center. If only he could be in there for just a moment—two strokes and he would come undone.

Enya made tiny sounds that sent Bran wild as his finger worked. He licked his lips and gazed into her face—mouth spread apart, pure joy radiating from her countenance. She was ready to explode. Moisture spilled from the tip of Bran's manhood.

Enya arched up, every sinew taut, trembling. She cried out with her release, barely able to catch her breath. Bran steadied his hand against her and showered kisses along her neck and breasts. His cock jutted hard against her hip. God, he would come with only one stroke.

"I never thought it would be that miraculous," she cooed between breaths.

"'Tis a sampling of what could be."

When her panting eased, Enya rose up on an elbow and cast her gaze to the rigid shaft pushed against her hip. "Did you...do you...how do I?"

He wanted her hands on him, but he could not expect a woman like Miss Enya to pleasure him. "Would ye touch it for me?" He nearly slapped himself for asking.

Enya cupped his face with her palm. "I want to touch it. Show me how."

Bran guided her hand under his kilt and wrapped her fingers around him. "Ye stroke it like this."

"'Tis so hard."

"It wants to be inside ye."

"Why did you not take me?"

"'Twould no' be right. Besides, ye could conceive." He lay back and watched her beautiful face as her hand worked magic.

His ballocks on fire, he slid his hand down and touched himself. His hips thrust in time with Enya's stroking. The fire in his groin blazed out of control. He pictured himself inside her core and his seed exploded with a bellow that could wake all of Halkhead.

---

Enya rested her head upon Bran's chest. His heart beat a steady rhythm, lulling her into a dream-like trance. "I want to stay here forever."

Bran stroked his hand over her hair. His large hands caressed her gently. Enya marveled at how hands that could wield a sword with crushing force could also be incredibly tender. His lips kissed the place where his hand had just been. "I wish ye could, but ye must go back to yer own bed. I still canna believe ye risked so much to come to me."

"I couldn't stay away."

Bran pulled her nightdress closed. "I'll see ye back safely, lass. Ye shouldna do this again."

Her heart squeezed. "Do you not feel as I do? Being close to you is like breathing."

"I ken, but ye're highborn. Ye're no' meant to be in me arms, no matter how right it feels to us."

*How could he share such intimacy with me and then push me away?* "Do not give up. Please tell me you will find a way for us to be together. We can sail the seas. You have your cottage on Raasay. Please tell me."

"I will always treasure you in me heart—no one will ever able to take yer place." He brushed his lips across her cheek. "Not ever."

"I feel the same way too." Enya rose up on her elbow and studied him. Though he smiled, he could not hide the anguish in his eyes from her.

Before she could say another word, Bran sat up and reached for her dressing gown. "Come, we must spirit ye back to the keep."

He held her hand as they skirted through the garden.

When they arrived at the secret passage, Bran pulled her into his embrace. His body was like a furnace, taking away the chill of the night air. He kissed her with all the passion he had before.

If only they could stay together. But Enya was no fool. To expose their love now would be folly. Her father would surely issue strict punishment for her, and most definitely would put Bran's neck in a noose. The mere thought sickened her.

"Ye must away, 'tis nearly light."

Not trusting herself to speak, Enya gave him one last squeeze and slipped into the passageway. How the biting chill swarmed around her without Bran's protective arm. She had never thought she needed the protection of a man, but with him, she wanted it. In his arms she could do anything, mayhap even stand up to her father and tell him this union with Claud Hamilton could never be.

The candle she'd left in the alcove had burnt down to a nub, wax spilling in blobs over the brass holder. She tilted the candle so the wax pooled at the top wouldn't singe her skin. The flame leapt with the long wick. Enya guessed there was just enough wax left to make it to the solar.

She slipped out from behind the bookcase and closed it carefully to not make a sound. When Enya stole away to ride, she would always enter through the kitchens. Entering through the solar added a risk that her escape route might be uncovered.

Relieved her sisters were all married and gone, Enya tiptoed down the corridor to her chamber. Robert and her parents occupied the floor below. Heavy footsteps might wake them. She grasped the latch of her chamber door. It creaked loudly. Enya stiffened. Her chamber was not as she'd left it.

The candles had been lit. Standing in the center, Heather crossed her arms, her lips hidden beneath an angry white line. "And where have you been, slipping away in the dead of night?"

Enya's stomach lurched. From the glint in her eyes, Heather already knew the answer to her question. "I had to see him."

"Holy Mother Mary." Heather crossed herself. "What have you done?"

Enya rushed to Heather and grasped her hands. "Please. Tell no one."

Heather pulled away and paced. "And to think I encouraged you to embroider the panel for that rogue."

"He's no rogue. He told me not to come."

"Did he lay his hands on you?"

"He did not take me"—Enya dropped her gaze to her folded hands—"as a man takes a wife." *Though I wanted him to. Oh God, if he only would have, I would be his no matter what happened now.*

Heather yanked the panel from the table and stormed to the hearth. "This must be burned."

"No!" Enya darted across and tore the keepsake from Heather's hands. "It will not be burned." She clutched it to her chest. "This is difficult enough. Father is forcing me to marry a man I cannot love, while a man who stirs me like never before sleeps on a pallet in the stable loft—chained to his low birth status, unable to shower his love upon me solely because he was born poor."

"You spend far too much time dreaming about what could be. You must face the world as it is."

Enya shook where she stood, her blood about to boil over. "Can you not see I am trying to make sense of the innumerable inequities that surround me?"

Heather clenched her fists to her chest, but the crease between her brows eased, and then her shoulders sagged. "Look at me, lass. I'm not nobly born, and my lot in life is to serve you—'tis the best I can hope for. Would you ever see me lusting after the likes of Robert?"

That struck Enya as odd. "But you are so much older."

"If I were young. Think on it."

Enya studied her maid. The years had lined her face, but she was attractive under her grey wimple. Had Heather once found love? Enya had never thought to ask, but everyone deserved to find their mate. "Why not? If you loved him and he loved you."

"Aye, that is a lovely dream, but 'tis not acceptable in noble society."

Enya's gut clenched. "My sisters and I have been used for trade like fine horses."

"Unfortunately, that is the way of it." Heather glanced toward the door. "I should report this to her ladyship."

"No! You cannot." Enya dropped to her knees and crawled to Heather's skirts. "Please. Sir Bran did not take my innocence—it was he who said he would not ruin me, though I wanted nothing more." A tear slipped from Enya's eye and she kissed Heather's hem. "Please, I beg of you—please do not go to Mother."

Heather crossed herself again. "Dear Lord Jesus, forgive my folly. I never should have left you alone in the tent with him." She pulled Enya up and embraced her. "Of all your sisters, you have been the most difficult—but you are also the most endearing. You love him, do you not?"

"Yes. More than anything."

"You are foolish, but I remember being young once." Heather held her at arm's length. "I will hold my tongue because your knight has acted like a gentleman, as I would expect."

"Thank you. Oh, Heather, I'll do anything to repay your kindness."

"First, you must promise never to see him again. If I find your bed empty, I shall have no choice but to alarm her ladyship. I could lose my position if she ever finds out I've kept something this grave from her."

Enya averted her eyes and nodded. *I could no sooner stay away from Sir Bran than I could stop breathing. But if I atoned to that fact, I would never see him again for certain.*

Heather led her to the bed. "Rest, have a bit of sleep and I'll wake you when 'tis time to dress."

"Thank you." Enya crawled beneath the bedclothes. "I shall not forget your kindness."

"Always remember, a lady acts with discretion." Heather snuffed the candles and slipped out the door.

Enya still had the panel in her hands. She ran her fingers across the ornate embroidery. She would find a way to give it to Bran. And she would find a way to lie in his arms even if only for one more night. She would lock the tenderness of his touch in her heart and prize it for all eternity.

---

Bran slept later than usual, though dawn was just bringing her light. His rendezvous with Enya had him tossing through the wee hours. God, she was so delectable, so full of life. This was the first time in his life he had regretted his lowly birth. Laird Calum had always treated him with respect—Bran had earned it through hard work and devout loyalty. Lord Ross was quite the opposite. All Bran represented to the baron was a sword for his army. That was bloody right. Ross invited the Hebride clans for a tournament to recruit fighting men. Why not put good fighting Highlanders in the front line so Ross's clan would be spared?

He swiped his fingers across his nose and moaned. The flowery perfume of a woman's treasure spilled through his senses. Hot desire swelled beneath his kilt. If only he could actually make love to her—slip inside her womanhood and claim Enya for himself.

He sat up and ground his fists into his forehead. He had nothing to give the lass. She wouldn't take to a life on Raasay, living in a small cottage, wearing simple kirtles. He closed his eyes to a vision of Enya in a barrel, raising her skirts to stomp on the washing. The creamy alabaster of her skin made the longing wash over him like a rogue wave, but the idea of a fine lass performing the work of a serving maid tied his gut in knots. Enya might be able to handle a bow like a man, but Bran was certain she'd never done a day of common work in her life. She was born for privilege and he'd best not forget it.

He took Griffon for a quick jaunt to the loch. Kneeling, Bran splashed the sleep out of his eyes, attempting to clear the lust from his head. He would march with Ross's army soon and Miss Enya would become a pleasant memory—but far sweeter than the wench in Tortuga.

Bran splashed another handful of cold water into his face. There was no comparison, aside from the two being female. Enya would always be on a pedestal—a woman so exquisite, she remained far beyond his reach. The wench in Tortuga paled in comparison. He doubted he would even want to lay a hand on her now that he'd had Enya in his arms.

Bran dunked his whole head in the pond. Holy falcon feathers, he had to leave the Lowlands. He most certainly did not intend to go through life as a monk. He may be forced to take a *leman* if he could not clear his mind.

The horn sounded, calling the guard to practice. Bran ran the drying cloth over his hair and headed for the courtyard, claymore swinging from his hip.

"There you are," Malcolm said. "Spar with the guard before you ride out. Rewan needs a partner."

Bran nodded toward the Lewis henchman. At least he'd have a challenge. Rewan drew his sword and circled. His eyes darted up to the window that looked out over the courtyard. "I see the little lassie's come to watch ye spar. Ye'd best keep yer shirt on or she'll be swooning from her perch."

Bran's gut flipped. Enya was watching? He thought she'd still be asleep for certain.

"What? Did I strike a nerve?" Rewan sneered. "Yer face looks like ye've been caught with the lassie's skirts hiked up around her hips."

Bran didn't need a mirror to know the heat burning the back of his neck had spread to his face. "Dunna speak about Miss Enya with disrespect. I'll no' stand for it."

Rewan lunged in. Bran deflected the attack. Rewan laughed. "So ye rescue the damsel from a mob of rutting Gypsies and now she's the honorable daughter of the baron who intends to send us to Hades?"

*Be patient with the scoundrel.* Bran wanted to attack like a raging boar, but that's what Rewan was hoping for. *Control yer anger, channel it into yer soul. Watch the shift of yer opponent's eyes and pick the moment.* When Rewan's eyes strayed to the window, Bran seized his chance. With one swift upward swing, he knocked the claymore from Rewan's grasp. "Ye'd best keep yer eye on the task at hand, lest I disarm ye and knock ye senseless."

Rewan stooped to pick up his blade. "Ye're the senseless one."

Bran planted his foot in Rewan's arse and laid him out flat. "I'm no' the one with me face in the mud."

The Lewis henchman cast a hateful glare over his shoulder. "But ye will be."

Rewan sprang up swinging, but Bran was ready. Well matched, their swords clashed in a battle of strength. Rewan had some sort of barney to settle and he went after Bran like a rabid dog. Bran had faced this kind of anger before. His inner voice reminded him to be patient. It was Calum's voice, really. The angry fighter would soon tire—and then make a fatal mistake.

# THE HIGHLAND HENCHMAN 119

Bran deflected a direct lunge. "Why are ye fighting like ye have a thistle up yer arse?"

Tiring, Rewan swung his blade across his body with both hands. "Why do ye stay away from the men and sleep in the stable with the animals?"

Bran deflected every slash as if he were scything hay in the paddock. "I need a quiet place for Griffon."

"And why does that lassie look at ye as if ye're some kind of bonny prince? Ye're as ugly as me nursemaid's arse."

Bran resisted the urge to glance up to Enya's window. One errant move might see him killed. "Ye still have a nursemaid?"

Rewan bellowed and charged, swinging his sword like a madman.

Bran ducked. If he hadn't, his head would no longer be attached. "Och, ye onion-eyed varlet." He pounded the pommel of his sword into Rewan's back, sending him stumbling to the ground. "Are ye out for blood?"

Rewan arched his back against the blow and bellowed. "Aye. Since ye won the tournament, ye've been in good with Malcolm, riding beside him, talking about strategy—flirting with Ross's daughter. But have ye included me in any of this? And I'm yer superior from Lewis—ye're just from the puny Isle of Raasay."

"If ye havena realized I'm a pawn in this bloody scheme, just like you, ye're a greater fool than I thought." Bran pulled his dirk. He couldn't resist dropping to his knees and holding it against Rewan's throat. "Now who's the *superior*?"

Rewan bared his teeth.

Bran thrust his face an inch from Rewan's. "I'm no' yer enemy, but if ye come at me like that again, ye'd better be ready to finish it. I'll have no man from Lewis thinking he's better just because he was born on a bigger island." He pressed the knife down a little harder. "And I'll have no man speak poorly of Lord Ross's daughter. Ye ken?"

Rewan's feet squirmed. "Aye, now hop up off me, ye bastard. Och, yer no captain of the guard."

"Neither are ye."

Bran stood and sheathed his dirk, stealing a glance to the window above. He smiled at Enya's darling face gazing at him just as she had last night. But then the dour frown of Lady Ross appeared and Enya was gone.

Malcolm stepped in beside him. "I didn't just see you flash your smile at Miss Enya."

"No, sir."

Malcolm whacked Bran's shoulder. "Time to saddle your mount. Riding the perimeter will keep you out of trouble."

Rewan chuckled. Evidently he found some amusement in Bran's new responsibilities. Bran welcomed it. Riding the estate's vast grounds would keep his mind off Enya—or at least keep his mind *away* from Enya.

## Chapter Thirteen

"Step away from that window this instant."

Enya jolted at the sound of her mother's voice. Instinctively, she stepped back as if caught pinching a morsel of holiday pudding.

Lady Ross stepped up to the window and frowned. "And just what are your feelings for that barbarian?"

"Are you referring to Sir Bran?"

Mother's eyes narrowed with the line of her lips. "You know exactly what I'm asking."

"He's quite adept with weapons." Enya shrugged nonchalantly. "Amusing sport to watch. 'Tis all."

"If I catch you watching him again, I'll send you to Alison for a month. I'm sure she could use more help with the baby."

Enya shuddered at the thought of her colicky nephew screaming into the night. "Please, not Alison."

"And haven't you anything better to do? When was the last time you wrote to William?" Mother grasped Enya's hand and frowned. "And look at your fingernails. Have you been digging a swine's bog?" She turned Enya's hand over. "What on earth? You have calluses on your fingertips."

"'Tis from the bow. Queen's knees, Mother, do you expect me to slather myself in tallow and roll my body in bed linen to prevent all possible blemishes?"

"If that's what it takes." Lady Ross pinched Enya's shoulder then pushed her down the corridor and into her chamber. "I'll not stand for your impertinence. Have Heather prepare a salve for those calluses...and when I next see you, your nails had better be immaculate."

Enya could have blown steam out her nose. Her nails weren't all that bad. "Yes, Mother." *Oh dear, my tone was sharp and clipped.*

Folding her arms, Mother frowned. "I believe you need a lesson in respecting your betters." Lady Ross held up her key. "You can spend the next day locked within."

Enya watched the baroness walk out and slam the door. Sometimes Enya found it difficult to believe she had actually been birthed from that rigid woman's womb. They were about as similar as a magpie and an eagle. She smiled. If she were an eagle, she could spend her days riding on Bran's shoulder. Enya held her hand to her mouth to muffle her laugh. *I'd much rather ride on Bran's lap.*

---

Claud Hamilton sat across the chessboard from Lord Seaton, but neither could concentrate on the game. When the mantel clock launched into twelve droning gongs to mark midnight, a nervous tic pulsed above Claud's right eye. "She should have arrived by now."

A much older man, George Seaton's sagging jowls shook in opposition to his head. "The plan is sound. They'll be here anon. Mark my words."

"We never should have trusted Willy and George Douglas to spirit her away."

"Oh? I thought the idea of a May Day parade with Willy playing the part of a drunken fool was the perfect ploy to sink all the Lochleven boats—pray the one he would use for the queen."

"'Tis foolishness if you ask me. And stealing horses from Laird Douglas's stables? George is asking to be strung up on a sturdy oak."

"Laird Douglas would never hang his own brother." Lord Seaton slid his pawn forward, taking out Claud's rook. "Keep your mind on the game, lest I capture your queen."

Claud shifted in his seat. "I'm not amused by your pun, my lord." Had something gone awry? If only his uncle would have allowed him to lead the escape, all would be well. Meeting the queen at Niddry Castle was not his preference, but Rutherglen was too far to ride in one night. He wanted to spirit Queen Mary to his keep as quickly as possible. Few would think to look for her under a Hamilton's roof. The most likely place would be Stirling Palace, where she could be with her infant son, but that was far too obvious.

Claud sipped his goblet of whisky and savored the sharp bite as it burned a trail down his gullet. He slid his bishop down a diagonal path. "Check."

Lord Seaton's rheumy eyes widened. "It appears we both need to concentrate."

Faint horse hooves clattered on the gravelly path. Claud stood. "It is time."

Dressed in black hoods, the party appeared more sinister than regal as they rode into the torchlight.

Claud watched Lord Seaton drop to his knee, then knelt beside him. "Welcome to Niddry, your grace."

Taking George Douglas's arm, Queen Mary ascended the steps of the earl's castle. A weight lifted from Claud's shoulders. After ten months of captivity on Lochleven, once more his queen was at liberty.

The queen first offered her hand to Lord Seaton. "I cannot express enough how good it is to be received by my loyal subjects."

He kissed her ring. "I only wish we had a greater party to greet you. But I felt we needed to exercise the utmost secrecy."

Her cloak parted, revealing a simple red kirtle, and she turned to Claud. "Lord Hamilton, I commend your indiscretion."

Claud took her hand and pressed his lips to her ring. "My queen. Your servant's armies are gathering at Rutherglen Castle. Your throne shall be restored."

"'Tis music to my ears. I look forward to meeting with them."

Lord Seaton stood and gestured inside. "Come, your grace. You must be hungry and tired."

"Thank you, my lord." She turned to her escort of half a dozen knights and beckoned them to follow.

"You brought no *femme-de-chambre*, your grace?" Claud asked.

George Douglas stepped beside him, assessing Claud with a flat line to his lips. "'Twas too risky. They shall join us at Rutherglen."

Lord Seaton bowed. "I shall wake Lady Seaton's chambermaid to attend you."

"Gratitude, my lord." A deep sadness darkened the queen's face. "I was forced to flee wearing common women's clothing with little else."

Claud bowed deeply. "I shall see to it you have a gown befitting your station for your ride to Rutherglen. All the countryside will be agog with the sight of you."

"Excellent. I want the people to recognize me. It shall be a triumphant march to Stirling Castle."

Claud held up his finger. "To Rutherglen, and then I will lead the march to reclaim your throne."

The queen pursed her lips. "We shall speak more on this when my lords assemble."

---

Enya was still fuming about being locked in her chamber merely for watching the guard spar. She'd watched them hundreds of times, but because her parents were prejudiced against Highlanders, it had now become a sin.

Released from two days of bondage, Enya headed to the stables. She climbed the ladder to the loft, but Bran's pallet was empty, as if deserted. He was gone again, and God only knew when she'd see him next. The ire coursing through her blood inflamed her. She hopped down, clenching her fists. She needed the wind in her hair—a fast gallop.

She found Rodney working in the tack shop. "I want to ride. Are you game?"

"It beats oiling Robert's saddle for the hundredth time. I swear your brother's more worried about how he looks riding into battle than how he fights."

"That sounds like Robert. What do you expect? He'll be the next Baron of Ross." She examined Rodney's trews. "Are those new?"

"Aye. I tore the arse out of me old ones."

With a chuckle, she cast her gaze to the top of his head. "I do believe you're taller than me now." Enya pulled her sidesaddle from the rack. "Come. Help me saddle Maisey."

"That crazy Galloway mare again?"

"She's got spirit." Enya grinned over her shoulder. "Just what I need after being locked in my chamber for the past day."

"What did you do this time?"

"I watched the guard sparring in the courtyard."

"Hells bells, you were locked in your chamber for that?" Rodney walked into Maisey's stall, slipped a snaffle bit into her mouth and buckled the bridle leathers behind her ears. "What about all the times you've stolen away? I'd think that would be a far worse crime."

Rodney knew nothing about Enya's escape route and the fact she kept their early morning jaunts to herself. She'd be locked in her chamber for a year if her mother discovered what she'd been up to. But Rodney didn't care. The son of Lord Ross's groom, the boy was happy to have Enya to mull about with.

She smoothed a blanket over Maisey's back and placed her saddle atop. "Go saddle your gelding and I'll race you to the loch."

"You're on. I want my farthings back."

Enya threw her bow and arrows over her shoulder and led the white mare to the mounting block. She needed no assistance to mount, and she wasn't about to hang about waiting for Rodney. She wanted to feel the freedom of the wind at her face and in her hair. She yanked the veil from atop her head, cast it aside and ran her fingers through her tresses. "Come along," she called over her shoulder, slapping the reins against the horse's neck.

While she exited the stable doors, the breeze picked up Enya's hair. Tension fled from her shoulders as she cued the horse to a canter. Laughing, she leaned forward in the saddle and clapped her riding crop against Maisey's rump. The horse bolted forward in a full-on gallop. Enya held her hands forward to give the mare her head, steering her straight for the loch and the surrounding wood. Spending over a day in her chamber had nearly driven her to madness. If she could not be in Bran's arms, the fresh air on her face would take the pain in her heart away.

She cared not that dark clouds loomed overhead. If it rained, so be it. She'd welcome the wet splashes on her face. Rodney hollered behind her. Enya urged Maisey faster. She would spend this day riding—blast her mother and blast her parents' narrow-minded plans for her future. This moment was hers.

She pulled up and Maisey skidded in the mud, stopping only inches before plunging into the water.

Rodney rode in beside her. "That's not fair. You didn't wait."

"Very well." Enya steered her mare on the path that circled the loch. "What shall be your next challenge?"

Rodney pulled his bow from his shoulder. "The targets are still up from the tournament. Hit the bull's-eye while riding at full gallop."

Enya grinned. "I like your idea of fun, young squire."

"I'll go first this time."

Enya relaxed in her saddle while she watched Rodney load his bow and race for the target. Once his horse sped up to a gallop, its movement was level enough to fire. Enya held her breath. Rodney pulled the string back and aimed. *Now*. Rodney released his arrow. It hit low on the target as he groped for his reins.

"Not bad for your first try," Enya hollered, trotting Maisey in a circle.

She pulled an arrow from her quiver and eyed her target. Shoving the reins in her teeth, Enya dug in her heels and swatted the mare's rump. Holding her gaze, the horse reared and took off at a raging gallop. Her heart racing, thundering in her ears, Enya pulled back the string and stared at the red center of the bull's-eye. As if transformed by the harmony of the world around her, Enya's reflexes took over. The arrow sailed straight for the target like a lightning rod. With a clap, it struck the bull's-eye.

Enya threw her head back and laughed, her heart pounding against her chest, the thrill still coursing beneath her skin. She lived for the rush from riding at breakneck speed, knowing with one errant move she could be flat on her back on the soggy ground.

She relished her morning with Rodney and his carefree, boyish outlook on life. Together they rode through the wood and shot their arrows at targets. When it came time for the noon meal, Rodney pulled some smashed oatcakes from his pocket. Enya didn't mind. That would be enough to sustain her until supper.

When they dismounted to water the horses in a brook that fed the loch, Enya estimated they were about a mile from the manse. Movement in the distance caught her attention—and the tingling that spread from the base of her core straight up to the tips of her breasts told her who it was.

"The guard has returned." Rodney gave her a tap on the shoulder. "Enya? Are you all right?"

"Huh?"

"Leaping lords, I thought the queen of the fairies jumped into your body and stole your mind—you looked as if the entire meadow was abloom with wildflowers."

"Mayhap it was for a moment."

Rodney took off his bonnet and scratched his brown curls. "You're becoming odder and odder."

"Perhaps you're right. I suppose 'tis time to return."

"Aye. Robert will already be sore with me for being gone this long."

Enya gave him a wink. "Tell him I kidnapped you."

"A lass?" Rodney stooped to give her a leg up.

"You are well aware I'm not just any lass." Enya cantered her mare straight for the stables, but when she rode inside, Bran was nowhere in sight.

Once again, Rodney brought up the rear. "Hells bells, Enya. You barreled out of here like the stable was afire, and now you're racing back as if you've got an engagement with Queen Mary."

Enya glanced over her shoulder. "Wheesht. I was just giving Maisey some much needed exercise." She slid her leg off the lower pommel of her sidesaddle and prepared to dismount. Bran appeared from nowhere—a raw, hungry man with a shadow of thick beard, laced with the musky scent of campfire. Enya couldn't breathe.

His warm hands encircled her waist. Oh heaven help her, if only they were alone. "May I help ye down, Miss Enya?"

"You are a gentleman," she managed to squeak out. Enya arched her brow at Rodney, hoping her antics masked her deep-seated desire. "Thank you, Sir Bran. A young squire would have much to learn from you."

"You never asked me to help you before," Rodney groused.

Bran lifted Enya in his hands as if she were as light as her saddle and placed her gently on the ground. "A lady shouldna have to ask, laddie."

"Bah." Rodney kicked the dirt and headed out.

Enya rested her hands on Bran's arms, her fingers trembling as if she hadn't eaten in days. "And how was your turn with the guard? Did you see any more Gypsies?"

"Nary a one."

Malcolm appeared in the stable door and cleared his throat. "Stand back, Highlander."

Bran dropped his hands. "Simply assisting the lady to dismount."

Malcolm tugged on his gloves, splaying his fingers. "Do not grow accustomed to your pallet. You'll be back on patrol come dawn."

"As I expected." Bran stepped to the mare and loosened her girth. "Shall I stable her for you, m'lady?"

Enya liked it when Bran used a formal address, though as a baron's daughter, "Miss Enya" would do. "Yes, thank you." Bran pulled the saddle off. She touched his arm and whispered, "Keep your candle lit tonight."

His lips parted and Enya didn't miss his quick inhale. But before he could respond, Malcolm sauntered over and grasped Maisey's reins. "Miss Enya, 'tis nearly time for supper. Do you not need to dress?"

Enya would have liked to tell the meddling toad to mind his own affairs, but he was right. The last thing she needed was Lady Ross locking her in the chamber because she'd come to the table looking like the proverbial guttersnipe. She curtseyed. "I bid you good day."

# Chapter Fourteen

The two days scouting for Lord Ross did nothing to cool the fire in Bran's heart. If anything, the time away from Enya had made him yen for her more. With nothing else to do but ride and scan the horizon for interlopers, Bran considered every possible alternative to enable him to marry the lass. *Him?* Yes, Calum MacLeod's henchman was smitten with a Lowland lass who could make his heart soar with the eagles.

Bran's skin pricked with awareness when she rode into the stable. Her lovely feminine fragrance wafted into the stall where he unsaddled his horse, and when she moved to dismount, he'd acted without thought. It was all he could do not to hug her body against his and let her slide down his length. He wanted to kiss her, hold her to his chest and tell her how happy he was to see her again. Transfixed, he watched Enya slowly peruse his body as he filled his senses with her hypnotic scent.

But no, he bit back his urges and reminded himself she could never be his. Nor could he show her the affection smoldering deep inside.

His heart skipped a beat when she whispered, asking him to keep his candle lit. He clenched his arse cheeks together to stop the longing, else Malcolm would string him up on the spot. Of course, Bran would give anything to hold Enya in his arms for one more night, but she shouldn't risk it. He ran his hand along her saddle. It was still warm where her exquisite bottom had been. If she came to him, he would need to control his urges again. Bran might be able to resist—if she milked him.

A soft groan escaped his throat. Remembering her silken fingers around his manhood was nearly as magical as the thought of being inside her.

After he'd climbed to the loft, a serving wench, rather than the stable boy, brought Bran's supper. Her head, thick with brown curls, popped through the trapdoor. "I've brought your supper."

Bran had seen the lass in the kitchens. "Gratitude. Just leave it there."

She paid him no mind and climbed up, placing the trencher on a bale of hay.

Bran didn't need to look at her to know what she wanted. The sooner he could spirit her out of the stable, the better. "I dunna want to keep ye from yer work."

"I *am* working." Her bodice laced unusually low, the wench arched her brows and leaned over, giving him a good look. "Lord Ross told me to come."

Bran clenched his fist and then stretched his fingers. The baron sent a peace offering to cool the fire beneath his kilt? How gracious. Bran averted his eyes. "Thank ye for the meal."

She sat on his pallet and rubbed her breasts against his arm. "That's not all I came for."

"Ye've made it quite clear why ye're here." Bran stabbed his meat with his dirk. "I've no mind to take a turn with ye."

Her bottom lip jutted out. "So the big Highlander thinks he's too good for the likes of me?"

She swished her hair away from her face. Her fingers slipped to his kilt. Bran snatched her wrist before she could run her hand across his groin. "Ye best leave. Now."

She snapped her hand away and pranced to the ladder. "There's one difference between Miss Enya and me." She gave him a hateful glare. "You can rut with me all night and no one will give a damn."

Bran shooed her away with a flick of his wrist and reached for the trencher. He shoveled the food in his mouth. If that wench had come to his pallet before he'd met Enya, he would have given her a turn, but now the sight of her flaunting her wares disgusted him. He wanted nothing but his beautiful redheaded *leannan*. Heaven help him.

Satiated by the first decent meal he'd had in two days, Bran fed Griffon and poured some water into the washbowl, reserving half in the ewer. He unwrapped his cinnamon soap from the leather parcel. The cake was nearly gone. He hadn't anticipated being away from Raasay for so long.

Bran stank of campfire and horse sweat, and his beard itched. Regardless, if Enya could steal away, he needed to bathe. The thing he missed most about his cottage was the hearth. He could warm his bath water—had a tub by the hearth too, though he'd never admit he preferred such a luxury to anyone. Washing in cold water was...well, it was bloody cold.

After stripping naked, he leaned over to wet his hair. Making quick work of lathering up, he used the remaining water in the ewer to rinse. He scrubbed every inch of skin and then wrapped his plaid around his waist and fished in his satchel for his shaving kit. It wasn't much—a polished brass mirror and a small folding blade he kept sharp—but it was better than shaving blind.

By the time he dumped the water, darkness shrouded the estate. Bran pulled his shirt over his head and lit two tallow candles to cast good light. Reclining on his pallet, he reached beneath and grasped the piece of wood he'd been whittling and examined it. He'd been carving it for Enya. All it needed was a bit of finishing and he'd have it done—the figurine was of a lady archer lining up her shot. He fashioned a twig for the arrow, and he tied strands of horsehair in place for the bowstring and then oiled it to bring out the rich beauty of the wood.

He hoped Enya would like it. A lass like her would have so many fine things, she might think it trite. Bran stopped oiling and held it up. She'd like it. Especially since the woman was an archer. He set it on the barrel beside his pallet and lay back. Sleeping on the trail was fitful at best. He closed his eyes, relishing the comfort of the hay beneath his back.

He had no idea how late it was when Enya's voice softly called from below. "Bran."

Gooseflesh rose across his skin. He leaned his head over the trapdoor. "I canna believe ye came."

She smiled up at him. "How could I stay away?" The white lace of her nightdress peaked from beneath the V formed by the crossing of her red dressing gown. Again she'd come in her chamber clothes.

He offered his hand and helped her climb up. "I'm glad yer here." The worries of the world were mollified as he enfolded Enya in his arms and brushed his lips across hers.

"I missed you so incredibly."

Enya rose on her toes and kissed him fully. A raging-hot fire swelled across Bran's skin. Her touch sent him into a maelstrom of desire. Her tongue had become far more practiced since the incident in the tent, and her mouth showed him what she wanted. Instantly erect, Bran clenched her dressing gown in his hands, fighting an internal battle. Every fiber of his being wanted to enter her, lay her down and claim Enya as his own. Bran forced himself to use restraint. He would not defile Miss Enya. She needed him to be gentle, to woo her and protect her innocence. Clenching his eyes shut, he blocked out the ragged desires that drove him mad. When he opened them, the figurine caught his eye.

After taking a deep breath and readjusting his priorities, he led her to the pallet. "Will ye sit with me?"

Her lips red and swollen from his forceful kisses, she nodded.

"I have something for ye."

A coy grin spread across her face, her eyes filled with mischief. She reached inside her dressing gown. "I do as well." She pulled out a parcel and held it on her lap. Her giddy excitement reminded him of the day he found Griffon—a mere chick in the nest.

Would she never stop surprising him? He leaned in and peered at the folded cloth. "What is it?"

Biting her adorable bottom lip, she unfolded a work of embroidery. She held it up—the likeness was undeniable.

"Halkhead." He brushed his fingers across the ornate stitching. "Ye've used such detail—'tis exquisite." His eyes trailed to the splashes of color in the garden. "Ye made this for me?"

"Aye. I thought you could hang it in your cottage." Enya pointed to the flowers. "And I used a lock of my hair to embroider the azaleas."

Bran grasped the panel and touched the shimmering buds. "That makes it even more special."

Her smile could make fairies dance in his stomach. "Do you like it?"

"'Tis the most beautiful thing anyone has ever given me."

Bran twisted his mouth as he eyed the figurine. She hadn't seen it resting on the barrel he used for a table. It wasn't half as ornate as her embroidery, but he wanted to give it to her.

Her eyes followed his gaze and she gasped.

He reached for it and held it in his palm. "I whittled this for ye. 'Tis no' much, but I thought ye would like it."

"An archer woman?" She carefully picked it up and turned it over in her hand. "The likeness is remarkable." She held it to her lips and kissed. "I shall always cherish it."

Bran set the gifts aside and kissed her, pulling her close in his embrace. He wanted this moment to last. He would lock it in his heart for all eternity.

Trembling in his arms, she pulled away. "I do not think I can live without you."

"I want to be with you as well." Bran reached out and cupped her cheek, losing himself in her fathomless eyes. "No matter how I try to block it, I canna help meself. I'm in love with ye."

Watching the smile spread across her face was akin to seeing the first time Griffon spread his wings and took to flight. Enya made him feel powerful, as if he were the lord of all Scotland. "That's all I wanted to hear you say." Enya threw her arms around him. "I love you too, Bran. More than anything."

"I've thought about spiriting ye away, but yer life would be hard and I canna expect ye to suffer for the likes of me."

Enya's hands slid to his shoulders. "Do you think for a moment I need all the finery my father provides?"

"'Tis no' that, but ye have a sheltered life. How could ye ken what it would be like to be henchman's wife?"

"I've been to the crofters' cottages. They're warm and full of happiness."

Bran remembered all too well the winter when his clan survived on pickled herring and seaweed. "And sometimes their bellies are empty."

Enya said not a word, but stood and unbelted her dressing gown. Slipping from her shoulders, it cascaded around her feet.

Bran drew in a ragged breath. Her nightdress was so sheer, he could make out the round buds of her nipples. He reached for her hands, but Enya stepped back. Her lips moist, her green eyes fanned by luscious auburn lashes, she clutched her skirts and lifted.

Unable to move, Bran watched as she pulled the gown up and revealed the creamy alabaster of her slender calves. She let out a nervous chuckle and exposed her thighs. Bran could scarcely breathe. His heart thundered in his ears. He must see the rest. In one swift motion, she pulled the nightdress over her head and cast it aside. He knew he should close his mouth, but never in his life had he seen such beauty.

Swallowing hard, he feasted his eyes on two impeccably formed breasts that stood proud—not inordinately large, but far from small, they were perfectly round, tipped by rose-colored nipples. *Perfect*. Bran's mouth watered with his need to suckle them.

His gaze dipped to her slim waist, and below it curved hips ending in a fiery red that made his cock jut from his loins as if he were a stallion overcome with the scent of a mare in heat.

She stepped toward him, and Bran pulled her into his lap. "Ye are the most stunning sight I've ever seen."

A low chuckle rolled from Enya's throat as she took him into her mouth. Her hips rocked against the erection, pushing through his plaid. Her mouth claimed him with every delicious swirl of her tongue. She pulled back, her eyes dark with desire. "Please show me how to love you."

His resolve washed away with her words and he laid her down on his pallet. Kneeling over her, Bran spread Enya's knees.

"I want to see you naked."

Unable to speak, he yanked his shirt over his head and then watched her eyes as his hand slid down to his belt. Her breasts rose and fell with her quick breaths. He wanted the moment to linger.

Enya sat up and caressed his chest, running her fingers over his abdomen. "You are beautiful."

Bran chuckled. Of everything he'd been called in his life, "beautiful" was not a word ever used. That she admired him made his heart swell. With a flick of his wrist, his belt unclasped and his plaid dropped around his knees.

With a quick gasp, Enya licked her lips and cast her gaze to his manhood. He was so hard, it tapped against his abdomen. She reached out and caressed it with silken fingers. Bran jutted his hips forward. "Heaven help me, I want ye."

He needed a moment to regain his senses, and he covered her with his body, seeking her mouth. He showered her with kisses over her long, silken neck. His lips trailed down to her breasts and he cradled them in his hands. Running his tongue across her delicate flesh, he suckled her nipples until she cried out.

"I want to feel you inside me."

"'Twill hurt the first time."

"Please."

Bran grinned. He had never tasted a woman, but he must have Enya in his mouth. He slid his tongue down her belly and inhaled the intoxicating perfume that was only Enya. Exploring her in the candlelight excited him beyond any imaginings. Her treasures were exquisite, each inch of her flesh perfect, and then he beheld her glorious womanhood. Trembling, he rubbed his thumb over her and slipped down to the pool of moisture he so desperately needed to enter.

She moved against him, heightening his desire. Nothing touched his cock, yet he could come just by inhaling her. Bran flicked out his tongue and lapped. Enya gasped, her hips rocking. She tasted of sweet cream butter mixed with nectar. He swirled his tongue against her and slipped his fingers inside her womb. Relentlessly, he licked her as Enya bucked against him, mewling like a woman possessed.

When her body stiffened with a frantic gasp, he knew she had arrived at the peak of desire. Her thighs shuddered and he rose on his knees, watching the pleasure on her angelic face. Her breasts heaved with every breath. "How can you make me feel like this?"

He grinned and trailed kisses from her hips to her slender neck. "You give me unimaginable pleasure." The pewter of his tankard flickered in the candlelight and he reached for it. Enya would need a reprieve before she would be ready to come again.

"Are ye thirsty?" She sat up, sipped and then licked her lips. Setting the cup aside, she stroked his manhood. "There's more."

Bran's eyes rolled back as he shuddered. "Aye, lass, so much more."

Again he laid her down and showered her with kisses, kneeling over her. Enya rocked her hips beneath him. His manhood slipped between her legs and she rubbed her moist core along it. She slid her hand between them and grasped him.

"Please." She placed him at her entrance.

Bran rocked his hips forward, and the head entered her. Every sinew in his body tightened as he strained to keep from coming. Enya grasped his arse and pulled. He slid deeper, met by resistance. She tugged harder and gasped as he plunged through the length of her. Her breath ragged, she moved against him, showing him she was ready. Bran didn't move for a moment, allowing her body to become accustomed to his size.

Enya moaned and swirled her hips, her eyes dark, steeped with desire.

Something in Bran's head snapped. He no longer had control. He was completely at the mercy of the hot core that milked him and the demands of Enya's fingers sinking into his buttocks, dictating the tempo. Giving in to the raging fire in his loins, he drove his need into her over and over again. Enya's cries escalated. Her body stiffened. She was close. He needed to come with her. The world spun as his hips matched her thrusts. As if possessed, Bran threw his head back and roared.

Connected by a power beyond anything she'd ever experienced, she watched Bran's eyes as he claimed her. Never before had she wanted to belong to a man, but Enya could no longer imagine herself without her Highlander. They were now joined, one body, and she would remain by his side no matter what anyone said.

When he shuddered and cried out, her own release burst around him. It was as if the secret of the universe unfolded around her. Enya clutched him against her breast and showered him with kisses until his breathing steadied. "I love you."

"And I you. So much it hurts."

For the first time since she met Bran, fear pricked the back of her mind. "My father will never approve."

"I ken."

"We must spirit away."

"Aye. That is our only choice." He cupped her face with his hands. "Are ye sure this is a life ye can live?"

"I would have it no other way."

"Then pack what ye must in a satchel. I'll steal away from the patrol. Come to the stable after supper—as soon as ye can slip away. We shall ride to Newark and take a galley."

"Sail to Raasay?"

"Aye, if Calum will have me." Bran spread his plaid over them. "I'll be going against his wishes by leaving yer father before Queen Mary regains her throne."

"But surely he will be compassionate. After everything you've told me—how he fought Thomas Wharton so he could be with Lady Anne."

"I'll remind him of that before he bludgeons me to death."

Enya hadn't thought through all the repercussions. "Do you think he would?"

"Nay, but he'll be awful cranky—especially if yer father follows with an armada of Scottish ships."

Enya cuddled into the crook of Bran's arm. "Everything will be all right. We are meant to be together."

Resting in his arms gave her happiness beyond anything she dreamt possible. And she was so tired. As Bran's breathing slowed, hers did as well.

# Chapter Fifteen

Bran had no idea how long they'd been asleep, but the candles had nearly burned down to nubs. He had to take Enya back to the manse before Heather noticed her missing.

He gazed upon her face and could hardly believe it possible for her to look more beautiful, but in sleep, she resembled an angel.

Bran closed his eyes and pressed his lips against her forehead. There was no reasoning for the love that swelled in his chest. It just was. He gave her a light squeeze. "Enya. Ye must wake, my love." Oh how sweet those words sounded as they rolled off his tongue.

With a sigh, she stretched. "I must have fallen asleep."

"We must spirit ye back to the keep afore they find yer bed cold."

He helped her dress, noticing a ray of light streaming from the trapdoor. "'Tis already light. We need to move quickly."

"I'll skirt around the woods. But you should remain behind. You cannot be seen with me."

Bran didn't like the idea of Enya going to the keep on her own, but the alternative would be devastating for them both. "This will be the last time."

He descended the ladder first to help her down. As his feet touched ground, hands grasped his arms and Robert stepped in, holding a dirk against his neck. "Stinking, putrid filth."

His heart pounding in his ears, Bran bucked and strained to break away from his captors, but they held him fast. His arms were wrenched behind his back and the grating rasp of hemp rope cut deep into his wrists. Lord Ross stepped into Bran's line of sight. "Where is my daughter?"

"I'm here."

Bran cast his eyes to the loft.

Ross threw his fist into Bran's gut. "What have you done?" He shook his finger at Enya. "Get down here this instant."

Enya held her skirts to the side and climbed down. Facing her father with a thin line to her lips, she folded her arms tight to her body.

Ross whipped his hand back and slapped her across the face. "Did you lie with this man?"

Bran twisted his wrists against his bindings. If he had the use of his hands, he'd make Ross pay for striking his woman, but four men held him back.

A red welt rising on her cheek, Enya stood proud as if unscathed. "I love him and I intend to marry him."

"You stupid girl. You are ruined." He turned to Robert. "Take her to Paisley Abbey. I cannot bear the sight of her."

Sentries seized her arms. Enya shrieked. "No. Bran, help!"

The ropes on Bran's wrists cut into his flesh. He jerked away from his captors and staggered forward, watching them pull her away. "Release her. She is innocent!"

Ross faced him and sauntered forward. "You will pay with your flesh for sullying my daughter." He pulled back a fist.

Bran steeled his gut against the blow, but it landed square and the air whooshed from his lungs.

"Tie him to the post."

It took all four guards to drag Bran to the courtyard and winch his arms up the whipping post. The wheels of a carriage creaked over the cobblestones. Enya's sobs echoed from within, twisting Bran's gut in a knot. Paisley Abbey? At least she would be safe there.

Malcolm's solid form blocked his view. "I told you to stay away from her. But now I can no longer be lenient." He lowered his voice. "Lord Ross ordered two dozen lashes, and I have no recourse but to make you bleed, lest he double it."

"Do what ye must," Bran growled through clenched teeth. Enya was his now. They could take her no place he wouldn't find her. The only thing that would part them would be death.

Over his shoulder, Bran watched Malcolm run the bullwhip though his hand. Bran would bear the whip, and when his torture was over, he would go after her. Malcolm gave a nod to the guard, who tore the shirt from Bran's back.

Bran arched as the first lash ripped through his flesh like the slice of a dagger, but he uttered not a sound. He'd been cut before. Wounds of the flesh would heal, but he doubted the hatred that built with each ensuing lash would ever subside. Bran hated Lord Ross for his condescending, pompous right to rule over all under his watch because of his birth. He hated the gentry for the stench of their unfair and oppressive laws. He cursed Calum for leaving him in the godforsaken Lowlands.

Lash number twenty-three crisscrossed Bran's back, blinding him with the screaming pain of open welts streaming blood down his legs. His mind spun. Bran's head dropped forward. The ground steeped with his blood as Malcolm drew out the final lash. Bran heard the crack before it struck him. With a roar catching in his throat, his back seized against the last shred of flesh tearing away.

Bran would make his peace with the captain of the guard—once he could stand.

---

Enya sat upon a cot, alone in a cold, dank cell. Far above the bed, there was a tiny window that cast a shadowy light. Aside from the bed and an iron cross hung on the wall, nothing else filled the cell—not a candle, no hearth for a fire to keep away the night chill, no warm Bran to cover her with his plaid. A single blanket was her only comfort during the three nights in which she had been imprisoned.

How could her father dump her here? But the thing that worried Enya most was Bran. The last thing she'd seen before the carriage rolled out the gates was Bran being tied to the whipping post. Was he still alive? What had her father done to him? She looked at the tiny window above. How could she escape?

Still wearing her dressing gown, she fingered Bran's carving in her pocket. She kept it there, afraid the monks would take her precious keepsake. It was the only thing she had that connected her to him, gave her hope.

The only people she'd seen since her arrival were the monks who brought her food. None of them spoke, nor did they acknowledge her questions. She stood and paced. A hundred times she had shaken the latch and pounded on the door. Her fists were bruises, her throat raw from screaming. Yet no one even spoke to her.

She had to find a way out. She must get back to Bran.

Enya pressed her ear to the door when two sets of footsteps echoed down the corridor. There had only been one set when they brought food.

"I hope she is receiving good care."

*Heather!*

Enya clutched her fists against her chest as the key creaked in the lock. She rushed into Heather's arms. "Och, I've never been so happy to see anyone."

Heather ran her hand over Enya's head. "There, there, lass. We have much to discuss and little time."

Enya gestured to the bed. "What news of Bran? I must know."

"He is still in the pit."

She tensed. "He's alive?"

"For now. Word among the servants is he will be the first of Queen Mary's army to be sacrificed."

A death sentence. Enya clutched Heather's hands and knelt before her. "I must go to him. Please help me."

"No, child." Heather solemnly shook her head. "As soon as transport can be arranged, you will be transferred to the nunnery on Iona."

"A nunnery? But I do not want to become a nun."

"You will remain there until things settle—Lord Ross still holds hope Lord Hamilton will have you."

"Claud? But I chose Sir Bran. He's a knight."

"Knighted by a Highland laird. Do you not understand? A marriage to Sir Bran would never suffice. He owns no property."

Enya threw up her hands. "This is mindless posturing."

"Your father intends to wait. There is no need for Lord Hamilton to know you have been...compromised."

"You make it sound so damning."

Heather slowly shook her head. "It is very grave indeed, Miss Enya."

"All my life I've wanted to travel, but never like this." Enya kissed Heather's hands. "Will you go with me?"

"Alas, no. Lord Ross has forbidden all the servants from contacting you. As it is, I took a great risk to come here today."

Enya squeezed Heather's palms together. "Please send word to Bran. Tell him I will always love him. Tell him to carry my panel for luck."

"No one can speak to Bran." Heather looked away. "He's suffering."

Enya's mind raced. In addition to needing a healer, Bran would be starving, mayhap dying of thirst. "And what of his eagle, Griffon? Is anyone feeding him?"

"I believe Rodney has taken on his care."

Enya wrung her hands. She had not even a quill or parchment to write upon. "Please. If there is any way to slip a message to Bran—you know he's a good man. Please, Heather. Tell him I love him."

Heather looked toward the door. "The monks only gave me a moment. I must go."

"No." There was another way to contact Bran. "Tell Rodney to release Griffon."

"That makes no sense at all."

"Do it. If you feel anything for me, you'll promise me you'll tell him."

Heather stood and shook out her skirts. "Very well, but I don't see what good that would do."

"The eagle will call to him—give him hope." Enya steepled her hands to her lips, silencing herself from speaking further of Griffon's virtues. "There is one more thing I need to ask."

Heather nodded.

"How did father know I was missing?"

The older woman took a step back, raising her chin. "I told you I would be forced to report it if you slipped away again."

A lead ball sank to the pit of Enya's stomach. "It was you?"

"You gave me no other choice. Part of my employment is to protect your virtue."

"But what if I had been out shooting arrows with Rodney?"

Heather's face fell. "You weren't, were you?"

The door opened. With one last glance, Heather slipped away. Enya's own serving maid had betrayed her.

---

For two days, Bran had been lying face down on the cold stone floor of the pit. A circular hole, twenty feet deep, lined with stone. He was lucky he didn't break a leg when they tossed him in. Exposed to the cold of night, his lash welts raw and as painful as a blanket of angry hornets, the least miserable position was on his stomach.

His lips chapped, his belly empty, Bran's thirst had nearly driven him mad.

A droplet of rain splashed on his shoulder, followed by more droplets stinging his exposed skin. Though it hurt like hellfire, Bran welcomed it. He pushed himself up and opened his mouth, catching the life-giving droplets.

In minutes, the sky opened to a deluge. Icy rain pelted him. He feared the pit would soon fill with water, but it must have been built to withstand the weather. Bran watched the water. The floor sloped to a drain in the center. At least he wouldn't drown. And though he shivered, Bran welcomed the cleansing bath. It stung, but he'd not developed the fever—at least he hoped not, though he'd slipped in and out of consciousness. He inhaled deeply. The rain washed away some of the stench of piss and shite that builds up in a prison with no doors.

Bran ran his hands across his wet face. He thought he'd been in the pit for two days, but it could have been longer. One thing he knew for certain—if someone didn't come for him soon, he'd die of thirst, starvation, exposure, or all three. He rolled back to his stomach and let the rain cleanse his wounds.

And then he heard it. As clear as a bell, an eagle called overhead. *Griffon*. He opened his mouth to sing, but his throat rasped. Without water, he'd gone dry. He held his head up and let the rain slide down his throat. Swallowing, he sang again. Though his voice croaked, he managed a bit of volume this time. He prayed Griffon would recognize the voice as his.

Bran cupped his hands, catching more water. He drank and sang once more. Griffon squawked above, perched on the upper edge of the pit. "Well, come down here, laddie."

The bird swooped down and latched his giant talons on Bran's bare arm. This wasn't the first time Bran had handled the bird without his leather glove, and the sharp claws punctured his skin, but the pain nothing compared to his back. "Who released ye from yer perch?"

He found an arrowhead lodged inside Griffon's jesses. He pulled it out and rubbed it between his fingers. *Enya?* But she was taken to the abbey. Had she returned? Bran cast his gaze around the rim of the pit. Nothing—no one—but her spirit surrounded him.

"Go find us a pigeon." Bran flung his arm forward, praying Griffon would find something to hunt in the rain. The bird would be back. Of that there was no question. Bran might not die of starvation. Death from exposure was still a possibility, however.

The rain had ebbed to a misty drizzle when the eagle returned and dropped a rabbit from its talons. His hands trembling with hunger, Bran picked it up. "Good lad." His voice didn't rasp quite so much.

Perched on the stone across from Bran, with keen yellow eyes, Griffon watched him use the arrowhead to cut out the rabbit's heart. Bran placed it in Griffon's beak. Though starving, the thought of eating raw flesh turned his stomach sour. Blood filled the carcass. Bran held it above his head and let the warm, iron-tasting liquid drain into his mouth. He gagged in the back of his throat, but he held his arm across his lips and forced himself to swallow. *Blessed be Mary and all the saints.* Almost as soon as the blood hit his stomach, his strength began to return.

Bran studied the carcass in his hands, contemplating the repulsive prospect of sinking his teeth into raw flesh.

# Chapter Sixteen

Lord Ross sat in the library with Robert, sipping fine aged whisky, when Malcolm entered. "I've a missive from Rutherglen."

Ross held out his hand. "Bring it here." He didn't need to read the missive to know what it contained. He slid his finger under the Hamilton seal and unfolded it. Yes. The queen had arrived as planned.

"We leave for Rutherglen on the morrow."

Robert reached for the missive. "This is it, then?"

"Aye, all the nobles have been summoned. The queen wishes to assemble her troops immediately."

Malcolm took a step forward. "I'd like to pull the Highlander out of the pit—clean him up before we take him into battle."

Robert tossed the missive on the table with a smirk. "Give him a bath and a meal before his death?"

Malcolm shrugged. "Something like that."

Ross wished he'd never invited the Highlanders to Halkhead, but seeing the bastard cut down in battle would be much easier to explain to the MacLeod army than hanging the arse. His gut clenched. He'd like to hang Bran now—but he'd be dead soon enough. "Pull him out and bring him to me. I want to ensure he understands the terms of his...*freedom*."

"Very well, my lord." Malcolm bowed and made his exit.

Robert folded his arms. "We should have strung him up when we discovered him with Enya."

"But this will be so much more amusing." Ross clapped his eldest son's back. "Mark my words, the Highlander will die—and the

Ross family will not be to blame for it." He gestured to the game board. "Come, let's have a game of chess while we wait."

---

Lord Ross could smell him even before the footsteps slapped the hardwood in the hall. His hands bound in front of his kilt, the MacLeod henchman stood, dripping wet, without a shirt. Christ. The man looked more bull than human. Ross pulled his kerchief from his sleeve and held it to his nose. Clearing his throat, he assumed a practiced look of disgust. "You smell like shite."

Bran kept his gaze averted. Ross didn't like that. He wanted to see the hate in Bran's eyes.

"Did you hear me, Highlander?"

"Aye." The man's voice grated, as if one single word caused him pain.

Ross stepped up to the hearth and stared at the mantel. Keeping his back to the man would demonstrate his contempt. "We've kept you alive so we can watch you die when you lead the Marian army into battle."

Ross waited for a response, but none came.

"Men like you never amount to anything." He turned. Ross wanted to see the Highlander's face with his next words. "You could never be good enough for my daughter—never provide for a real lady, never rise beyond your own pathetic cesspool of poverty."

Aside from the twitch of his jaw, the Highlander made no outward sign of his ire, but Lord Ross was no fool. It was there, boiling under the surface, and that anger would make him all the more exciting to watch as Regent Moray's men cut him down. Ross had no doubt Claud Hamilton and the others would go along with his plan—though he'd mention nothing of Enya's *situation*.

"Take him to the tower and keep him under lock and key."

Malcolm bowed. "I'd like to have the healer attend him, my lord."

Ross flicked his wrist, waving his captain off. "Whatever is necessary to keep him alive. We ride at dawn."

Lying on his side, Bran closed his eyes and sank into the pallet of straw. After sleeping on stone, this was a luxury. He willed sleep to take him away, but Ross's words echoed in his head. *Men like you never amount to anything.*

Ross was right. Bran got himself into this mess because he couldn't control his heart. He couldn't resist Enya. True, she'd encouraged him, but he should have been stronger. It was his duty to resist her. Now they both were condemned—he to death and she to a life cloistered in an abbey. God help him, Bran loved her. He would gladly die in exchange for her life—for her happiness.

Lord Ross could still marry her off. Bran's gut clenched. The thought of another man touching Enya filled him with rage. If he wasn't good enough for her, no one ever would be.

Ross wanted him dead. He expected him to lead the army into Regent Moray's cannons? Bran hadn't lost a fight yet, and he didn't intend to now.

The door opened and Malcolm pushed inside. Bran eyed him from his pallet. The friendship they'd developed was now forfeit. Malcolm worked for the enemy. But the captain of the guard's concerned expression was more sincere than Bran expected. "I've brought Heather to tend your wounds."

This meager act of kindness surely wouldn't make Malcolm think he'd repaid his debt. "Ye bring help now I'm nearly dead?"

"No one was allowed to tend you in the pit."

Heather bustled in with her basket in one hand and a candle in another. "Leave us be, Sir Malcolm."

"Very well." The door closed behind him and the heavy iron bar creaked into place.

Heather knelt beside him and tsked. "Look at you." She held her hand to his forehead. "At least you're not fevered."

Bran rolled to his stomach. "Is it festering?"

Holding the candle high, she leaned over and examined the welts. "There's some pus, but scabs are forming." She pulled a stoppered pot from her basket. "I'll apply a honey poultice to keep it from turning putrid."

"At least there willna be too much time for me wounds to go bad. Ross intends me to be the first man dead in battle."

"Aye? I've watched you spar. 'Twill take quite an army of men to bring down the likes of you."

Bran chuckled. "I've never seen a man stand up to cannon shot."

"At least there's hope." Bran winced as Heather's fingers worked in the cool cream. "I've a message from Enya."

Bran pushed himself up, but Heather pressed on his shoulder. "She asked me to tell you she loves you."

Bran's throat closed. He would give anything to hold her in his arms right now. "Thank you, mistress. That means more to me than you could possibly know." He had to ask. "Did she send Griffon to me?"

"Rodney released him, but she asked me to have him do so."

The salve started to soothe as it seeped into his exposed welts. "And how is she?"

Heather stoppered the pot. "She's nearly gone mad, locked in a cell."

"Miss Enya isn't one to be caged. She needs to spread her wings and fly."

"Aye, she does." Heather held up a bandage strip and applied it to his back. "Lord Ross is sending her to Iona until he can finalize her marriage."

"Iona?" That was farther away from Renfrewshire...and on an island, easier for a sailor to reach. It surprised him the abbey was still in operation, having been hit hard by the Reformation—parts of it were in ruins. "Finalize? He's still proceeding, then?"

"It appears so—after the uprising."

"When will ye see her again?"

Heather applied another bandage across his angry welts. "I've asked Lady Ross to allow me to take her a change of clothes. I plan to return as soon as I'm allowed."

Bran pictured Enya sitting in a lone cell still wrapped in her red dressing gown, subsisting on bread and water. "I must see her."

Heather shook her head. "Unfortunately, it doesn't appear that will be possible."

He had to find some way of reaching her. "Please tell Miss Enya I return her love tenfold."

"It would be best if you would both forget you ever met."

Bran grasped Heather's hand. "But we did meet, and I love her like no other. Promise me ye'll tell her."

"Aye," Heather whispered. "'Tis the least I can do."

With a jingle of keys, the lock scraped and the door opened. Rewan MacLeod stepped in, carrying a bundle. "I've brought yer things from the loft."

*Rewan doing something considerate? Does every warrior at Halkhead want to give me charity now I've been bludgeoned?* "Gratitude." Bran recognized his chainmail and clothing, but saw no weapons. "Where's me sword?"

"Malcolm's holding on to it. Ye'll have it afore battle and for practice." A slow whistle passed Rewan's lips. "Ye look like hell."

"I'm sure he doesn't need you to tell him so." Heather tugged Bran's arm. "Sit up so I can tie these bandages in place."

Bran complied, though he wasn't happy Malcolm had his weapons. It would be a long time before he could trust Ross's captain of the guard.

Heather wrapped the roll of bandage around him at least a half-dozen times before she tied it off. "I'll leave you the poultice. Have someone to reapply the dressings in a couple of days."

"I'll do that. If I'm still alive."

She stood and brushed her hands. "I have an inkling you'll find a way to survive."

Bran grasped her hand and kissed it. "I thank ye, Mistress Heather."

It tickled him to see the matron blush. With a nod, she picked up her basket and swished out the door.

Rewan sauntered over and sat on the pallet beside him—another unusual move for the Lewis henchman. "I never like to see me own kin tied to a post and whipped. Even if ye are from Raasay." He pulled a flagon from beneath his plaid. "But why did ye have to mess with the lass?"

"She came to me." Bran reached for the flagon and took a long draw. "But dunna take me wrong. I'm in love with her."

"Yer feelings will see ye killed."

Bran stoppered the flask and passed it back. "We'll all be dead if Ross has his way."

"Och, ye're bloody right." Rewan clapped his shoulder and Bran winced at the pain radiating across his welts. "The Highlanders will stay together. I'll do what I can to watch yer back."

Bran grasped Rewan's arm at the elbow, a sign of kinship. "And I'll watch yers. Let us disappoint the bastard."

"Aye, I want to see Lewis again afore I die."

"I have me own plans as well."

"I hope that doesna include a stop at Paisley Abbey."

"It does."

"God have mercy on yer soul." Rewan pulled the stopper. "Here. Another tot of whisky will help ye sleep."

Bran took it and savored the fiery liquid as it slid down his gulled. "Ye're no so bad are ye?"

*Rutherglen of Hamilton ~ 8$^{th}$ May, 1568*

Claud Hamilton could take no more posturing from the nobles who were all supposedly on the same side. Even the queen had her own damned agenda.

He paced in front of the hearth where nine earls, nine bishops, eighteen lairds and over a hundred lesser supporters crammed into Rutherglen's great hall, all with something to say. The queen sat on the dais in his velvet-upholstered chair and struggled to listen to countless simultaneous petitions.

Archbishop Hamilton stood beside her and pounded his staff on the floorboards. "Silence! I will never read through this proclamation if you do not hold your tongues until the end."

Lovely Queen Mary with her red tresses, masked by a veil held in placed by her bejeweled crown, turned to him and frowned. "I did not overlook the fact that as a Hamilton you are seizing the ripe opportunity to emphasize your nephew's claim to the succession if both my son and I disappeared." She shook her finger. "Let it be known there will be no skullduggery here."

The archbishop bowed. "Of course not, your grace. I am only saying should something happen to your highness, the Hamilton succession would act as governors for the prince until he comes of age."

Claud ground his back molars. The one way to make the queen shy away from his potential suit would be to pressure her into thinking he *only* had eyes for the throne.

Mary shook her finger at the archbishop. "I believe I should be the one to determine the succession."

"But we want Moray"—the Archbishop rattled his head vehemently—"a bastard conceived in shameful adultery, removed as regent."

She gave one firm nod. "On that we are agreed." Her gaze darted to Claud. It was more the look of a wild cat telling him to keep his distance than that of an enamored woman. Claud possessed a number of fine qualities, but patience was not one of them. He would prove his worth to the queen. Once she saw him in battle, she would understand his superiority and choose him to sit beside her.

Archbishop Hamilton droned on until he got to the proclamation of allegiance. Every man in the hall stood and cheered for the queen. Once again, the archbishop called for silence.

The queen stood. For the first time, Claud could hear the fire crackle in the hearth.

She gazed across the crowd, the power of her presence captivating every man in the hall. "There are many brave souls to recognize for my escape from my half-brother's unlawful incarceration of my person on Lochleven. As you are aware, under duress, I was forced to sign a document abdicating my throne. 'Tis time to push aside the usurper and take it back."

The hall erupted in cheers.

She raised her hand and dipped her head. "Though I prefer to proceed peacefully, I gravely fear my throne will only be reclaimed by force."

The Earl of Eglinton shook his fist. "I shall be the first to lead my men against the usurper!"

Again the rafters resounded with shouts, everyone wanting to be a part of the battle that would seal their legacies for all history.

Queen Mary held up her hands and requested silence. "In appreciation of his great numbers brought to defend my honor, I hereby name the Earl of Argyll as lieutenant of the kingdom."

Claud's gut knotted. That post should have gone to his father, the Earl of Arran—regardless of the thousand untrained pikemen Argyll brought. Argyll was a blubbering buffoon. Once again, the hall erupted into an earsplitting roar as everyone voiced objections about the queen's declaration.

She motioned to the archbishop, who called for silence, pounding his staff.

"I ask all my loyal subjects to sign this joint proclamation of support." The queen gestured to the parchment on the table. "Together we will depose the usurper and the prince will once again be in my arms, where he belongs."

The noise in the hall escalated in volume as, one by one, Queen Mary's supporters stepped up to the dais and made their mark, pledging their allegiance to her.

## Chapter Seventeen

Enya inhaled a deep breath of fresh air. The abbot had finally seen fit to pay her a visit, and subsequently allowed her to walk the secured cloisters of the abbey—with a meddling monk trailing five paces behind. Would there be no chance for escape?

She'd also asked the abbot to send for some clothing. Had Lord and Lady Ross forgotten she still wore her dressing gown? She walked a bit faster. Her parents most likely cared not about her state of dress now she was imprisoned away from Halkhead.

On Enya's fifth trip through the airy hall, Heather bustled in, her hands clasped to her breast.

Hit with a myriad of emotions, Enya wanted nothing to do with the disloyal maid, but then, Heather was her only contact with the world outside the abbey and she might have news from Bran. She planted her fists on her hips. "Good day, Mistress Heather."

Heather reached out her arms, but pulled them back, bowed her head and curtseyed as a serving maid ought. "I've brought you some clothes and have had them placed in your cell, Miss Enya."

Enya looked to the archaic arched ceiling and sighed. It was a small act of kindness, but it meant a great deal. "Thank you." Enya outstretched her arms and beckoned Heather in.

The matron welcomed the gesture, her matronly frame providing comfort that brought tears to Enya's eyes.

Heather trembled, obviously holding in her tears. "I begged Lady Ross to allow me to bring you a kirtle and undergarments."

"Would she prefer her daughter be seen in her nightdress?"

"Nay, but your father insisted you have no visitors—said you should be wearing a habit and wimple by now. He doesn't know I've come."

"I wouldn't think they'd have nun's clothing here, and it would be rather embarrassing attending mass in a monk's habit—or my dressing gown."

"Aye, Miss Enya."

Enya grasped Heather's shoulders. "And have you news of Sir Bran?"

"I dressed his wounds last eve. Though the welts are grave, he was in far better condition than I would have expected after spending three days in the pit with no food or water."

"Did Master Rodney release the eagle?"

"Yes, and I had him attach an arrow so Sir Bran would know it was your doing."

Enya's heart soared. Though Heather had betrayed her to her parents, she'd given Enya a warning, and then acted on her word. "That was very thoughtful of you." Unable to hold a grudge, Enya slid her elbow through Heather's arm and continued on her walk. "With Griffon released, Bran would not have starved—though I doubt he'd savor an uncooked bit of meat."

"Ah. That explains it." Heather's brow creased.

Enya's insides churned with unease. "You're not telling me everything, are you?"

"The men left for Rutherglen this morning." Heather squeezed Enya's arm. "I suspect we shall have news of fighting soon."

"If only I could break free of these walls. I could find a vantage point and fire arrows to protect him—protect all our men."

"Well then, 'tis probably best you're here. For if you take up a weapon, you must expect to have it used against you." Heather shook her head. "That is the way of war."

Enya clutched her arm across her stomach. "I hate being caged in this abbey while danger is about. I can be of no use at all."

---

Once they arrived at Rutherglen, Malcolm returned Bran's weapons. "I ken you live by a knight's code of honor. In returning these, I expect all misgivings you harbor for Lord Ross to be cast aside."

Bran snatched his claymore, dirk and dagger and issued a thin-lipped nod. If his oath of fealty had not been for Calum, he'd challenge Ross's captain on the spot. He doubted he would ever forget the baron's hospitality, and mayhap one day he would prove how much it meant to him. Christ, if Lord Ross weren't Enya's father, Bran would seek his vengeance and deal with Calum's ire.

"You've got the look of a killer in your eye." Malcolm wrapped his fingers around the hilt of the sword on his belt. "Your punishment could have been far more severe."

Bran grabbed the neckline of Malcolm's mail and pulled the captain of the guard to his face. "I fight for me chieftain, Calum MacLeod, and to honor the word he gave yer lord." He took one more step in. "When me debt us paid, I shall no longer owe fealty to Lord Ross."

Malcolm batted Bran's hand away. "Are you making a threat?"

"I'm merely stating the truth." Before he did something that would see him thrown into Hamilton's pit, Bran headed to the courtyard.

He removed his shirt and bandages to spar. He'd been idle for too long, and Bran needed to regain his strength. Heather's poultice had worked magic, and the air against his healing wounds soothed the burn, but he must to lock away all pain, for if Ross had his way, Bran would need every tactic in his arsenal to stay alive.

He sauntered over to a pair of men wearing Hamilton tunics. They both showed promise, using advanced maneuvers. Bran drew his sword. "Ye mind if I have a go?"

"With us both?"

"Aye."

The two men exchanged grins. "You want to be killed?" one asked.

"Nay, but I could use a good run." Bran turned and showed them his back. "I've been waylaid for a bit."

"Holy Christ. It looks as if you had a fight with a lion and lost," the tallest one said.

"Let's just say I had a disagreement with a baron." Bran swung his sword in a two-handed figure eight. "Show me what ye've got."

He didn't need to ask again. The both charged in, swords held high. Bran's instincts took over as he deflected their blows. Spinning out, his sword caught a blade and clattered to the ground.

"Perhaps you should find a lassie to spar with," the shorter one said.

Bran watched him while picking up his sword. "Me muscles are warm now. Come again."

Bran's mind clicked. The only thing that existed was his opponents. They came at him relentlessly, using maneuvers he only had the occasion to practice on Raasay. His blood rushed and he fought faster and harder, keenly anticipating each man's move. The two were exactly what Bran needed to regain his edge.

Vaguely, it registered the warriors around him had stopped sparring, but Hamilton's men continued to come at him with vicious sword thrusts. Unable to tear his attention away, he swung his claymore with lightning speed. Beads of sweat dripped from his chin and ran down his chest. He wanted to push harder. "Come, lads, show me what ye're made of."

"Hail the queen!" a deep voice bellowed only feet away.

Bran scooted back as the other two lowered their swords. The entire courtyard of soldiers was on bended knee, heads bowed. Chest heaving, Bran dropped to his knee, just as gold silk skirts swished into view. Her slippers tapped the cobblestones, heading straight for him.

Bran's heart not only pounded in his chest, his temples throbbed. Holy falcon feathers, she was going to reprimand him for certain. Another bead of sweat dripped from his chin and splashed on his bare chest. He should have left his shirt on. The queen would think ill of him, of that he had no doubt.

The ample skirts stopped inches from his bowed head. "Rise." The queen's voice was commanding, yet gentle, with a French lilt.

Bran grasped the hem of her skirts and kissed before he stood. "Yer grace, ye honor me. Please forgive my unsightly appearance."

The queen was inordinately tall for a woman, even taller than Enya. With her auburn tresses pulled away from her face, tucked beneath her coronet and veil, he understood why the legend of her beauty followed her—though she was not as lovely as his Enya.

Regal, pale and statuesque, her blue-grey eyes assessed him. "You fight well, swordsman. What is your name?"

"Sir Bran of Clan MacLeod." He bowed, careful not to bend too far, else she catch sight of his mangled back. "At yer service, yer grace."

"A knight, are you?"

"Aye, knighted by me laird, Calum, Chieftain of Raasay." Bran dipped his chin. "But I've no royal order, yer grace."

She raised her royal chin. "Are you here to fight for the Kingdom of Scotland?"

"For Scotland and for you, my queen."

She held out her hand. "Give me your sword."

If only she would move along to someone else—a soldier who still had his shirt on. Blast it all. He took hold of his blade and handed her the hilt.

"Kneel."

Bran's stomach flipped twice. Surely she wasn't going to attempt to cut off his head herself? He bowed, and knelt as asked.

Lord Ross's voice carried from the portico. "He's merely a Highland scrapper, that one."

"Silence." Her voice had lost its buttery smoothness. "All Scots are my subjects, hail they from the Lowlands or Highlands."

She turned full circle, holding Bran's claymore above her head. "Bran of Clan MacLeod, do you promise to uphold the values of faith, loyalty, courage and honor?"

Stunned he still had his head, he managed to croak, "I so promise."

"You shall join my personal guard." The blade tapped his right shoulder. "I knight you into the Order of the Thistle, in the name of the Kingdom of Scotland, to protect this nation from any and every evil." She tapped his left. "Rise, Sir Bran."

He couldn't believe his ears. She'd knighted him—without his shirt—right there in the courtyard with Ross and everyone present? His chest swelled as he met her gaze for the first time. Her eyes sparkled when she smiled at him. "Gratitude, yer grace. I shall fight for ye with me life."

"As I would expect." She returned Bran's sword and turned toward her groom. "Willy, see to it Sir Bran is fitted with a royal tunic and bunks with my personal guard. I would like him to ride beside me as we march to Dumbarton."

"I shall see it done, your grace."

With a turn of her head, she proceeded down the row of fighting men. Bran let out long breath. Across the courtyard stood Lord Ross, looking as mad as a badger cornered by a fox. Bran pulled his shirt over his head and swallowed his grin.

Rewan slipped beside him. "Ye're the luckiest bastard I've ever seen in me life."

---

The tent erected for the queen's guard provided more luxury than anything Bran had experienced since arriving in the Lowlands. The pallets were filled with ample amounts of straw and covered by new linens. In the center, a table laden with an array of fruits and meats made Bran's mouth water. But he had more pressing things to attend to.

No longer under the scrutiny of Malcolm and Ross's men, he snatched a lamb shank and headed for the stables with his satchel of bandages and Heather's salve. Uneasy with the prospect of running into Malcolm, he crept through the shadows, saddled his horse in the stall and led it through the back stable door.

Now he had his freedom, no one could prevent him from seeing Enya before he marched into battle. At a fast trot, Bran estimated he could make it to Paisley within two hours.

The sunset behind the stone abbey made the building hard to miss. Certain the structure was designed to strike the fear of God in all who beheld it, Bran steered his mount around the outside, looking for the best mode of entry. Of course Enya would not be in the church, but built alongside the cloisters, a four-story dormitory clearly housed the monks—and, most likely, Enya.

Surrounded by an iron fence, festooned with sharp pikes, the sanctuary doors would be his best way to access the adjoining building. The difficult part would be finding Enya, and he had little time.

He tied his horse and slipped inside. The nave was empty, aside from the dark wood pews lining the walls. His footsteps echoed. He entered the robing room and shuffled through the rack of garments. Finding a brown hooded habit, he threw it over his clothes, claymore and all. Though big enough around, the sleeves only reached his forearms, and the hem was a good three inches from the floor. It didn't matter. The habit would be disguise enough to see him inside.

As he crept back into the vestibule, rustling came from an alcove. Bran pressed himself against the stone wall and craned his neck. Inside was a small chapel. On his knees, a monk held vigil over a single candle.

Bran hated to interrupt a holy man during prayer, but this was urgent. In two steps he seized the poor monk and slapped a hand over his mouth. "I mean ye no harm, but I must find Miss Enya Ross."

The monk nodded.

"I'll release ye now. Dunna cry out or I'll be forced to silence ye for good." Gradually, Bran pulled his hand away. The monk faced him and used his finger to draw a line across his lips.

"Ye've taken a vow of silence?"

The monk again nodded.

"Please, take me to Miss Enya. For tomorrow I ride into battle to fight for the queen. I must make peace with the lady before I die."

He beckoned Bran with a wave of his hand and led him into the cloisters. Bran's eyes darted from under his hood. The monk could betray him, but Bran had no choice but to trust, else he'd be kicking down every door until he found her.

After climbing four flights of stairs, they entered a narrow passage with many doors, all closed. The monk pulled a key from under his habit and stopped at a door at the end of the corridor. Bran opened his robe and wrapped his fingers around his claymore, ready for anything.

The monk pushed the iron key into the lock, but before he could turn it, Bran placed his hand on the monk's shoulder. "Are any of these rooms vacant?"

He signaled to them all with an uplifted palm.

Bran grasped the key and pulled it over the man's head. He led him across the hall and unlocked the door. "I canna take a chance on yer sounding the alarm. I'll slip ye the key when I leave."

The monk frowned, but Bran pushed him into the empty chamber.

"Apologies, but I have nay other choice." He closed the door and turned the lock.

Facing Enya's chamber, he took in a deep breath and placed his hand on the latch. When he opened it, he pulled the hood from his head.

In a heartbeat, Enya's face went from sorrowfully drawn to stunned disbelief. "Bran?"

His heart thudded against his chest. Before he could step inside, Enya flew into his arms. Sweet Mother Mary, he'd arrived.

"How did you find me? I thought you had marched to Renfrewshire to meet the queen."

Bran lifted her up and kicked the door closed behind him. With a deep inhale, he smothered her mouth, kissing fiercely, barely able to keep his heart from thundering out of his chest. Enya's questions could wait, but first he had to savor the warmth of her body against his.

"My God, Enya. Ye feel like heaven on earth."

"I cannot believe you're here." Enya closed her eyes and pressed her lips against his. "I've been sick with worry—h-how did you slip inside?"

"'Tis a long story." He carried her to the bed and cradled her on his lap. "I locked a monk in the cell across the hall."

She wrapped her arms around his neck. "You didn't."

"What else could I do? I couldna risk having him sound the alarm while I ravished ye." He kissed her forehead. "Dunna worry. I'll release him when I go."

"Go?" She frowned. "You're not taking me with you?"

"There's something I must do first."

Enya brushed her fingers along his jaw. "You must tell me everything. The only news I've had is from Heather's two visits—which wasn't much."

"I did ride to Rutherglen with yer father's men."

A crease formed between her pretty brows. "And my father is going to attempt to have you killed?"

"That was his plan." Bran batted the air. "It seems our mother queen took a liking to me—she knighted me into the Order of the Thistle right on the spot."

Enya clapped her hands together. "Oh, Bran, how exciting!"

"She commanded me to ride beside her."

Enya pushed a stray lock of hair from Bran's face. "That means you will not be in the front line as father wished."

"Nay. I shall guard the queen as we march to Dumbarton Castle."

"Dumbarton? Why not Stirling?"

"'Tis dangerous. Moray has Stirling too well fortified, and Dumbarton has the biggest cannons in the region. Word has it Regent Moray's army is in Glasgow. We can expect a bloody battle."

Enya wrung her hands. "'Tis awful. I hate war."

"As do I." He ran his fingers over her luminous auburn hair. "And how are ye, m'lady? I've missed ye so."

"Other than feeling caged, I am well. Father intends to ship me to the nunnery in Iona."

A tic flickered above his eye. Her father was a damned fool. "Heather told me. But I doubt he'll have the guard to take ye until this skirmish with the queen is over."

"Have you ever been there?"

"Iona?" He nodded. "Sailed past, aye."

"Is it dreary?"

He glanced at the barred window of the tiny room. "From the sea it appears no more foreboding than this abbey—some parts are in ruins owing to the Reformation. But I will no' allow him to send ye there."

"No?" Enya splayed her palms outward. "How can you prevent it?"

"When the fighting is over, I'll come for ye...and *if* they take ye to Iona, I will find ye. Dunna worry, Enya. I shall never give ye up."

"Och, I love you, Bran." Enya ran her hands down Bran's back. The wince came out before he could steel himself to the pain. She clasped her hands over her mouth. "Oh heavens, 'tis bad, is it not?"

Bran stretched. "The welts are healing. Thanks to Heather's salve." He pulled the pot from his satchel. "Would ye apply it for me?"

Enya grasped it and stood. "Yes, of course."

Bran removed the robe and his shirt then Enya helped him unwind the bandages.

"It looks awful, angry."

"'Tis on the mend."

Bran lay on the cot and Enya stood over him. "Will it hurt?"

"Not with yer fingers upon me."

---

Enya's stomach roiled as she gazed upon the angry, blood-encrusted welts on Bran's back. "My father is responsible for this."

"The only one to blame is me. I kent better, but fell in love with ye anyway."

Her heart squeezed. How could her father do this to him—and a man who had agreed to fight for his *noble* cause? Enya dipped her fingers in the pot. Bran's back tensed as she began to spread the poultice as gently as possible. "I do not think I could have stopped myself from loving you."

Bran exhaled and the muscles in his back relaxed. "I reckon ye're right. I had a mind to wrap ye in me arms and kiss ye when I saw ye up on that hill with yer bow slung over yer shoulder."

"You did?"

"Aye, if ye didna shoot me first."

Enya laughed. She couldn't remember the last time so much happiness had filled her entire soul. She set the pot down and blew on the open wounds. "Does it feel better?"

"I scarcely ken the welts are there." He sat up. "Will ye wrap it for me?"

Enya reached for the bandages he'd brought. "Yes." Her eyes dropped to his well-muscled chest. Involuntarily, her tongue flicked out and tapped her top lip. Here he was in pain and she couldn't stop thinking about his incredible body. Her skin had tingled since he opened the door, but looking at the bands of muscle rippling across his abdomen made a rush of heat swirl between her hips. She ran a trembling palm across his chest. Her need for him spun so tight inside, she might burst.

He held his arms out and watched her while she unwound the cloth strips. Aware of every breath and every beat of her heart, she tended him, desperately wanting, needing more.

Fanned by dark lashes, his half-cast eyes watched her. "I didna just come here for ye to tend me."

Enya's breathing became shallow as she tied off the bandage. Bran cupped her cheeks and pulled her to his lips.

"Ye are so fine to me, Enya Ross."

"And you to me." Her kisses trailed down his neck, and she savored his sweet, salty taste. She needed him, body and soul. "Make love to me."

He pulled her between his legs. Her mons pushed up against his erection. "Ye'd make love to the likes of me in a house of God?"

"I'd lie with you in the sanctuary if you asked." She joined her mouth with his and desperately searched inside, her breasts screaming for pleasure as she surged against him. "Lying with you could be no sin. Not with the love that burns in my soul."

Bran groaned and kissed her, clamping his hands to her buttocks and pressing her hips against him. With a wicked grin, he unlaced the front of her kirtle, slowly pulling the laces from each eyelet. Enya moistened her lips, the tips of her breasts inflamed with desire. She was dying for him to hurry and free them from her constricting bindings.

His breath ragged, his eyes filled with longing, Bran opened her bodice. He nudged aside the neckline of her linen shift and flicked his tongue across the mounds peeking above her stays. Closing her eyes, she savored the heavenly fluttering of his lips that caused a magnificent flutter inside her womb. She ran her fingers through his hair, nuzzling into him.

He tugged at the neckline of the unyielding wooden slats that bound her breasts. Enya fumbled with the laces.

Bran clasped his fingers around her hands. "I'll do it." His voice rasped as if he were in pain. He worked faster and soon Enya's stays dropped to the floor. Inhaling, her breasts stretched against her shift and she ached for him to place his hands on her.

Enya watched Bran's hazel eyes as he unfastened the bow on her shift. His lips parted while he slipped it from her shoulders and cupped her. Enya threw her head back with a deep moan as he took her breast into his mouth. Shuddering, she could have exploded with joy.

His deft fingers kneaded her right while his mouth made love to her left. Moisture pooled between her legs, her need for him building to the point of madness. Enya pushed against him, her body frantic to feel the hot friction of their joining.

Enya's fingers trembled as she worked loose his buckle. Bran lifted up as she tugged away his kilt and exposed his rigid manhood. Her thighs quivered at his magnificence. Oh how deliciously excruciating this torture.

Scarcely able to breathe, Enya's gaze meandered up his body, taking in every exquisite inch—every sinuous muscle, the vein pulsing along his sturdy neck, leading to a bold, masculine jaw, a jaw no man would trifle with. Bran was so unbelievably beautiful. When his hazel eyes met hers, the intensity of their love took her to a plateau she'd never imagined. At no time had Enya been thus connected to another human being. She now knew what God meant by one body. She belonged to Bran, as he belonged to her.

Standing naked before him, her thighs quaked, though she had no urge to cover her nakedness.

He reached out and caressed her breasts. "I love ye, Enya, *mo leannan*." The words rolled off his tongue like sweet cream.

Oh God, she had to have him. Reaching between them, Enya stroked him with her fingers—using a soft touch, running her fingers along him. Bran's hips jutted forward as a groan ripped from his throat. In one move, he swung Enya down. She lay flat on the cot with Bran kneeling above her. "I want ye so bad, I canna wait."

Overpowered by the emotions coursing through her blood, she could not bring herself to speak. Opening her legs, she grasped him and guided his manhood to that sacred place that only he could enter. He slipped in so much easier this time, without the pain. The ecstasy was enough to transport Enya to the moon. Watching her eyes, ever so slowly, Bran slid deeper, filling her.

Enya's hips rocked in tandem with his thrusts. The tension spun so tight within her core, it almost hurt. But she needed to savor this moment. Her lover was heading for battle, and only God knew when they would be together again. The friction of their love took charge of her mind and she could only focus on their heavenly joining. This had to be perfect—a moment she would carry in her heart for eternity.

Not once did Bran avert his eyes from her. Together their breathing quickened. A deep moan escaped Bran's throat. The sound of it took Enya beyond the realm of control, and she cried out. Her womb shuddered in a concert of spasms as if the world had reached utopia. Enya smoothed her hand over Bran's muscled chest, his eyes telling her he had reached his peak. With one final thrust he channeled his bellow into a long, rugged groan.

Panting, he dropped to his elbows and gently kissed her neck, her cheeks, her eyes, and finally he found her mouth. Bran owned her soul. Enya would find a way to be his. Only death would stand in her way. She closed her eyes and prayed he would return to her soon. She prayed for his safety, and then savored the blessed feeling of holding him in her arms.

# Chapter Eighteen

After making Enya promise not to break out of the abbey, Bran tore himself away, released the very irritated monk and headed back to Rutherglen. He hoped he hadn't been missed. The completely unexpected attention from the queen had renewed his sense of duty. He would see her grace reclaim her throne, and then he would marry Enya, regardless of what Lord Ross had to say about it. Bran was a knight of the Thistle now. No one could argue his station.

He reckoned it was well past midnight when he slipped into the tent. The moonlight shone through the white shrouds, casting an eerie glow over the sleeping men.

Willy Douglas sat up on his pallet. "Where have you been?"

"I had a matter to attend."

"Meeting Moray's spies? I should have you whipped and thrown into the pit."

Bran held up his hands and grimaced. "Nay, 'twas nothing like that. Simply seeking the comfort of a woman's arms."

"Then why didn't you tell me where you were going?"

"The woman's a bit higher born than the likes of me."

Willy grinned. "You not only fight like a scrapper, you love like one too, aye?"

Bran unbuckled his claymore and dropped it on his pallet. "Something like that." The less Willy Douglas knew about his affairs, the better. If word got to Ross he'd been to Paisley Abbey, the bastard might demand the queen lock him in the dungeons. A lot of good that would do. Bran intended to stay out of prison holds for the rest of his life.

None too happy about the queen's decision to march to Dumbarton, Claud Hamilton joined the nobles in the great hall. The queen had been cool toward him since his uncle pressed her about the line of succession. She'd immediately insisted on marching to Dumbarton Castle, a decision that could be dangerous. Claud feared the move had nothing to do with the size of the stronghold's cannons. The queen clearly desired to remove her person from Rutherglen. He would discuss his concerns with the archbishop. The path to Mary's bed and the kingdom must be won with more subtle tactics.

The queen had made quite a spectacle of knighting the damned Highlander in the courtyard. Clearly she was drawn to men with practiced skill. And it seemed women were drawn to that bastard...

In the midst of a barrage of shouts, Argyle stood on the dais. "One hundred of my best pikemen will march at the head of the procession."

Claud ignored the boisterous exhortations, climbed up to the dais and stood beside Lord Argyle. After all, this was Claud's castle and his rightful place was on the dais. Everyone else was his guest.

Flushed from his collar up to the top of his head, Argyle glared. "What do you want, Hamilton?"

"Lord Argyle. Your pikemen are impressive indeed." Claud offered an obsequious bow. "I've fifty of the queen's best-trained cavalrymen ready to lead us. Do me the honor of allowing mounted men to demonstrate our might."

Argyle's eyes narrowed, but the queen daintily dabbed at her mouth and stood. "In gratitude to Lord Claud's hospitality, I agree. He and his horsemen shall lead us."

Claud dropped to his knee. "You honor me, your grace."

Argyle bowed to the queen. "Very well. My force of men shall bring up the rear."

"Word has it Moray and his army have assembled in Glasgow," said Lord Eglinton.

Argyle nodded. "Then let us skirt the city and show him our numbers. That alone will send him back to Edinburgh with his tail between his legs."

"'Tis a dangerous game you play," Lord Ross said. "I'd wager they are amassing troops as we are."

Claud glanced at the queen and stepped forward. "I agree with Argyle." *This once.* "Perhaps we can draw them in and annihilate the usurper's forces—quickly, before they have a chance to further build their numbers."

Again the crowd erupted in a cacophony of shouting, everyone proffering his agenda. Claud could care not. He'd won a small victory, and with luck, he would demonstrate his exceptional fighting skills. He would impress the queen, and with his birthright, she would be unable to refuse him.

---

Dressed in his battle armor, Claud assembled his men and waited for the army of six thousand to pull into ranks.

He eyed the Highlander, sitting tall in his saddle while watching Willy Douglas assist the queen to her mount. Dressed in a red silk gown, covered by a female breastplate of silver, with an ermine bonnet perched atop her head, she exuded Claud's ideal of royalty, as if embodying the reincarnation of Zenobia riding into battle.

The queen took charge of her reins. "Ride beside me, Sir Bran."

"Aye, yer grace."

*That rutting bastard will have her swooning by the day's end.*

She pointed her riding crop forward. "Argyle. I do believe we are ready."

The earl held his sword in the air for all to see and then pointed it straight ahead. "Onward!"

Claud spun his horse and galloped to the head of the procession with an air of flamboyance. He would have recognition this day. He first marched the army to the shore of the River Clyde, where the lookout of Glasgow would spot them for certain. Claud ensured they took their time—carrying pennants and weapons, six thousand men shook the ground as they sent a daunting challenge to Regent Moray. From there, he turned west toward Langside, three miles away.

The Hamiltons had suffered much at Moray's hands—his occupation of the regency was a flagrant insult to Claud's family's ancient position in Scotland. Claud would seize his opportunity to obliterate his enemy, and with an overwhelming show of force, the odds would be weighted in his favor.

Entering the small village, Claud saw his chance. Enemy soldiers lined the common land that sloped up a hill beyond the town. Clearly, the King's Party accepted the challenge he'd issued by riding past the River Clyde. Claud glanced over his shoulder. A tickle of doubt crept up his spine. Walking rather than marching, weapons casually tossed over their shoulders, Mary's men appeared more like a mob than well trained and organized ranks.

But doubt could not plague him now. With a stutter of his heart, Claud drew his sword and bellowed the charge. Galloping forward, he led his men through Langside's narrow streets. Musket shots clapped. Claud barely flinched, barreling toward the onslaught of the enemy's cavalry. With cries of war, he met the usurper's men head on, slashing down foot soldiers to his left and right.

Claud spun his horse, brandishing his sword, the thrill of battle driving him to the brink of bloodthirsty madness. He would appraise well in the queen's eyes indeed.

---

As soon as the battle cry sounded, Bran took charge. He'd watched the ineptitude of the nobles and he would not see Queen Mary fall due to their incompetence. "This way, my queen."

She pulled up her reins. "I do not wish to leave my subjects."

Bran pointed up the hill. "No' to leave, only seek a vantage point to direct the fighting."

A cannon blasted. The queen's horse reared. Bran grabbed her reins and pulled the mare into a circle beside his mount. The mare quieted and Bran urged her forward. "I will see to yer safety, for ye'll be no use to Scotland dead." He turned to Mary's guard. "Follow me."

Behind them, Lord Argyle argued with Lords Ross and Eglinton.

Wearing a cumbersome coat of armor that sported every protection known to man, his helm with mere slits for him to see through, Argyle teetered on his horse. "Lord Ross, move your men in behind Hamilton."

Eglinton waved to his forces and trotted ahead. "My men should be next."

Ross rode in behind the earl. "Pull back, Eglinton. My army will take on the usurper." Ross waved to Malcolm and the Ross guard, signaling them to march forward. Eglinton did the same. Like a mustering of cattle, the two forces attempted to push and shove through the narrow street.

Argyle kicked his horse with brutish force, but the beast refused to move. "I am in command here. You—" Argyle's horse reared, sending the earl flying through the air. He landed with a thud, his heavy armor clanking loudly on the stony ground.

Still holding the queen's reins, Bran glanced at the downed earl while a squire dismounted to tend him. Faced with a decision as to whether to take control of the confusion or save the queen, Bran opted to stay by Mary's side. He urged their horses faster toward the summit as soldiers rushed in every direction. The battle quickly turned into mayhem.

After arriving at the vantage point, Bran pulled up and surveyed the carnage. Moray's men, though fewer in number, tore through the Hamiltons. Leaderless, Argyle's men, the queen's greatest force, fled from Moray's pikemen, scattering like a mob of cockroaches exposed to a ray of sunlight.

The enemy fast approached the hill, leaving Claud and his few remaining cavalry in their wake.

Bran turned to Willy. "Lead the queen out of here. I'll create a diversion."

"But—"

"I said ride. Now!"

In a blink of an eye, the queen and her guard disappeared over the hill. Bellowing his battle cry, Bran zigzagged his steed across the advancing army, swinging his sword, cutting them down.

Spinning, taking on more men at once than ever sparred with before, he fought blindly. Someone grabbed him from behind and pulled him off his horse. Bran stood his ground and fought the encroaching mob.

"Spare them," a powerful voice hollered from beyond. "I do not wish for bloodshed."

Bran whirled around as the soldiers, at least ten of them, backed away, their weapons trained on Bran's heart. He leveled his claymore and slowly turned in place, anticipating the next onslaught of attack.

The crowd parted for a man clad in royal armor. Regent Moray raised his visor, staring straight at Bran. "You are surrounded, Highlander. Lay down your arms."

Bran had never seen a regent before. Though touted as a bastard, the man had an air of command, of competence. Bran bowed and tentatively rested his claymore on the ground.

"Seize him. We shall march these rebels through the streets of Glasgow and show them our hospitality in the tolbooth."

Bran didn't fight as the enemy soldiers bound his wrists behind his back and removed his dagger and dirk. He said nothing when a bastard with black teeth and foul breath admired the only keepsake he had from his father. "This'll look good hanging off me belt."

Bran committed the face to memory. If he ever had the chance, he'd take his dirk back.

Corralled into a collection of prisoners, Bran surveyed the faces. Some of the Hamilton men were among the captives, but there was no sign of Claud. Bran saw Malcolm, but not Rewan—had the Lewis henchman been killed?

James Hamilton, the Earl of Arran, stood with his hands bound behind his back, along with Lord Ross, his son Robert and Lord Seaton. Of the queen's six thousand, Bran estimated Moray had only collected fifty prisoners—enough to make a mockery out of the queen's attempt to regain her throne, but not so many as to cause another uprising. *Smart of him.*

Enya knew something was wrong the moment the monk opened her door. When he led her to the carriage, she thought it might be her escort to Iona, until she climbed inside and found Heather weeping. Cold perspiration prickled Enya's forehead.

She clutched Heather's arm. "What is it?"

Heather dabbed her eyes with a kerchief. "All is lost."

"Where is father? Robert?" She had to ask. "Bran?"

"All taken prisoner—Sir Malcolm too. Some of the guardsmen escaped with the news."

"All?" Enya's throat thickened and she clutched her neck. "This is very grave indeed."

"Aye, your mother needs your comfort."

"Mother needs me? What about father and Robert?" *And Bran?*

The ride to Halkhead took an eternity. Enya couldn't understand why they were heading to the manse when they should be racing to Glasgow. She would talk some sense into Lady Ross as soon as she arrived.

The carriage pulled into the courtyard and Enya leapt down before it came to a stop. Henry opened the door as she ran up the stairs. "Where is my mother?"

"In her chamber, miss."

Enya raced up the stairs. Her mother sat in a corner while her serving maid piled dresses into a trunk. "Enya. We must away."

"Yes, we must. Quickly."

"We shall leave as soon as our things are packed."

"Pack? Surely we do not need more than a change of clothes. We must ride anon."

Lady Ross wiped her eyes. "I don't know if I can stand the stress."

Enya grasped her mother's shoulders and gave a firm shake. "You must be strong. Father needs you now. Do you have shillings to let a room?"

"Nay. I think—"

"I'll fetch it and send a groom to collect your things. Be ready to ride in the half-hour. "

Enya ran to the solar and pulled a black-bound bible from the bookcase. Inside was the key to her father's bank box, which he kept hidden in a secret antechamber just off the passage she used for escape. She took a candle, slipped in and opened the box.

Though she knew of its existence, she'd never looked inside before. Unset jewels and gold sovereigns mixed in with innumerable silver shillings. "Blessed be the saints." Enya took a handful of coins—more than enough to support them for a month in Glasgow if need be.

After locking the box and returning things exactly as she found them, Enya ran to her chamber. Heather was already there, preparing a valise. "At least someone has some sense. Mother is in her chamber, packing her entire wardrobe. Meet me downstairs."

"Aye."

Enya reached under her bed and pulled out her bow and quiver of arrows. Counting only five, she headed for the armory. The supplies had been depleted by the guard and not much remained on the shelves, but she found a dozen or so arrows shoved into a dark corner, and a dirk. She grabbed them both, stopped by the kitchen, wrapped some oatcakes in a cloth and headed for the courtyard.

Lady Ross was right behind, clutching her fists under her chin. "I'm not sure if Lord Ross will want us there. Mayhap we should stay at Halkhead and await his summons."

Enya grasped her arm. "If you were in prison, would you want Father to come to you straight away?"

"Well, of course, dear, but that's different."

"How so?" Her mother gaped, but Enya held up her hand. "No need to answer. Father will be relieved to see us. I am sure of it. Besides, it is our duty."

---

Hands tied, roped by the neck and forced to walk single file, Bran shuffled through the streets of Glasgow as citizens jeered and spat. How could they taunt him and the others? He'd fought to see the true queen regain her throne—her very birthright. If these people had the chance to meet the queen as he had, if only for a moment, they would understand no other person on earth could possibly have been born to be their sovereign.

"Parading the lambs before the slaughter," said the prisoner behind him.

A woman spat. "You're a disgrace to Scotland."

Bran looked in her eyes and saw only hate.

He never should have allowed Calum to leave him with Lord Ross. Bran had run into disaster at every turn. Falling in love with Enya felt so right, but he would most likely never see the lass again. Surely every man in this procession would be hanged, drawn and quartered, with their body parts strewn across the country to be used as deterrents to further uprisings.

A sickly heat radiated under Bran's skin when he recalled how utterly incompetent the Marian Party had been in comparison to the King's Party. For Christ's sake, Argyle, their supposed leader, fell off his horse and had some sort of seizure. That moron, Claud Hamilton, charged without receiving the order from Argyle or the queen. Bran didn't blame the masses for scattering. They had no leadership.

Hungry, angry and humiliated, Bran could do nothing to help his situation. The welts on his back throbbed, ached, threatened to eat him alive. The sentries assembled the prisoners in the center of the tolbooth courtyard, surrounded by a wall of guardsmen armed with poleaxes.

# Chapter Nineteen

The eight-mile carriage ride into Glasgow seemed to take as long as the ride across the country to Edinburgh. Enya sat at the edge of her seat the whole way. After instructing the driver to take them straight to the tolbooth, they arrived just in time to catch the end of the procession.

Filled with onlookers, the street was impassable, and the carriage stalled.

Enya patted her mother's arm. "I'm going to move in for a better look."

Mother clasped Enya's hand. "No. Stay with me."

"I can hear nothing from here. I'll be back with news." Enya gathered her skirts, pulled on the latch and hopped down.

"Enya!"

If she stayed, Enya's mother would argue until the excitement was over.

Wearing an ornate coat of silvered armor, none other than Regent Moray climbed the steps of the tolbooth portico. He removed his helm and glared across the masses, a deep frown stretched against his black-whiskered face.

"As you are aware, Mary, the former Queen of Scots, escaped Lochleven a week ago today. I had hoped we would capture her without bloodshed. But it wasn't to be."

Enya tried to push into the crowd, but the wall of people was impossible to penetrate.

"She raised an army and the king's men met her at Langside. Though strong in numbers, her forces were unorganized, and after only an hour of fighting, we quashed her lawless uprising."

"Where is the queen?" a disembodied voice hollered from the crowd.

"She has escaped. Fear not. Her army is deposed. She will be arrested and tried for treason." Regent Moray gestured into the mob. Enya rose up on her toes, but could only see a line of crossed poleaxes. "These prisoners shall be tried as well."

Though a cool breeze blew over her skin, Moray's cold words caused her to sweat as if in a bread oven. Holding her elbows tight against her sides, she forced herself to listen.

The crowd erupted in boisterous shouts and taunts. Moray held up his hands, requesting silence. "But it shall be far worse for those who slipped through my hands. The Archbishop of St. Andrews, Lord Claud Hamilton and Lord Eglinton are declared traitors and their lands forfeit to the crown."

Enya clutched her palms against her stomach. *Claud and his uncle have fled? How could all be lost in a day?* She shoved against the man in front of her. "Let me pass."

Driven by the frantic need to see her father and to find Bran, Enya shoved her way to the front of the crowd. "Father!"

Soldiers crossed their poleaxes and blocked her from rushing to him.

Shoulders hunched, Lord Ross looked years older than when she'd last seen him only weeks ago. "Enya? Why are you not in the abbey?"

"Mother sent for me."

Her father stared at her with a distant glaze to his angry eyes. "I did not give you leave."

Robert peered from behind a guard. "Go home and take care of Mother, Enya."

"She is with me, waiting in the carriage. What can I do?"

Lord Ross's knitted brows eased as if he'd come upon a plan. He grasped her wrist through the crossed poleaxes. "Find the magistrate. Tell him I will reward him handsomely for my release." Ross looked to his son. "And Robert's."

Enya shook her head. "Very well, and what of your other men?" She glanced across the crowd of prisoners and recognized a few faces, but did not see the one she desired most.

The cold steel of her father's ruthless eyes turned her blood cold. "They might be more lenient with the nobles, but if we make it out with our own lives, it will be a miracle."

"March the prisoners inside," the sentry's voice rang out.

Enya reached in. "No!"

But the pikemen kept her from holding her father's arm, moving the prisoners along. Enya's chest clutched tight and then she saw him, a head above the others at the rear of the mob of captives. Enya ran to him and slipped beneath the pole of a deadly pike. "Bran!"

His bound hands cupped her face. "Enya? How in heaven's name did ye get here?"

"It doesn't matter. Father told me to speak to the magistrate. I will see you released."

Bran's shoulders sagged. "I doubt yer father has any notion to barter for me release."

"How can you say that? I will speak for you."

A guard grasped her arm and yanked her back. "Get the blazes out of here, you shifty wench."

Enya reached out. "I will fight for you."

Bran mouthed, "I love you."

A sentry slammed him in the back with the shaft of his poleaxe. "Get moving, you bastard Highlander."

Enya tried to break free but the guard's grip tightened. "Bran!"

"Sing to Griffon," Bran bellowed over his shoulder.

"He's heading for the gallows, that one." The soldier shoved her to the cobblestones. "You'd best crawl back home and be glad it won't be yer neck in a noose."

A tear slipped from Enya's eye as she watched the procession disappear behind the stone walls of the Glasgow Tolbooth. That wretched place was as notorious as the Tower of London. A term in there could sap any man's wits, even a man as strong as Sir Bran MacLeod.

Too late to visit the magistrate, Enya situated her mother in their rooms. Though she tried, Enya couldn't sleep. At daybreak, she had one of the Ross footmen and Heather accompany her back to the tolbooth. After she located the magistrate's quarters, the factor advised her to wait in a in a corridor lined with wooden benches where scraggly people sat, mostly dressed in rags, smelling as if they'd crawled out of a gutter.

Heather sat beside her and held a kerchief over her nose. "They should at least have a comfortable pad upon which to sit."

Enya surveyed the long, dirty faces around her, conscious of the rich damask gown she'd decided to wear—the only one Heather had packed. "I doubt they want to encourage people from staying here overlong."

With little time, it was of utmost importance to make a good impression on the man who held so many lives in the palm of his hand. The deep dong of the clock-tower bell rang at each quarter-hour. The first time it hit the hour, the bell tolled nine sorrowful peals. Enya sat with her back erect, her stays cutting into her ribs. At ten tolls, she reclined against the stone walls. At eleven peals, her stomach grumbled, complaining Enya had skipped the morning meal.

She counted another three quarter-hours when the factor addressed her. "Miss Ross, Mr. Fisher will see you now."

She swooned when she stood and steadied her hand against the wall. Heather scooted to the edge of the bench, but Enya held up her hand. "Stay. I shan't be long."

Mr. Fisher rose when she entered, offering a curt bow. "Miss Ross. I assume you are here for your father?"

"Yes."

He pulled out a chair and gestured for her to sit. "You are aware he laid down his arms?"

Enya hadn't heard about the surrender. "Ah, yes," she hedged. "That's what I understand." Perhaps this news would help her cause.

"I'd like to make this quick. I'm late for my nooning."

Enya's stomach growled. A midday meal might repress the tremors in her hands. "I came to plead for leniency. My father has offered to compensate you."

Mr. Fisher tugged on the sleeves of his velvet doublet. "Interesting. Go on."

Enya had no idea what this man would expect, but it would take something substantial to allay a charge of treason. Aware of her father's wealth, she picked a sum. "I can have a hundred gold sovereigns delivered to your office upon my father and brother's release."

He smiled with a malicious curve to his lips. "If your father agrees to divulge the conspirators, I just might accept your offer."

"Since he willfully surrendered, I'm sure he will be eager to impart such crucial information."

"Most fortunate. I shall meet with him after my nooning."

Mr. Fisher stood and inclined his head toward the door. Enya followed. "There is one other matter I'd like to discuss." Though he gave her a foreboding frown, she stood her ground. "You also have a Highland knight under your guard. Sir Bran MacLeod. I should also like to negotiate the terms of his release."

He brushed his finger across her cheek. "Ah, Miss Ross, will you have me release every rebel from my gaol?" His eyes fell to the tops of her breasts, peeking over her stomacher. "Though you are tempting, I suggest you return to Renfrewshire and leave the executions to me."

Enya's vision blurred and she forced herself to take a deep breath to keep her wits. "Executions? Will there be trials?"

"Yes, the day after next, though a formality."

Enya leaned against a chair. "Please, Mr. Fisher. Allow me to negotiate Sir Bran's discharge. I promise his will be the last."

"I'm afraid your appointment has come to an end. Unless..." He reached out and lightly brushed his finger across the flesh above Enya's bodice. "Lovely." His tongue shot out like a snake's and moistened his lips. "Unless you are willing to raise your skirts."

Enya clasped her hand over chest. He took a step closer, reeking of tallow and lilac oil, which covered some other ungodly odor. Enya's stomach churned as she recoiled.

He grasped her elbow and opened the door. "I thought not."

Chained to the stone wall, Bran leaned into his manacles, his legs too tired to bear his weight. The stench of stale piss surrounded him, burning his eyes. A single stream of light shone through a crack at the top of the cell. The dirt floor was crowded with men huddled miserably, some rocking and some mumbling to themselves as if they'd lost their wits. In a solid stone chamber with a thick wooden door, the manacles weren't necessary, but since it had taken four soldiers to restrain Bran, it appeared Regent Moray was taking no chances.

Bran turned his head to the side. The only other man in chains stood beside him, his hair hung over his face, but Bran would recognize Malcolm anywhere.

Ross's captain turned his head. "What are you looking at?"

"Me service for Lord Ross has ended."

"Unfortunate we're in chains. I'd sooner die fighting."

Bran chuckled without humor. "Mayhap ye'll feel the slice of a bullwhip on yer back afore they hang us."

Malcolm yanked his arms against his chains. "You ken I'm a paid soldier, just like you. I pulled you out of the pit and fetched the healer, did I not?"

"Aye, after nearly letting me starve." Bran ran his tongue across his cracked bottom lip. "Forgive me if me gratitude is wanting. I've four and twenty jagged cuts on me back to remind me of yer hospitality."

Iron scraped as the door unlocked and creaked open. Bran willed a splash of saliva into his mouth, hoping they were bringing food and water, but the miserable guard only replaced the slop buckets, mumbling curses under his breath.

Bran slid down the wall and crouched, his wrists dangling in the manacles above. His head slumped forward. All was lost. He'd never hold Enya or sing to Griffon again.

When Lord Ross entered the magistrate's office, they removed his manacles. Ross never much cared for Mr. Fisher, a reformist, but unfortunately Regent Moray attributed a great deal of power to the man, and Ross would do whatever necessary to keep his head intact.

Mr. Fisher didn't rise, but eyed him from head to toe, seated behind a dark walnut table. The ass apparently harbored no respect for his betters. "Your daughter visited me this morning."

Having not been offered a chair, Ross opted to take the seat opposite.

Mr. Fisher's thin lips twitched. "She's quite pretty."

"Thank you." Enya might be a thorn in Ross's side, but her bold spirit was of use this time. She'd negotiated a good compromise for his release. "I shall dispatch my factor to pay you a visit upon my return to Halkhead."

"That is most generous." Fisher drummed his fingers on the desk. "Can you tell me who the queen's key men were? Of course, notwithstanding your involvement."

"As you are aware, Claud Hamilton and his uncle were at the helm of the uprising, including the Earl of Argyle."

"And who else?"

"Lord Eglinton and Lord Seaton played roles. Of course, George Douglas had a hand in her escape."

Fisher lifted his quill and dabbed it in his silver inkwell. Ross leaned forward and watched him record the names he'd mentioned. This was an opportunity too great to let pass. He licked his lips. "There was a Highlander who got close to the queen. She even knighted him before her entire army."

"Knighted, you say?" Fisher raised an eyebrow. "And whom might this be?"

"Sir Bran MacLeod. He fights like a pack of dogs, but the men followed him—would still follow him anywhere if he were released."

"MacLeod, did you say?"

"Aye, a large bull of a man."

"Why, I believe Miss Enya mentioned him." He squinted as if filing through his memory. "Yes. She requested his release as well."

"Oh, no. That man is more dangerous to Scotland than any other."

"Interesting. I wonder why your daughter spoke highly of him."

"I apologize for her outspoken nature. I do believe she is infatuated with him—he's quite an impressive male specimen."

"I suspected something afoot." Fisher rested his quill in a silver stand that matched the inkwell. "Tell me, Lord Ross. Would you like me to take care of this problem between your daughter and the Highlander?"

Ross folded his arms and smiled smugly. "I trust you will proceed with punishment as you deem appropriate."

"Regent Moray gave me two directives. First, I am to show adequate leniency, especially to the nobles. Second, I'm to select a number of commoners to be made an example of."

"Hopefully my information has been of assistance."

Fisher stood and gestured toward the door. "Yes. We will try this Highlander as well as your man, Malcolm. I suspect both have little time left on this earth."

The back of Ross's neck pricked. He needed Malcolm, but if his captain's life was part of the price of freedom, then so be it. He just needed to spirit Enya back to Halkhead before she made a damned fool of herself, asking everyone to help the MacLeod henchman. Thank God that bastard would soon be condemned and no longer be a thorn in his side.

# Chapter Twenty

Calum MacLeod strolled along the wall-walk of Brochel Castle's outer bailey with his cousin, John Urquhart. Together the two had sailed the waters of the many a foreign sea for nearly two decades. Calum inhaled. Enjoying the panoramic view of the Sound of Raasay, he loved the brisk air and a wind strong enough to pick up the sails of his beloved galleon, *The Golden Sun*.

The hankering for a new adventure always grew stronger with a chilling breeze at his face. "When Bran returns, I want to take another run to Tortuga."

"Aye? Last time we sailed home with little else but our lives."

"Are ye going soft on me, John?" Calum swatted his cousin's shoulder. "We need to plunder the Spanish silver before Francis Drake, the bastard."

"Havena we enough silver?"

"Ye can never have enough."

A commotion at the lookout caught Calum's attention. William MacLeod waved his arms over his head. "A galley approaches from the south!"

Calum pulled his spyglass from his belt. His eyesight had begun to wane, blast it all. He practically needed the spyglass to see his ships in Brochel Cove. He scanned across the Sound of Raasay and saw it, though he could not make out the sailors. "Man the cannons. Call the archers."

"Ye expecting someone?" John asked.

"Nay—mayhap Bran."

Calum climbed down the worn turret steps and headed to the beach. He didn't want to alarm anyone as of yet but his wife, Lady

Anne, could sniff out unease all the way from Dunvegan Castle on the Isle of Skye.

She met him at the heavy iron gate. "A galley approaches."

"Aye, do we have all of Brochel Castle on alert?"

"Yes, of course—one can never be too careful, especially with your notorious *privateering* activities." She winked. Though she nagged him endlessly about giving his seafaring activities away and staying put, she loved him all the same.

He gave her a fond squeeze. "Take the boys up to the solar. I'm sure 'tis nothing, but I'd prefer it if ye were safe within."

She crossed her arms. "Visitors come to call and you wish me to hide in the solar?"

"Och, woman, must ye challenge me at every turn?"

"Why yes, my laird." She offered a deep curtsey. "Did you not know, 'tis a wife's sole purpose in life."

He laughed and patted her backside. "Go inside and keep the boys safe." Calum adjusted his sword belt and turned to John. "Let's head down to the beach afore yer wife comes along to badger us as well."

"Aye. When Lady Anne and Mara join together, we've nay chance of winning."

They zigzagged down the path to the beach, arriving minutes before the galley. Calum could see clearly now. Ruairi's henchman Rewan stood at the bow. From the frown on his face, the news wasn't good.

Calum bounded into the water and caught the rope. Together he and John hauled the small galley until it touched the sands. Rewan hopped over the side and faced him. "Mary's army was quelled at Langside. Moray has Bran locked in Glasgow Tolbooth."

"He's alive?"

Rewan frowned, trudging through the sand. "Me guess is no' for long. The regent will be looking for a pawn, and Bran's the reason the queen got away. I watched him take on a whole cohort of Moray's men while she fled with Willy Douglas."

A rock the size of his fist formed in Calum's stomach. "How much time do ye reckon he's got?"

"A day, mayhap two."

Calum whipped around to John. "Provision two galleys, we leave at once."

John pointed to the bay. "What about *The Golden Sun*? The galleon's got eighteen guns."

"Aye, but we won't make it up the Clyde with a big ship, the river's too shallow. Besides, I'm no' planning to sail into Glasgow with me guns a-blazing." Calum turned to his man, William. "Run up the tower and sound the horn. We'll no' be flying the MacLeod pennant—the flag of Scotland will be the only colors gracing our bow."

"Not the Jolly Roger?" John asked with a wicked twinkle in his eye.

Calum glanced over his shoulder to ensure Rewan hadn't heard. "No' this time. Now go give yer wife a kiss and have her load us up with mutton and oatcakes."

"And whisky."

"Aye, that too." He turned to Rewan. "Thank ye for bringing the news. Ye're welcome to sail with us."

"As much as I'd like to head home, I'll go." Rewan held up Bran's satchel. "I've brought his things—what I could find, anyway. I've much to tell ye."

Calum marched Rewan up the trail. "Aye?"

"He fell in love with Ross's daughter and got thrown in the pit for starters."

"I was afraid of that." Calum sped up his pace. "A young buck like Bran would have difficulty keeping his cock under his kilt with a pretty lassie batting her eyelashes his way."

"And the queen knighted him into the Order of the Thistle."

Calum stopped. "Ye don't say? The bastard's been mighty busy, and now he's gone and got his arse thrown in the Glasgow Tolbooth?"

Enya had the carriage ready when Robert and her father were released. She stood with determination beside her mother, watching them approach.

Lady Ross stepped forward and embraced her husband. "Thank heavens they've released you from that deplorable place."

"Not to worry, Jean. Moray would have anarchy on his hands if he killed half the gentry."

Enya embraced Robert and then Lord Ross. "Father, we are truly blessed."

"You did well negotiating our release, though I daresay one hundred gold sovereigns is quite a hefty price to pay."

"I wanted to ensure he knew I was serious." Enya took a step back and steeled her nerves. "I would like to remain in Glasgow and attend the trials. Heather and a groom can remain with me."

"Are you daft, daughter? We must away to Halkhead forthwith and put this ugly business behind us. Remaining in Glasgow during these unsettling times will only invite misfortune."

Though she had no doubt her father would react this way, Enya had to ask. She bit back her frown. This meant she must resort to her alternative plan and steal away once they returned to Halkhead.

Robert folded her hand in his. "Come, sis. Board the coach. 'Tis time to go home and lick our wounds."

Enya gaped at the stern faces staring at her then climbed inside. "What of Malcolm and your other men? Are you leaving them to the wolves?"

Ross followed all into the coach. "Mr. Fisher's terms were thus. It cannot be helped."

"Enya." Mother used a scolding tone. "We shall hear no more. Sit back and enjoy the ride home—for tomorrow it will all be forgotten."

Heather looped her arm through Enya's and encouraged her to rest against the padded carriage seat. Enya had absolutely no inclination to forget about the men who had loyally ridden into battle with her spineless father. If she did nothing, Bran would surely die.

It was well past dark when the wheels rolled over the cobblestones of Halkhead House. After her mother alighted from the carriage, Lord Ross took hold of Enya's arm. "I'll not have you make a mockery of me," he growled. "Watching you glare across the coach, you've left me with no other choice but to lock you in your chamber until this whole business has come to an end."

Enya tried to jerk away, but he held fast. "You wouldn't."

"You should still be tucked away at Paisley Abbey." He squeezed her arm harder. "Frankly, I cannot trust you."

"How can you say that? I negotiated your release."

"Anyone could have bribed that codfish." He shoved her to the bench. "You are my greatest disappointment."

Her father's words knifed through her heart. Tears welled. How could he say that? It wasn't as if she'd escaped and fled the abbey. Mother sent for her.

Lord Ross stepped to the ground and faced a sentry. "Take Miss Enya to her chamber and post a sentry outside her door. No one is allowed to enter except her serving maid and Lady Ross."

"Yes, my lord." The young guardsman bowed, and Enya wondered if this was Malcolm's replacement. How convenient that her father could disregard and replace men who were once important to him.

The guard grasped her arm, and Enya snatched it away. "I am quite capable of walking to my chamber without being restrained."

While she marched up the stairs, hundreds of thoughts coursed through Enya's mind. She'd promised Bran she'd sing to Griffon. Now she'd have to attempt it from her chamber window. Who knew where the eagle was now, if still alive? But she had made a promise. It was one her father couldn't prevent her from keeping.

More pressing, however, was her need to return to Glasgow. Posting a sentry outside her door was something Enya hadn't expected. How would she slip past a guard?

Sucking back her desire to throw herself on the bed, Enya pulled a chair up to her window and opened it. At the top of her lungs, she fa-la-la'd Bran's tune, wishing she'd asked him to teach her the words. She scanned the dark, dreary sky, wondering how on earth Griffon would hear her, let alone come to her when she'd only handled the bird once.

As she sang, sloppy wet droplets fell and soon a downpour forced her to pull the window closed. In the dim light, she could see nothing.

Enya slumped into the chair. Curling her arms over her head, she rocked. Tears spilled from her eyes, splashing her gown. Her chest tight, she wailed aloud. This could not be happening. She must do something to help Bran. She would not remain in her chamber while he faced trial and, most certainly, the executioner. The mere thought of Bran's life held in the hands of that pungent, rheumy-eyed magistrate filled her with such panic, she could scarcely breathe. *Heavenly Father, please help me.*

Enya staggered to the bed and threw herself across it, sobbing and wailing out of control.

---

Recovering from her lapse into the depths of despair, Enya fought to steady her breath. She pulled Bran's archer figurine from her pocket and ran her thumb across the smooth wood. Touching it renewed her strength. Wallowing in self-pity would not help Bran or anyone else. She marched across the room and shook the latch with such force, the door rattled in its hinges. "I must see Mistress Heather. Now!"

"Heather has retired to her chamber," a deep voice resonated from the corridor.

"Fetch her."

"But your door must remain guarded."

"She's only paces away. Besides, how can I escape with the door locked?

Footsteps clomped away and soon Enya heard a muffled rap. Fingering the sovereigns, she dashed to her wardrobe and pulled out a satchel. She wouldn't need much, but to promote the air of nobility, a regal mantle to wear over an embroidered kirtle would be lightweight enough to carry. She stuffed a lovely red kirtle inside.

Enya settled for a black velvet mantle lined with golden silk. With a hood, she could use it to hide her identity. She tossed it on the bed, ready to throw over her shoulders when the time came.

The door opened and Heather slipped within.

Enya pulled her to the far end of the chamber so they would not be overheard. "Dearest Heather." She kept her voice low. "If you care anything for me, you shall help me escape this night."

"Enya, have you not noticed? An armed sentry guards your door."

"Help me to distract him."

Heather covered her face with her hands. "Oh heavens..."

"Can you honestly face me and say you care nothing of the lives of Father's men? Even if you wish Bran dead, what of Malcolm?"

Heather's eyes grew round at the mention of the captain's name. "Malcolm?" She clasped her hands together. "Even if I could convince the sentry to leave his post momentarily, it would be only hours before your father would discover you missing."

"Please, Heather."

"If I help you, neither of us will ever be able to return to Halkhead."

"I understand." Enya met Heather's tortured gaze. "Will you ride with me this night?"

"Aye. I there's no other place for me but beside you, my dearest." Heather shook her head. "Every time I close my eyes, I see Malcolm's face. I'll never reconcile with myself if we don't try something."

Enya threw her arms around Heather and squeezed. "I knew I could count on you." She held her at arm's length. "Now. How do we distract the guard?"

Heather sat on the bed and chewed her thumbnail. "Believe it or not, I've been thinking about this all night. I shall tell him I'm going down to the kitchen to fetch you something to eat."

Enya nodded. "And?"

"I'll return with a parcel of oatcakes—for us to take along—and give him a full tankard of ale."

Enya's heart skipped a beat. "And when you leave, you'll offer to stand guard while he relieves himself—and I'll slip across to the solar."

"Exactly. Upon his return, I shall pretend to go to my rooms, but once I round the corner, I'll follow you to the solar and meet you in the passageway."

Enya hugged her. "The plan is perfect. But Halkhead is your home—can you risk so much?"

"It has been a home, but with all the girls grown, I suspect Lord Ross would no longer have use of me once you're married and gone. I had hoped to follow you when you married."

"Well, it may not be exactly as you planned, but as long as you are willing, you will always have a home with me."

"I thought you would never speak to me again."

"As did I, but I realized you believed you were doing right. And now you've proved I have your loyalty." Enya pulled Heather to her feet. "Make haste, for we must be far away before dawn."

---

For once, Enya took Heather's advice and secured her tresses under a snood. Besides, it would prevent her hair from whipping out from under her cloak. With her bow and arrows over her shoulder, the dirk in her pocket, Enya waited for Heather in the secret passageway. "Do you think the guard suspected anything?"

"Nay, he was too grateful for the reprieve. We didn't even need the ale. His relief never arrived. I think he'll be stuck there all night."

"Poor man."

"Aye, and he'll be a mite poorer once your father realizes you escaped under his watch."

Enya led Heather through the tunnel. The rain had ebbed to a heavy mist. "I hope he isn't punished too severely."

"Me as well." Heather held up her palm. "'Tis a shame God didn't see fit to keep the rain at bay."

Enya tugged her through the shadows. "'Tis a blessing. We'll be harder to spot in the darkness."

"Lord help us."

In minutes Enya had Maisey and a gelding saddled. "Put up your hood and follow me. I ken how to avoid the guard."

Heather climbed the mounting block. "Precious child. I knew there was a reason the good Lord saw fit to make you so adventurous."

"With any luck they won't notice us gone for some time. Mother always punishes me by staying away, and Father rarely visits my chamber." Enya chuckled. "They'll probably discover you're missing before me."

# Chapter Twenty-one

By the time they reached Glasgow Road, the rain had completely stopped, though the dark clouds above and heavy fog made it difficult to see more than a few feet ahead. Wet and shivering beneath her cloak, Enya urged the horses to a steady trot. She could barely feel her numb fingers grasping the reins. Her sole motivation was to spirit to Glasgow as quickly as possible and save Bran from the gallows.

Her teeth chattered while white mist billowed from her mouth with each exhale. "Are you doing well, Heather?"

The gelding pulled alongside Maisey's flank. "I'm holding up. Though we could have done without this miserable fog."

"Not to worry. We'll be there soon enough."

The darkness got blacker and the trail became further blurred by the mist. The cadence of the horse hooves grew louder with her lack of sight.

"I do not like this." Heather's voice warbled.

Enya tapped Maisey with her heel. "It will pass."

The air grew heavier, more humid. Enya breathed a sigh of relief when she heard the lazy flow of the Clyde River. Any moment, the trees would open up to the bridge.

She spurred Maisey to a fast trot. "Come on, Heather, we're nearly there." Enya glanced back only for a second. Something slammed into her midriff, ripping her from the saddle. Enya's heart shot to her throat. Midair, she flung out her arms and flapped them wildly, trying to grasp anything to break her fall.

Completely blinded by the darkness, Enya could see nothing. Time slowed until her backside slapped into a muddy bog. Her hands filled with moist peat. Sucking in a breath of air, she tried to push up. Male laughter cackled behind.

A dreaded memory of the Gypsies made ice run through Enya's veins. She reached for her bow, but it was gone. Patting the forest floor, she desperately searched when something smashed into the side of her head.

She cried out with the pain. Stars clouded her vision. Footsteps slapped the mud as she raised her hand to staunch the throbbing.

"We've a ripe one," a deep voice growled in her ear.

Enya tried to spring to her feet, but hands grasped her wrists and dragged her into the trees.

"Release me this instant." Enya thrashed and wrenched her arms against the force, the illusion of stars completely blinding her. Her head spun like it was engulfed by a swarm of bees. Vaguely it registered that hands searched in her pockets, around her neck, all over her body.

"We're in luck, lads. The wench has a stash of coin in her pocket."

Voices laughed.

Enya's head throbbed. The world spun. "Heather!"

"This old crow didn't survive the fall."

Bile burned the back of Enya's throat. *Old crow? Heather?* Enya struggled to sit, but she couldn't tell up from down. The pain overcame her. At once, everything mercifully went black.

---

Enya awoke to the sound of horse hooves. Violet streams glowed against the clouds, announcing the sun's appearance. Though her head throbbed, she opened her eyes. Surrounded by trees, Heather lay in a heap a few feet away.

Enya pushed up, the trees around her spinning like the slow churning of the blacksmith's wheel. "Heather?"

Nothing moved. Enya turned her ear to the nearing horse hooves. Colors fluttered through the trees. She clutched her arms against her chest. It could be another mob of thieves. Praying for a miracle, Enya tried not to make a sound as she crawled to Heather and placed a hand on her shoulder. "Heather. You must wake."

Tears stung her eyes, but she sucked them back and held a trembling hand to Heather's nose. A warm, faint breeze caressed her finger. A shaky laugh slipped past Enya's lips. "Heather." She shook her shoulder vigorously. "Please wake."

Heather moved under Enya's hand. "What happened?" she rasped.

"We were attacked by brigands." Enya pulled Heather into her embrace and squeezed. "Praise God you're alive. Are you hurt?"

Heather hung her head and ran a hand over her face. "My head's throbbing."

"As is mine. One minute I thought we'd made it to the bridge and the next I was on my backside."

Heather lifted her head and cupped Enya's face with both hands. "Did they violate you?"

Enya tensed, her mind racing back to what she could remember. Hands searched her, mayhap not to violate, but to rob. "I think not." She reached inside her pocket and gasped. "They've taken my shillings and my dirk." Her gaze darted around the clearing. Bran's figurine floated in a puddle.

"You had a dirk?"

Enya picked up the archer and wiped it dry with her dirty skirts. The horsehair bowstring was missing, but the rest survived the attack. "Aye. We needed more than a bow and arrow for protection."

"A lot of good that did us." Heather brushed the dirt from her hands.

"I neither heard nor saw them coming." Enya glanced toward the road. "The sun is rising. We best be on our way if we're to reach Glasgow in time for the trial. Thieves shouldn't bother us now we look like we've been wallowing in a swine's bog."

Heather pressed her palms to her cheeks. "And there's nothing left to steal. What are we going to do without coin?"

"I'll think of something." Enya swooned as she stood. After a moment, she steadied and held out her hand. "Come."

Heather eyed her and grimaced. "You look a sight. Mud from head to toe."

Enya shrugged. "As you say, I always manage to turn into a guttersnipe when I leave the manse. Now you ken why."

Fortunately, it wasn't far to cross the bridge over the Clyde and enter the city. The brigands had lain in wait on the outskirts of town, watching for their chance to attack an unsuspecting party. Enya offered a prayer of thanks they hadn't seen fit to kidnap her. She shook her head and vowed she would never allow herself to be so gullible again. But this couldn't be helped. She had no choice but to leave Halkhead without a guard. Blast being female. If she were Bran, she would have skewered them all and left them bleeding on the road.

They stopped at a fountain near the river and washed the caked mud from their faces and hands.

Heather tugged Enya's arm. "Come here and let me tidy your tresses."

"But we have no comb."

"Nay, but I can work a little magic with my fingers."

Enya complied and sat on a bench while Heather removed her snood and made quick work of re-securing it in place. She stood back and gave Enya a good look from head to toe. Heather slapped Enya's mantle and brushed out the dust. "You're marginally presentable."

"I do not know what I would do without you."

"I have no idea why I let you talk me into this."

"There's no turning back now." Enya looked past Heather and spotted a flash of red hair on one of the galleys moored at the riverbank. Recognition tickled the back of her neck. "It can't be."

"What?"

She shook her head. "Nothing. Just my imagination getting the better of me."

---

Weakened by two days with little to eat or drink, Bran followed the procession into the courtroom, barely able to raise his hands. The manacles had worn strips through his skin. With every step, they jostled against his raw flesh.

The courtroom was hot and crowded and stank of captives who had gone far too long without bathing, as the prisoners were processed into a large hall, its walls richly inlaid with wooden paneling. At the far end, the magistrate sat at a long bench with a council of men wearing black robes topped with white ruffs.

Malcolm filed in front of him. "The lambs being led to the slaughter."

Bran gritted his teeth. "Death beats another three days in hell."

"Word is Lord Ross was released yesterday. He's not among the faces here."

Bran tossed his head to scatter the hair away from his eyes. "Left ye here to hang with me, did he?"

"Aye, the bastard. And after all I did for him."

Surrounded by pikemen, the prisoners stood while the council frowned down at them from behind the dark maple bench. Bran scanned the public, standing, crammed into the hall. Like vultures, they waited for the spectacle to begin.

As his gaze shifted, he hoped to find one familiar face, though he knew Enya wouldn't be there, especially not since her father had been released. The same jeering faces he'd seen when they forced him to parade in shame through the streets of Glasgow now glared at him.

They hailed the first prisoner to the platform, called him by name. Bran wondered if they were going to pass sentence upon each individual. He got his answer when they called the next and the next.

It was a sham. Each man stood in chains, head bowed, while the magistrate read a list of charges against him. The worst part was the chilling sentence. *At dawn on the morrow, you will be hung by the neck until dead.* The timeline extended a day after the fifth man. The gallows must only hold five. Such a pity they were forced to draw it out.

They ushered each man out the side door once his sentence passed, some crying, others pleading for leniency.

The tower bell tolled eleven times. Bran had stood in the hall for three hours. Malcolm received his sentence to hang. Ross's former captain of the guard uttered not a word, and the sentries led him away as they had the others.

"Bran of Raasay," a sentry bellowed.

To the taunts and jeers of the crowd, Bran shuffled awkwardly in his leg irons and climbed the two steps to the platform.

The magistrate pounded the bench with a wooden gavel. "Order. Order, I say." When the noise ebbed, he peered down the length of his nose. "I have a sworn statement from the Honorable Lord Ross revealing you were personally responsible for the queen's escape at Langside."

Bran clenched his fists and jerked them against the chains. Ross had betrayed him? He'd done it to save his own neck, no doubt—the spineless codfish. "I wasna the only—"

"Silence!" The magistrate glared. "You have been found guilty of treason against the Kingdom of Scotland in the highest order. You are hereby sentenced to be hung in chains. At dawn on the morrow, alive, you will be gibbeted in an iron cage until your bones are picked clean by ravens."

Blood surged through Bran's veins. He wanted his hands around Fisher's scrawny neck. Lurching forward, he reached out as sentries seized his arms.

"Bran," Enya's disembodied voice called above the crowd.

He wrenched his head around. Where was she? Bran planted his feet and used his weight to fight against his captors' grasp. A horde of soldiers swarmed toward him, but he saw her. One last time, her lovely face lit up his heart. *Enya.*

The sharp point of a pike stabbed into his shoulder. "Get moving, you bloody bastard."

---

Putting the distaste of his incarceration behind him, Lord Ross opted to ride out on a hunt after breaking his fast. Accompanied by Robert, a morning in the saddle chasing red deer was what he needed to clear his head.

In time, all the ugliness would be forgotten. Word came Claud Hamilton had fled to England. Curses. It looked like Ross would need to find another match for his wayward daughter. A thorn in his side, she was.

Movement ahead snapped his mind to the task at hand.

"Three does and a young buck," Robert whispered.

Ross raised his musket to his shoulder. He had one shot. If it missed, the chase would be on. Hell, the chase would be on even if he hit his mark. The deer grazed in the green meadow beyond the trees. He lined a doe up in his sights. She raised her head, sniffing the air. She'd sense him if he hesitated. He pulled the trigger and the gun blasted. The deer dropped.

"Excellent shot, Father." Robert loaded his bow and took off at a gallop with Ross on his heels. He could smell the fear on the air as they made chase, the deer scattering for the shelter of the forest.

Out of the corner of his eye, Ross saw movement. His mind clicked. *Maisey?* He reined his horse to a sliding stop. "Robert. Come."

Enya's saddled mare grazed beside one of his stock geldings.

"Did you see your sister this morning?"

"I thought she was still locked in her chamber."

"As did I." He kicked his heels against his stallion's sides. "Boars ballocks, we must ride to Glasgow. When I find the twit, she will spend the rest of her life on Iona."

"If she's still alive." Robert's grave tone twisted around Lord Ross's spine like the chilling knell of a funeral bell.

---

Enya tried to push through to Bran before the sentries muscled him out of the courtroom. He started struggling when she called out his name, and then they skewered his shoulder with a pike. She only wanted him to know he wasn't alone.

Hung in chains? An unimaginable death. Enya clutched Heather's arm. "We must find a way to free him."

"But how? There are hundreds of sentries guarding the gaol." Heather's shoulders dropped. "I've no idea where we'll find the next meal. We cannot go much longer."

Enya's stomach growled at the mention of food. With her bow and arrows lost, there was little hope of killing a rabbit. Besides, one didn't hunt in the middle of town. "We can set a snare in the wood this eve."

"Except it's crawling with thieves."

Enya followed the crowd. "Have you a better idea?"

Heather struggled to keep up. "I'm thinking on it. Oh, Enya, if we could only return to Halkhead and ask forgiveness."

Enya pushed through the big double doors to the street. "That's the one thing I will not consider."

She saw it again, the ginger hair, but this time the man sporting it was in full view. Enya tugged on Heather's arm. "Come."

Dressed in red plaid, the likeness was uncanny. It had to be Laird MacLeod. Had he come for the trial? Enya hurried after him—heading for the docks. He walked beside a man wearing a blue and green plaid. After turning the corner, he headed straight toward a moored galley. Enya broke into a run.

"Slow down," Heather hollered, but Enya couldn't stop.

Nearly out of breath, she raced up behind him. "Laird MacLeod. May I have a word?"

The man turned and eyed her. She hadn't noticed before, but his features were quite striking—crystal-blue eyes, a bold nose that pointed to full lips. "Miss Enya Ross, is it?"

"Aye." Enya sucked in a deep breath. "You must help me free Bran."

His gazed slipped to her dirty gown. "What the blazes happened to you?"

Heather huffed up beside her. "We were attacked by thieves in the night. Haven't had a morsel to eat or drink all day."

Calum's jaw dropped. "You brought the healer?"

Enya grasped her nursemaid's arm. "If you may recall, Heather is my maid."

Understanding washed over his face. "Ah."

Enya pressed on. "We need to formulate a plan, and fast."

Calum stroked his neatly cropped beard. "A plan, yes. We, no. Ye should take Mistress Heather and go home to yer father afore ye end up in serious trouble."

He stepped onto the gangway but Enya lunged forward and caught his arm. "Please. You must help us. Bran told me about Lady Anne—how she was from English nobility, how you fought for her. If anyone can understand, 'tis you."

Calum stopped and glanced at the blue-plaid man, who looked to the skies and shook his head. "Bloody hell, Calum, do ye always have to mistake yerself for Robin Hood?"

Calum's mouth twisted in a devilish grin. "Me quartermaster isna too happy 'bout the prospect of having a woman aboard."

"Women." Enya dragged Heather along. "Please. We shan't be any trouble."

"To that, I beg to differ." He beckoned her with a wave of his hand. "Come aboard and put some food in yer belly. The least I can do is feed ye." He turned to his quartermaster. "John, go muster up some oatcakes and bully beef."

Enya hurried behind him. "Thank you, m'laird. Your kindness shall be rewarded."

"I doubt that," John mumbled from behind.

Enya followed Calum up the gangway, her mind racing with questions. "How did you know Bran had been captured?"

He stepped aboard the galley. "Ruairi's henchman sailed to Raasay."

He offered Enya a hand and she caught sight of Rewan coiling a rope. "Weren't you in the battle at Langside?"

Rewan held the rope between his hands with a crooked grin as if he'd been smitten. "Aye, and I hightailed it to Raasay as soon as I saw the soldiers seize Bran."

Enya fanned her face. "Oh, thank heavens."

Calum led them below decks to a tiny room with a round table and four chairs. "Apologies for the cramped space. A larger ship canna sail up the Clyde."

"'Tis no problem."

John set a trencher of food on the table. Enya's mouth watered as she reached for a piece of bully beef.

"'Tis an answer to prayer that you're here."

"Aye, well, the greater question is what are ye doing in Glasgow without a guard?"

Enya started from the beginning. Heather cringed as Enya explained how her relationship with Bran blossomed, how they were caught, and his visit during her stay in Paisley Abbey.

Oddly, Calum listened with no outward sign of surprise. "And yer father. I expected to see him standing on the trial platform. What happened to him?"

"I negotiated release for him and my brother with Mr. Fisher. I tried to do the same for Bran, but he would hear none of it."

"Of course the lad had to play the hero for the queen."

Enya nodded. "It seems as though he did." John placed a tankard of ale in front of her and she guzzled greedily. "My, that's good." She swiped her hand across her mouth and looked at Calum expectantly. "Please tell me you have a plan."

"Aye, I do."

"And?"

Calum scratched his head. "I dunna like the odds of the king's men *and* yer father chasing after us."

"I can help. Bran told me you used to put him in the crow's nest with a bow and arrow." Enya pointed to her chest. "I can do that."

Calum arched a brow, giving him the look of a pirate. "What else did me henchman tell ye?"

"H-he would fight beside you to the death."

Calum grinned. "That's me boy."

"Please. Allow me to help. Station me with a longbow anywhere and I'll see to your safety."

Heather slid her hand atop Calum's. "She's very skilled, m'laird. Better than her brother."

Enya smoothed her hands over her unkempt hair. "As good as Sir Bran."

"Aye?" Calum's eyes popped and then narrowed. "Ye must swear fealty to Clan MacLeod."

"Of course. I'd pledge my life if it means saving Bran."

"Very well. We will take him under cover of darkness. I want as little bloodshed as possible. If we wait until daylight, no doubt Scotland will declare war on Raasay and we'll all be fleeing for our lives." Calum lifted his tankard. "If ye're as good as ye say, we'll post ye on the gallows."

Enya's hand slid to her neck. "The gallows?"

"'Twill give ye the best vantage point, and I'm planning to moor the galley directly beneath it." He waggled his eyebrows. "No one will suspect us so close to the hangman's noose."

Enya pictured it in her mind. The plan made sense. "I cannot believe you are so cunning."

"If ye'd prefer no', I had thought to post Rewan there, but it would be a blessing to have his sword beside me."

"No. I want to help."

Calum turned to Heather. "Ye'd better stay below, mistress."

"I'll be here to tend any wounds." She crossed herself. "Heaven help us."

---

Lord Ross took Robert and half a dozen men on the ride to Glasgow. He wanted to take a full army, but he could not leave the manse unprotected, and he'd lost over half his guard in the fighting at Langside.

It was late afternoon when their horses clomped across the bridge. "There are only a few inns. Let's start there. Lie low, men. For Mr. Fisher most assuredly still has a taste for blood."

He pushed through the door of the George Inn, renowned for its unsavory clientele, with rooms above and a bar filled with boisterous, distasteful men drinking ale at wooden tables while loose women flitted about. Ross sincerely hoped his daughter had the sense to stay away from this place.

He walked up to the barman and leaned across to be heard. "Has a young lass with auburn tresses let a room?"

"That sounds like Queen Mary, and word has it she's fled to England."

"I'm speaking of my daughter, Enya Ross."

"No ladies here." His eyes strayed to Ross's ermine bonnet and badge, which signified his noble status. "M'lord, is it?"

Ross eyed him with haughty contempt. "Have you rooms available?"

"Aye."

"I'll pay for the night's accommodation for myself and my son. Can my men bed down in your stable?"

"Two shillings for the room and five pence for the stable."

Ross untied the pouch from his belt. "You drive a hard bargain."

The barman shrugged. "'Tis the going rate—same as Mule Deer Inn down the road."

Ross tossed his money on the bar. "Thank you, friend." He added a shilling. "A pint of ale for me and each of my men as well."

Ross found an empty table and led Robert to it. "Keep your eyes open." The ale was welcome after an afternoon of hard riding. "I think we should pay a visit to the tolbooth. See if she's been there."

Robert shuddered. "You think it's wise to show our faces so soon after our release?"

"Have you a better idea?" A bow slung across a patron's chair caught Ross's eye. There was only one bow like that on earth, and he'd carved it himself. He shoved his chair back and crossed the floor. The man, who sported a thick beard and an unshaven neck, turned to him with a hateful glint in his eye.

"May I have a look at your bow?"

The man slid his hand over the pommel of his dirk. "And why should it interest you?"

"I collect such artifacts." Ross leaned down to inspect it. No question, this was the one he'd carved for Enya. His eyes shot to Robert in silent warning. "The craftsmanship is exquisite."

The man took a gander at Ross's well-tailored attire. "I might be persuaded to sell it for the right price."

Ross slipped the bow off the chair, taking inventory of the man's four mates as Robert and the guard surrounded their table. He checked the inside shaft and ran his thumb over his initials—*JR*. In one swift move, he unsheathed his dirk and held it against the man's hairy neck. "I'm only going to ask you once, and you'd better speak quick, for my knife is sharp and itching for blood. Where did you find this?"

Ross's guard drew their swords as chairs scraped against the floorboards and the table of men prepared for a fight.

"I found it last night."

"Where?"

"On the Glasgow Road just before the bridge."

"And where is the young lady it belonged to?"

A bead of sweat dribbled down the man's temple as he made eye contact with an ugly blighter across the table—who nodded his head.

"Once we realized it was a lass, we left her and the old woman in the trees. We didn't do nothing to her, I swear."

Ross looked at his men. "Take these thieves to the tolbooth. Robert, come with me."

---

Her belly full, Enya pulled a plaid over her head and climbed onto the galley deck. She cast her gaze to the sky. She hummed Griffon's lullaby, not too loudly, as she didn't want to draw attention to herself in the busy dockyard. Had her father noticed her missing? Surely he had, but would he come looking for her? Probably. He might even be searching the streets of Glasgow at this very moment.

Enya fa-la-la'd a bit louder. Clouds still loomed above, but they weren't as ominous as the night before. Why she had to mount her escape in a thunderstorm, she had no idea. She sneezed. Queen's knees, the last thing she needed was to catch a cold.

She slid her hand in her pocket and pulled out Bran's archer figurine. Where was the panel she embroidered? Did Bran still have it? She doubted he would. But the figurine gave her hope. He'd fashioned it with his hands. Enya held it up to the sky and sang the words with the pronunciation she'd heard Bran use. Though she didn't know the meaning, she prayed the bird would come.

Calum slipped beside her. "Ye're searching for Griffon?"

"Aye."

"If he's no' hereabouts, he's most likely headed back to Raasay."

Enya rubbed her thumb across the warm wood. "I hope so. Bran loves that bird."

"They're kindred spirits." Calum pointed to the archer. "Did Bran whittle that?"

Enya opened her palm and stared at it. "'Tis all I have to remind me of him."

Calum wrapped an arm around her shoulders and squeezed. "Dunna worry. He's a fighter if I ever saw one. We'll get him out."

Enya closed her eyes and relaxed into the warmth of the laird's arm. She was exhausted. The world seemed like a whirlwind of uncertainty, and she was spinning out of control within it.

*Caw.*

Griffon perched atop the center mast.

# Chapter Twenty-two

Bran hoped he would hear Enya's voice call to him from the tiny window at the top of the cell. Though he'd told her to run, he thanked everything holy he saw her in that fleeting moment. He swallowed against his parched throat. If only he could hold her in his arms one last time and say goodbye, his mind would find peace. But that was not going to happen. Enya must to return to Renfrewshire and forget him—marry Claud Hamilton or some other noble.

He hung his head. She was there when they called him a traitor and passed the worst death sentence imaginable—gibbeted in a cage and left to die, sitting in his own shite. It would take three days or longer for a man to succumb to thirst. The only positive thing about his miserable treatment in the tolbooth was he was already thirsty and half starved. With any luck, he'd die in a day or two, before the birds started pecking away his flesh.

Bran slumped down the stony wall. This would be his last night in this hellhole. The light from the window faded. He'd be shrouded in complete darkness soon—along with his cellmates and the resident rats.

His belly growled, long since empty from his single meal of porridge mixed with lard that morn. He'd refuse his meal on the morrow. The miserable fare would only serve to postpone his death.

The rims of his eyes stung. He'd had so many plans for his life and now he would see none fulfilled. He would never wed a woman or hold a bairn in his arms. His tongue swiped across his arid lips. He'd never wed Enya. He closed his eyes and tried to block the memories.

The cell had gone dark and the rats rustled across the dirt floor, scurrying between the sleeping forms of the condemned. Bran pulled his knees to his chest. He'd kill the next vermin that gnawed on his toes—they'd already eaten through his boots. Dropping into a stupor between sleep and awake, Bran tried to force his mind to blank, but all he could see was Enya's stricken face.

Feet shuffled in the corridor beyond the cell. Had they come for them already? The tower clock had struck twelve bells only moments ago.

The prisoners stirred as the door opened with a flood of torchlight. Bran shaded his eyes with the crook of his elbow.

"Merciful God," a prisoner cried, crawling for the passageway.

A large man stood over him with a raised battleax, the light glowing behind him. Bran could not see his face. "Spread yer legs."

Recognizing the deep voice, Bran did as asked. "Calum?"

"Aye. A fine lot ye've got us into."

"How did ye ken?"

Calum swung the blade and the chains smashed apart. "Rewan brought word right after Langside. If he'd have been a day later we wouldna made it."

Bran spread his hands against the dirt floor. "Praise Jesus ye did."

Calum busted his chains and offered him a hand. "Can ye swing a sword?"

"Was I born a MacLeod?"

Calum held up a claymore. Bran snatched it. "We must hurry. This place is swarming with the enemy."

Bran took a few wobbling steps to the door and nodded at Rewan and John, who stood guard in the corridor. He inclined his head back to Malcolm. "Release him too."

John shook his head. "We canna have any others slow us down."

"Give him a chance."

John made quick work of releasing Malcolm's chains. The older man held up his hands. "I'll not forget this. My sword now belongs to the MacLeod."

"Ye think ye can make it to the galley?" John asked.

Bran inhaled. "I can run back to Raasay without stopping. Let's go."

Stumbling over a body in the passageway, Bran hesitated. He recognized the face. The bastard who had stolen his dirk lay dead, eyes gaping as if frozen in shock. Without breaking his stride, Bran reached down and reclaimed his father's dirk.

---

On the platform, Enya crouched beside the support post of the Glasgow gallows. A place no person would intentionally hide. An eerie calm blanketed her nerves. The gallows was erected on the shore of the tidal river to hang thieves at low tide and watch them drown while the tide rose. After dark, Calum had moored his galley directly beneath it. The tower clock had just knelled twelve bells, and yet horse hooves still clamored over the bridge, bringing travelers to and from the Scottish town.

A musket blasted in the distance. Voices rose in indiscernible shouts and echoed off the stone buildings. Enya snatched an arrow from her borrowed quiver and loaded the bow, her eyes trained up Saltmarket Street, where the tower of the tolbooth loomed in the moonlight.

Her mind flashed with an image of the Gypsies who'd attacked her in the forest. She'd killed them to survive. She could do it again.

The shouting voices neared, and she saw movement through the shadows. Musket fire cracked from the cathedral's barmkin walls.

Men ran toward her. She couldn't make them out at first, but as they neared, she spotted Bran. A tad taller than the others, he limped. Enya couldn't think about that now. Right on their heels, soldiers made chase across the cobblestones. If only Bran and the men would round the corner to give her a clear shot. She pulled back the string and held her breath. Her view cleared.

Without hesitation, Enya clenched her teeth and released. The arrow skimmed the air and silently hit its target. No one noticed as her victim fell to the ground. She whipped her arm back. Number two. Another arrow. Number three.

Grunts came from below. The Highlanders were caught up in a clash of swords, as iron clanged with iron.

"Pull the oars!" Calum bellowed.

Enya snatched another arrow as the second onslaught approached on horseback. She had the man in her sights. Familiarity crept up her spine.

*Robert.*

"Climb aboard," Calum roared over the clatter.

Her gaze flashed to the man riding beside her brother—*Father*. Crouching on the gallows, Enya shifted her gaze to the galley. With the sail unfurled, it listed away from the pier as every man strained to pull their oars.

Slinging the bow over her shoulder, she took a running leap and hurled herself through the air. Enya crashed into the deck just as the men pulled in the wooden gangway.

"Fire the cannon!" Calum commanded.

Enya covered her ears as the galley's single cannon blasted a fiery lead ball into the onslaught. Muskets cracked from the shore. Musket balls slapped the water and the galley's thick hull. The boat rocked beneath her. Enya sat upright, scanning the dark figures for Bran. Her heart thundered against her chest. He had his back to her. Her legs trembled as she stood. "Bran!"

The wind picked up the sail and the galley lurched. He turned. A musket cracked. Something smacked Enya's arm. It stung. Bran crossed the deck and caught her as she fell.

"Enya!" Bran cradled her in his arms. "She's been shot."

---

"Cease fire!" Ross shouted over the barrage of musket blasts. He had no doubt the woman's scream came from his daughter. He surveyed the carnage. Dead and injured soldiers littered the dock.

Robert rode in beside him. "She's on the boat. I saw her."

"We must commandeer a ship. Come."

Ross pounded on the door of the magistrate's rooms until answered by an ancient valet. "What business have you?"

"I must speak to Mr. Fisher at once. Prisoners have escaped."

The valet looked from Lord Ross to Robert as if he was going to protest, but then he nodded. "Wait here."

Mr. Fisher appeared in his dressing gown and cap, carrying a candle. "Lord Ross? I thought I sent you back to Renfrewshire."

"Where I was quite happy to retire until my daughter went missing. Robert and I returned to Glasgow just as Laird Calum MacLeod led a raid on your gaol."

"My word. Why has no one alerted me?"

"The watch is most likely dead," Robert said.

"I must send word to Edinburgh."

Ross pointed in the direction of the Firth of Clyde. "We need a ship and men. They've absconded with my daughter."

"With hangings scheduled every day for the next week?" Fisher tugged on the sash around his waist. "I hardly have enough men to keep peace in the burgh of Glasgow. Near all our fighting men have made chase with the king's army."

The tower pealed two knells. Ross jammed his finger into the magistrate's sternum. "Have you lost your mind? I *gave* you Bran MacLeod. He's the most notorious of all the condemned."

Fisher cocked one thick brow. "Have you forgotten, *my lord*, you could easily be substituted for the Highlander?"

That was exactly why Ross would have preferred to remain in Renfrewshire. He gripped the hilt of his sword. "I have not, nor would I be here if the circumstances were not dire."

"I shall send word to the regent in the morning. Once the frenzy from the hangings has ebbed, we shall see about chasing this brigand. I suspect you know where to find him?"

Ross pulled on his beard thoughtfully. "The Isle of Raasay." They would hide in the protection of his fortress, and after a fortnight, their guard would wane. That would give Ross time to recruit new men for his own army. He mustn't underestimate the Highlanders. Bran learned his fighting skills somewhere, and Ross had little doubt he'd meet a formidable force.

Mr. Fisher reached for the door latch. "I suggest you find a bed, for I am certainly heading back to mine."

Bran cradled Enya in his arms and pressed his hand against the wound in her upper arm. Her precious blood streamed through his fingers.

She nestled into him. "I cannot believe we're together."

"Aye, lass, but we need to tend yer arm."

"Heather," Enya called out weakly.

At first Bran thought Enya was delirious, but then Heather tapped him on the shoulder. "Carry her down to the hold. 'Tis too windy out here to burn a lamp."

Bran stood with Enya in his arms, but had to lean against ship's rail for a moment while his head cleared. The past few days had taken their toll. It didn't matter. He was headed back to his beloved Raasay, and Enya Ross was in his arms. He could go without food for another week.

He took her down the cramped hold. Calum had altered this galley to resemble a pinnace, with a small hold beneath a platform that held a single cannon. The chieftain preferred not to sail anywhere without guns.

Heather had the ship's parcel of remedies opened on the table. Friar Pat at Brochel Castle always ensured Calum sailed with a healer's kit. But Bran assumed Heather would want her own. "Ye dunna have yer basket?"

"We lost everything on the road to Glasgow last eve."

"What?"

Heather pointed to a wooden chair. "Set her down. She needs to be tended first."

Bran did as asked but kept his hand pressed against Enya's arm. "Tell me what happened."

Her face white, drained of blood, she still grinned. "I couldn't stay locked away in my chamber during the trial." She glanced at her maid. "Heather helped me escape."

"I need to see to that arm. You'll have to go above decks, Bran."

Enya clasped her hand around his wrist. "No. I want him to stay."

Bran knelt beside her. "I'll stay if that's what Miss Enya wants."

"Bloody insolent children," Heather said. "You can help if you do as I say. Remove her mantle, but only remove her kirtle from her shoulder. I'll not have the young lady exposed, not until you're married."

Bran grinned. He liked Heather's train of thought. Enya stiffened as he slid the mantle from her wounded arm. "I dunna want to hurt ye."

"'Tis not too bad. I can move it a little."

"You'll be right." Bran carefully unlaced her kirtle and slid it from her shoulder. He glanced at the cache of herbs and bandages on the table. "Friar Pat is a good healer. Ye should find all ye need there."

"The problem is he's made notations, but I cannot read." Heather lifted a pot to her nose and sniffed. "I think this is a honey poultice."

Bran reached for it. "Let me have a look."

"You read?"

"Aye." He turned the stoppered clay pot in his hand. "Ye're right. 'Tis honey poultice."

"Splendid." Heather pushed the sleeve of Enya's shift up to her shoulder and pressed a linen bandage against the wound. "Find me the witch hazel or peppermint water."

Bran held up a bottle. "Here's the witch hazel."

"Dab it on a cloth and hand it to me. It'll help stop the bleeding."

Enya hissed when Heather applied the remedy. "It stings."

Heather peeked under the compress. "It looks like your arm was grazed. I feel no musket shot inside."

A grand weight lifted from Bran's shoulders. "'Tis good news. It's a slow death when the lead ball is buried inside."

"Aye," Heather agreed. "We would have had to remove it straight away."

Enya listed against him, even whiter now. "How did you learn to read?"

"Calum's wife, Lady Anne, saw to it when I was a lad."

"It seems she taught you a great deal."

"Aye, she did."

Heather reached for a rolled bandage. "Hold her arm up."

Enya grunted as he raised her delicate arm high enough for Heather to wrap it. Bran hated to see her in pain. If only he had been the one shot, she would not have to endure it.

Heather tied off the bandage and patted Enya's hand. "You need to find a corner where you can rest."

Bran held Enya's hand. "I can care for her from here."

The older woman tipped her head to the side. "Sir Bran, I daresay you look a mite worse than Miss Enya, and smell...well, the only word for it is foul."

"Apologies. I've no' had a chance to wash." He turned to Enya. "Mayhap I should leave ye here with Mistress Heather."

"No." She sat forward. "Heather, you must tend the wounds on his back. We can cleanse him with a cloth."

Heather shook her head. "But—"

"I'll be fine. You said it was but a graze."

"You've lost a lot of blood."

"It won't take but a moment." Enya pointed to a chair. "Sit."

Bran looked from Enya to Heather. "There's no use fighting."

Enya stood, but Heather eased her back into the chair. "I'll tend him. You stay put."

"But I have one good arm."

Heather tapped her foot. "And your eyes are rolling back as if you're about to swoon. Do as I say for once."

Bran removed his shirt and folded his arms on the table, resting his head atop them. Heather unwound the bandages that hadn't been changed since he'd visited Enya in the abbey. She sniffed. "It's foul."

"Mayhap ye should let it air."

She saturated a cloth with witch hazel. "'Tis a good idea, once it's cleansed. We'll reapply a honey poultice in the morn."

Bran tried not to grimace at the stinging pain. When Heather finished, she poured a tankard of whisky. "You both look like you could use this."

# Chapter Twenty-three

Enya spent what was left of the night nestled in Bran's embrace. Though her arm throbbed, contentment washed over her body with the waves that carried the ship to sea. Their plight, the unpleasant smells that soured below decks—nothing mattered. She was in Bran's arms, and naught would take her away from him this time.

A ray of daylight glimmered from the hatch. Footsteps clomped down the wooden stairs.

"Time to break our fast." John searched inside a hemp bag and pulled out two parcels wrapped in gauze. "Mutton and oatcakes."

Bran stirred. "Sounds like a royal feast after sampling the fare in the tolbooth."

"I'll take it up top. We left Glasgow with a fair bit more people aboard than we'd planned."

Enya and Bran followed the food up through the hold. Though hidden behind clouds, the sunlight glared. Enya rubbed her eyes and pulled her mantle close under her chin. A stiff breeze cut right through to her bones.

"Ye have a good sleep, lass?" asked Calum, manning the rudder.

"Aye. A mite bit better than the night before."

Heather moved out from under Malcolm's blanket. "Where we were both knocked silly by thieves on Glasgow Road."

Enya couldn't hide her grin. *Malcolm and Heather?* She never would have thought, but Heather deserved to be loved just as every soul.

"Ye havena had a good time of it, have ye?" Calum handed Enya an oatcake. "And how is yer arm?"

Enya flexed her fingers, which was about all the movement she could manage without sharp pain. "It aches a bit, but will be good as new in a few days."

Bran pointed to a castle looming in the distance. "That's Dunvegan on the Isle of Skye. They're MacLeod allies."

"We're in the Highlands?"

"Aye, the Hebrides, which are part of the Highland territories."

Enya's eyes glazed with tears—partly caused by the chilling wind and partly because this was everything she'd dreamt of. She was on an adventure, and she would have none other along than the man standing beside her. Bran tore off a piece of mutton and popped it in Griffon's beak. The bird flapped his wings and dug his claws into the roost. Aside from Enya's musket wound to the arm, they'd come out of danger fairly well.

Rewan handed Bran a satchel. "I found this at Langside. I reckon it fell off yer horse in the fighting."

"Thank ye." Bran opened it and pulled out the panel. "I thought I'd lost it."

"'Tis very kind of you, Rewan." Enya tapped her fingers to her mouth. "But I thought you and Bran weren't the best of friends."

Rewan shrugged. "Bran would have done the same had it been me."

A blast of wind blew Bran's hair across his face when he turned to her. "War has a way of mending disagreements."

Enya ran her fingers across the embroidery. "'Tis the only nice piece I've ever finished."

Bran wrapped his hand around her waist and squeezed. "When we arrive at Brochel, I shall hang it on the wall of me cottage and 'twill never go missing again." As they rounded the point of Skye, Bran pointed. "'That's the Isle of Rona. 'Tis too rocky but for a band of cutthroat pirates." Then Enya followed his finger to the right. A larger isle came into view, covered with rock and bracken fern. "And that's Raasay."

"A sight for sore eyes," Rewan said. "No' as mighty as Lewis, of course, but a bonny sight all the same."

Calum clapped him on the back. "That it is."

Heather and Malcolm stood beside the group, all lining the rail of the boat, making it list slightly.

Calum smoothed his hands over his hair, worry creasing his brow. "We'll have no rest when we arrive. Ross and the king's men will be after us." He regarded Malcolm. "Where do your loyalties lie?"

Malcolm glanced to Heather and then looked the laird in the eye. "Ross would have let me hang to save his own neck from the gallows." He nodded to Enya. "No disrespect, miss."

"None taken."

Bran squeezed her hand. "I can vouch for Malcolm. He's true to his word."

The galley sailed down the east coast of Raasay. Enya gasped. Rising from a stony crag, a magnificent castle surrounded by stone outer bailey walls presided over the white sands of a moon-shaped beach. Bran nuzzled against her hair. "Brochel Castle, m'lady."

"'Tis enormous."

"She supports some two hundred seventy odd souls."

As they approached, the beach swarmed with people running down a zigzag path. Men splashed into the water and John threw them a rope. Calum jumped over the side and waded through the surf to a lovely blonde woman. He swung her in a circle and then picked up two boys and twirled with them.

"That's Lady Anne and the lads. Alexander is the eldest and Ian the stout little tyke."

"They look happy."

"Aye."

It took several men to drag the galley onto the sand. Bran helped Enya alight and Malcolm did the same for Heather. Mayhap this was a blessing for them as well.

Calum addressed the crowd. "We've brought our brother, Bran, back from the gallows of Glasgow, but with it, we've unleashed a dragon. Regent Moray will soon be at our gates. We shall celebrate Bran's return with a gathering tonight, and on the morrow, we will strengthen the guard and send word to Lewis." He turned to Rewan. "Will ye stay and fight with us?"

Rewan stepped beside him. "Aye, I'll stand beside ye—make no bones about it."

Calum wrapped his arm around Lady Anne's shoulders. "Very good. Kill a steer, for we shall have a gathering and celebrate our good fortune this eve."

Lady Anne stepped forward and grasped Enya's hands. "Welcome to Brochel." And then she turned and greeted Heather with the same warm address. Her accent was English, and she had an aristocratic air, as if she were bred for royalty.

Bran made the introductions. "Lady Anne, Miss Enya Ross and Mistress Heather."

A spry woman in a white wimple bustled through the sand. "And I'm Mistress Mara, John's wife."

Anne gestured toward the path leading to the castle. "You must be exhausted after your ordeal. Come, we shall find some clean clothes for you and a hot bath."

Enya glanced down at her filthy mantle and gown. "Thank you, m'lady. That would be lovely."

Bran tugged on Enya's waist and pulled her against him. "We'll find ye some clothes and then I've other plans."

His warmth heated her skin. Enya liked the sound of that.

A portly friar with a ring of grey hair, wearing a brown habit, stood at the top of the path. He leaned on a wooden staff. "I see ye've brought a number of souls from the Lowlands."

"Friar Patrick MacSween." Bran wrapped him in a smothering hug. "'Tis good to see ye."

---

Bran took the friar aside. "I need a pot of yer honey poultice. Musket shot grazed Miss Enya's arm and me back is healing from a round of two dozen lashes."

Friar Pat grimaced. "Ye got yerself in a bit o' strife, didna ye, lad?"

"Let's just say I've never been so happy to be home."

The friar slapped his back. "We'll see ye fixed up."

Bran's knees nearly gave out with the stinging pain. "Aye, and after, I need to discuss a wedding with ye."

The friar's eyes grew round as shillings. "Oh? That pretty ginger-haired lassie has turned yer head?"

Lady Anne looped her arm through Enya's and led her through the big oak doors of the great hall. Bran waved when Enya regarded him over her shoulder, and grinned at the friar. "Aye. She's won me heart, I canna deny it." He cocked his head toward the galley, where Griffon cawed from his perch. "I'll take Griffon to his mews and see ye in the hall."

---

Bran leaned against the doorjamb and watched while Mara and Lady Anne doted over Enya and Heather. They hadn't noticed him yet, allowing him to observe without the women being inhibited. He couldn't remember seeing four women have so much fun, not ever. Mara held a green kirtle against Enya's shoulders. "Ye're about me size, and this one will go perfectly with yer eyes."

Lady Anne dug in a trunk and shook out a linen shift. "One of the elders passed, and I stowed her things, thinking they might come in handy one day." She turned to Heather and held it up. "Yes, this will suit splendidly."

"Thank you so much." Enya took the green dress and twirled in a circle. "Your generosity is too kind."

"'Tis the least we can do." Anne pulled out every womanly garment imaginable and tossed them on the bed. "And I do hope you'll be staying a long time. 'Tis rare to receive visitors on Raasay."

Malcolm stepped beside Bran and the women looked his way.

"Sir Bran," Anne said. "I'm told you were knighted into the esteemed Order of the Thistle."

Lady Anne could make the heat rise to Bran's face like no other. She'd been doing it since he was two and ten. "Aye, m'lady."

"Well, there's not a young man who deserves it more than you." She beckoned him inside. "Come and look at all the pretty things we've found in these old trunks."

Bran shrugged at Malcolm. "I guess we've been captured."

"Och, I should have stayed in the armory." He pointed to his hip. "At least I found an old claymore to use until I can have the blacksmith fashion me a new one."

"Have ye found a place to bed down?"

"Aye, there's an empty chamber in the tower."

Bran placed his hand on Malcolm's shoulder. "Good. I hope ye plan to stay. We'll make a Highlander out of ye yet."

Enya reached for Bran's hand. "I desperately need to bathe before I change into these things. 'Tis so thoughtful of Mara to lend them to me."

"Gratitude, Mara, ye are a fine matron." Bran bowed. "But I'd like to borrow Miss Enya for a bit."

Lady Anne shot him a knowing smile and held up Enya's pile of garments. "Do not be late for the gathering."

Bran took them. "Yes, m'lady."

Heather looked from Bran to Enya with her mouth gaping, but Malcolm gave her shoulders a firm squeeze. "Aye, Heather. I've ordered a hot bath for you, and after, I'll be next."

Bran tugged on Enya's uninjured arm. "Come, let's away afore someone stops us."

Enya followed him down the donjon stairs. "Where are you taking me?"

"Ye'll see."

"Did you bring Griffon from the boat?"

"Aye, he's secure in his mews. I didna think an eagle could show emotion, but I daresay he was happy to be home."

Enya looked up at him. "As are you?"

"Aye."

They walked through the busy courtyard with chickens cackling and the clang of the blacksmith echoing across the stone battlements.

Enya's eyes darted everywhere, taking it all in. "My, 'tis like a town, so much different from Halkhead."

"Aye, Halkhead is an estate that serves one family. Brochel is an extended family. We all work for the good of the clan."

He pushed through the back gates of the outer bailey walls and pointed toward his home. "Come. I lit the fire in me cottage and hung a pot of water over the hearth."

Enya looked up the hill. "Your cottage?"

Bran bit his lip. "Aye. Like I said, 'tis small, but it's mine."

She rushed ahead. "'Tis darling."

Bran thought so too. With a thatched roof and strong stone walls, he'd even purchased glass for the windows on their last voyage. He clutched her clothing under his arm and hurried alongside her to open the door. "M'lady."

Enya stepped inside, her eyes wide as a child's. She turned a full circle in the center of the main room. "'Tis adorable."

Bran pointed to her panel, now hanging on the wall. "And this will always remind ye of yer home."

Enya cocked her head and admired it. "I think it suits there."

Bran ran his fingers around Enya's waist and pulled her into his embrace. "I'm so happy ye think so, *mo leannan*."

She rose on her toes and kissed his lips. "Your cottage is cozy, Sir Bran."

His heart thundered in his chest. He loved this place, loved the warmth and comfort of it, and it was ever so important she did too. He took her hand and led her to doorway of the bedchamber. "And this is the sleeping quarters." The large bed took up most of the space. "There's a small antechamber at the back for clothes and storage."

Enya spun into the room with her skirts circling wide. "It looks like you have everything you need, right here." She faced him, her expression quite serious. "I do believe this cottage has more space than my chamber at Halkhead."

Bran cast his mind back to the one time he'd seen it. The comparison had to be close. "Ye're probably right there." He took her hand and led her to the hearth. "Come."

He pulled the wooden washtub into the center of the room. "We both could use a bath." He picked up the iron tongs and clamped them around the kettle handle. "The water should be warm enough now."

Bran emptied the steaming kettle into the tub and then topped it off with a bucket of cool. He stood and stared at her, dipping his chin. Suddenly, this didn't seem like his cottage at all. Enya stepped into him and brushed her hand across his cheek. "There's nothing I'd like better than a bath."

It seemed she always knew the right thing to say. "Ye should go first." He took a drying cloth from the shelf and placed it on a chair. "Would ye like me to help? Um, s-seeing yer arm is injured."

A blush crawled up her lovely cheeks. "Aye."

As Bran stepped up to her, Enya's breath stuttered. She was as nervous as he. His fingers trembled as he untied her laces. "I've dreamt of this moment."

"I still can't believe I'm standing here with you."

Slowly, he removed her mantle overdress. He unlaced her kirtle and it slid easily down over her injured arm and hips. He toyed with the lace that secured her shift just above her stays. His gaze drifted down. Her breasts swelled proud over the thin fabric, breasts he feared he'd never see again when he was imprisoned in the tolbooth.

Licking his lips, he reached for the laces of Enya's stays. "Nearly done. I hope I'm no' hurting ye."

"You are far gentler than Heather."

He pulled away the contraption, enforced with wooden slats. Bran had no idea how women could tolerate the damnable things. He cast it aside, grinning at her. Bran slid his finger along the neckline of her shift. "Do ye think this will fit over yer hips? I canna imagine the pain of raising yer arms."

She blinked at him seductively. "It should. Loosen it all the way."

Bran managed to slip the shift from her shoulders. It fell to her hips and she chuckled. Bran's cock jutted against his sporran—one tug and her womanhood would be exposed to him. Oh how he wanted to forget about the bath and carry her to the bed. But it would be so much sweeter if they waited.

He could have come when he pulled the shift down past her hips—with one tug, it slipped away easily, exposing the alluring triangle of her precious treasure. Bran had to stop for a moment to steady his breathing. His long bout with little food and the pain in his back had sapped his stamina, or so he told himself.

Skin as smooth as pure cream milk, Bran could not tear his eyes away. "Ye're beautiful."

He reached out her good arm, but Bran gestured to the tub. "The water's growing cold, m'lady."

She stepped toward him and slid her fingers into the waist of his kilt. "I want you to join me."

His cock shot to rigid. "But there's no' enough room." His voice rasped, barely audible.

She unfastened his belt and let it drop to the floor along with everything else. "I can tell you want to." She cast her gaze down to his manhood, tenting beneath his linen shirt. "Besides, we'll both fit if we stand."

Bran grinned. He liked her way of thinking. "Ye have a way of scheming until ye have everything ye want."

She tugged open the laces of his shirt. "Aye. There's nay use of arguing with me."

Bran whipped his shirt over his head. With one hand, Enya untied his bandages and unwound them, dancing around him like a maypole.

Completely bare, he pulled her naked body against his. "Should we forget the bath?"

"Oh, no." She pulled him to the tub and stepped into the water. "This will be far too much fun."

# Chapter twenty-four

Tingles coursed across her skin in anticipation of Bran's hands upon her. Enya bent down, picked up the cake of soap and held it to her nose. "Mm. Cinnamon. It smells of you."

"Aye, we brought back barrels of it from Tortuga."

She lathered it into a washcloth. "I love it." He started to pull her into his embrace, but she shook her head. "Wait."

He took the cloth and soap from her. "Ye first, m'lady."

Enya opened her mouth to protest, but promptly shut it and moaned when he reached around and kneaded her back with the wet, warm cloth. As he moved along, gooseflesh formed where the cloth had been. She shivered with titillating anticipation.

He lathered every inch of her body with the soap but stopped at her womanhood. Hunger filled his eyes, his breathing shallow. "How?"

She parted her legs, longing for him to touch her at last. "There too."

His fingers trembled as he ever so slowly ran the cloth along her sacred spot. Erotically, his fingers brushed her through the thin cloth. Enya moved with him, her hips sliding across his hand. She swallowed, willing herself not to succumb to the friction. Not yet.

"I think ye'd best sit so I can wash yer hair."

Bran straddled his legs. There was just enough room for her to sit between them. He reached for a tankard and ladled it over her long tresses and massaged in the soap, his fingers lulling her.

"How do ye ever comb out the tangle?" His voice was but a whisper.

"Heather is quite skilled at it, though it feels like she's trying to pull it out one strand at a time."

When he poured the last tankard of water over her head, Enya stood, dripping wet. She filled her eyes with every ripple of his muscular form, and then to his swollen manhood. She wanted to touch it, but resisted. "Your turn."

"Och, 'tis too cold for you to stand and bathe me."

Enya calmed her shivers and reached for the washcloth and soap. "The fire will warm me fast enough. I wouldn't miss this for all the gold in my father's chest."

She swirled the soap in the cloth, considering how she would begin. She could wrap it around his proud manhood, which had teased her relentlessly, but she got a better idea. She stepped out of the tub. "You sit."

"But—"

"I want you to."

The water nearly flowed over the top of the barrel when he slid his large frame into the tepid water. The fit was so snug, his knees practically touched his chin. But Enya persevered, though she could use only one hand. She started by massaging the suds into his shoulders, careful to avoid contact with his lash marks.

"Does the water hurt your wounds?"

"Stung a bit at first, but it's eased now."

"Lean forward."

Enya gently poured water over his hair and massaged in the cinnamon-scented suds.

Bran moaned, long and soft. "Who would ken a bath could feel so heavenly? I never want ye to take yer hands off me."

She left the best part for last. After slathering the cloth with soap, she stroked it over his groin. Bran's eyes rolled back. "Blessed Jesus, ye are after me soul."

Enya kissed his forehead. "Aye, so you may as well relax and let me claim it." She cleansed his erection and the tight ballocks beneath.

Bran clasped his hands around her fingers. "If ye keep going, ye'll unman me."

She formed an O with her lips. "We certainly cannot have that. Not yet, at least." She tried to unfold his drying cloth with one hand, but it dropped to the floor. In seconds, Bran snatched it up and wrapped it around her shoulders, drying every last droplet that remained on Enya's skin.

He swathed her hair. "Would ye like me to comb out yer tresses?"

Gooseflesh of anticipation trickled along her skin. "I think they can wait." Enya reached for the cloth and smoothed it across his hard frame. "But there's something more urgent that cannot."

Running her hand over every inch of Bran's body had turned her insides to liquid. She led him to the bedroom and turned. Bran cupped her face in his hands and kissed her. His eyes closed tight. His face expressed the deep emotion that also burned inside her. She ran her hand to his back and he grunted a bit when her fingers hit scar tissue.

She rested her forehead on his chest. "How are we to do this with our injuries?"

"Can ye no' lie on yer back?" Bran chuckled into her hair. "There are other ways, if ye're an adventurous lass."

Enya's insides leapt. "Have you been keeping secrets from me now?"

"Nay, but ye are a fine lady, one who mightn't care to be bent over the bed or taken against the wall."

The insides of her thighs quivered. She rose up on her toes and kissed him, his manhood tapping against her abdomen, sending her insides fluttering with desire. "Are you full of undiscovered pleasures?"

"Would ye like to try?"

"Have you ever known me not to be willing to face adventure?" She lifted her arm slightly. It hurt, but she wouldn't let on. "Besides, my arm is healing. What would you have me do, sir knight?"

Bran rubbed his member against her belly, and then led her to the bed. "Bend at the waist and lay yer torso across it. Ye can rest yer head in the crux of yer good arm."

Enya did as told. Her anticipation grew hot with her bare bottom presenting over the edge of the bed. "Like this?"

"Aye, perfect." His voice trembled. "Now spread yer legs."

Enya did as he asked, and Bran slid a hand under her belly and stroked the spot that turned her sex molten. She arched her back. "Mm. That feels unbelievable."

He placed his manhood between her legs and stroked her with it, back and forth until it was slick with her moisture. Enya could see nothing, but his stroking took her excitement to a level near bursting.

Bran leaned over and showered kisses across her neck as his hand worked its magic. "I want to enter ye."

"Aye. I need you inside me." God, did she ever. She moved her hips with his rhythm. "Now. Please."

Bran tickled the front of her mons as he slid inside. "Does this please ye, Enya?"

She could scarcely breathe, let alone reply. "Faster," she uttered, pushing against him, his finger making her frantic with the need to burst. She rocked back with each thrust, his finger working in circles around that spot. She closed her eyes and dug her fingers into the bedclothes, every inch of her skin on fire. "Take me, Bran. Take me!" Her body tensed as spasms racked through her. Bran thrust deep inside and roared, moving his hands to her hips and holding his manhood inside as it pulsed.

Panting, he bent over her, his manhood still pulsing inside her body. "I love ye, *mo leannan*."

She relaxed into the soft folds of the mattress. "And I you."

"Ye must marry me, for soon I'll have ye with child."

Enya's heart swelled. "I would marry you with child or not."

He nuzzled into her neck. "I shall ask the friar to set the date and it will be done."

Enya rolled over and pulled him onto the bed beside her. "My father will not rest. I haven't had a chance to tell you I nearly shot Robert during your escape. He and my father were giving chase."

"Aye, Calum expects retaliation, but they willna come after us without ships and cannons. They ken the might of Raasay. No one walks onto our beach and makes demands."

Enya curled into a ball. Must her every action cause disaster? "'Tis all my fault."

Resting on his side, Bran gently caressed her. He ran his hand down the length of her good arm. "Nay, lass. Ye helped me escape.

'Tis yer father who's wrong. He doesna understand I love ye and will dedicate me life to seeing to yer happiness."

"I am happy, Bran." Her insides fluttered with his kisses teasing her neck. "So how many other positions are there for us to try?"

He cupped her cheek and chuckled. "Och, ye are full of surprises. Mayhap we can concoct a few of our own."

"I'd relish that." She stroked her hand along his member. "Shall we start now?"

"I'd like nothing more, but we're expected in the hall."

Enya's bottom lip jutted out. "Ah yes, the gathering."

## Chapter Twenty-five

It took longer to dress than it did to undress. With no head covering in her pile of borrowed clothes, Enya opted to wear her damp hair in a braid down her back. They managed to arrive at the great hall just as everyone was being seated. The chamber swarmed with family groups and people of all ages. Halkhead had entertained large groups, but it was a family manse, and the crofters who tilled Ross land and paid fealty to her father all lived and dined in their own cottages.

This was more akin to what she'd read about from the times of the great kings like Robert the Bruce. Of course, she was well aware Highland clans still lived as a community within the bailey walls of big castles, but it was not as common to see in Renfrewshire. After all, this was the sixteenth century.

Bran led her to the table where Sir Malcolm sat with Heather. "Do ye mind if we join ye?"

Malcolm gestured to the wooden bench. "Please do."

Bran helped Enya to sit then Calum bellowed from the dais. "I expect me henchman to dine with me."

Enya shot Heather an apologetic look. "I'm sorry. Are you settling in?"

Heather's cheeks glowed rosy red with a sideways glance at Malcolm. "Aye." She gestured toward the dais. "You'd better go."

"I'll find you later?"

Heather nodded and shooed her away with a flick of her hand. When the kitchen doors burst open, Enya's mouth watered with the tempting smells of roasted meat and fresh oat bread. Her stomach growled and she smiled inwardly. She'd worked up quite an appetite with the activities at Sir Bran's cottage.

Calum stood to greet them. "I see ye found a cake of soap."

Everyone at the table laughed. Prickly heat crept up Enya's cheeks. They all looked at her as if they knew what she and Bran had been up to—most likely they did.

Anne gestured to the seat beside her. "Miss Enya, you must sit beside me. I see Mara's kirtle fits you perfectly."

Enya reluctantly released Bran's hand as he took a seat across from Calum. She hated to be separated from him even for a minute. Mara sat directly across from her, and Bran sat next to Mara. If Enya stood, she'd be able to stretch across the table and touch him. Calum had his retinue with John, Bran and Calum's brother, Norman, at one end, and Lady Anne, Mara and Enya at the other. Friar Pat sat on Enya's right.

"Where are the lads?" Enya asked.

"We're allowing them to eat at their friend's table tonight." It was odd hearing Lady Anne's proper English accent in contrast to the Highlanders.

Mara leaned in. "They're with me Samuel, on strict orders to behave themselves."

"That'd take a miracle," Friar Pat mumbled into his tankard of ale, making the sign of the cross.

Trenchers of meat and vegetables arrived. Enya poured a tot of ale into her tankard. "Lady Anne, you must tell me how you ended up on Raasay, married to a Scottish laird."

She exchanged a knowing look with Mara. "Hasn't Bran told the story?"

"Only you were the daughter of an English earl, and Calum fought an entire English armada to win your hand." Enya fanned herself at the romantic adventure of the story.

Lady Anne glanced at Calum, who nodded his approval. "Well, my uncle arranged for me to be wed by proxy." She stabbed a piece of meat with her eating knife and looked up with a frown. "To a much older, despicable man."

"How awful."

"I thought so too, but then the ship taking me to him was pillaged by pirates."

Enya clutched her fists against her chest. "You must have been terrified."

"I was." She grasped Calum's hand and kissed it. "Until Laird Calum kicked in my door, brandishing his mammoth sword, mind you."

Enya gasped and gaped at Calum, her gaze trailing to Bran. "You're pirates?"

Bran stuttered with a panicked grimace, but Calum raised his tankard. "Privateers, if ye will."

"I call Calum the Robin Hood of Raasay," John added. "He's responsible for the clan's livelihood."

Wide-eyed, Enya again looked at Bran and mouthed, "Pirates?"

He leaned back in his chair, spreading his palms apologetically. "What can I say? I told ye we sailed to Tortuga—just like Captain Drake."

Drake? He was Queen Elizabeth's sea captain. Enya studied the jovial faces at the table and wondered what other unsavory things she might discover about them.

Lady Anne patted the back of Enya's hand. "Calum limits his activities to goodwill cruises for the health and wellbeing of the clan."

"Aye," Bran said. "We'd never plunder a ship that didna deserve it."

Enya dropped her jaw. "Deserve it?"

Calum winked. "An enemy vessel."

"I see." Enya looked to Friar Pat, who was now taking a swig from a whisky flask. "And what say you about their privateering activities, friar?"

His nose shone red as he stoppered the flask. "The good Lord has seen fit to provision us with bounty from the sea. Calum's a worthy laird, lassie. Near eleven year ago, the clan would have starved if weren't for him and his philanthropic ways."

"Philanthropic?"

"Aye, he saved the clan."

"What a remarkable place this is." Of course, Enya had heard the Highlands was a place that harbored lawless thieves and pirates, but had thought it all balderdash. She watched the happy faces at the table—they were definitely not scowling with danger, as the Gypsies had been when they attacked her in the forest. *Privateers?* That definitely did sound more respectable.

Lady Anne clapped her hands. "We shall have music and dancing."

Tables at the far end of the hall were being pushed aside while the piper filled his bagpipes with air, the familiar bray filling the hall.

Once they'd eaten, Bran walked around the table and bowed. "Will ye dance with me, Miss Enya?"

She loved it when he acted with chivalry, but she couldn't resist teasing. As she stood, she pressed her lips against his ear so only he could hear. "Aye, if ye'll promise to plunder me again this night."

He flashed on of his devilish grins. "On that ye have me word."

Enya couldn't recall seeing him smile quite so broadly as they moved to the dance floor for a high-stepping reel. She stood across from Bran, and down the line of dancers, Heather and Malcolm were a pair. Enya loved how they looked at each other. She would have to find out more when she could steal some time alone with Heather. How wonderful it would be if the matron had found love.

The music started and Enya curtseyed. Careful not to pull on her injured arm, she and Bran swung in a circle, but when they sashayed down the line, she was partnered with a man who looped his arm through hers and barreled around for the turn. Enya doubled over with the pain, clasping the sore arm against her body.

Bran was instantly beside her. "Enya! Are ye all right?"

The music stopped. "'Tis just my arm. I should have put it in a sling."

"Ye're white as a calla lily." He wrapped an arm around her waist. "Come—mayhap we should watch the dancing tonight. Ye need to rest yer arm lest it start bleeding again."

They spent the remainder of the evening sitting on the dais with Calum and Anne.

Calum tugged on Bran's shirtsleeve. "We can expect an attack, 'tis for certain."

"When?" Bran asked.

"A week, mayhap two. I want to meet with the guard on the morrow."

"Have ye sentries posted?"

"Aye, of course. We'll see them coming a day ahead. I want ye to stay in the keep."

Bran's gaze darted to Enya. "After tonight, m'laird?"

Heat crawled up her face when Calum raised a red brow and shot her a sideways glance. "Agreed, but be in the courtyard at dawn."

---

Before heading to the cottage, Bran took Enya to the kitchens. A woman he dearly loved, with a careworn face, her head covered by a grey wimple, opened her arms. "Son. 'Tis good to have ye home."

Bran encircled her in his arms. He inhaled the familiar sent of fresh bread and the cooking fire as his mother's matronly body embraced him. "I have someone I'd like ye to meet." He grasped Enya's hand. "This is Miss Enya, I've asked her to marry me."

Enya curtseyed, bowing her head. "'Tis an honor to meet you, mistress."

Mother grasped Enya's shoulders and studied her face. "Ye are a lovely lass. I can tell by yer eyes ye've spirit."

Bran chuckled. "Aye, that she does."

"Well, ye'll need it being married to the likes of Bran." She wiped her hands on her apron. "I never thought I'd see the day when a lassie would steal my lad's heart."

Bran gave her a peck on the cheek. "I need some oatcakes for the morn. Can ye fix up a basket?"

"Aye." She pulled a basket from under the table and lined it with a linen cloth. "I hear ye're from Renfrewshire, Miss Enya."

"Halkhead. My father—" Enya looked at Bran, biting her lip.

"Her da's a land baron. He's none too happy she's here."

Mother placed a handful of oatcakes in the basket and folded the cloth over it. "I ken there had to be a catch. Ye couldna come back here with a lass from Lewis, or Skye?"

"Well, what'd ye expect? Calum got his baroness."

Mother chuckled and handed him the basket. "That he did, and ye always had a fondness for Lady Anne. I suppose 'tis fitting." She clasped Enya's hand. "Ye have me blessing."

Enya raised his mother's hand to her lips and kissed it. "Thank you."

Bran took her out the kitchen door to avoid being stopped in the hall. They were both exhausted and he wanted Enya alone—at least for the night. A week would be preferable, but he'd take what he could.

"What will I do when you're staying in the keep?" Enya asked.

"I'll try to find an empty chamber for us. Dunna worry. I'll see ye're cared for." He pushed through the door to his cottage and pulled her into his embrace. "But I dunna want to think on it tonight. For right now, in this moment, there is only you and me and this cottage. 'Tis all that matters."

---

The cock had begun to crow when Bran stood at the side of the bed and pulled the bedclothes over Enya's sleeping form. In slumber, her hair cascaded across the pillow in silken waves of auburn. Devoid of a blemish, her profile reminded him of a goddess. He would love her forever. He would protect her with his life. If her father came, the baron would have to kill him before Bran would let her go.

Bran hated to leave Enya alone, but Calum needed him in the courtyard. Last eve they'd made love until they both were so tired neither one could stay awake for a moment longer. After finding a slip of parchment, he took a cooled cinder from the fireplace and carefully wrote, *I love you.* With a kiss, he rested it against the basket and slipped out the door.

Malcolm stood off to the side as the MacLeod guard surrounded Calum. Bran cuffed the former Ross captain on the shoulder. "Come. Ye're one of us now."

Calum stood with his fists on his hips. "Ye're all aware we have a few new faces among us. In addition, our brother Bran was sentenced to be gibbeted at the Glasgow Tolbooth."

The crowd rumbled with disapproval.

"I couldna stand by and allow Regent Moray's men to send Bran to such a long, agonizing death." Calum scanned across the crowd. "And Bran has brought Miss Enya with him, daughter of Lord Ross of Renfrewshire. There will be retaliation. Of that I have no doubt."

"And now we have Ross's henchman fighting alongside us?" asked William MacLeod.

"Former henchman," Malcolm replied. "Ross left me in the tolbooth to rot along with Sir Bran."

Bran placed his hand on Malcolm's shoulder. "If any man doubts Malcolm's loyalty, ye can take issue with me. I would fight beside him, though I've four and twenty lashes on me back to tell me differently. Ross betrayed Malcolm just as he betrayed me and our cousin, Rewan of Lewis."

Calum drew his sword. "We need to prepare for what may come. Let no enemy breach the walls of Brochel."

The men cheered as Calum thrust his claymore into the air.

Bran drew his sword and gave Malcolm a nudge. "Spar with me today. The men will grow to accept ye. It just takes time."

The night's rest had done Bran some good and he lunged into action. He liked sparring with Malcolm and they would both need to rebuild their strength. The tension from impending calamity grew with each clang of the swords.

---

Calum watched Malcolm appreciatively. "Ye fight like that and ye can be a part of the MacLeod guard for as long as ye are able."

Bran gave the older man a good run, but if Calum had to choose, Bran would be his man. He'd grown stronger since he'd left him in Renfrewshire. A grand mistake that was, coming back with a highborn lass. Calum was too old for this. He'd already met the wrath of the English nobility when he fought for Anne ten years ago. He surely didn't need a battle now, but there was little doubt Ross would come with an army. Especially with Bran a fugitive.

"Malcolm." Calum beckoned the Ross man with a wave of his hand. "Come. We've things to discuss."

Calum led the Lowlander into the donjon and up to the solar on the second floor. He closed the door and reached for a flagon. "A tot of whisky?"

"Aye, thank you, m'laird."

Calum poured two tots and gestured to a chair at the table. "Please, sit."

Malcolm complied and sipped the whisky. "'Tis a fine castle ye have here. Secluded from the mainland."

"Aye, and that's how I like it." Calum threw back his drink and swiped his sleeve across his mouth. "What are Ross's forces like now the effort to reinstate the queen failed?"

"I'd reckon he has about a third of what he had when we marched on Langside—mayhap fifty men."

Calum poured another round and sat in the chair at the head of the table. "Do ye ken if the regent will be inclined to help him?"

"I think so, especially since Bran escaped the tolbooth." Malcolm tapped his finger against the cup. "Me as well, I suppose. Ross will want to come after Enya and he'll leverage the fact we escaped to bend Mr. Fisher's ear."

Calum looked out the window and watched a wispy cloud sail by. "But the hangings will delay them for a fortnight at least. Wouldna ye say?"

"Aye, I doubt they would pull forces out of Glasgow until the spectacle's over—too much risk of retaliation."

"They'd no' want to lose any more prisoners either." Calum sipped his drink. "Anyone who knows these waters will bring cannons."

"But there are no ships with cannons the size of yours. Not in Glasgow for certain—they'd have to sail around from Edinburgh."

Calum swirled the amber liquid thoughtfully. "That's a good thing for us, but I'd like to avoid bloodshed. 'Tis no' a wise thing to be on the wrong side of the regent. It could make me old age very uncomfortable."

Malcolm scratched his chin. Arching his thick brows, his eyes bugged wide and a slow smile spread across his face, as if he'd come up with an answer to this miserable parcel of woes.

## Chapter Twenty-six

Enya wrapped a plaid around her bare shoulders and looked for Bran. Though clean, the cottage was rather stark. The only hanging on the wall was her panel. Near the door was an assortment of weapons—including a longbow, of course. She ran her finger along the cold barrel of a musket—a dangerous weapon that had become increasingly popular. Her arm throbbed, reminding her she could have been killed by a similar weapon.

The main room had an enormous hearth with a wrought-iron kettle suspended over the fire by a swinging arm. Neatly stacked beside it were a bake stone and a butter churn, with a ladle and other cast iron utensils hanging against the stone.

The embers of the fire glowed, and sitting on the hearth's step was a ewer. How thoughtful of Bran to warm water for her. Enya sat at the table and reached in the basket, pulling out an oatcake. A piece of parchment flopped over. With a grin, she picked it up. *I love you.*

She raised it to her lips and kissed. So much had changed since Bran had ridden through the gates of Halkhead House. He was so unlike other men. He respected her, did little things for her, like leaving a note and a ewer of warm water. Taking a bite of oatcake, she cast her gaze across the warm cottage—the wooden table, a rocking chair in the corner. She could be content here, but she'd have to improve her needlepoint and add some splashes of color. Perhaps she could learn to weave.

She found her archer figurine and placed it on the mantel. When Enya resumed her seat, she looked at it and smiled.

Bran would be a fine husband and a caring father. She ran a hand over her flat belly and hoped she would bear his children one day. She had never given much thought to the prospect of being a mother, but now Bran shared her life, it seemed as natural as breathing.

She only hoped she would be accepted by the clan. If Anne was any indication, there should be no trouble. But she had noticed some slanted looks when she danced with Bran last eve. Mayhap it was because of her injured arm. She must have looked awkward holding it against her body. Enya moved the offending appendage, raising it higher than before. A good night's sleep had helped it heal some.

Enya frowned at the last of the oatcake sitting on the table. Her stomach churned a bit—odd, she'd never had trouble finishing one before. With a shrug, Enya took the ewer into the bedroom and filled the bowl. She cast aside the plaid and gave herself a quick splash bath. Mara had given her a clean shift and she pulled it over her head. Her good arm slipped through the sleeve just fine, but she couldn't pull it down far enough to slip her injured arm in. Finally, she gritted her teeth and forced her arm through, the pain tearing her skin and stinging. It was far easier when Bran was there to help.

But she was no ninny. Enya must learn to endure hardship, and this was a good place to start. She wrapped her stays around her torso with the laces in front. Holding one side in place by clutching her sore arm against her body, she tightened the laces. Her breasts ached as the stays tightened, her nipples sensitive to the slightest pressure. She opted to keep the laces relatively loose.

Having learned from her shift, she stepped into her kirtle and pulled it over her hips. She secured the laces and tied the front bodice. Then she picked up the dirty clothes she and Bran had cast aside the night before and stepped outside in search of the well and washbasin. If this was the life for her, she'd start by doing the washing. Enya chuckled. Her mother would have one of her spells if she could see her now.

With the washing hanging in front of the hearth, Enya set out to look for Bran. She wanted him to see her handiwork—she'd even accomplished it with one hand. Well, she'd hiked up her skirts and stomped on the washing in the barrel to ensure the clothes were clean. She'd seen the serving maids do that before. If she'd known how satisfying doing the washing was, Enya would have hiked up her skirts and sloshed in a barrel ages ago. Besides, the work would be much easier once she regained full use of her arm.

Bran would be so pleased. She couldn't wait to show him. Enya skipped through the back gate of the outer bailey walls and found him sparring in the courtyard. Where else would that man be at this time of day? Without his shirt, of course.

Enya found a bench where she could watch. Bran wielded his sword like no one she'd ever seen. He sparred with Malcolm, who was giving him a good run, but was clearly not as strong or agile as Bran, the younger man. Her solar plexus tightened in concert with every ripple of Bran's muscles. She could stare at him all day—a human sculpture in action.

Friar Pat ambled beside her, leaning on his walking stick. "He's a strapping lad, our Bran."

"Aye. He taught the men at Halkhead a thing or two." Enya smiled. "You ken Queen Mary got away at Langside because Bran fought off Moray's men? 'Tis why he was caught."

"I heard as much from Calum, but it didna surprise me." Pat gestured to the path. "Would ye like to take a stroll through me garden, Miss Enya?"

"Aye. I've heard ye are quite skilled with healing herbs."

"I do what I can."

"You should talk to Mistress Heather. She was the healer at Halkhead."

The friar led her to a path that cut into a tall hedge bordering the courtyard. "I would enjoy that. One can never stop learning."

Beyond the hedge, the garden opened up into rows and rows of sprouting plants. Friar Pat waved his staff across the picture. "Thank the good Lord winter is gone and God has seen fit to bless us with a fine start to the season's crops."

"My, yes. I daresay you'll have a wonderful harvest."

"Do ye like to work in the garden?"

"I'm embarrassed to admit I never have, but I'm not afraid to try."

"There's a good lass. I'd enjoy your company any time ye have a mind to till the soil." He walked on a bit and gestured to a bench. "Would ye sit with an old friar?"

"Of course."

His knees cracked as he leaned forward and popped down. Enya took a seat beside him, wondering how old he was.

The friar's blue eyes sparkled when he looked at her. "Bran spoke to me about marriage."

Enya's heart fluttered. "Aye. He told me he would."

"I can see he cares very deeply for ye."

"We are kindred spirits. I love him very much."

"But me guess is Raasay is a far cry from the life ye're used to."

Enya nodded. "My life in Renfrewshire is over. I can never go back."

"Is that why ye want to marry Bran?"

"Of course not. I would marry him no matter what." Enya smoothed her hands over her skirts. "The only thing keeping us apart was my father."

The friar inhaled deeply and looked toward the sky. "But yer father's desires are important. The Bible tells us to honor thy father and mother."

"Aye. I'd like to honor him, but he does not honor me—he only wishes to lock me in the nunnery on Iona until he can arrange a marriage that will benefit the family."

Friar Pat shook his head. "The way of highborn marriages has always escaped me. 'Twas the same when Lady Anne and Calum were courting, and it caused a great deal of bloodshed and heartache."

"In watching them last night, my guess is it was worth it."

His eyes glazed with a faraway glint. "Aye, it was." Friar Pat tapped Enya's knee. "Though I must say I'm concerned about yer father coming to claim ye. Ye wouldn't want his blood on yer hands, would ye?"

Enya tightly folded her hands in her lap. She recalled having Robert in her sights and how awful she'd felt knowing she could have killed her own brother. So much had happened and she'd little time to think about it. "I'd prefer a peaceful resolution, of course." Her voice was but a whisper. "But Bran was convicted of treason—the might of Scotland could very well befall us."

The friar leaned all his weight on his staff and stood. "I think we should hold off on this wedding until all this uncertainty is behind us—mayhap a month."

Enya's stomach clenched. She didn't want to wait, not even a few days. "That long?"

He placed a warm mitt on her shoulder and squeezed. "When ye've been on this earth as long as I have, a month passes in a blink of an eye."

Bran strode through the garden, pulling his shirt over his head. "I thought I saw the friar spirit ye back to his plot of dirt."

---

They bid good day to the friar and Bran led Enya through the labyrinth of shrubbery, which was filled with the brilliant greens and blossoms that came with spring.

Enya's brow furrowed. Bran immediately stopped. "Is something ailing ye?"

Enya studied her feet. "Nay."

He lifted her chin with the crook of his finger. "Then why the long face? Has someone said something to offend ye?"

She let out a long sigh. "'Tis just the friar wants to wait a month before we are wed."

Bran brought her into his arms. "He said the same to me, but surely a month is no' long to wait—no' when we have the rest of our lives."

"I suppose not. 'Tis just..."

"What?"

"I'd like it to be done before my father finds us."

"Dunna worry. The friar is a wise man. I trust him." Bran took her hand. "Come, I've something to show ye."

He savored her lovely profile as they walked. Her nose was straight and came to a point just above her lips. He wanted those lips on him with a passion that could drive him to madness. "I've found a chamber for us, though 'tis only as big as a privy closet."

Enya threaded her fingers through his. "'Tis only temporary. Anything should suit."

Bran's chest swelled as he held her small hand in his larger one. His ragged passion needed to wait until he could see her alone. "That's what I like about ye. Ye're no' prissy like other noble lassies."

"Will we be able to steal away to the cottage?" She grinned. "I ken why ye like it so much. It has a homey warmth to it."

"Aye—mayhap during the day. Calum's afraid we willna hear the ram's horn if we're attacked during the night."

Bran stopped outside the mews door, a wooden shed with slats an inch apart on one side to let in the light and keep the eagles within.

Enya tried to peer through one of the gaps. "What is this?"

"'Tis the eagle mews. Griffon shares it with Lady Anne's female eagle, Swan."

"Griffon has a lady friend?"

"Aye."

"Lucky duck."

Eight-year-old Ian came running up the path. "Bran, are ye going hawking?"

Bran used the lad's momentum to swing him onto his hip. Ian's looks took after his mother's, with blue eyes and blond curls, but his physique was more like Calum's. The boy was solid muscle and probably outweighed his ten-year-old brother by half a stone.

"Yer father doesna want us to wander far from the keep, but we could take Griffon down to the beach if ye'd like." Bran flashed a sheepish grimace. "That's if it's all right with Miss Enya."

She popped her eyes wide, grinning at the lad. "Of course, I'd love to."

Ian studied her. "Are ye Bran's missus?"

"Ye shouldna be so brash." Bran set him down. "But the lady is soon to be me wife."

"She's bonny, if ye ask me." Ian grasped Enya's hand and tugged. "Come."

## Chapter Twenty-seven

Once Enya's arm had healed to the point where she could raise it over her head with little effort, Lady Anne invited Enya and Mistress Mara to the lady's personal chamber. It was a spacious room, and though there was a bed, a long table stretched across the middle of it. Trunks lined the wall as if it were used for storage and crafts rather than living.

Enya spied bolts of fabric piled on one end of the table as Anne pulled Enya inside. "We need to pick some fabric for your gowns."

Enya sighed. "I wish I had my wardrobe from Renfrewshire. Then none of this would be necessary."

Anne gracefully gestured her hand to the fabric. "But 'tis always so much fun to receive new clothing."

Enya felt a tad awkward. She'd accepted too much charity from the laird's wife already. "You think so? I never cared for the fancy gowns my mother had made for me. Heavy things they were."

Lady Anne gestured to her kirtle with a beautifully embroidered bodice. "I've dressed as a Scottish countrywoman since coming to Raasay. Though I daresay I love to add a touch of embellishment."

Mara held up a bolt of red wool. "What color suits?"

Enya looked at the fabric. "Green matches my eyes, and I'm partial to yellow."

"Hmm." Anne crossed her arms and drummed her fingers against her lips. "Have you ever tried lavender?"

Mara gasped. "Ah yes, lavender would be bonny, especially with yer auburn tresses."

Enya crossed to the table and ran the lavender wool through her fingers. "'Tis pretty."

Anne lifted the bolt and held a swatch under Enya's chin. "I say, it suits you. And we'll embroider a string of thistle blossoms along the neckline."

"As long as someone other than me does the needlework." Enya couldn't help but join in with their excitement. "Do you think Bran will like it?"

Mara nodded enthusiastically. "That young man is so rapt with yer darling face, he'd not notice if ye were wearing a flour sack."

Enya twirled in place. "I still cannot believe we are to marry."

"Nothing can pull you away from your destiny." Anne set the fabric down. "'Twas the same with me and Calum. I never would have believed I'd marry a brawny Scottish laird, but here I am."

Mara laughed. "I kent Calum was in love with Lady Anne afore she stepped ashore. But they both were so pigheaded, they had to incite a war before either one admitted to it."

"'Twas not all that bad." Anne held up her finger as if struck by an idea. "Have you thought of a gown for your wedding?"

Enya looked down at her borrowed kirtle. "I could wear this."

"Rubbish." Anne tugged Enya to one of the large trunks, unbuckled the hasps and threw open the lid. "I've a number of fine gowns remaining from my days as an earl's daughter. I'm sure one of these will suit."

Mara peered over her shoulder. "I'm partial to the blue damask."

"Have you anything in emerald?" Enya asked.

Lady Anne filed through to the bottom of the trunk and tugged. "This would be ideal."

"Och aye." Mara reached for the gown and held it to Enya's shoulders. "It matches yer eyes perfectly."

Anne glanced down. "Though 'tis a bit short. You are taller, I daresay." She bent down and inspected the hem. "We can have the tailor alter it."

The gown had a matching stomacher with intricate floral embroidery. Enya ran her fingers across it. "'Tis so beautiful. Are you certain you don't mind lending it to me?"

Anne waved her hand through the air. "What else will I do with these fancy gowns? Let them draw moths?"

Enya rubbed the finely woven silk cloth between her fingers. "I do not ken how to thank you enough. Both of you have been ever so kind, making me feel welcomed into the clan."

Lady Anne brushed Enya's cheek with her forefinger. "You are marrying a fine young man. He's got a heart of gold, that one—Master Bran."

Mara lowered the gown. "Ye mean Sir Bran now."

"Ah yes, I do not know if I can ever erase the lanky cabin boy from my mind." With a nostalgic smile, Anne stared off into the distance as if recalling fond memories.

The ram's horn sounded two short blasts, announcing the noon meal. Enya rubbed her stomach. "Thank heavens. I haven't been able to take the morning meal as of late. I'm famished."

Anne and Mara exchanged glances. Anne bit her bottom lip. "Are you feeling a bit queasy in the morning?"

"Aye." Enya rubbed her stomach again. "And I've no idea why."

Mara tapped her finger to her lips. "And when were your last courses?"

Enya felt the color had drain from her face. "Oh my, things have been so frantic, I hadn't thought about it." She pressed her palms to her cheeks. "Do you think I could be?"

"Aye," Mara said.

"Most definitely," Anne agreed.

Enya turned and paced. "I wanted the friar to marry us sooner." She whipped around. "Please do not tell anyone. I would be mortified if word got out before..."

Anne drew her into an embrace. "Your secret is safe with us." Anne giggled. "Calum and I couldn't wait either."

Mara clapped a hand over her mouth. "Nor could I with John."

Lady Anne faced her with a broad smile. "You never told me about that."

"Aye, well, I was lucky enough not to get with child until after the ceremony."

Enya deliberated over how she should break the news to Bran. She contemplated waiting until after they were married, but two things made her decide against the idea. First, Bran was the type of man would want to know straight away, and second, she was too excited to hold it back. Besides, with her morning sickness growing worse, he just might figure it out.

She packed a basket and took him to the cottage—the place where they would spend their lives together.

As soon as the door closed behind them, Bran nuzzled her hair, as he often did when they stole away for the solitude of the tiny home. "I wanted ye to meself all day."

"I thought I'd never lure you away from Calum."

He ran his lips along her neck. "He's driving us hard—afraid we'll go soft while we wait for attack."

"Do you really think they'll come? It has nearly been a fortnight."

"Aye, they'll come, and the longer it takes them, the more guns they'll have."

"Do you think we'll be able to defend the keep?"

"Brochel? No walls were built stronger than our solid stone outer bailey. Twelve foot thick it is."

Enya walked into the main room and set her basket on the table. Bran stepped in behind and slid his hands around her waist.

"I want ye."

She looked toward the bed. It could wait for a moment. That's all it would take. She pulled a white linen infant gown from under the basket's cloth and held it up for him to see. Lady Anne had given it to her, saying it had been Ian's. "Do ye like this?"

Bran buried his nose in Enya's hair and slid his hand into the top of her bodice. "Aye, but 'tis a bit too small for me."

"That it is...but not for a bairn."

His body stiffened against her back. Grasping Enya's shoulders, he turned her around. His eyes were wide and filled with happiness. "Are ye?"

"With child?"

He nodded.

"Aye. 'Tis why I've not taken the morning meal."

He drew her into his arms and squeezed. "We're going to have a bairn. When?"

"I think mayhap I conceived the first time we joined. The babe should come in seven to eight months."

"'Tis a miracle."

Enya slid her arms around his waist and inhaled the masculine scent that had become so familiar. "I love you more than you could know."

"I think I have a good understanding of how ye feel." He led her to the chair and had her sit then knelt beside her. "We must take precautions."

"I'm fine, truly. I hardly even know it's there except in the mornings." She placed her hands on his shoulders. "We mustn't tell a soul. Not until we are properly wed."

Bran nodded. "Does Heather know?"

"Only Mara and Lady Anne—they figured it out when I complained of queasiness." She held up her hand. "But they've taken an oath of secrecy."

"Very well, if that's what ye want. We shall avoid a scandal for certain." He pulled her into his lap. "Now kiss me, woman."

# Chapter Twenty-eight

As the days passed, the tension in the keep grew. Bran had prepared for battle too many times to miss it. Fortunately, the evening meal always provided a needed reprieve.

When the tables were pushed aside, the fiddler and the piper tuned their instruments for the evening's festivities. Calum filled Bran's tankard with ale. "Ye've had that pretty lassie to yerself for far too long. 'Tis time I had a turn with her on the dance floor."

Bran lifted his tankard and gave Enya a wink. "Ye think yer old bones can keep up, m'laird?"

"Stick it in yer arse." Calum offered Enya his elbow. "M'lady."

"A strathspey ought to be a tempo ye can handle," Bran called after them.

Calum eyed Bran over his shoulder. "I can still out-dance ye."

Bran cupped his hands around his mouth and raised his voice. "Mayhap I should challenge ye to a sword dance."

Bran thought Calum wouldn't hear him, but the laird stopped and turned. "Ye're on, Sir Bran. Just as soon as I finish showing this fine lassie how the laird of the keep dances."

Lady Anne laughed and clapped her hands. "You've gone and done it this time."

"What do ye mean? I can sword dance as well as any Highlander."

"Of course you can, but you threw a challenge to Calum—one he cannot resist."

Bran was crushed. "Ye think he will out-dance me?"

"I cannot say, but he will try." Anne nodded toward the dancers. "Enya is glowing tonight. I believe the brisk Highland air agrees with her."

Bran gave her a knowing wink and then looked at the others. No one appeared the wiser. He watched Enya smiling and laughing, wearing a new yellow kirtle. She did glow, her face alive with color, her lovely ginger tresses worn loose, swaying across her bottom with her every step. She was as beautiful as a rose in bloom.

Anne reached over the table and covered his hand. "It is wonderful to see you so gay."

"I am happier than I've ever been."

"I can tell." She smiled thoughtfully. "Remember the day when I wrapped your arm on the *Flying Swan*? You were but twelve at the time."

He rubbed it as if he could still feel the pain of his fall from the ship's rigging. "Aye, I'll never forget."

"You have always been like a son to me, Bran. I hope you know that."

"Thank ye, m'lady. Yer blessing means a great deal."

The strathspey ended and Calum beckoned Bran with a wave of his hand. "Come up here, ye young buck and lay yer sword on the floor."

The hall erupted in a roar of hollers as everyone pounded the tables with their dirks and eating knives.

Bran strutted down the steps and gave Enya a peck on the cheek.

She gave his hands a squeeze. "Don't be too hard on him. He is your lord and master, after all."

"I'll only give him a dose of what he deserves." The laird thought he could jump higher? This would be fun. Bran strutted onto the dance floor. "Ye remember the steps, do ye, m'laird?"

Calum set his sword down and rested his scabbard across it. "Stop yer swaggering and line up yer claymore."

Bran did as asked and Calum nodded to the piper. Bran chuckled. The laird was known throughout the Hebrides for his high-leaping sword dance. The piper launched into the familiar tune and, heels together, they bowed with their hands on their hips.

Alexander and Ian filled the side benches with their young mates, stomping their feet and clapping. The entire hall followed suit, clapping a beat that nearly drowned out the bagpipes. Bran held his hands up and out as he kicked to the side and leapt.

Calum leapt through the air with the spring of a young man, his rolling laugh reaching Bran's ears. Bran used all his strength to match the laird, not quite laughing as hard, but enjoying the challenge every bit as much.

As he rounded the corner of the imaginary box made by the sword and scabbard, Bran thought he heard the ram's horn sound. But he had no doubt when Calum stopped. Calum sliced his hand through the air and the drone of the pipes brayed into a clash of unharmonious notes as the bellows emptied of air. The hall fell silent. The horn sounded again.

Bran's pulse raced. William MacLeod burst through the big double doors. "An armada just rounded Aird of Sleat."

"How many boats?" Calum asked.

"Twenty galleys all filled with pikemen."

"And cannon?"

"At least one per boat, m'laird."

Calum scratched his chin. "Four hundred men and twenty guns. They could be here before daybreak."

Bran picked up his sword and scabbard. "They may have us outnumbered, but we have them outgunned."

Calum looked him in the eye. "Pick yer crew. I need ye aboard the *Sea Dragon*." He raised his voice for all to hear. "Norman, ye'll man *The Golden Sun*. Board tonight and sail round the south end of the island. Robert will light the southern torch once they've sailed into our cove. The big ships will flank them and we'll have them surrounded."

Benches scraped across the floor as everyone set to task.

Enya raced down the steps of the dais and into Bran's arms. "I want to go with you." She clutched his shirt in her hands, terrified to release him.

Calum sheathed his sword and placed his hand on Enya's shoulder. "We need ye here, lass. I'll post ye on the battlements with the other bowmen."

Enya started to object, but Bran held her at arm's length. "Ye must do as Calum says. Ye'll be safer here."

Her stomach clenched. She wanted to be with Bran, but knew nothing of ships. She looked at the hard, determined line of Calum's jaw. He appeared completely changed from the jovial man she'd just danced with. He took charge of the keep, bellowing orders. Every single person in the hall jumped into action. She had no doubt they would be ready to face her father when he arrived.

Enya cast a worried glance to Bran. "You cannot kill my father."

Bran grasped her arm and led her up into the antechamber off the great hall. He closed the door. "I only have a moment. It would bring the clan a great deal of strife if we kill one of Scotland's barons. But dunna take me wrong. He's the one attacking us and we've a right to defend our home."

"But he's my father, and Robert could be there too."

"I'll do what I can to see to their safety. But ye dunna come to Brochel with an armada of ships filled with fighting men and expect to return home."

Enya couldn't breathe. Bran enfolded her in his arms. She knew this moment was coming, but never expected the wave of emotions crashing over her. The man she loved was facing her father and brother in a battle that could see all three of them killed. And she would not be by Bran's side. She wanted to drop to her knees and retch.

Bran squeezed her tighter. "Ye must be strong for me. 'Twill all be over afore ye ken."

He cupped her face and kissed her. Enya ran her hands around his waist and pulled him against her body. His fingers slid over her shoulders. With his lips, he showed her the depth of his love, claiming her as his own.

Bran pulled back and smoothed the rough pads of his fingertips along her cheek. "No one shall ever part us."

Enya squeezed his hand and held it to her lips. Closing her eyes, she kissed the hand that could wield his sword with ruthless and practiced fury, and then caress her gently as if she were as delicate as a rose.

"I must away. Remember I love ye, lass."

A tear streamed down her cheek. "I love you too."

It took all the courage Enya could muster to release his hand. Bran headed toward the courtyard, and Calum caught her arm as she exited the antechamber. "Ye proved yerself in Glasgow. I want ye with yer bow and arrows in the crenel notch over the main gate. William has command of the wall-walk. Ye'll report to him."

Enya nodded numbly. All her life she'd dreamt of what it would be like to be a man and fight in battles. But now the time had come for her to be a part of a conflict, she wanted to take Bran and run. Her palms grew slippery with sweat. The great hall was spinning. Enya ascended the winding donjon stairs, feeling withdrawn from the activity around her. Clansmen raced past, laden with arms, but somehow everything moved slowly, as if she were watching the frenzy from the rafters.

Would the king's men pursue Bran and Malcolm if she wasn't there? Would her father ever give her up? He'd already proven how much he hated Bran, and Enya was fully aware he considered Highlanders barbarians.

---

Bran and his crew launched their skiffs to board the *Sea Dragon*, Calum's carrack. Though heavier in body, which made it slower than the racing galleon, *The Golden Sun*, it carried forty-one guns and could blast any armada of Scottish galley ships out of the sea.

A full-rigged ship with a rounded stern, Bran usually enjoyed taking the helm of the *Sea Dragon*, but this assignment left him with no control. Enya would be at the castle and he wouldn't be able to protect her if something went awry. He wanted to argue with Calum when the laird assigned him to the carrack, but he would never shirk an order from his chieftain.

The skiff thudded against the *Sea Dragon*'s hull. With no pier, Bran and his men used the rope winch to board, and then hauled the skiffs aboard for the return journey.

The men worked quickly to unfurl the sails. Bran was about to give the command to weigh anchor when a thud from a skiff echoed from below.

"Ahoy the ship."

Bran strode to the wooden rail and peered over the side. John and Friar Pat waved from the skiff and Murdoch had begun his ascent to the deck. "What the blazes are ye doing here?"

Murdoch swung his legs over the rail and hopped from the wooden seat supported by ropes of rigging. "Calum sent us."

"Doesna he ken I can handle this on me own?"

Murdoch shrugged. "I didna ask him."

The winch started creaking again as John worked his big frame up the side of the ship. "Calum wanted more men for the guns. Said our greatest weapons are at sea, where his men should be."

"Bloody hell. That leaves him with William's archers and a few fighting men?"

"He's confident we'll take them by sea."

Bran didn't like it. "Who's watching the laird's back with all of his best swordsmen aboard his ships?"

"Malcolm's there."

Dragon's teeth. Yes, Malcolm was a warrior to be reckoned with, but it was only a few weeks ago he'd been one of Ross's men. Though their friendship had been rekindled, Bran wasn't sure he liked the idea of him standing beside Calum if Lord Ross stormed the beach.

When John tied off the winch, Bran glanced over the side. The friar had turned the skiff around.

John followed Bran's line of sight. "There was no use winching another skiff onto the deck just for two men."

Bran thought to row back and ask Calum what the bloody hell he was thinking. He sucked in a deep breath and looked up at the three masts—the wind billowed the sails, the rigging groaning against the force, asking to be set free. "Weigh anchor!"

Though they were only sailing to the southern tip of Raasay, a mere two leagues away, the fresh salt in the air and the wind on his face helped to shed some of the anxiety that had Bran's gut twisted in knots. He had only respect for his laird. But still, he worried about Enya's safety, though he had faith Calum would act in the best interests of the clan. Owing to their engagement, Enya was now a member of Clan MacLeod of Raasay.

Bran's chest squeezed taut. *If anything happens to her I'll nay forgive meself.*

It took less time to sail to the southern point of Leac than it did to start the ship underway. Bran climbed to the poop deck and pointed his spyglass toward the Brochel Castle lookout. He couldn't see it, though he knew the tower Calum had built was tall enough to be seen once the fires were lit. Yet that knowledge didn't give him peace.

He cuffed the cabin boy on the back of the head. "Climb the crow's nest." He hollered over the deck, amassed with men working to secure the ship. "I want a lookout in the crow's nest all night. Spell the watch every two hours and leave the sails unfurled. As soon as the cauldron is lit, we sail back to Brochel."

---

Lord Ross choked back his bile. He hated the sea. Since they sailed from the protected waters of the Firth of Clyde, he'd had his head hung over the side of the galley while he puked his guts out. He glared over his shoulder at the men behind him. If anyone said a word, he'd make an example of them. He wished they would. He'd been waiting over two weeks for blood.

When the armada rounded the tip of Skye, Ross gave the command to strike the sails and wait until just before dawn. He'd surprise the filthy MacLeods as they were waking to take their morning shite. He'd purchased twenty new muskets and found the best shots to man them. Twenty guns ought to be enough to take the Highlander down. He wasn't about to waste his time chasing him with sword and pike.

Ross reclined in the bow of the ship and waited.

After a night without sleep, his insides raw, Ross shivered under his cloak as he watched the horizon until a grey-blue glow arced over the eastern sky. At last he would have vengeance. He would show the beastly Highlanders he was not a man to reckon with, and then he'd take his wayward daughter and lock away her in the nunnery. At this stage, he couldn't care less if Claud Hamilton returned. Besides, the man's lands were forfeit. What good would an alliance between their families be now?

# Chapter Twenty-nine

Calum sat before the hearth in his chamber. Guilt needled up his spine. He should be on the wall-walk with his men, but he couldn't face them. What he was about to do would make him appear ruthless in the eyes of the clan.

Lady Anne placed her gentle hands on his shoulders and squeezed. "I've not seen you this agitated since you took me to Carlisle all those years ago."

"Och. I always end up on edge before a battle."

"I know you too well. With your plan of surprise, this battle is all but won. Something else is bothering you."

He couldn't look her in the eye. "I should be out there with the men."

"But you're not." She kneaded harder. "My guess is it has something to do with the fact you sent Bran to the *Flying Swan*, leaving Enya to stand with the archers."

"She's an excellent archer."

"She's Lord Ross's daughter."

Calum clenched his fists. "She will be hidden well enough."

Anne walked around him and confronted him. "What have you got planned?"

He dared glance at her face. "All I ask is ye do no' judge me until this is over. I can live with the clan's ire, but no' yers."

"You're not going to fight, are you?" Christ, she was too smart for her own good, and she could not leave well enough alone.

He lifted his chin. "Fight with the crown when there's another way?"

Anne turned her back and faced the fire. "Saints preserve us, Calum."

---

Ross watched the galley's sail pick up a strong wind when they turned south.

The navigator pointed ahead. "We'll see Brochel Castle any time now. She looms over the beach near the north of the island."

The queasiness of his empty stomach quelling, Ross crossed to the bow and opened his spyglass, but he didn't need it when the boat rounded the point. Brochel Castle indeed presided over the beach, its grey walls rising above the white sands. A fortress as impressive as Edinburgh Castle. He swallowed hard. He assumed he'd see a larger fleet in the bay, but only a few small galleys moored, rising and falling with the surf.

He held his fist in the air. "Ready your weapons, men." His command repeated along the line of galleys as they sailed into the cove. The tension that fills the air before a battle raced through Ross's blood. With a flick of his arm, he tossed one side of his cloak over his shoulder.

Robert stood beside him. "I see no one on the battlements. Should we fire a warning shot onto the beach?"

"And alert them of our presence? The cock has barely begun to crow. Let's meet the laird at his own gates—I wouldn't spoil the surprise with a blast."

Robert grinned. "Mr. Fisher was right—give them some time. Let them think we're not going to pursue them."

But it was too quiet. There was no movement on the battlements—no horn sounded. Why would a man like Calum MacLeod make it so easy? Ross's gaze darted to the moored galleys. "I thought MacLeod had a larger fleet."

The Lowlander captain shrugged. "I doubt a poor Highlander living on an isle this small would have many boats."

A resounding boom blasted behind them. Crouching, Ross covered his head with his arms. Another blast shook the seas. A cannonball slammed into the surf, sending their galley bobbing like it was on the open sea. When Ross looked up, his blood ran cold. A mighty carrack and a galleon trapped the armada of small galleys in the cove. They were surrounded and outgunned.

A battle cry came from the beach as fighting men pushed cannons into view. Archers with loaded bows aimed at them from the crenel notches. Ross glared at his son. "You thought this would be easy?"

Robert crouched behind the hull. "As did you." He peeked over the rail. "We might need a slight change in plans."

Ross pointed to the nearest soldier. "Give me your shirt."

"Pardon, m'lord?"

"You heard me. I need your shirt, and make it fast, else you'll have no tongue with which to question your betters."

Ross tied the shirt to the flagpole and gave the order for the oarsmen to row the galley to into the beach, motioning for the other boats to hold back.

Calum stood behind the big iron cannon at the center of the beach. "He wants to parley."

Malcolm folded his arms. "Lord Ross is no fool."

"Fortunately, he played right into my hands. Go fetch the lassie."

Calum stepped out from behind the cannon and sauntered onto the beach. In seconds, a dozen clansmen flanked him. He would have preferred it if Bran and John were at his side, but this could be handled without his greatest muscle, and God willing, without a single drop of blood.

Calum had seen many galleys like the ones that accompanied Lord Ross to Raasay. In fact, he owned two very similar boats. With eighteen oars, there would most likely be eighteen to twenty fighting men aboard each one. The galley came to a slow stop when it slid into the smooth rocks of Brochel Beach.

Lord Ross hopped over the side, splashing into thigh-deep water. Calum smiled. The water was cold enough to freeze the ballocks off a bull. After his son handed him the white flag of parley, the men moved to disembark. Calum held up his hand. "Only Lord Ross."

The baron gave his son a sharp nod and marched through the surf. Calum counted the muskets trained on his heart. Twenty.

"How kind of you to pay a visit to Raasay." Calum made a point of staring at Ross's wet hose, following up to his velvet trews and the water streaming from the bottom of his cloak. He then focused on the white shirt tied to the flagpole. "Ye didna need to bring such a large fleet of fighting men if ye wanted to parley."

"You ken why I'm here."

"I have an inkling. But I dunna like leaving things to chance. Exactly why are ye here?"

Ross slammed the base of the pole into the sand. "I'm here to claim my daughter and to see your traitorous henchman is brought to justice."

Calum balled his fists. How easily Ross had swapped sides for his own gain. "As I recall, Regent Moray declared ye a traitor, right there on the steps of the tolbooth."

"I was pardoned along with my son."

Calum squinted. "For a grand fee, I've no doubt." He moseyed forward until he was within a hand's breadth of the "traitorous" baron. A head shorter, Ross craned his neck and looked him in the eye. Calum read a hint of fear, but the man's eyes reflected something that disgusted him more. Ruthlessness.

Ross didn't blink. "Do you honestly want to become an enemy of the king?"

"Do ye honestly think I would let ye sail out of here with yer life?"

"We're ready to fight, and with God as my witness, you will be the first to die." Ross stood his ground, feisty for a noble.

"Ye don't say." Calum scratched his chin. The time had come to show his hand. His ploy better work, or ten-year-old Alexander might very well be the next Laird of Raasay. All Ross need do was give the command, and Calum had little doubt the muskets would blow a hole through him the size of a cannonball—though Calum would use the baron as a shield, which would stop the first dozen or so musket balls. "Given the circumstances, I'd like to propose a trade."

Ross blinked for the first time. "Go on."

"I'll give ye yer daughter, if ye'll convince the crown to grant a pardon to Sir Bran and Sir Malcolm."

At the mention of his captain of the guard, Ross scanned the beach. "Malcolm is here?"

"Aye." Calum rested his hand on the hilt of his sword, ensuring Ross's body blocked him from any twitchy musket fingers. "I need yer answer now."

Ross gave him a nod. "Very well. A pardon in exchange for my daughter."

"Two pardons."

"Agreed."

"Then call off yer guns."

Ross turned and gave the signal to lower the musket barrels.

Calum looked up the hill and beckoned to Malcolm. He led the pretty little lass out the castle gates and down the winding hill. Calum could hear the death knell on the breeze as she walked toward him, her hands bound behind her back.

Calum had never seen a pair of green eyes hold so much contempt. Malcolm led her by the elbow, but when they stopped, she twisted out of his grasp. "That's why you sent Bran to man the ship."

Grinding his teeth, he faced Ross. "I had to do what was best for the clan."

"You're a filthy traitor. You would sell your soul to the devil for your own gain." Her words sliced through his heart, worse than being stabbed by a dagger.

Lord Ross grasped Enya by the elbow and yanked her beside him. "Have you been treated badly, daughter?"

If Enya could shoot darts from her eyes, the baronet would be dead. "Hello, Father. Has Lord Hamilton returned from his exile in England and paid for his pardon?"

"That is a splendid idea." He grasped her arm. "Come, before we impose further on Laird Calum's hospitality."

It took five men to restrain Bran when he watched Malcolm muscle his woman onto the beach. And the bastards were in on it. John and Murdoch stood beside him at the ship's rail. Bran twitched to order the cannons to fire when he saw Ross waving the white flag of parley. And then it didn't take a mind reader to figure out what had been negotiated when Enya appeared with her wrists bound.

Bran abruptly raced to the main deck to launch a skiff. He had to reach to the beach before Ross could put her in a boat, but John reached in and pulled Bran's sword. Murdoch and Hamish grasped Bran's arms, with two men diving for Bran's feet. "Ye're bloody traitors, the lot of ye!" Bran twisted and struggled, dragging all four men while John finished disarming him.

They wrenched Bran's arms behind his back. The rough surface of hemp rope scraped around his wrists and ankles.

"Ye planned this, ye backstabbing whoresons."

"Tie him to the main mast until Calum arrives," John ordered.

Bloody Calum. Whether he was laird or not no longer mattered. Bran had been deceived—his loyalty chewed up and spat out in the sand as if years of dedication meant nothing. While the rope was wound around his body, fury expanded in Bran's chest. Pulling against the grating hemp, he watched the king's armada sail up the Sound of Raasay.

"Enya!" he roared at the top of his lungs. Bran strained against the ropes as they cut into his flesh. He would never rest until he found her.

John said Calum would arrive soon and board the *Flying Swan*. The chieftain had much to atone for, but he would no longer be Bran's lord and master.

*What must be going through Enya's head? She'll think the lot of us betrayed her.*

When Lord Ross grasped her elbow, Enya jerked away so hard, she almost fell over. Hands tied behind her back, she marched into the surf with her father close behind.

He loosed her bindings. "You'll thank me for this one day."

"I'll never thank you for anything as long as I live."

"I knew you had a mean streak." He gestured to the rope ladder. "But I liked your idea of purchasing a pardon for Claud Hamilton. That just might be how we get you out of this mess."

Enya started to climb. "Me? This was no mess until you showed up on the beach."

"Watch your tongue. You're dangerously close to overstepping your bounds."

Robert reached over and offered a hand. "I see you fared reasonably well with the barbarians." Not even her brother could show a shred of sympathy.

Ross tossed up the rope. "Tie her aft. I'll not have her doing something stupid like jumping ship and trying to swim back."

Enya shoved Robert in the chest. "You wouldn't."

Robert's face twisted with an apologetic look, and then he glanced at Lord Ross as he climbed into the boat. "It won't be for long."

Ross climbed into the galley. "I'll say when she'll be released."

Robert wound the rope around her midriff, binding her hands in front for comfort. "I'm sorry we have to do this."

She stared directly into his eyes. "But you're doing it all the same."

Robert sat on the bench across from her. "What were you thinking? Did you honestly believe Father would allow you to run after a Highlander, a lowborn one at that?"

Her blood boiling, Enya strained against her bindings. "Father cares naught about me. Why can he not leave me be and let me live my life?"

"Because no daughter of his will make him look foolish."

"And you support him."

"I am his son and his heir."

Her brother was as bullheaded as their father. "Can you not see this is wrong? Have you no love for me?"

Robert reached out and brushed her cheek. Enya snapped her head away. "Ah, sister, your eyes are filled with stars. Marry Claud Hamilton. Once his lands are returned, he will provide a good home and you'll never want for anything."

"If Father can find him."

"He will."

Enya clenched her fists. "I will never marry that strutting peacock." Could no one understand? For the love of God, Bran was her man.

"Robert," Lord Ross bellowed. "Leave her be. You could learn a thing or two from the navigator."

"Wait," Enya whispered loudly. "Where is he taking me?"

Robert stood and adjusted his belt. "Iona."

"Why?"

Robert shook his head.

She wasn't about to him by without explaining. "I want to hear it."

White lines formed around Robert's pursed lips. "He said he cannot trust a deceitful wench under his roof."

Enya wanted to scream as she watched Robert climb over the oar benches to stand beside her father at the stern. *I'll wager he said far worse than that.*

The sail billowed with wind, and Enya was hit with the sickly realization she was sailing away from Bran. She tried to stand, but her bindings held tight. She craned her neck, but all she could see was the shore and the flurry of activity on the beach. How could this be real? It was as if Calum reached down her throat and tore her guts out. She'd *trusted* him. Bran had trusted him.

Her mind darted back to the moment in the antechamber when Bran told her not to worry. Was he in on the betrayal too? She squeezed her eyes shut, remembering the passion behind his last kiss. Calum had sent him aboard the *Flying Swan* to ensure he was nowhere near the beach when Calum betrayed her. Malcolm was a party to it—and she thought the former captain of her father's guard had declared fealty to Clan MacLeod. Calum, mayhap, but he was not loyal to the clan, else she would never had been deceived.

Enya half expected Bran to jump over the side of his ship and swim to her rescue, but he had not. Nor would he have been successful, with twenty galleys filled with fighting men.

Traded to the devil so the charges against Bran and Malcolm would be dropped? Her worth in this world had always been that—a pawn to be moved by powerful men to enable them to earn what they wanted.

Enya needed to talk to Bran. He promised he would come for her...but why had Calum done this? Would Calum restrain Bran? But why, why, why? Her chin dropped to her chest. She couldn't think straight.

Numbing pinpricks stabbed at her fingers. Though it was cold, she didn't shiver. Enya crouched against the hard wood at the back of the galley and stared into space. She'd be cloistered in the nunnery at Iona until her father saw fit to marry her off to Claud or some poor, unsuspecting cad. Mayhap she'd give her life to God. Mayhap she'd hide behind the walls of the abbey so no one could ever take her dreams and stomp on them as if a piece of horse dung.

Then a lump formed a solid ball in her throat. Enya began to shiver uncontrollably. She must protect her unborn bairn.

# Chapter Thirty

When Calum boarded the *Flying Swan*, Bran could have shot daggers through his eyeballs. Worse, Malcolm, that arse-kissing traitor, walked behind Calum as if he'd become the laird's new henchman. As soon as Bran could wrap his fingers around the hilt of a sword, he'd run the former captain of Ross's guard through.

Calum held his palms up and walked forward. "'Tis no' what ye think."

Bran's chest heaved. "I'm tied to a *bloody, stinking, unbendable* mast!" Bran's voice started low, but increased to a roar. He stretched his neck and twisted against his bindings. "What else can it be? Ye betrayed me and ye betrayed the only woman I've ever loved."

Bran scanned the faces on the deck to ensure all were watching, his every muscle wound tight.

"Ye better be quaking in yer boots 'cause I will no' be tied here forever." He glared at Calum. "Unless ye plan to ship me back to Glasgow to see out me sentence."

Calum glared back, his fists on his hips. "Are ye finished now so I can explain?"

Blood boiling, Bran fought against his bindings. The ropes were slipping and he'd bust out sooner or later. "Ye better talk fast."

"Or what?" Calum said. "Ye'll slip yer wrists out of the rope and wrap yer fingers around me neck?"

That was exactly what he wanted to do. "Aye."

Calum glanced at John, who held a sheathed sword in his hands. "The bastard's madder than I thought."

John frowned. "Och, Calum. Stop toying with him. We all want to ken yer plan." As Calum's cousin, John could be more persuasive with the laird. "This is madness."

Calum waved everyone in. "Gather round, lads." Though everyone on deck could hear, Calum looked directly at Bran. "I couldna let the king's armada sail into Brochel Cove and blast them all to hell."

Bran splayed his fingers. If he could work loose his bindings, he'd wrap them round Calum's thick neck and kill him. "Why no'?"

John nodded. "Aye, they threatened us—"

Calum sliced his hands through the air, demanding silence. "Will ye let me finish? If we killed them all, there would be retribution, and the lot of us would be fugitives. The regent could declare our lands forfeit. I had to think of something that would be a victory for everyone involved."

Bran strained against the ropes, his muscles aching to slam his fist into Calum's jaw. "So ye gave them Enya's head," he growled.

Calum took one more step toward Bran. "For now." He scanned the deck and looked every man in the eye. "I purchased a pardon for Sir Bran and Sir Malcolm with a loan of Lord Ross's daughter."

The deck erupted in a chorus of bellows. Clearly the clan did not approve.

John pounded the sword on the deck. "Silence!"

Calum gave him a nod. "Do ye all have so little faith in me that I would deliver Bran's bonny lassie into the hands of a tyrant without a plan to fetch her back?"

"Ye did," Bran groused.

"Aye, but Malcolm confirmed he'll take her to Iona. All we have to do is bide our time and wait until his ships are clear of the Sound of Iona, and we walk right in and have words with the abbess."

Bran's ire slipped a notch, though the fire burning in his belly still inflamed. "But why didna ye just tell us? Why did ye have to put us through hell?"

"If Enya didna think she was going to Iona for an indeterminate amount of time, do ye think Lord Ross would have bought it? She had to be terrified. She had to feel like the whole world abandoned her."

Bran dropped his chin. "For the love of God." He snapped back up. "Do ye ken what ye've done to her?"

Calum squeezed Bran's jaw. "Och, are ye going soft on me?"

Bran lurched forward, only to have the ropes cut into his flesh. "Loosen me bindings and I'll show ye exactly how soft I am."

The chieftain dropped his hand. "I'll release ye when ye've come to yer senses."

"When do we sail for Iona?" Malcolm asked.

Bran eyed him. He was in on Calum's plan. The image of Malcolm marshaling Enya down the beach and into the arms of that tyrant was emblazoned upon his mind. "Ye will no' be going with us."

Calum ignored Bran's remark. "We canna arrive before Ross and his men have returned to Renfrewshire. I will dispatch spies to watch from Mull."

Bran didn't blink. "I want to go."

"At the risk of doing something stupid?" Calum shook his head. "Nay, I cannot allow it."

Damn Calum and damn his wretched scheming. With every fiber of his being, Bran wanted to weigh anchor and blast Ross and his rutting armada out of the sea. It was an ugly game Calum played, one that could be very bad for Enya. God only knew what went on in a nunnery on an isolated island.

John placed his hand on Bran's shoulder. "Ye've naught but to put this behind ye and go with Calum's plan. The lassie's gone and we need to work together to bring her back."

"Unbind me."

White lines formed around Calum's lips. "Do I have yer word ye'll no' be swinging yer fists like a raging boar?"

Bran looked at Malcolm. He wanted to slam his fist into that ruddy face, damn it all. But if he started swinging, everyone on the deck would jump on his back. Besides, what good could he be to Enya tied to the mast or locked in the tower? Though the lash marks had closed, the sting still clawed at his flesh. Bran couldn't clear his mind of Ross's thirst for violence. The man could kill her before they reached Iona.

"Och, fine." Bran watched Malcolm's eyes. "Ye have me word."

The sun had traversed to the western sky when the galley moored on the beach of the tiny isle of Iona. Separated from the abbey, the nunnery looked like a condemned and crumbling labyrinth of steepled grey stone buildings connected by stone walls and cloisters made of the same dreary rock.

Enya slumped in the back of the galley, her mind unable to focus. When they left Raasay she'd been so angry, her mind raced through the events of the past day, and she tried to formulate a reason for her betrayal. She'd thought everyone accepted her, liked her. She couldn't remember seeing Heather on the beach. Was she working for her father all along?

Enya didn't know what to believe. Her mind was numb and all she could manage was to sit and stare at the floorboards of the damp boat that reeked of dead fish.

The galley stopped rocking when the hull skidded onto the sandy beach.

Lord Ross pointed to the oarsman nearest Enya. "Untie her."

"Aye, m'lord."

Still wearing his helm and mail, the man leaned into her, emitting the foul stench of stale masculine sweat and rotten teeth. He untied the knot and the rope fell away from her wrists. "It looks like the rope cut into yer flesh a bit."

Enya said nothing.

Lord Ross ordered Robert and the crew to stay behind as he dragged Enya through the bubbling surf and sand. "At least you'll be off my hands. There's no place to run on Iona, unless you fancy a very cold swim." He strengthened his grip on her arm. "But if you attempted it, the cold would kill you before you reached the mainland, even if you weren't pulled under by the weight of your gown."

Enya stumbled in the sand, her skirts soaked up to her knees. "I am your daughter. Do you care nothing for me?"

"You showed me how little you cared for me when I found you in the loft with that barbarian. Besides, you are one of six daughters.

Do you know how difficult it's been to find suitable husbands? And you are the most insufferable."

Enya tried to pull away, but his fingers were wrapped completely around her arm. "Father. Please, I beg you. Do not leave me here. 'Tis a prison."

"You've left me with no other choice."

Enya grimaced against the pain as her father marshaled her to the gate, guarded by a lone sentry. Standing immobile in his chainmail and helm, a poleaxe in his grasp, he reminded Enya of a crypt effigy.

Marching past Sir Postmortem was the least of Enya's worries. In the courtyard stood a woman so gaunt, she couldn't have been a day younger than two and seventy. If the guard were a candidate for an effigy, this woman could pass for the bones beneath the crypt.

Flanked by two nuns in like dress, she wore a black woolen gown with wide sleeves, her head topped with a white wimple shrouded by a black veil. Everything but her sallow, wrinkled face was covered, and her dark eyes glared, as if they had already passed judgment.

Lord Ross bowed deeply and Enya managed a polite curtsey. "Mother Abbess, I trust you received my missive."

With a dour frown, she held her chin high while her beady eyes assessed Enya from head to toe. "We've been expecting you for weeks. 'Tis fortunate you caught me on my way to vespers." She motioned to the nun on her right. "Sister Martha will take your daughter to the chamber, where we shall begin the cleansing process."

"Cleansing?" Enya asked.

"As a daughter of Christ, you must atone for your sins."

Enya stared at her father's hateful glare as Sister Martha pulled her away. How could he abandon her without one kind word? Had he no compassion under his stoic façade?

Lord Ross watched the nun lead Enya away, confident the abbess would break her damnable spirit.

"I've only a few minutes. Walk with me." Mother Abbess tapped his elbow. "From your missive, I assume you daughter has engaged in fornication?"

"Aye. I'm afraid she's lain with a barbarian."

"Is she with child?"

Ross's gut squeezed at the image her question conjured. "I haven't seen any signs, though she would not yet be showing if she were."

"We could administer a tincture to ensure no bairn takes root. She would suffer days of misery, though it most likely will not kill her. Under the circumstances, I would recommend it."

His head gave a sharp nod. "'Tis best."

The abbess steepled her gnarled fingers. "As you are aware, we insist fallen women atone for their sins with blood."

"I understand. Enya needs a firm hand to mollify her adventurous spirit."

"That we can do, Lord Ross. Mayhap we can persuade her to dedicate her life to God."

"I would be content with Enya accepting her duty to wed whichever suitor I choose."

"I trust your job will not be difficult, once she is cleansed." The abbess stopped outside the chapel's double doors, the chant of women's voices echoing within. "I must bid you good eve."

Lord Ross bowed politely and hurried back to the galley. Robert offered his hand as Ross boarded. "Have MacLeod's ships followed us?"

"If so, they haven't sailed into open waters."

"He's too smart to come after us, having negotiated a pardon for his henchman. I suspect he saw his chance to buy absolution and he took it."

"Aye, and Malcolm."

Ross knit his brows. It displeased him to see his former captain in MacLeod's service. But then he did abandon the man at the tolbooth. What was he to do? Ross scarcely slipped away without having his neck stretched on the gallows.

Robert looked to the north. "I did not see MacLeod's henchman on the beach."

"No. He was most likely on one of the mammoth ships that flanked us."

"Might I suggest we leave one of the galleys behind to patrol these waters? God only knows what that Highlander may try."

Ross ran his fingers along the rail. "But he'll expect Enya to be in Renfrewshire, not Iona."

Robert leaned against the galley's rail. "Are you certain about that? Malcolm and Heather were both well aware of your plans to ship Enya to Iona."

"But Malcolm delivered her into my arms. I expect he still harbors some loyalty to me. After all, I've supported him, helped him become a knight."

"True. But it cannot hurt to remain cautious."

Ross patted his son on the shoulder. "You have learned well, Robert. Commandeer one of the galleys and run your patrol. But do not stay for more than a fortnight. I may need you to help locate Claud Hamilton. Enya gave me a splendid idea. The sooner I can marry your sister to an acceptable suitor, the sooner she will be off my hands for good."

# Chapter Thirty-one

Sister Martha, who was not quite as weathered but every bit as gaunt as the abbess, led Enya to a small, pie-shaped chamber with three stone walls and no windows. In the center of one wall was a hearth, a peat fire smoldering within and a pile of rocks stacked like a cairn set off to one side. Apart from a stool and a table, upon which sat a single candle, a bucket and ladle, the room was completely bare.

"Remove your cloak and kirtle." It surprised Enya when Martha spoke—the monks at Paisley had never uttered a word to her.

Enya unfastened the brooch at the neck of her cloak and looked at the door. Closed. She wondered if she could make a run for it—but to where? Her fingers fumbled with the laces at the front of her kirtle. Holding vigil on the wall-walk the night before, she hadn't slept. Her limbs were heavier than the dull ache in her heart.

Sister Martha pointed to the stool. "Sit."

Enya complied and stepped out of her kirtle. Martha set the bucket on the floor and handed Enya the ladle. "Slowly pour a ladle of water over the rocks and breathe in the steam."

Enya did and the rocks sizzled. Vapor wafted up to her nose. It did clear her head for a moment.

"This is the first step in a very long process of cleansing. I shall return after vespers."

Enya watched the sister leave, the click of the lock sending a resounding scrape across the walls that made gooseflesh rise on her arms.

Numbly, she scooped another ladle. She watched the mesmerizing water trickle over the rocks as the steam engulfed her. If only the entire cleansing process would be this relaxing, but even Enya was not so naive to believe it would be.

---

Bran slumped in his chair and stared at the remains of the fire in the hearth. Calum had ordered him to his cottage until word came. How could he wait? Reminders of Enya were everywhere. How could he rest his head upon the pillow knowing she was in the clutches of the Abbess of Iona? The woman had a reputation for taming wayward lassies.

Bran froze. What if they discovered Enya was with child? Surely she would be punished severely. He'd never witnessed them used, but he'd seen breast rippers in the torture chamber at the tolbooth. Cast-iron tongs fired to red hot were designed to crush a woman's breast and rip it off. A wave of nausea crashed over him. This form of torture was often used with the unwed mother's bairn writhing on the ground before her. The babe would be drenched by its mother's blood as her breasts were torn from her body.

Bran could take no more. It was impossible to bow to Calum's unreasonable demands. Besides, Bran would attract far less attention if he traveled alone. And if he stayed off the waterways, they would have no idea he was coming.

He could row to Applecross and take one of the clan's horses. He reached for his claymore. The only problem with his plan was it would take him days to reach Enya, and he would have to rely on others to ferry him from the mainland to Iona. He buckled his belt. It didn't matter. At least he would be doing something.

Bran grabbed a satchel. If he stopped by the kitchen, his mother would fill it. She wouldn't even ask him where he was going. He reached for the latch, but the door opened on its own.

Calum's gaze shot to the satchel. His eyes narrowed. "What the blazes do ye think ye're doing?"

"I could ride. At least I wouldna be sitting here staring at these walls with the memories driving me mad."

Calum held up a flagon of whisky. "Take off yer sword and have a seat. I've much to discuss. And I expect ye to honor your vow of fealty and stay put."

With one hand, Bran unclasped his damned sword belt and let it clamor to the floor.

"Sit yer bad-tempered arse down." Calum pulled two cups from the shelf and sat at the table opposite Bran. "When we receive word the seas are clear, Friar Pat will sail to Iona with us."

"Och, that makes sense—take the holy man to fight our battles. He can carry the cross of St. Columba so the nuns quake under their habits."

"I've had enough of yer bellyaching." Calum picked up Bran's cup and slammed it down hard. He unstoppered the flagon and poured. "Drink this down, ye blasted bleating mutton-heid."

Bran tossed the whisky back. "Next thing, ye'll be handing me a needle and thread so I can embroider with the ladies."

Calum poured himself a tot. "'Tis no' a bad idea."

"I want to fight."

"Ye'll have yer chance." Calum tossed back the drink and wiped his mouth with his sleeve. "As I said, Friar Pat is going with us. I'm taking him along to talk to the abbess."

Bran reached for the flagon. He needed another drink, else he might do something he'd regret. "Keep talking."

"We're going to tell her ye're married."

Bran held the cup to his lips. Could they do that?

Calum shook his finger. "After all, according to Gaelic law, ye are. Ye've taken Enya to yer bed, have ye no'?"

"Aye."

"Then ye're wed. Whether or no' there was a ceremony is no matter."

Bran turned the cup in his fingers. "Will the abbess side with Gaelic laws?"

Calum shrugged. "She doesna have to ken there was no ceremony as long as the friar makes it clear ye're her lawful husband."

"So why didna Friar Pat tell Ross I was her bloody husband?"

"I dunna ken Ross would be as accommodating as Mother Abbess. Besides, I needed to secure yer pardon."

Bran tipped back the cup and let the fiery liquid slide down his gullet. Then he eyed Calum. "There's another, more sensitive matter."

The laird sat straight. "Aye?"

"Enya's with child."

"Bloody hell." Calum shoved his chair back. "How far along?"

"No' far. I canna even tell by looking at her." Bran held up his hands and rounded his fingers as if he were imaging her breasts. "Aside from her...er...ye ken."

Calum chuckled, sort of a nervous tic, as if he knew exactly what Bran meant but wasn't happy about it in the least. "Does she have the morning sickness?"

"No' too bad—a bit queasy, nothing more."

"That changes things."

Bran gave a sharp nod. "I ken."

"If they discover she's with child, they'll abort it and could kill her in the process."

"Why do ye think I had me sword strapped around me waist and a satchel over me shoulder?"

---

When Sister Martha returned, she carried yet another bucket. "This water has been blessed by Mother Abbess. It will purify you from sin." Using a key she wore around her neck, the nun locked the door behind her. "Rise."

Enya obeyed as Sister Martha placed the bucket on the table. "Put your arms at your sides."

Again, Enya did as she was told, but she gasped when Martha's icy hands grasped the neckline of her thin linen shift. Using a pair of shears, she cut a straight line down the center and yanked it from Enya's shoulders.

Stripped naked, Enya shivered, watching Martha wring out a cloth. "I can bathe myself."

"'Tis too late for that. The abbess has commanded I scrub the filth from your body."

Enya covered her face with her hands. Her head spun. How could her father agree to subject her to this humiliation? Then Martha ran the cloth along her back. Enya grimaced against the coarse friction.

"Does it hurt?" Martha asked.

Enya gasped as the next swipe drew blood. "Aye."

"The sackcloth is made of goat's hair, woven with strips of wire, designed to cut through your skin." Martha held up her palm, revealing a bloodied hand. "It cuts through mine as well. I suffer with you."

Enya recoiled. "Why would you do such a thing?"

Martha ran the cloth over Enya's breast. "God expects us to atone for our sins. Our flesh is weak. This helps us to understand how weak."

Enya pulled away. How could someone be so insensitive to pain? She clenched her teeth and balled her fists, choking back her tears. With every swipe of the cloth, the muscles beneath her skin contracted. Sister Martha took her time, as if painting a work of art—but in Enya's blood. A lashing would have been preferable to this slow torture.

When Martha finished by swiping the bottoms of Enya's feet, she stood back and gazed upon Enya with a rapt expression, as if she were beholding a masterpiece. Every inch of Enya's skin burned, scratched by the wire, blood smeared across her skin, giving her an orange hue.

Martha tossed the cloth in the bucket and wiped her bloodied hands on her apron. "Now for your tunic."

Enya eyed the garment as the sadist nun held it up. It was roughhewn, and clearly the coarse brown fibers were designed to further irritate her skin. "Why are you torturing me?"

"Cleansing," Martha said. "This is made of goat's hair. Wear it and purge your mind of sin. Putting on the sackcloth of Christ is a token of humiliation."

The coarse cloth needled into Enya's raw flesh as Martha pulled the tunic over her head. The fibers clung to her skin. Enya wanted to tear it from her body. She grasped the collar and pulled, but the cloth was woven tight, and gave nothing.

Martha answered a rap upon the door. Enya thought she saw the abbess's gaunt face in the shadow. The women spoke in low tones, but Martha turned with a cup in her hands. "The abbess has prepared a tincture for you."

"Thank heavens. I've had naught to eat or drink all day." Enya reached for the cup and guzzled. The refreshing taste of spearmint swirled across her pallet.

Martha watched her with the same fascinated, almost daft smile. She rolled her hand. "Drink it all."

Enya held the cup to her lips, but a tickle at the back of her neck made her stop. Before Martha could move, Enya turned the cup upside down. "What's in it?"

Martha frowned at the small puddle. "Something to cleanse you within."

The cup fell from Enya's grasp. Dear God, they couldn't have. How could she guzzle the tonic without asking what it was first? Had she caught it in time? Would she lose her bairn? Her head spun. A sharp pain stabbed her stomach. Enya doubled over with a grunt.

Martha moved toward the door. "I shall return in the morning. By then your insides should be fully cleansed."

Her entire body shaking, her mouth salivating, Enya lumbered to the door. The lock clicked. She bore down on the latch and pulled with all her might, but the door did not budge. The pain ratcheted up, seizing her insides. She dropped over the bucket and retched until bright yellow bile filled the base.

Enya folded into a ball, her skin bloodied, every nerve scratched raw, her stomach roiling as if the tincture had reached inside her body with iron gauntlets and ripped out her bowels. Tears streamed from her eyes as she tried to block the pain. "Dear God. Please do not take my unborn child."

---

Cloaked in a crofter's woolen mantle, the hood pulled low over his brow, Claud Hamilton watched Lord Ross disembark at the wharf in Glasgow. Claud had paid a visit to Halkhead House, though Lady Ross had been too distraught to meet with him. The only thing he could pull from the valet was Ross had commandeered the king's ships in Glasgow—something about taking Miss Enya to a nunnery. Boar's ballocks, what had happened while his attentions had been elsewhere?

Claud had been on the run for weeks. Initially he fled into England, but found no hospitality among the border barons. His only recourse was to return to Scotland and reclaim his lands. After hearing Ross had successfully secured a pardon, Claud and the half-dozen men who followed him donned peasant clothing and crossed back through the Scottish Marches.

In the shadows, Claud crouched like a beggar and watched from under his hood. When Lord Ross disembarked, Claud removed the cloak and swiftly approached. "Lord Ross."

The baron lifted his chin and squinted. "Hamilton?" He observed Claud with a disgusted frown. "I daresay I never thought I'd see you dressed as a commoner."

"Desperate times..."

"'Tis fortunate I've found you here." The crease between Ross's brows eased. "I had planned to seek you out."

Claud's pulse quickened with hope. "Oh? And why, may I ask?"

Ross grasped Claud's elbow and glanced over his shoulder. "Walk with me. We need to talk away from prying ears."

"I heard you took Miss Enya to Iona."

"Aye." Ross's eyes narrowed. "What else have you heard?"

"You managed to buy your pardon." Claud leaned in. "I thought we might come to an arrangement—and renew our negotiations for Enya's hand."

Lord Ross actually smiled. This toothy grin spread across his face, as if he'd heard wonderful news. "I believe now would be an excellent opportunity for us both to arrive upon an amicable settlement."

Claud clenched his fists. Before he could take this conversation further, he had to know if what he suspected was true. "Why on earth did you take Enya to Iona?"

Ross's frown vanished as he knit his beetle brows. "'Tis grave. She followed the Highlander to Raasay."

A lump formed in Claud's throat. Enya was even more beautiful than Queen Mary. That bastard Highlander wouldn't have been able to resist her. All she needed to do was grace him with her smile and he'd be smitten. Claud stopped and gazed over the dark swells of the river. He didn't want to compromise. He tensed when Ross firmly placed his hand on Claud's shoulder.

"I will buy your pardon and petition for your lands to be reinstated if you will accept her hand in marriage."

"And if I do not?"

"I will raise the alarm before you can wrap yourself in that filthy cloak and resume your disguise."

Claud cracked his thumbs.

"The abbess assured me Enya would be cleansed. Once they complete the process, she will again be a virgin in the eyes of God." Ross squeezed his fingers tighter on Claud's shoulder. "Her wild spirit will be quelled, and then you can rescue her from hell. She will adore you forever."

Claud stepped out from under Ross's grasp. Cleansed in the eyes of God and his lands returned? 'Twould be far preferable to living like a wild animal. He picked up a stone and threw it into the river. "Very well. A full pardon and my lands returned."

"I can petition the magistrate on the morrow."

With Enya's wandering spirit broken, she would worship him. And a purification by God he could abide, as long as she remained beautiful. "Let it be done. I'll commandeer your galley and mount my rescue."

---

Bran stood on the main deck of *The Golden Sun* as they rounded Calgary Bay on the Isle of Mull. He used Calum's spyglass to scan the waters to the south. Iona lay off the southern peninsula of Mull and was now in their sights. Though Bran wanted to sail directly to the tiny isle and blast any enemy out of the water, they needed to be cautious. Ross could still be lurking with his twenty galleys. No matter how large Calum's ship was, it would not withstand a cannon shot below the water line. On one thing Bran was firm—he would rescue Enya and he needed to stay alive to do so.

"One galley with Ross's pennant."

Calum reached for the glass. "Only one?" He scanned for half an eternity and then lowered it. "It looks as though they're tacking across the abbey's beach—guarding it."

John stepped in behind them. "I say we turn round and sail down the Sound of Mull. There's an outcropping of rocks at the south of the isle where we can hide the ship. It'll see ye close enough to row a skiff across and stay out of sight from the Ross galley."

Calum nodded. "I like it. We might even slip through unawares—avoid a fight."

Bran gripped the rail. "There's nothing I'd like better than a good barney with that bastard and his son."

Calum gave Bran's arm a shove. "I ken one thing."

Bran folded his arms and arched his brow.

"To wrap yer arms around yer fine lassie." Calum cuffed the back of Bran's head. "Calm yer blood. Ye may have cause to swing yer sword yet."

"Good. Let's turn this beast around. With the wind at our backs, we should reach the outcropping before dusk."

To pick up time, Claud made the men row in concert with the galley's sail. If the wind cooperated and the sailors used their muscle, there was a chance they'd arrive at Iona before nightfall.

Fortunately, an angry wind blew in from Ireland, filling the sail and the boat skimmed along nicely. Claud stood at the helm, watching the masses of land pass. Growing up inland, Claud hadn't done much sailing, but Ross had lent him a worthy crew—or so he said. At the moment, Claud had no reason to doubt it. They were making far better time than he could ever hope on horseback. In addition, until his name was cleared, it wasn't safe to be seen in any Scotland burgh, and no one would see him on a galley.

With nothing left to do but wait, Claud curled against the hull and closed his eyes. He must have fallen asleep straight away, because the next thing he knew, his man-at-arms shook his shoulder. "Iona ahead, my lord."

Claud first glimpsed a tall ship sailing around Mull. He followed the direction of his man's pointed finger. The isle looked tiny from the sea, but as they approached, it grew in size and the grey stone of the abbey came into view, as did Robert's galley.

"Blow the ram's horn to alert Robert. I'd prefer him not to opt to fire his cannon before he realizes 'tis us."

By the time Robert's men tossed the rope across the hull, it was nearly dark. The wind was markedly colder, with heavy, dark clouds rolling in above.

Robert stood on the deck of his ship, hands on his hips. "Where in God's name did you come from?"

---

There was no way Bran would allow Calum to row across to Iona without him. The skiff lay low in the water with Friar Pat, Calum, John and a handful of clansmen rowing to Iona's western shore.

Another galley had come up alongside the Ross boat. Calum peered at it through his spyglass. "I don't like the looks of that. Ross has either sent in reinforcements, or there are other galleys mulling about." He slammed it closed. "Be wary, men. Bran might just find the fight he's been itching for."

They quickly pulled the skiff ashore. They hid in the heather and marched north as the looming clouds opened with a torrent of rain. Calum pulled his plaid over his head. "This could be a blessing. The rain will make it difficult for the Ross guard to see us from the sound."

Bran didn't bother covering his head. Only one thing drove him forward, and nothing would stand in his way—not the weather, and most certainly not a galley or two filled with the stragglers from the Ross guard.

By the time they'd marched a half-mile to the abbey gates, the rain had soaked them clean through. Water dripped from Bran's hair to his shirt and streamed from his kilt down his legs and his sloshing boots. Calum lifted the huge iron doorknocker and pounded it twice.

# Chapter Thirty-two

Enya's womb cramped so fiercely, stars crossed her vision. Curled on her side on the stone floor, she writhed in pain. Saliva drained from her mouth and her throat constricted. The pounding of her head stabbed against her temples and crept up her neck as if her brain had turned to stone. She squeezed her eyes shut, begging for mercy.

With an agonizing rush, the floodgates opened. Hot blood pooled on the floor beneath her hips. Shrieking, she clutched her knees against the unimaginable cramping that came in torrents. Tears poured from her eyes as she wailed. The babe was lost and she was next.

---

The nun who ushered them through the cloisters was none too friendly. "I do not know if Mother Abbess will grant you an audience. Compline has just ended. 'Tis time for the evening meal."

Friar Pat ambled beside her. "We shan't be long. We've word the lad's wife is here. Once we find her, we'll be on our way."

The nun regarded the breadth of Bran's shoulders and her eyes went stark, as if she were terrified. "No married woman has been brought here in some time."

Bran cleared his throat, ready to bellow curses, but Friar Pat flashed him a glare that demanded silence and then turned to the sister. "If we can just have a word with Mother Abbess, we shall take our leave."

The nun nodded once. "Wait here."

Only Bran and Calum had been allowed inside with the friar. The rain streamed down from the cloister arches. Bran thought he heard a woman cry out, a sharp, muffled sound. Bran whipped around to face the source. "Did ye hear that?"

"Aye," Calum whispered.

Bran gripped the hilt of his sword. "'Tis Enya. I ken her voice."

The friar grasped Bran's arm. "If ye want to slip out of here with the lassie in yer arms, ye'll follow the plan."

Calum nodded. "It willna be long now. Besides, we dunna want Ross sailing back into Brochel Cove, especially now he's seen the extent of our guns. He's likely to bring enough cannon to blast the keep off the isle."

Bran held his breath and listened, but only heard the water dripping from the cloister arches. If their plan went awry, he would find her.

Footsteps pattered from the rear. The sister approached. "Mother Abbess will see you now. But mind you, she is most upset about being late to her table."

The friar bowed obsequiously. "May God's blessing be upon you, sister. As I said, we shan't be long."

Bran wanted this business done. If it had been left up to him, he would have charged through the passage and beat down every door until he found Enya.

The abbess, clad in black, sat behind a table and did not rise. Her eyes were dark, quite the opposite of Friar Pat's sparkling blues. These eyes looked like they'd seen the devil—that she'd sold her soul, even.

The friar bustled in, grasped her hand across the table and kissed her ring. "Mother Abbess, gratitude for seeing us on such short notice."

She eyed Calum and Bran as if they were vile serpents. "I take it your business is urgent, thus unable to wait until morning."

"'Tis very grave indeed." The friar made the introductions.

The abbess's eyes rested on Bran and narrowed.

*She's been warned.*

Friar Pat continued. "We've word Lord Ross has interned his daughter Enya into your care."

The abbess continued to stare at Bran. "You're the Highlander."

"Husband," the friar said.

The woman's eyes snapped to the holy man. "Pardon me?"

Friar Pat folded his hands in front of his habit and bobbed his head. "Sir Bran, knighted into the Order of the Thistle by Mary, Queen of Scots, is *Lady* Enya's husband."

Calum stepped forward. "I witnessed the wedding meself. Lord Ross unlawfully trespassed upon my lands and abducted Sir Bran's wife."

The abbess narrowed her eyes. "And just how did Lord Ross take the woman out from under your"—she looked to Bran and crossed her arms—"sizable knight?"

The friar held up his hand. "Ross lay in wait and snatched her as she exited the privy."

Bran nodded, stretching his frown downward. The friar's quick story surprised him. The holy man would need to atone for a week for that fib.

Mother Abbess appeared to shrink a mite smaller. "You understand we accepted the woman into the abbey under the pretense her father requested she be cleansed." Her gaze traveled from Bran's head to his toes. "From fornication with a common man."

"I am no commoner." Bran walked up to the table, placed both hands on it and leaned forward. "And I'm here to claim the right of a husband."

Mother Abbess's hard expression returned. "You shall not bully a woman of the cloth."

"I—"

Friar Pat stepped beside Bran. "You might sympathize with Sir Bran's plight. If only ye can lead us to Lady Enya, we shall be on our way."

"It is impossible for us to release her this night. Come back tomorrow."

Bran wanted to wrap his fingers around the woman's neck. "What did ye do to her?"

"She is in the midst of her cleansing—"

"Where is she?"

Calum ran his fingers across his dirk. "There best no' be impropriety here."

"This is a house of God. I assure you, nothing we have done exceeds the edicts of the written word."

"Ye would deny a man from his wife?" Bran drew his claymore. "Ye wouldna want us to take her by force."

Mother Abbess shuffled backward. "I cannot be bullied by the weapons of men."

The friar held up his hands. "Sir Bran, sheathe your sword."

Calum stepped in beside Bran and folded his arms. "Ye'd best take us to Lady Enya now, for I'll no' be responsible or me henchman once we leave yer chamber."

The abbess stood, her hands shaking as she slipped a key from around her neck. "If I take you to her, you must hold the abbey harmless. We followed Lord Ross's instructions in good faith."

"What did ye do to her?" Bran growled.

The friar wrung his hands. "We shall give the lady any healing she needs from here out. Thank the good Lord we've found her—agreed, Sir Bran?"

Bran said nothing, but Calum grasped his elbow as the abbess led them to the corridor. Calum pressed his lips to Bran's ear. "Dunna behave like an angry bull when ye see her. We've managed a peaceful entry. I want our exit to be the same."

Bran offered a single nod of understanding.

Leading them through the cloisters, the abbess spoke over her shoulder. "You must understand, the first day of repentance is the most painful. Our methods have been sanctioned by the pope. Many fallen women have been reborn and have returned to their homes to live fruitful lives."

Bran kept his hand on the pommel of his sword. Yes, Calum wanted a peaceful exit, but he didn't trust a word from Mother Abbess. "Enya has no' fallen."

"That may be so, but we took her in good faith."

Enya couldn't stand when the nuns entered her chamber. They cut the sackcloth from her body. Her skin burned when they ran a sponge over her raw scratches. Two sisters held her up by her armpits. Working quickly, they tied rags between her legs to absorb the blood, and then wrapped her in a black woolen robe.

Enya stared at the large puddle of blood as a nun sopped it up with rags. Martha had said she would return in the morning—but surely it had only been a few hours. Enya's insides cramped. She doubled over as the pain racked her body and a gush of hot blood soaked the linens between her legs.

Enya could barely move while they dragged her across the hall to a cell containing a bed with a straw mattress. Without a word, Enya fell onto it and curled into a ball. The waves of pain had grown further apart, but when they came, they gripped her with remorseless iron teeth that scraped her insides raw.

The door closed. The lock clicked. In utter darkness, Enya bore down as her womb purged. Cold sweat dampened her brow.

No sooner had Enya closed her eyes to pray for a swift end than the key rattled in the door. "She's in here," a crackly woman's voice said.

Enya lifted her arm and shaded it from the torchlight. "Please leave me alone."

Through the blinding light, she couldn't tell who was there.

"Enya?"

Her heart lurched and Enya pulled her shaking hand away. "Bran, is it you?"

His face came into view as he stepped away from the torch and knelt beside the bed. Before she could stop him, he wrapped her in his arms. "Ye're as pale as the pulp of a turnip."

Enya clamped her fists together and stiffened, sucking in a hiss of air. "My skin."

Bran eased his grasp and pushed up her sleeve. Angry red scratches ran along her forearm. "My God."

With a wretched cry, Enya doubled over as a cramp seized her gut.

"What is it?"

"Th-they gave me a purging tincture."

Friar Pat stepped beside them and examined her arm. "This is shameful."

"She has been cleansed." Enya recognized Mother Abbess's voice from the doorway.

Bran caressed Enya's cheek. "I'm going to lift ye in me arms."

She bit her lip and nodded. "Take me home." Enya would tell him about the baby, but not here. The abbess had said the bairn was the spawn of the devil. The witch would be pleased to learn it had been lost.

"Come." Calum waved the torch. "We must away."

Ever so carefully, Bran wrapped Enya in his arms. Enya clenched her teeth and tried not to cry out. She was in Bran's arms. Enya pressed her ear against his chest and listened to the rhythmic beat of his heart. A cramp seized her gut, but she ground her teeth and bore it. In his arms, she could bear anything.

Mother Abbess stood in the passageway. Enya turned her face into Bran's chest to block the image. She prayed all the stones of this wretched place would crumble to the ground and finish what the Reformation had started.

---

The moon eerily peeked through a break in the clouds as Bran carried Enya out the gate.

"'Tis about time." John looked at Enya. "Can she no' walk?"

Bran shook his head. "She's half dead."

Calum pointed to the sound. "Ross's boats can see us. Hurry."

They had nearly made it to the edge of the beach when the cannon blasted from the Ross galley. Bran broke into a run. "We must make it to the skiff."

Calum was right on his heels. "If Norman hears the blast he'll meet us in the sound."

Enya whimpered.

"Are ye all right?"

She hissed. "Keep going."

"Pat," Calum shouted from behind.

Bran glanced over his shoulder and stopped. Ross's men had seized the friar. Swords drawn, a fight was on, and Calum faced none other than Claud Hamilton.

"I must help them." Bran stooped and gently placed Enya beside a rock. "Ye'll be safe here."

"I don't want to let you go." Enya grasped his hand. "I can't lose you again."

"Who says ye're going to lose me?" Bran kissed her palm. "I must finish this."

Bran hated to leave her, but if he turned tail and ran, Ross and Hamilton would never rest. Breaking into a run, he drew his sword. Robert Ross approached on Calum's flank.

"To yer right," Bran warned, deflecting a vicious blow from Claud.

Hamilton's eyes popped. "We meet at last."

The two men circled. Bran studied his opponent for weakness. "Ye nearly got us all killed with yer storming ahead at Langside."

"If it weren't for me, we'd all be dead."

Bran watched Claud cross his right foot behind his left rather than in front, which would give him better balance if attacked. "Ye're wrong."

Claud let out a nervous chuckle. "Argyle couldn't lead the ladies to Sunday mass."

Bran had enough of the arrogant bastard's drivel. When Claud's right foot again crossed behind, Bran lunged sideways, aiming a cut at his left flank. Claud barely deflected it, but stumbled, just as Bran predicted. Spinning around, Bran took advantage of Claud's lack of balance with a direct hit, slicing open Claud's side.

With a bellow, Claud dropped to his knees, clutching at the blood spewing from his wound. Bran stepped in and rested his blade along the pulsing vein on Claud's neck. Blood streaming from his wound, Claud lifted his sword. Bran pushed his blade in tighter. "Throw down or I'll run me blade across yer neck and ye'll be dead afore yer face hits the sand."

"Stop this!" Enya hobbled onto the beach, arms clutched against her waist.

Robert and Calum circled. Enya threw herself to her knees between them.

"Enya!" Bran reached out one hand while keeping Hamilton in check with the other.

Calum and Robert eased away, but only slightly.

Enya pushed her sleeves back from her arms. The bloody tracks looked black in the moonlight against her alabaster skin. "Is this what you want for me? To be tortured and killed?" With a shriek, she doubled over.

Claud collapsed to the ground. Bran dashed to Enya.

She held up a hand, stopping him. "No." Trembling, she stood over Claud. "I love Bran. Nothing will change that. You can send me to purgatory and tear my flesh. You can feed me poison." She doubled over again. "I am Bran's woman, and if you cannot live with that fact, you can burn in the fires of hell."

As she crumpled to her knees, Bran lifted her into his arms. "Let this battle be done. Ye all heard her. Enya will choose no man but me." His gaze dropped to her lovely face. "I love ye."

Enya's ice-cold hand reached up and brushed his face. Her smile was faint. Then her eyes rolled back.

Bran smoothed his hand across her face. "Enya?" He glanced at the stunned faces of the warriors before him. "To the ship. Now."

# Chapter Thirty-three

A *week later*

Enya watched Bran rub the salve into her arms. "The scabs are nearly gone."

"Aye. I think the scars will fade after a time." Bran looked into her eyes with a sad smile. "And are how are ye feeling, *mo leannan*?" His voice took on a husky lilt.

Enya liked that he'd referred to her with the Gaelic term for sweetheart—it sounded sensual rolling off his tongue. "I'm glad Martha didn't cleanse my face with that wretched cloth."

"Martha should be committed as daft with the rest of them." He threaded his fingers through hers and kissed. "Calum has sent a petition to have the nunnery closed."

"Good. I'm only sorry it wasn't completely destroyed during the Reformation." Enya looked away. "And..."

Bran nuzzled into her hair. "And what?"

Tears stung her eyes. "I'm so sorry I lost our child."

"Ah, *mo leannan*." He gently rubbed his hand over her belly. "More bairns will come, of that I am certain. Our love is too great."

"But what if...what if my womb is scarred?"

"It will be all right."

"What if we cannot conceive again?"

"Ye worry overmuch, but dunna doubt me. If it doesna happen, I will have ye to love, and that is enough to fill me heart clear full."

Enya clasped his stubbled cheeks between her hands and stared into his swirling pools of hazel. She could watch Bran's eyes for the rest of her life, and soon she would be bound to him officially. "You need to shave."

He pulled her dressing gown around her shoulders. "And ye need to dress."

As Enya tied her sash, a knock sounded from the cottage door. "Are you ready for your wedding day, my lady?" Lady Anne peeked inside. "We have your gown."

Enya stood. "Aye, come in. Where is Heather?"

Heather ambled across the threshold with her arms laden with trappings. "I'm here. I wouldn't miss this for anything."

After draping the gown across the bed, Anne faced Bran with her hands on her hips. "You haven't left this cottage in days."

Bran cast a worried glance Enya's way. "I havena been able to leave her side."

"Well, now she's awaken from her slumber, 'tis time the friar made good his fib. Calum's waiting in the great hall."

Bran ran his hand over Enya's hair. "I dunna want to leave ye."

"Go. How can the ladies work their magic with you worrying over me?"

"Are ye sure ye're strong enough?"

"What? Are you trying to postpone our wedding again?" Enya turned in a circle and smiled. "I am absolutely certain nothing could keep me away from taking our vows."

The sun favored them, making a brilliant appearance as the clan gathered in the gardens, which were awash with roses of every color. Bran stood next to Calum and Friar Pat as they waited for Enya to make her appearance. Calum had given him a new linen shirt embroidered by Lady Anne. Bran proudly draped his best plaid across his shoulder and fastened it with his bronze brooch.

He'd dressed in the laird's chamber, which had a great mirror. Everything was in order. Black flashes tied his hose just below his knees. Around his waist he strapped an ermine sporran. His claymore hung at his left hip, his father's dirk at his right. In his hose, he wore his dagger, just as he always did. It wasn't that he expected a battle, but this was the dress of *An Gille-coise*—a henchman—and he wore it with pride. Today, however, he did not wear his iron helm with the nose guard that blocked his face. With his hair tied at the nape of his neck, upon his head he wore a Scot's bonnet, adorned with eagle feathers he'd found in Griffon's mews.

The crowd erupted with oohs and ahs, and Bran searched for her. As his clansmen and women parted, he saw he, clad in an emerald-green gown, her long auburn tresses flowing out from under her matching silk wimple. Enya looked like a goddess. He had never beheld a woman so incredibly beautiful. Her green eyes sparkled like precious gems, bringing the garden around him to life. Enya's face, clear as sunshine, glowed with radiance as she steadily walked toward him.

Bran's stomach flipped and swirled with ecstatic joy. He would never behold another woman as beautiful as the *leannan* he would marry this day.

# About the Author

*An Image*

Known for her action-packed, passionate romances, *USA Today* Bestselling Author Amy Jarecki has received reader and critical praise throughout her writing career. She won the prestigious RT Reviewers' Choice award for *The Highland Duke* and a RONE award from InD'tale Magazine for Best Time Travel for her novel *Rise of a Legend*. In addition to being a *USA Today* Bestselling Author, Amy has earned the designation as an Amazon All Star Author. She holds an MBA from Heriot-Watt University in Edinburgh, Scotland and now resides in La Crosse Wisconsin with her husband where she writes immersive historical and contemporary romance novels. Become a part of her world and learn more about Amy's books on amyjarecki.com!

# Also by Amy Jarecki

**Highland Force Series:**
*Captured by the Pirate Laird*
*The Highland Henchman*
*Beauty and the Barbarian*
*Return of the Highland Laird (A Highland Force Novella)*
**The Kings Outlaws series**
*Highland Warlord*
*Highland Raider*
*Highland Beast*
**Highland Defender Series**
*The Fearless Highlander*
*The Valiant Highlander*
*The Highlander's Iron Will* (a novella)
**Lords of the Highlands Series:**
*The Highland Duke*
*The Highland Commander*
*The Highland Guardian*
*The Highland Chieftain*
*The Highland Renegade*
*The Highland Earl*
*The Highland Rogue*
*The Highland Laird*
**Guardian of Scotland (Time Travel) Series**
*Rise of a Legend*

*In the Kingdom's Name*
*The Time Traveler's Christmas*
**Highland Dynasty Series:**
*Knight in Highland Armor*
*A Highland Knight's Desire*
*A Highland Knight to Remember*
*Highland Knight of Rapture*
*Highland Knight of Dreams* (a novella)
**Devilish Dukes Series:**
*The Duke's Fallen Angel*
*The Duke's Untamed Desire*
*The Duke's Privateer*
*Secret Longings of a Duke (a novella)*
**The MacGalloways series**
*A Duke, by Scot*
*Her Unconventional Earl*
*The Captain's Heiress*
*Kissing the Twin*
*A Princess in Plaid*
*Charmed by the Wily Lass*
**Blitzed series:**
*Defenseless*
*Unintentional*
*Tackled*
**ICE Series (romantic suspense)**
*Hunt for Evil*
*Body Shot*
*Mach One*
**Pict/Roman Romances:**
*Rescued by the Celtic Warrior*
*Celtic Maid*
**Stand Alone Titles:**
*My Genes Don't Fit*
*Time Warriors*
*Defenseless*
*Virtue*: A Cruise Dancer Romance
*The Chihuahua Affair*
*Boy Man Chief*

Printed in Great Britain
by Amazon